WESTWARD CHRONICLES

3

A Veiled Reflection

TRACIE PETERSON

BETHANY HOUSE PUBLISHERS
MINNEAPOLIS, MINNESOTA 55438

Published by Bethany House Publishers
11400 Hampshire Avenue South
Bloomington, Minnesota 55438
www.bethanyhouse.com

Bethany House Publishers is a Division of
Baker Book House Company, Grand Rapids, Michigan.

Printed in the United States of America

Library of Congress Cataloging-in-Publication Data

Peterson, Tracie.
    A veiled reflection / Tracie Peterson.
        p.   cm. — (Westward chronicles ; 3)
    ISBN 0–7642–2114–0
    1. Fred Harvey (Firm)—History—Fiction. I. Title.
PS3566.E7717 V45   2000
813'.54—dc21   99–006884
                                                            CIP

With thanks to my editors at Bethany House,
Sarah Long and Barb Lilland,
who have helped to see me through
some rough spots in the road.
May God richly bless you.

Books by Tracie Peterson

www.traciepeterson.com

Controlling Interests
The Long-Awaited Child
Silent Star
A Slender Thread • Tidings of Peace

BELLS OF LOWELL*
Daughter of the Loom • A Fragile Design
These Tangled Threads

DESERT ROSES
Shadows of the Canyon • Across the Years
Beneath a Harvest Sky

WESTWARD CHRONICLES
A Shelter of Hope • Hidden in a Whisper
A Veiled Reflection

RIBBONS OF STEEL†
Distant Dreams • A Hope Beyond
A Promise for Tomorrow

RIBBONS WEST†
Westward the Dream • Separate Roads
Ties That Bind

SHANNON SAGA‡
City of Angels • Angels Flight
Angel of Mercy

YUKON QUEST
Treasures of the North • Ashes and Ice
Rivers of Gold

NONFICTION
The Eyes of the Heart

*with Judith Miller †with Judith Pella ‡with James Scott Bell

TRACIE PETERSON is a popular speaker and bestselling author who has written over fifty books, both historical and contemporary fiction. Tracie and her family make their home in Montana.

CHAPTER

1

Kansas City,
March 1895

"YOU JUST HAVE TO DO THIS for me, Jillian."

Jillian eyed her twin sister with suspicious curiosity. "Oh, really? I just *have* to?"

The exasperated blonde plopped down on the bed to plead her case. Jillian steadied herself for anything—from an onslaught of tears to a beautifully illustrated story of intrigue and romance. Judith was a master with detailed expression. Some people painted on canvases, but Judith created entire landscapes with words.

"I'm in love, Jillian."

Jillian smiled at her sister tolerantly, gazing sympathetically into blue eyes identical to her own. "I understand that part." Her sister had long ago attached her affections to a shopkeeper's son named Martin Schein, much to their parents' dismay. "What I don't understand is why I need to pose as you and go west to the Arizona Territory."

"It's that silly job with the Harvey Company," Judith explained, her eyes pleading with Jillian to understand. "Mr. Harvey made me sign a contract to work for his restaurant for one year. My year won't be up until June."

"So wait until June to be married."

"I can't wait until June," Judith wailed, a hint of desperation in her tone. "I love Martin and I want to marry him now. We have a wonderful future planned."

"So send a letter of regret to your Mr. Harvey and explain the situation."

"I can't do that either. One of the stipulations I agreed to was not to marry before my contract was up. If I do, I have to forfeit part of my wages."

"So forfeit them," Jillian flippantly replied.

"I can't afford to forfeit anything," Judith admitted softly. "I gave all my savings to Martin so he could invest in a business. You know Father and Mother will never understand my running off with Martin. Mother has it in her mind that I should marry her aunt Gertrude's second cousin, who just happens to be a duke in line for some minor principality in only God knows where."

Jillian nodded. Her mother had a way of meddling in her daughters' lives.

Judith continued. "We'll be completely on our own once we're together. Father will certainly never offer any financial support."

"No, I don't suppose he will," Jillian replied thoughtfully. She tried to imagine herself going west in her sister's place. A part of her longed to break from her confined environment, but another part was equally terrified. At least here in her confinement she knew safety, even luxury. Out there in the West—well, who knew what dangers might await?

"You really are asking a great deal, Judith. You know that, don't you?" Yet Jillian knew what her sister asked of her was really no different than any other time. Judith always expected the impossible from Jillian, and this was no exception.

"Please, Jillian, I wouldn't ask if it weren't so important. Besides, you'll have the time of your life. Think about the adventure. You were just telling me yesterday how much you longed for a bit of change."

"This is considerably more than a bit," Jillian replied. But even as she answered, her heart began to soften to the idea. Her fears of the unknown were nothing compared to her love for Judith.

Jillian studied her twin for a moment and sighed. There wasn't much she wouldn't do for Judith. She adored her sister and admired her free spirit and adventurous approach to life. Jillian had always longed to be more spontaneous—more willing to take chances and risks—but apparently Judith had received all the ability in those areas. Jillian faithfully remained the tame and quiet one.

"So will you do it? Please!" Judith begged.

"But, Judith," Jillian tried to reason, "I know nothing about Mr. Harvey's system. You've written me enough letters to make me realize how intricate and focused on detail your job as a Harvey Girl can be. How can I hope to understand my duties—much less pull off a believable impersonation of you—when I haven't a clue what will be expected of me?"

"I can teach you," Judith said, getting very excited as she sensed Jillian's defense slip. "I know I can. There's really nothing to it once you know the routine."

"But you're expected back there in four days. Your train leaves tomorrow. How can I possibly learn everything that quickly?"

"It'll work out," Judith replied, coming to where Jillian stood. She reached out to take hold of Jillian's hands and smiled. "I know you can handle this," she encouraged. "You've always been able to deal with the unexpected. Look at how well you handled Grandma coming to live with us, and now her death and funeral."

Jillian shuddered involuntarily. Death was not a subject she cared to discuss. Even the mere mention of it caused the hair on the back of her neck to stand taut. "I didn't handle much of anything connected to Grandmother's funeral." She looked away and tried to steady her nerves. It was silly to get so upset simply thinking about such matters. But in truth, Jillian found this to be her Achilles' heel.

Judith patted her hand. "Forgive me. I forgot how hard these things are on you. I didn't mean to cause you grief."

Jillian shook her head. "I don't know why it's so hard to face up to. I was such a ninny when Grandma took sick. I guess I just kept thinking of all her superstitions about sick and dying people. 'Don't look them in the eye or you'll be next. Don't kiss a dying person on the mouth or they'll try to steal your soul.' I mean, I know it's all ridiculous, but that old woman had me tossing and turning with nightmares for the past five years! Every time someone opened an umbrella or broke something a certain way, we were all cursed and needed to look for death on the horizon."

Judith nodded. "Why do you think I fled to work for Mr. Harvey? I figured at twenty-two, I deserved to put my sights on life, not death. Now a year later, I decided I might as well try married life."

"You make it sound as if you're trying on a new outfit. Marriage is a lifetime commitment," Jillian told her sister quite seriously.

"Silly goose, of course it is. I wouldn't think of it any other way. It's just that some women go into marriage acting as though their life is over. I plan for it to be just the start of yet another adventure."

Jillian shook her head. "I wish I could be like you." She honestly meant every word. Just thinking about Judith's proposition caused her heart to beat a little faster. Could she really do it—just go and start a new life?

"Here's your chance," Judith replied, squeezing her sister's hand. "Go take my place in Arizona. It's just until June—barely three months. And you can keep the money you earn. Not that you'll have much need for it. Mr. Harvey houses and feeds you and even has your laundry done for you. It's a pampered life on some counts."

Jillian raised a brow and looked at her mirrored image. "Since when is working ten to twelve hours a day serving food and cleaning up afterward a pampered life?" Hard work had never frightened her, but in all honesty, she'd never really been called upon to do such a task. Until now.

Judith laughed. "It has its moments. Haven't I made that clear in my letters? I mean, look at me now. I came home on a railroad pass for Grandmother's funeral. I didn't have to pay a cent. They gave me two weeks' leave for the funeral, and they will even provide meals on the trip back to Arizona. Please, Jillian." Her voice lowered to a whisper. "I love him so much."

"I just don't see why you can't wait," Jillian said, carefully studying her sister's flushed features. "There's something more, isn't there?"

Judith turned crimson at this. "You always know, don't you?"

"I can sense something's going on. I just don't know what."

Judith looked away. "I . . . let things get out of hand with Martin."

Jillian immediately understood her sister's meaning. "Oh, Judith."

Her twin held up a hand. "Please don't lecture me. I know it was wrong. But the moon was bright and the air crisp and cold, and . . . well, he was so dashing in his brown wool, and when he took me to show me the place he's been living . . ." Judith hesitated, her expression forlorn. "I just couldn't help myself."

"So now you may well carry his child, and by June your actions would be evident."

Judith nodded slowly. "There's no way to know for sure—not this soon—but it is a possibility." She looked genuinely remorseful. "It wasn't the way I planned it. It just happened. Please, Jillian—do this for me. I know I've been foolish, but I do love Martin and there isn't any sense in putting off our marriage. Not now."

Jillian sighed, knowing that she would do whatever Judith asked of her, no matter the cost to herself. But then again, the cost didn't seem that bad. Arizona did sound like an adventure, and who knew what might await her there. She smiled at the thought of actually taking a chance at something. "Mother and Father will positively rupture an organ," she said conspiratorially.

Judith grinned. "Oh, thank you! I just know you'll love it in Arizona. It's so warm and dry, and the scenery is so very different from Missouri."

"I hardly imagine I'll have time for sight-seeing. You'd better start filling me in on what I have to do."

"Well, if you were paying attention to my letters, you pretty much know the rules."

Jillian nodded. "No fraternizing with other Harvey employees. If I wish to date, I must have my housemother's permission. Change my clothes if they get dirty. Curfew is at ten." She glanced upward, as if to find the rules written on the ceiling of her bedroom. "Service with a smile, right?" She looked back at Judith, who was staring at her with the most overwhelming look of love and adoration.

"This means the world to me, Jillian. I can't thank you enough." Judith's voice was husky, and tears threatened to spill down her cheeks. "I honestly didn't mean for things to happen this way. I know what I did was wrong, but I know this is the only way to make it right. I promise I'll never ask another thing of you so long as we both live. But even so, please forgive me."

Jillian hugged her sister tightly. "You are forgiven as far as I'm concerned. You know very well that my love for you could never be disrupted by your antics. At least I won't have to endure Mother's parade of suitors on a daily basis."

"Is she still tormenting you with that?"

Jillian pulled away and nodded. "It's as bad as ever. She's located some distantly related baron who needs a wife. If he won't do, then there's a bevy of commoners that she'll settle for in this country. You know how Mother is about being descended from Bavarian nobility; she won't be happy until she sees us sitting on thrones or dancing with dukes. I simply haven't written to tell you about it because I figured why bother? She wants her daughters married well and living as happily as she is."

"Given Father's overbearing nature, I don't see how she can be so happy. The man is positively impossible!" Judith declared. "He has berated me since I walked in the door. Chiding me for signing a contract without his approval. Admonishing me that I have done irreparable harm to the reputation of this family."

Jillian laughed. "If he only knew the half of it. Still, I can hardly see your joining up with the Harvey Company as a harm to our reputation. We've managed to maintain the second pew on the right-hand side in church. Mother and I are still invited to tea by the best families, and as far as I know, Father has made more money in his many investments over this last year than he ever made in the past. So if that's harming us, by all means, Judith, harm away."

Judith giggled and looked toward the bedroom door suspiciously. She sobered instantly. "You don't think we've been overheard, do you? If someone tells Mother or Father of our conversation, then our plans will be for naught." She shook her head and dropped her gaze to her hands. "I should have been more like you, Jillian. I can't imagine life without Martin, but I couldn't bear to lose you over this. I thought going away to work would get Martin out of my heart, but if anything, it just planted him there more firmly. I want to spend my life loving this man and raising a family with him." She looked up, and her expression broke through any final reservations Jillian harbored.

"Don't worry about anything." Jillian went to the door and glanced out into the hallway. The entire floor appeared deserted. "I doubt anyone would tell or do anything to interfere with your happiness. Even Charlotte finds Mother's constant harassment toward matrimony to be an annoying inconvenience. I'm certain she would applaud your desire to marry for love."

"How long has Charlotte worked as Mother's personal maid? Fourteen, fifteen years?" Judith questioned, wiping at her tears. "You'd think after being around this family that long, Charlotte would long to run away to Arizona herself."

Jillian imagined that might well be true. In fact, the more she thought about her sister's appeal, the more attractive the idea sounded. Why not go west and pose as Judith? After all, what harm could there be? The two were identical in looks, and even though their personalities were a definite contrast, Jillian could pretend to be outgoing and exciting. Couldn't she?

———

Silently contemplating her next move, Jillian barely heard the supper conversation around her. Her father grumbled and growled disappointment in Judith's plans to return to the Harvey Company, and her mother addressed the issue of taking Judith and Jillian to Europe, where she could get both of them married off before they passed an acceptable age for matrimony.

Jillian gazed at the immaculate room with its gilded gold-framed paintings and portraits. Bavarian ancestors stared down at her from the wall as if to question her decision to help Judith, while overhead a crystal chandelier bestowed electric light in a warm and steady glow. Would she miss it? Would she find the rustic nature of Judith's tiny Arizona water stop to be an unbearable punishment?

I'm twenty-three years old and I've never even contemplated living on my own, Jillian reasoned. And in truth, she hadn't. For all of her mother's meddling and continuous parade of suitors, Jillian had simply taken it in stride like a good daughter. She had been raised to be ornamental and lovely, gifted in singing and playing the piano, and graceful and elegant in dancing and formal entertainment. She had been trained for one purpose and one purpose only: to be the wife of an affluent, noble-born man. And if not of a noble birth, then certainly one given over to privilege and wealth.

"Jillian, you haven't said a word all evening. You aren't ill, are you?"

Jillian snapped to attention at her father's words. "No, Father. I'm just a bit weary."

He nodded. "Yes, well, with my mother gone to her reward, I believe it might do you and your mother both a great deal of good to travel abroad."

Gretchen Danvers smiled lovingly. "But it would be tiresome without you by my side. I cannot even think of it unless you would consider joining us."

"I'm afraid that's impossible," Colin Danvers said, wiping his mouth with his linen napkin. He dropped it down beside his plate and signaled the servant to remove his dishes from the table. "I have an elaborate affair to see to, one that will take me to Chicago for the better part of two weeks. I leave tomorrow."

Jillian and Judith exchanged concerned glances. If their father was to be at the train station anywhere near the time of Judith's planned departure, it could prove to be a problem.

"Judith leaves tomorrow as well," their mother interjected before either of the girls could question their father. "Perhaps you could ride together to the station." Jillian tensed and tried hard not to look in the least bit concerned.

"I'm afraid that won't work. I'm leaving first thing in the morning. Judith's train isn't until evening."

Jillian exhaled rather loudly, causing all eyes to turn her direction. Putting her hand to her mouth, she feigned a yawn. "I'm sorry. I suppose I'm more tired than I realized."

"An early evening would do well for all of us," her father replied, apparently unconcerned with Jillian's reaction.

No doubt had it been Judith, he would have questioned what the young woman was up to. But Jillian had never given her parents any reason to believe ill of her. It had always been Judith who had climbed the trees and gotten herself hurt, Judith who would shimmy down the drainpipe at night and slip off to do all manner of nighttime marauding with her friends.

Jillian caught her sister's gaze and smiled. And now it would be Judith who was venturing into matrimony and married life.

"I quite agree with your father. I suggest we retire directly," Gretchen said, slipping her own napkin quietly beside her plate. "I have several letters to write, and I know Judith must still have packing to see to."

And with that it was decided. Jillian felt relieved that her father would not expect her to entertain them at the piano. And better still, that he would not spend what might have otherwise been a pleasant evening berating Judith again for her decision to take up a job with Fred Harvey.

After waiting for their father to give them the signal to rise, the women graciously swept from the room, pausing at the stairs only long enough to exchange good-night kisses.

"Sleep well, Jillian. Tomorrow evening I have arranged for that dashing Mr. Nelson to come and join us for dinner. I think you will find him most pleasant now that he's had that bad tooth pulled. His face isn't swollen at all anymore."

Jillian looked to Judith, hoping her sister would interject something, but it appeared Judith was struggling just to keep from laughing out loud.

"Good night, Mama," Jillian said, kissing her mother's cheek.

"Good night, my dears."

Judith quickly kissed her mother, then looped her arm through Jillian's. "Come along, sister. I shall see you to bed."

Jillian took hold of her pink silk skirt and lifted it in the precise way her mother had taught her. There were rituals and routines for every part of life, and even ascending the stairs had its do's and don'ts. A lady was never to climb the stairs in a hurry; in fact, a lady was never to do anything in a rushed manner. She should appear, as her mother had stated on many an occasion, as if she had all the time in the world to accomplish her task. This was to be true whether mounting stairs or visiting with guests. One showed poor manners when appearing pressed for time.

When they reached Judith's room, she quickly pulled Jillian inside and let out a laugh that could no doubt be heard throughout the house.

"I thought I would die when she talked of Mr. Nelson. As if that bad tooth was the only reason his face was swollen. Why, the man must weigh three hundred pounds if he weighs an ounce. See, my sending you to Arizona will be a lifesaving event."

Jillian smiled and nodded, feeling her budding excitement override her previous apprehensions. "No doubt you are right. I sat there tonight and wondered if I would miss the grandeur and opulence of our home, but I've decided there are things that make life here seem anything but lovely." She sobered. "I just hope Mother won't be too disappointed in me. I hope she won't be lonely."

Judith patted her sister's arm. "Mother will be fine. She has her charities and socials, and of course she has Father to tell her when and where to go. He will no doubt be just as pleased to tell her whether or not she can feel sorrow in your absence."

"I know what you're saying, but seriously, she will have no one after I go. Grandmother Danvers has passed away. You'll be married and living somewhere else, and I'll be in Arizona."

Judith seemed to comprehend the situation for the first time. "Yes, I suppose you're right. Well, you will simply have to write her many, many letters, and I shall endeavor to see her on a daily basis. Father will not like my marrying Martin, but he will settle down soon enough. Then I will be able to come and visit with Mother often. Maybe Father will even help Martin in his new business."

"Which is to be what?" Jillian asked.

Judith beamed proudly. "He's setting up a shop to sell books! Won't that be marvelous?"

"For your sake," Jillian replied, "I hope it is. I hope you are inundated with customers."

Judith nodded. "We're sure to be. Now, here." She went to the closet and pulled out her suitcase. "I've packed what little I brought with me. Your uniforms are back at the Harvey House. Just take your cue from Kate and Louisa."

Jillian stiffened at the mention of Judith's roommates. "I nearly forgot. What about Kate and Louisa? Won't they realize I'm not you? I mean, you've shared your hopes and dreams together. I know because you've written to me about things they've said."

"And because of that, they'll never have a clue as to you being anyone else but me."

Jillian looked at the suitcase and then at her sister. "I have a sneaky feeling someone will figure it out rather quickly."

FROM THE MOMENT JILLIAN nervously stepped off the train in Pintan, Arizona, it became clear that things were not going to be as easy as Judith had planned. The Harvey House, clearly marked and situated beside the depot, beckoned her in a brick and adobe welcome. Judith had explained that there were two floors, the upper one being devoted to housing the girls who worked there and the bottom floor containing the dining room, kitchen, and gathering rooms for off-duty activities and entertaining.

With an appearance of confidence that she herself did not feel, Jillian boldly braved her new world. Suitcase in hand, she entered the Harvey House with the other passengers, only to be inundated with questions and greetings.

"Miss Danvers, it's good to have you back with us," a rather plain-looking woman said as Jillian moved out of the rush of passengers. Jillian studied the woman and decided that this had to be the house-mother, Gwen Carson. She opened her mouth to acknowledge the woman's words when a vivacious young woman with a wet apron appeared.

"Miss Carson, I'm off to be changin' me apron. Oh, Judith!" she said, spying Jillian. "It's really yarself come back to work. I wasn't at all sure ya'd be gracin' our halls again."

Jillian smiled weakly. "Well, here I am."

Miss Carson nodded. "Go on and change, Kate, before all the passengers get seated. Hurry now."

Jillian sighed with relief. She'd managed to meet Kate and Gwen without any mishaps or misunderstandings, but that was to be her last moment of ease.

"Look, Judith, we're shorthanded," Gwen stated rather quietly. "I've had two girls quit since you left, and you know we were already two girls short at that time. So I need you to go right upstairs and get changed. I'll need you to work this shift."

Jillian felt her mouth go cottony. "Very well, Miss Carson."

"Thank you, Judith. I knew I could count on you!"

Gwen hurried off to see to the passengers now being seated in the dining room. Jillian picked up her case and cautiously moved down the hall to where she'd seen Kate disappear. Judith had informed her that the front stairs were normally quartered off, and sure enough, there was a red velvet rope, much like the Kansas City Opera House used, barring the way upstairs. The back stairs, Judith had explained, were down the hall from the front entrance and past the last of two parlors.

Jillian hurried to make her way through the house. She knew her mother would disapprove of her unladylike conduct, but she supposed there would soon be much that her mother would disapprove. Juggling suitcase and skirts, she mounted the stairs quickly. Perhaps she would catch Kate in the process of changing her apron and then ask any questions that came to mind. But Kate was rushing out of the room just as Jillian topped the stairs.

"So yar to be put to work, are ya?" Kate called out as she raced past Jillian.

"Yes, I suppose what with being shorthanded, it's to be expected."

"Aye. Lana and Betsy left inside of two days of each other. Yarself wasn't gone an hour before Lana came bounding down the stairs announcing her intentions of marriage. Betsy showed up a day and a half later and said nearly the same thing. Miss Carson was fit to be tied."

By this time Kate was already halfway down the stairs. "Go on with ya now, I'll cover yar station until ya get there."

Jillian could only nod, but Kate didn't see her. The tiny black-haired woman was already on her way to the dining room. Jillian glanced down the hall and drew a deep breath. There were four doors on each side of the hall, two sets on either side of the stairs. Judith had said that the first door to the right was the bathing room. The door after that was Miss Carson's, and the room across from hers was the one Judith shared with Kate McGee and Louisa Upton.

Timidly, as if intruding on a stranger's privacy, Jillian opened the door to this room and stepped inside. Three beds were positioned in dormitory fashion with a chest at the foot of each one. This was where they were to keep any personal articles.

The bed nearest the door was Judith's. The sides of the simple brown wool cover had been tucked neatly under the mattress, and the iron frame of the headrail and footboard stood soaking in jars of water. This, Judith told her, was to discourage scorpions and any other manner of pest from climbing into bed with you while you slept. It was also the reason that covers were tucked in tight and not allowed to drape along the floor.

Putting the suitcase down on the bed, Jillian tried to remember all of Judith's admonitions about life in the desert. There was much to remember, for it seemed that danger and harm could come at nearly every turn.

With this in mind, Jillian went to the closet and opened the door cautiously. She easily found the iron poker that Judith had directed her to use for the purpose of beating her clothes before taking them out of the closet. Again, this would lower the risk of sharing her uniform with the strange desert vermin that had a tendency to be poisonous.

Judith's uniforms were neatly hanging to the right. They were positioned just as the beds were with Judith's, then Kate's in the middle, and Louisa's on the left. Licking her lips, Jillian picked up the poker and began pounding it against the first of Judith's starched and ironed aprons. She felt quite silly doing so. What kind of life was it where a person had to beat at their clothing as a ceremonial routine?

Convinced that she'd adequately abused the apron, Jillian pulled it from its hanger and moved on to the rest of her uniform. Within moments she had stripped from her forest green traveling suit and donned the regulation Harvey Girl attire. The uniform fit her a little loosely. Judith had always carried a bit more weight on her hourglass figure, but not enough that it should matter. Folks would merely believe her to have cut back on desserts or perhaps even think she had simply laced her corset a bit tighter.

Checking her hair, Jillian made a few brief adjustments, then decided it would suffice for service in Mr. Harvey's dining room. Now all that was left was to trade her cream-colored heels for the regulation black shoes.

Shoes! Where did Judith say her black shoes were kept? Jillian searched the room but couldn't find them. She shook her head and strained to remember. Where were her shoes?

Deciding there was nothing to be done about it, Jillian prayed that her skirt would cover her feet and keep the others from noticing the obvious deviation from the prescribed uniform. Realizing the time, Jillian hurried back downstairs to face her new job.

The dining room was utter chaos, as far as Jillian was concerned. Black-and-white clad Harvey Girls bounced back and forth from the kitchen to tables, their hands full of a variety of articles. Some held pitchers, others carried plates teeming with mouth-watering food. It dawned on Jillian as a whiff of succulent roast beef assailed her nose that she was quite hungry.

"Miss Danvers, is there a problem?" Gwen questioned, coming up from behind Jillian.

"I guess I've just been away too long," Jillian said, in awe of the entire operation. The scene that had appeared chaotic only moments ago now proved to be neatly ordered. Each girl held a specific task and knew without a second thought exactly what was required of her. Every girl with exception to Jillian.

"Well, get over there and help Kate with the coffee," Gwen suggested with a chuckle, "and I'm sure it will all come back to you." Jillian nodded and hurried to join Kate.

"I'm sorry I took so long," she apologized as Kate swept by her.

"Don't be frettin', just grab up the pot. Some of the passengers are ready for a second cup."

Jillian went to the sideboard where an artfully crafted silver coffeepot awaited her attention. She picked it up, surprised at the weight, and headed out across the dining room floor.

It wasn't long before any remaining semblance of her sanity fled. Jillian was confused by the questions asked of her by the passengers, as well as frustrated by the whispered comments of greeting offered her by the other Harvey servers.

I was crazy to ever consider this, she thought. Leaning over, she poured a cup of coffee, only to hear a woman shriek at her.

"I was drinking tea!"

"Oh," Jillian said, noting the slice of lemon that now floated rather strangely atop the black liquid. "I'll get you another cup of tea right away."

She said it without thinking, then glanced up to see what was to be done about the situation.

"Take the cup and saucer, Miss Danvers," Gwen told her as she approached the table, "and bring this woman another cup of tea immediately."

Just then a gong rang out amid the clatter of noise. A dark-skinned man in an immaculate white coat announced, "No need to rush now, folks. This be the fifteen-minute warning. Enjoy your meal."

Jillian felt her hand shake as she picked up the cup and saucer and headed toward the kitchen. Before she made it that far, however, Kate popped out the door with a white china cup and saucer.

"Here's yar tea. I'll take that coffee."

Jillian nodded and headed back to the table feeling rather breathless. What else could go wrong?

It was not a question she should have contemplated. Before the passengers exited the dining room for their final boarding call, Jillian had managed to break two dishes, spill coffee on three tablecloths, and burn her own fingers. It was only as the train was chugging out of Pintan that Gwen made her way to Jillian's side.

"I'm sure Cook will spare a little butter for those burned fingers. Are you sure you're all right? You don't seem quite yourself. In fact, if I didn't know better, I would think you to be an entirely different

Judith than the woman I sent back to Kansas City."

Jillian swallowed hard. "I'm afraid my grandmother's death has left me feeling out of sorts," she replied honestly. In truth, Grandmother Danvers' death had left her quite shaken and upset, but that was hardly the reason for her poor performance that afternoon.

"Well, I'm sure we can all understand that," Gwen replied sweetly. "I've lost dear loved ones myself."

Jillian nodded and felt a sense of relief when Kate led her to the kitchen and helped her to butter her burns.

"Ya've not burned them bad," she informed Jillian after inspection. "For sure not as bad as that time ya spilled the hot water on yar arm." She smiled and gave Jillian a strange wink. "But had that man not pinched yar backside, ya might not have upset that pot on yarself."

Jillian had no idea what Kate was talking about. Hot water? Burned arm? Judith had said nothing about this.

"There," Kate said satisfactorily. "Ya'll be as good as new in the morning. Now, we'd best get out there and see who's come to be dining with us."

Jillian tried to remember what Judith had said about the dining room and what took place after the train had pulled out. She remembered there were stations to be cleaned and such, but she now feared she had grossly misunderstood the things required of her.

The dining room held only a handful of new customers. Most were railroad workers, sweaty and greasy from their hard labor. One man, a tall, beefy sort of fellow, stood for a moment listening intently to Miss Carson before finally taking his seat.

"Miss Danvers, please bring Mr. Matthews some coffee."

Jillian nodded and went to where the silver serving pots were lined up on the sideboard. She lifted one pot and found it nearly empty. Bypassing that one, she found the next one to be nearly full. Feeling more confident with fewer people to demand her attention, Jillian moved across the room at a quick pace. She had nearly reached the table where Gwen remained in conversation with Mr. Matthews when her heel caught the edge of the chair and she stumbled forward.

The pot surged forward, barely remaining in Jillian's grasp, while the lid popped up to allow the contents to pour out and rain down on the seated man.

Gasping an apology as the man leaped to his feet, Jillian felt a complete sense of horror as she realized she'd emptied nearly half the pot on Mr. Matthews' jean-clad legs.

"I'm so sorry! I'm so sorry!" she kept repeating even as the man assured her he was all right.

"Judith! What has gotten into you!" Gwen declared. "I've never seen you so incompetent."

"It's all right, Miss Carson," the man soothed. "I'm no worse for the wear."

Jillian wanted to crawl in a hole and never be seen again. She couldn't begin to explain her clumsiness, and it was only after allowing herself to look upward again that she noticed the badge on Mr. Matthews' shirt. *Great,* she thought, *not only do I assault this man, but he's a lawman as well.*

The man seemed to notice her fixed gaze and laughed. Jillian felt even more embarrassed at his response.

"Zack Matthews," the man announced, holding out his hand for her to shake. "I'm the new sheriff."

"Oh my," Jillian managed to say as she put the coffeepot on the table before greeting him properly. "Jil . . . Judith Danvers," she said, stumbling over the introduction.

"Miss Danvers has generally been one of my better workers," Gwen added. "Today, however, she is greatly preoccupied. No doubt she's just tired from her trip. Are you certain you're not seriously burned, Mr. Matthews?"

"Nah, I'm fine. Don't go worryin' about it." He smiled at Jillian and Gwen, then sniffed the air. "I'm too hungry to think about anything else."

Gwen smiled and Jillian picked up the coffeepot. "We'll have you served in a quick minute," Gwen stated and reached out to take the coffeepot away from Jillian. "Miss Danvers, you must go change your uniform. You know what Mr. Harvey says about stains and spills."

Jillian looked down to see that her once white apron was dotted and marred with coffee. "Yes, Miss Carson. I'll see to it right away."

She left the dining room feeling a great amount of relief. *I wonder when the next train comes through?* She mulled the idea of giving up Judith's job and returning to Kansas City. She had a little bit of money saved up. Maybe she could pay back whatever amount of forfeited wages Mr. Harvey required. Judith said it could be as high as half her wages for all the months she'd actually worked. Doing mental calculations, Jillian headed down the hall.

Before she could reach the back stairs, however, a couple of Harvey Girls grabbed her and gave her an endearing embrace.

"Oh, Judith, it's so good to have you back. The place just isn't the same without you!"

"I thought I would die of boredom without you here to keep us entertained," the other one stated after giving Jillian a quick peck on the cheek. "Sorry you had such a bad day."

Jillian tried to laugh off her earlier mishaps. They were all so sweet, and she didn't know when she'd felt more welcomed or cared for. Too bad those feelings were really reserved for her sister.

"It's good to be here," she lied. "I suppose none of us shall be bored any longer."

CHAPTER

3

AT THE END OF HER FIRST WEEK, Jillian found herself more exhausted and sore than she'd ever been in her life. She had never had to get on her knees and scrub hardwood floors before this, and her kneecaps were so tender from this exertion that she wondered if they would ever feel normal again. Not only that, but every muscle in her body seemed to scream in protest. Even the one day off she was given in the middle of the week did little to restore her to her full strength.

But perhaps the biggest problem to contemplate came in the form of a letter from home. Judith wrote to say that she'd eloped with her beloved Martin, and after spending a night in what she scrawled as "wedded bliss," they had returned home to deal with Judith's parents. It hadn't gone well. From the moment they realized that it was Jillian and not Judith who'd boarded the evening train, there had been no peace. Judith joked about how preoccupied their mother had been with arranging a meeting between "Jillian" and her latest potential suitor that she hadn't even noticed that Jillian was the one who had gone to Arizona. Their mother was the only one who could ever tell them apart by simply looking. Others relied on the girls' behavior to distinguish the twins from each other. Their father had never even given it serious thought. After all, children were the responsibility of mothers and governesses.

But, Judith wrote, when their mother learned the truth, she took to her bed in complete misery, causing even Judith to feel a bit guilty. Their father, upon seeing his wife so ill disposed, railed at the servants and Judith until she thought he would bring down the rafters.

Judith's letter did little to put Jillian at ease. If she were to make it at the Harvey House until June, she would have to have the co-operation of her overbearing father. Visions of Colin Danvers de-barking the next train, ranting and raving at the top of his lungs for his daughter to return to Kansas City, haunted Jillian even in her sleep.

Hastily penning a note to her mother and father, Jillian appealed to her father's business sense. She pointed out the situation with Judith's wages and made a comment about the senselessness of having to turn over a lump sum of money to Fred Harvey when Jillian was happy to help Judith out. Then midway through the missive, she humbled herself and appealed to his good nature—although she wasn't entirely convinced that her father had a good nature. She knew, however, that he was a fair man. For all his tirades and seeming insensitivity to the needs of his women, Colin Danvers would listen to reason. At least on occasion.

The letter was left with the house manager, Sam Capper, before Jillian headed to her station in the dining room. By now she knew most everyone and greeted them cheerily. Louisa smiled and called out from behind a stack of freshly ironed linens.

"Good morning, Judith!"

Louisa Upton proved to be an amiable young woman, albeit a rather quiet one. With her mousy brown hair tucked into a tight little bun, Louisa wiped away any potential for actually capturing attention for her looks. Her manners were rather appalling at times; Jillian would catch her scratching her head in public or even raising her skirts to adjust her stockings without giving the slightest glance to see who else might be watching. Louisa came from a poor family in Chi-cago and had so many brothers and sisters that pushing her out the door at age eighteen seemed to be the family's only hope for survival. She faithfully mailed all but a dollar of her monthly wages to her family. She had told Jillian in passing that she knew it would likely be the difference between them eating or going hungry.

Jillian couldn't imagine. Knowing only wealth and plenty, there had never been any concern about what food would be available or how many it could serve. Jillian had never had to so much as make her own fire in the hearth. Yet in listening to Louisa and Kate, she knew they could both not only build a fire but also cut the wood or shovel the coal for fuel. It made her feel rather useless and sheltered.

So, too, did serving on the dining room floor. The work itself only seemed to prove to Jillian that she had been a spoiled and pampered child. How could it be that at age twenty-three she was only now experiencing what it was to work hard at something? Why, even dressing her own hair had become quite an ordeal. Once when Kate had helped her lace her corset, she had suggested *Judith* go back to wearing her hair like she had before she'd gone back to Kansas City for the funeral. Only Jillian wasn't exactly sure how that might have been. Fortunately, Louisa chimed in that she thought the new style more becoming. They had contemplated Jillian's hair for nearly fifteen minutes before Kate went back to tending her own raven locks. Jillian watched the young Irishwoman from the corner of the room. She tucked and twisted and pinned her hair in less than a minute. Not only that, but it looked quite appealing. Jillian had pleaded with her to teach her the trick, and while Kate had looked at her rather oddly, she did as Jillian asked. Now Jillian found her own blond hair easier to manage, and even Louisa declared it to be a triumph.

But given all of these things, Jillian began to contemplate her life. She had always listened to her parents, doing, for the most part, exactly as she was instructed. Judith was the one who would sneak out of the house in the middle of the night. Judith was the one who knew no fear. Jillian, on the other hand, had enough fears for both of them.

"I'm simply afraid of life," she whispered, refocusing her attention on shining the silverware.

"Judith, would you leave off with polishing and help Kate set the tables? Irene is ill and won't be down this morning," Gwen called out as she moved through the room.

Jillian nodded and put the polishing cloth and spoon to one side. Grasping a tray of china cups and saucers, she headed out across the dining room floor. But just as she did, Louisa came running from the linen closet, shrieking something about lizards, causing Jillian to lose her balance.

Cups and saucers clattered noisily to the floor, and Jillian herself landed in a ballooning puff of skirt and apron not far from the mess.

"I'm so sorry, Judith," Louisa said, her eyes brimming with tears.

The sound of the crash alerted Gwen, who frowned and shook her head in a most perplexed manner. "Are you all right?" she asked Jillian.

Jillian nodded. "I'm fine. I can't say the same for Mr. Harvey's china, however." She looked at the sorry mess and picked up one single cup that had escaped breaking. "This one only has a tiny chip," she commented, turning it to catch the light.

"You know Mr. Harvey's rules. Throw it all away. If there's so much as a chip, it must go. Louisa, you helped cause this mess; you help Judith clean it up."

"Yes, ma'am. I'll go for the broom and the dustpan right now."

Louisa scurried off as Jillian attempted to get to her feet. Though she didn't see the jagged piece of saucer that cut her little finger, she certainly felt it as it sliced down the side.

"Ow!" she cried out, clutching her wounded hand. Blood poured generously onto her white apron. Had her hand not throbbed painfully, Jillian would have laughed about the number of aprons she seemed to require. Certainly Judith had never needed so many.

"Oh, Judith, what have you done to yourself?" Gwen questioned as Jillian managed to get to her feet.

"I didn't see the broken saucer. I thought all the pieces were in front of me, but this one managed to elude me."

"Here," Gwen said, reaching out, "let me see how bad it is." Jillian complied, biting her lip to keep from crying out. "Well, you're going to have to see Dr. Mac on this one. I think you're going to need a few stitches."

"What!"

"Kate, walk with Judith over to the doctor's and then hurry back here."

"But wait," Jillian muttered. "I don't think it's all that bad."

"Now, Judith, do as you're told. You don't want to bleed to death, do you?"

Jillian was beginning to feel a little light-headed with all this talk of blood and stitches. She let Gwen bind her hand in the lower part of her apron, then stared dumbly as Kate took hold of her arm.

"We'll be havin' ya fixed up before ya can say jack-a-dandy." Kate took it all in stride, apparently unaware that her roommate was trembling from head to foot.

Jillian hated doctors. Well, she didn't really hate them; she feared them. She had always felt a strange sense of morbidity when the doctor had come to the house to check on her grandmother. It was really her only encounter with doctors, and this, along with her father's open disregard for their services, caused Jillian to adopt an uncertain attitude toward physicians. Doctors always seemed so stern faced and unfeeling, and they always knew things they didn't let you in on until it was too late. At least that's how it had been with Grandmother Danvers. The doctor had come faithfully day after day and finally after several months announced that the elder Mrs. Danvers had a terminal cancer. He assured them it was too late to do anything but make the old woman as comfortable as possible. Jillian shuddered simply thinking of the scene.

"Kate, I honestly don't think this is necessary," Jillian said, holding her wrapped hand tightly to her waist. "I mean, the bleeding will stop in a few minutes, and I hardly think I need to bother the doctor."

"Dr. Mac will be gettin' a real laugh out of seein' ya again so soon," Kate said.

Jillian knew nothing about what Kate was talking about and had no chance to question her on it as they stepped out the back door of the Harvey House and crossed the sandy dirt road to where the doctor's small wood and stone house stood.

Kate knocked loudly on the door, then grinned at Jillian. "I almost wish it were me to be seein' the doc. He's surely the handsomest man I've ever laid me eyes to. But no doubt he'd not be wantin' a poor Mick for a wife."

"Coming!" came the muffled call from within the house.

Kate turned on her heel and headed back to the Harvey House.

"He'll be havin' ya fixed up in no time at all."

Jillian thought to call after her, not exactly sure what she wanted to say but desperate to have Kate's bolstering support. She eyed the placard at the side of the door. *Dr. Terrance MacCallister.*

She glanced back over her shoulder to Kate's departing figure. "Aren't you going to wait until he opens the door?" she finally managed.

"He's already opened the door," a deep masculine voice stated from behind her.

Jillian turned to look up into the bluest eyes she'd ever seen. They were bright with amusement and well matched to the grin on the man's face. He looked nothing like any doctor she'd ever encountered.

"Miss Danvers. Can't get enough of my company, eh? Well, come inside. I see you're back from your trip back East. How did it go?"

Jillian wanted to call out again for Kate as the man took hold of her arm. Her quaking only increased as he led her into the house and closed the door.

"Why, you're shaking like a leaf. If I didn't know you better, I'd say you were scared to death. But that can't be the case. After all, this is the same woman who watched me pick out pieces of lint from her burn," he stated with a look of approval. "By the way, how's the arm doing? I hope those two weeks in Kansas City didn't ruin all my good work."

Jillian felt her mouth go dry. *Oh, Judith. What have you gotten me into?*

"My arm is perfectly fine," she told him. At least it was the truth. "It's my hand. Well, actually my finger. I cut it." She held up her hand as if to prove the fact. "I don't think I need to be here bothering you with it, however." She forced herself to remain calm.

"Well, now, I guess you must have received your license to practice medicine while you were back in Kansas City," Dr. MacCallister said with a laugh. He stopped in midstep, turned to her, and let his gaze linger on her face for just a moment. "I don't come to the Harvey House and tell you how to do your job."

"I might have been better off if you had," Jillian muttered.

The doctor laughed. "Why don't you let me be the judge of whether you bothered me for nothing."

Jillian nodded. "I'm sorry, Dr. MacCallister."

The man frowned. "What happened to just calling me Mac? You go back East and get all civilized? I thought we had an agreement."

Jillian wanted to protest that she'd never agreed to anything except her sister's ridiculous scheme. But instead she whispered his name. "Mac."

He nodded. "That's better. Now come sit in my examining room, and we'll see just what you've managed to do to yourself."

Jillian allowed him to lead her into his medical office. She took a seat on the chair he pointed to, glad that he'd not suggested she try to mount the spindly contraption that posed as an examination table. *Just stay calm, Jillian,* she told herself. *This will all be over in a few minutes, and you can go back to your room. And do what?* she wondered. After all, what she wanted to do was pack and leave without another word. But there was no hope of doing that. Judith needed her, and Jillian knew she would remain no matter how uncomfortable things got.

Mac went to a washbasin, poured water, and washed his hands before coming back to examine her hand. Carefully—in fact, tenderly—he unwrapped her hand while Jillian tried not to think about the blood or the pain. Or the warmth of his touch.

"My, my," he said good-naturedly. "Were you just desperate for attention or bored with Mr. Harvey's routine?"

Jillian didn't know quite how to take his teasing. "I fell with a tray of cups and saucers. Then when I went to get up, I cut my hand. It's that simple."

"Well, not exactly," Mac told her. "It's going to have to be stitched. Otherwise the bleeding will never stop. See here, it's already starting back up."

Jillian refused to look, but nodded and kept her gaze fixed on Mac's face. Kate was right. It was an extremely handsome face with its broad square jaw, dark brows, and those wonderfully blue eyes.

"Are you sure this is the only way?" Jillian questioned, fearing what was to come.

Mac shook his head. "What happened to you back East? You used to have more gumption than this."

Jillian realized she was in danger of being found out. Swallowing her fear, she squared her shoulders and replied, "It's just that there's a great deal of work to be done back at the dining room. I made quite a mess and it won't clean itself. My work—"

"Can wait," Mac interjected and added, "at least a few minutes while I tend to that cut. Now just sit tight, and I'll get a needle."

"A needle," Jillian murmured. Oh, this wasn't going well at all. How would she ever be able to sit here and pretend to have what he called Judith's "gumption," when all she wanted to do was cry? Judith might have taken up the job of stitching herself, but Jillian knew she would be more inclined to pass out in a dead faint from such an ordeal.

She watched the man move around his office with ease. He was something just over six feet tall and wore a simple dark suit of black serge. He looked like a doctor, she decided. Albeit a young doctor. The doctor who had tended Grandmother had been nearly as old as Grandmother herself. Jillian had no other memory of any other doctor, for doctors were common people as far as her mother was concerned. They were never invited to parties and certainly had never graced the Danvers' dinner table.

Mac returned with a tray of necessary equipment. Jillian spied the threaded needle and felt her heart begin to palpitate a little harder. She wished now she was more given to prayers and religiosity. If she were, she would ask God to make this all go away.

"Why, Judith, you're as white as a ghost," Mac stated in a serious tone. "You must have lost quite a bit of blood before making it over to see me."

Jillian just nodded. It seemed as logical an excuse as she could come up with.

He took hold of her hand and began washing the wound. Jillian bit her lip to keep from crying out, then discovered this pain was nothing compared to the actual process of Mac's stitching. Twice she nearly screamed, and throughout it all she fought waves of nausea and dizziness. She leaned her head back against the wall, grateful that

Mac had positioned the chair close to the corner. She had already determined to lean toward the left where the wall might better support her should she faint.

"There, four stitches ought to hold you," Mac said, eyeing his work appreciatively. "I thought for sure you'd be watching to make sure I did it right."

Jillian eased her head up and looked at her right hand. It didn't seem all that much worse for the wear.

"I'll wrap it up, and in a week, maybe ten days, I'll take those stitches back out. You ought to be good as new then." He began to wrap a bandage around the wound, admonishing her to keep it dry. "Tell your Miss Carson that you should not be given any task that will cause you to get your hand wet. Neither should you be lifting anything with this hand."

Jillian nodded. *Just a few more minutes,* she told herself. *A few more minutes and I can leave.*

"So how was your trip home? I mean, I know that you went there for your grandmother's funeral, but since you didn't like the old woman anyway—"

Jillian gasped at this. Had Judith really told him that she didn't like Grandmother Danvers? It was true—neither one of the girls cared much for the superstitious old woman—but that Judith would have actually told this stranger how she felt was almost unimaginable.

"Did I hurt you?" he asked gently.

"No," she managed to say, collecting her thoughts. There was apparently a great deal that her sister had shared with this man. Funny that Judith never mentioned him in letters home.

Mac smiled and went back to work. "So how did you find your parents and sister?"

"Oh, they were the same as always," Jillian managed.

Before she knew it, he was finished and pushing the tray aside. "Now," he said in that authoritative tone that seemed to precede any doctorly task, "I'll take a look at that arm."

"What!" Jillian exclaimed, yanking back the left arm that he had already taken hold of.

Mac gave her arm a gentle pull. "I said, I intend to see how you're recuperating." He was already unfastening the wrist buttons of her blouse.

"No, that isn't necessary," Judith protested, but in her weakened state, she was hardly up to matching the determined Dr. MacCallister.

Mac pulled up the sleeve and studied her arm for a moment, while Jillian looked up at the ceiling. Now he would know the truth, and for the life of her, she wasn't sure what she could say or do that would set things right. Jillian waited for him to say something—anything. But he remained silent, his hand still firmly gripping her arm. Finally Jillian dropped her gaze back to Mac's face when the silence became too difficult to deal with.

"Do you want to explain this to me?" he said, dropping his hold on her. He leaned back against the counter and eyed her in the same fashion one might consider a wayward child.

Jillian drew a deep breath. "I'm not Judith."

"Yes, I can see that for myself."

"I'm her twin sister, Jillian."

"And you're here masquerading as Judith because you were bored with life in the city?" he questioned.

She shook her head. "My sister asked me to come and pose as her." Jillian sighed, preparing to reveal the whole scenario. There was no sense in lying. She'd been discovered and would soon be sent back to Kansas City. Unless, she thought hopefully, she could convince Mac to keep her secret.

"You want to give me the full story?"

Jillian nodded. "I suppose that would be best."

"Yes, I think it probably would be," Mac said, crossing his arms.

"Well, you see, Judith was in love with a young man we've known most of our lives. She planned an elopement with him but knew if she didn't come back to work for Mr. Harvey, she'd have to pay back half the wages she'd already earned. She couldn't do that because she'd already given her fiancé the money, and there was no possibility of our father giving her the money as he had never approved of her taking up employment in the first place and would certainly never approve of her choice in husbands."

"So she convinced her twin sister to come to Pintan in her stead,"

Mac stated thoughtfully. Then he totally surprised Jillian by bursting into laughter. "That Judith! What a gal!"

Jillian didn't know whether to be relieved or jealous. He said it with such obvious admiration for her sister that Jillian couldn't help but feel a little envious.

"I realize I tried to deceive you as I have the others, but please understand . . ."

"Oh, I understand. I mean, Judith was involved, so it couldn't just be a simple matter. Nothing Judith ever did was simple."

"Do you always call women by their first names?" Jillian asked suddenly. It struck her as very strange that this man had insisted she call him Mac, while he constantly called her sister by her given name.

"I don't always," Mac replied, "but your sister was special. She just seemed so at ease with the world. She insisted everyone call her by her first name. She hated it when Miss Carson would get all formal in front of the train passengers. She thought it complete nonsense. If it makes you uneasy, rest assured I won't call you by your given name unless you grant me permission to do so."

"Well, you won't really have to worry about it, I suppose," Jillian replied.

"And why would that be?" He leaned forward and his black hair fell across his forehead in a way that made Jillian want to reach up and push it back into place.

"Because now that I'm found out, Miss Carson will no doubt demand I return to Kansas City."

"Miss Carson would only do that if she found out about your little deception."

Jillian eyed him very seriously. "What are you saying?"

"I'm saying that I think this will be great fun. What do you say we just be good friends and keep this between us? If you're anything like your sister, I know we'll get along just fine."

He was serious, Jillian realized. He was laughing and enjoying the situation, and he was willing to let her go on posing as Judith.

"Do you mean it? Truly?"

He laughed again. "I don't see that it will harm anyone. After all,

I know Miss Carson doesn't have any girls to spare. So if anything, it'll only be helpful."

Jillian breathed a sigh of relief. "Thank you, Dr. MacCallister. I can't tell you what this means to me."

"Mac," he said, reaching out to help her to her feet. "Call me Mac."

Jillian warmed to his smile and nodded. "Very well, and you may call me Jillian."

"I'd probably better call you Judith," he said, then gave her a wink. "Oh, and I'd keep that arm covered with a bandage if I were you. You go to changing clothes in front of anyone and they'll know right off that you're not Judith. That burn she had was pretty intense."

"But she was all right, wasn't she? I mean, I never knew in the whole of her visit that she was wounded," Jillian said, suddenly very concerned for her sister.

"Oh, Judith will get by just fine. She could sell sand in the desert. Your sister is quite a card. She'll always land on her feet. Here, let me put a bandage on your arm and no one will know the difference." He very quickly wrapped her forearm, then pushed her sleeve back into place. "There."

Jillian sighed and struggled to rebutton her sleeve. "I wish the same could be said of me," she murmured. Mac's confused expression caused her to add, "I mean the part about landing on my feet." She smiled weakly. "After all, I wouldn't be in here now if that were the case." She couldn't seem to coordinate the work required to secure her sleeve.

Mac pushed her bandaged hand away very gently, then took up the edges of the sleeve and buttoned it for Jillian. Where his warm fingers touched the sensitive skin of her wrist, Jillian felt a tingling sensation that seemed to move up her arm in waves.

"I think it would have been a pity not to have learned your secret, Jillian," he said softly, glancing up to meet her stare. "A very big pity."

CHAPTER

4

"THE SECOND CHAPTER OF JAMES states, 'For if there come unto your assembly a man with a gold ring, in goodly apparel, and there come in also a poor man in vile raiment; and ye have respect to him that weareth the gay clothing, and say unto him, sit thou here in a good place; and say to the poor, stand thou there, or sit here under my footstool: Are ye not then partial in yourselves, and are become judges of evil thoughts? Hearken, my beloved brethren, hath not God chosen the poor of this world rich in faith, and heirs of the kingdom which he hath promised to them that love him? But ye have despised the poor. Do not rich men oppress you, and draw you before the judgment seats?' "

Jillian shifted a bit uncomfortably in the hard pew of the tiny Pintan church. Reverend Lister, the round little man with a balding head and spectacles, held her captive with his words. Words that spoke of treating others badly simply because they were poor. She had seen this type of partiality for most of her life. She couldn't remember a time when her parents' social standing hadn't been an important mark of who they were. People looked up to her family. They were given places of honor. So why did that suddenly seem so wrong?

" 'But if ye have respect to persons,' " the pastor continued reading, " 'ye commit sin, and are convinced of the law as transgressors.' "

He gripped the sides of the pulpit and stared intently at the thirty-some people gathered in the little church. "Do we agree that the Scriptures tell us that we are all equal in God's eyes?"

A slight murmuring went through the crowd. A couple of weak "amens" were heard from the very back of the room, and Jillian thought it all rather queer. Her church back in Kansas City had been stately and beautiful in its cathedral-style setting. There had been lovely ornamentation and some twenty stained-glass windows to honor God up in His heaven. Jillian had never really felt inclined to think about God in one way or another. He obviously existed, because she existed. She never thought how pretentious this idea really was—it just seemed logical.

But in all her time of attending Sunday services back home, she had never once heard the minister address his flock in quite this manner. Scriptures were usually read in lengthy monotone liturgies, and these were always followed with long windy prayers that seemed to berate the unworthy congregation for even daring to draw breath without honoring God's generosity for overlooking their sin.

She had no idea what great sin it was that she had committed. She held to the commandments. She didn't steal or murder or lie. She honored her mother and father. Well, usually she did, when she wasn't running off on one of Judith's schemes. She sat faithfully in church to honor the Sabbath. She would never have considered uttering blasphemies against the Lord, and she had never replaced Him with a graven image or had any other gods before Him. But then again, neither did she honor Him in any particular way. Still, it seemed enough to her that she had upheld these rules as well as the other two commandments of the original ten. She certainly hadn't committed adultery. Finally, there was no need to covet anything of her neighbors' since she had everything her heart desired.

"It's rather easy to sit here in the comfort of our friends and say that we agree with the Bible—that we are all equal in God's eyes. However, I would like to point out that God had more folks in mind than those who sit here today. God also has made us equal to the Navajo—the Hopi—the Zuni—the Apache."

Gasps of discord and a general rumbling of disagreement rose up from the crowd. Reverend Lister waited patiently for the comments to die down before continuing. "I challenge you," he stated, his blue eyes piercing and ablaze with passion, "no, I demand that you show me where the Word of our God states otherwise."

The murmurings faded into a deadly silence. Jillian could feel the electricity in the air. This man had dared to compare heathen Indians with their pagan rituals—rituals that Jillian had heard included everything from animal impersonation to human sacrifice—to good Christian men and women. Surely God didn't mean that educated and religious folks were on an equal footing with those who were obviously ignorant of Scriptures and the rules of polite society.

"There is a disease in our midst called prejudice," Pastor Lister proclaimed. "It allows that our red-skinned brothers and sisters are not worthy to sit beside us in our place of worship. It allows that their hearts are not salvageable—that their ways are too corrupt. But Scripture says that God is willing that none should perish, but that all should be saved. Explain this Scripture to me if that does not include our red brothers and sisters."

The following silence held the group captive as Reverend Lister moved away from the pulpit and came to stand near the pew where Jillian sat.

"You sit here in your comfort and finery. Various reasons have brought you to Pintan. You come not as natives to the area, but as visitors. You take what you will and strive to build a town in the midst of a desert land. The Navajo were already here. They could teach us much, but we are a prideful people—and what can we learn from mere savages?" he asked, his tone edged with sarcasm. "They have lived off this land for hundreds of years, and yet we bring in our new methods and our ways are proclaimed as better."

He let his gaze travel to each person, making Jillian most uncomfortable.

"I want to remind you, in case you've forgotten, that the wages of sin is death, and from the Scripture we just read, if you have respect to persons, you commit sin and are convinced of the law as transgressors."

Jillian was afraid to look anywhere but at the pastor. Her conscience was soundly pricked. She had ignored the Indian women who sat near the edge of the depot and sold their wares. She had smiled at the chubby toddlers and lean athletic children who played with lizards and other desert wildlife, but she had never really given them much thought. They were dark skinned and different. They spoke another language and worshiped another god. They weren't like Jillian and her people.

Realizing she could have heard that final thought coming from her mother's lips, Jillian began to have an understanding of her own attitude and misconception toward the Indians. She hadn't set out to harm the Indian people, but neither had she considered them worth her time and trouble.

Reverend Lister spoke for another ten minutes, admonishing his congregation to be bearers of love and Christian charity. He prayed in a fervent manner that resonated within Jillian's heart. It was nothing like the pretentious and pompous prayers of her ministers back home.

Then, just when she figured things to be completed, Reverend Lister drew a well-rounded, short little woman to the pulpit with him.

"Most of you know Mary Barnes. She's been widowed now for nearly ten years, but she and her husband came to this territory a long time ago with a heart to work with the Indians. Mary is here today to join us for our church social and to gather used clothes and other supplies you might be willing to part with, to aid our Indian brother and sister. I hope you will give generously of your money and material wealth in order to help those less fortunate. Mary, why don't you tell us a bit about what you've encountered."

Jillian immediately liked the woman. Her face held a look of serenity, despite being tanned and weathered. Her gray hair was pulled back into a neat little bun atop her head, but it was her smile that captured Jillian's interest. It was most generous and sincere.

"Folks, listen up," the old woman said with a loud, clear voice.

Jillian almost laughed that such volume could come out of such a small package, for the woman couldn't have been over five feet tall—if that.

"Mostly I've been workin' with the Navajo. You've seen a good many of them sittin' around the depot selling blankets and baskets.

You've also known me to collect the same things in trade as I swap them for supplies and goods they can use. Those things you donate, I give freely. Those things I have to buy, I use monies I make in selling their trade goods. You know there's been a lot of sickness going 'round. The Indian has been inundated with our measles and small-pox. There's a good deal of need in the various villages, so I'm askin' you to seek the Lord on this matter. I've used up most of the money on medicine and such to help them in their sickness. This makes it kind of rough when it comes to helpin' them in other areas such as clothes, food, and household goods. I ain't picky," she added with a laugh. "I can probably find use for just about anything you want to donate."

She sobered and appeared to be studying each person to ascertain their heart on the matter. "The government agencies don't come near to helpin' as much as these folks need helpin'. I'd appreciate your donations of money or goods, and if you have a strong arm and want to help by donatin' time, that's just as good. Like I said, I ain't picky. If you want to talk to me after church, I'd be happy to answer your questions."

After that, Reverend Lister dismissed the congregation with a hymn, and Jillian found herself moving with the crowd down the short narrow aisle. She heard their murmurs of disapproval.

"Imagine, letting her in here. She's lived with those savages, you know."

"Why Mrs. Barnes thinks I should turn over my hard-earned money to help heathen brats is beyond me."

The comments were not declared very openly, but instead ran through the crowd in a barely uttered undercurrent. Jillian felt a sense of frustration from their words. She had been brought up to agree with such thinking. So why did it seem so ugly and distasteful now?

"Why, Miss Danvers, how nice to see you here."

Jillian startled at Mac's voice. She turned to find that he was not but six inches from her side. "Dr. MacCallister," she said with a nod. She supposed they were being formal because of the public setting, but since Mac had started the conversation in that manner, Jillian intended to follow suit. Besides, by calling her Miss Danvers, there was no chance of betraying her true identity.

He took hold of her elbow and smiled. "May I escort you to the tables? There is going to be quite a feast. You've not attended one of our monthly church socials," he said in an informative way, "but they are quite enjoyable."

"Dr. MacCallister," a thin, pinch-faced woman declared as they reached the door. "I must say, you are looking quite well today." She sneered down her nose at Jillian, then looked back to Mac. "Have you noticed my Davinia? I believe her to look exceptionally lovely today."

Mac grinned at Jillian, then gave the woman a curt little nod. "I'm sure she does, Mrs. Everhart. Have you noticed how well our Miss Danvers is looking today? She is the picture of health, despite a terrible mishap she endured last week at the Harvey House."

Mrs. Everhart gave Jillian a look that suggested she thought her little better than a servant. Jillian immediately threw back her shoulders and thought to say something to the woman about her true position in life, but Reverend Lister's sermon came back to haunt her, and she did nothing but smile blandly. It had never taken more effort to smile than it did in those moments, especially in light of Mrs. Everhart's persistent nature regarding her daughter.

"Davinia will certainly be disappointed if you don't share your time at the social with her," the woman stated quite seriously.

Mac started to answer but never got the chance. About that time Mary Barnes came up and gave him a hearty slap on the back.

"Why, Mac, you're too handsome for your own good. I see once again you have the prettiest gal on your arm."

Mrs. Everhart harumphed her disapproval before storming off toward the churchyard, where tables and chairs had already been assembled. Mac grinned at Mary, and Jillian suppressed a giggle.

"Mary, my dear, you always have a way of putting things right." Mac dropped his hold on Jillian in order to embrace the little woman. "You've been gone so long, I figured I'd have to come out and find you."

"Been busy, my boy," the woman said as Mac pulled away.

While Mary spoke of her exploits, they continued out of the

church and toward the picnic area. Jillian found the older woman's tales to be most fascinating.

"There's been some trouble," Mary admitted. "The government men are pushing the various tribes to put their children in school. It's not going well at all."

"But why?" Jillian questioned. "Do they not want their children educated?"

Mary smiled tolerantly. "Their children *are* educated, my dear. They're educated in the way of the Navajo and Hopi. Their children are more capable of fending for and defending themselves than are most of the folks you see here today. They don't need book learning to teach them how to plant and tend their sheep, and that's how they provide for themselves—probably how they will provide for themselves for the rest of their lives. They aren't looking to live back East in fancy houses or work in offices counting someone else's money."

Jillian felt embarrassed for showing her ignorance. Her expression must have revealed this as well, for Mary patted her arm gently. "Don't feel bad. Most folks would say the same. Somebody decided that everybody had to know the same thing in order to get by in life. I can't say that I wouldn't like to see the children learn to read and write English. After all, if they want to make a life outside of their village, they'll need it. But most of them only want to live their lives among their own people. They don't want our interference, and they don't appreciate our presence in their lives."

"Sounds like some of the Indians can be as prejudiced as the whites," Jillian said without thinking.

Mac laughed. "See, Mary, there are intelligent women in this world, and I just happen to be in the company of two of the finest today. Now, what do you say I go and get you both a glass of lemonade?"

"That sounds good," Mary agreed. "And while you're gone, Miss Danvers and I will have a conversation about you."

Jillian frowned. Mary had called her by name. She knew Judith. But how well? Judith had said nothing about Mary Barnes. She had commented on Indians and some of the trials concerning them and the people of Pintan, but she'd not said anything about this spitfire of a woman.

"Let's grab that table over there. We'll have a nice shade from the church building," Mary said, heading off to the table in question before Jillian could ever comment.

Once they were seated, Jillian's uneasiness made her tongue-tied. How could she say anything without appearing to have lost her memory as to the knowledge of their relationship? On one hand she could say too little, and on the other hand she could say too much and presume upon knowledge and intimacy that did not exist.

But as if God himself had understood her problem, Mary initiated the conversation and made their status clear. "I only know you through Mac, but I feel confident that we can be good friends."

Jillian nodded. "I felt rather curious when you called me by name."

Mary laughed. "Well, I saw you some months ago. It was that time you were heading out on muleback with a group of folks to go exploring the countryside. Since you were the only woman not being forced by some bullying husband to go on that trip, I asked Mac who you were. He told me, and there you have it."

Jillian smiled weakly. Judith and her adventures would be the discovery of her yet. "I was fascinated by what you had to say about the Indians. Do you work with them all the time?"

"As much as I can. I've been fairly well accepted by the Navajo women and especially by the children. I respect them and show them consideration, and they do the same for me. I also buy a great number of their pots, baskets, and blankets in order to sell back East. There's a man who comes to see me here a few times during the year. He takes the stuff with him and makes a tidy little profit on it by peddling it as authentic Indian goods.

"Folks back East seem quite fascinated with the stories they've heard passed down through the years. Stories about Indians in war bonnets, scalping settlers on the open prairie, doing their rain dances and such. Having some trinket from the Indian world seems to satisfy their curiosity, and it helps the Navajo at the same time."

"What about you? Do you make your living this way as well?" Jillian questioned.

Mary shook her head. "God provides for me, child. I use that money for the Navajo. I want them to know there is at least one white person in this world who isn't trying to use them. They've suffered a great deal at our hands." Her expression grew sad. "Many of their women were abused by our men. Men who most would consider to be upstanding citizens. But since the women are considered to be less deserving because they are merely Indian squaws, no one does anything about it."

"How awful," Jillian said, shuddering.

Just then a man of medium build stalked by the table. Rather nice looking, the man had an air of self-assurance that seemed to announce he was someone of importance. He appeared intent on catching the attention of another man in the congregation, but his presence made Mary Barnes' look of sorrow turn to anger. "He's one of the worst culprits. You have to watch him—he's quite the womanizer. I hope he hasn't already caused you problems."

Jillian noticed the man and recognition dawned. "Isn't that Mr. Cooper, the Indian agent? He comes into the Harvey House all the time, and I do remember him being quite the rogue. The other girls seem to enjoy his attention."

"Indeed. I suppose that's why he gets away with so much. But the Navajo are furious with him. He's been trying to force their children into schools and has constantly harangued them to cut their hair and dress in white man's fashions."

At that moment Mac returned with an apology and two lemonades. "I've just been informed that Mrs. Bennett is having trouble delivering her fourth child. I'm going to have to go."

"Do you want some help?" Mary asked, getting to her feet.

"Nah, Mary. You stay here and have some fun. Mrs. Bennett's mother is living with them now. If I need an extra pair of hands, I'll grab her or Mr. Bennett."

Mary nodded. "God's blessings, Mac."

He smiled and placed a worn black felt hat atop his head. "Take good care of our Miss Danvers."

With that he was gone, and Jillian felt a sense of disappointment. She'd not realized how much she was anticipating his company until that moment. There were times when Mac came to eat at the Harvey House, specifically seeking out her area, engaging her in conversation about everything from the railroad to the weather. And other times he caught her attention on the street as she was making her way to the dry goods store or enjoying a leisurely walk. But they never had long to talk, and Jillian found it pleasant to be able to just be herself around Mac. He was the only one who knew her secret, and that made him very special in her eyes.

"He's a good man," Mary said, as if reading her mind.

Jillian blushed. "Yes, he is. He has been most kind to me."

"Mac's that way. He's broken many a heart around these parts, however."

"Oh?" Jillian questioned, trying not to appear curious.

Mary nodded. "Poor Mrs. Everhart has tried to get him hitched to her Davinia for some time now. He's never shown the slightest bit of interest in her, however. Then there have been several Harvey Girls who found him to suit their desires. Only trouble is, Mac isn't lookin' for a wife."

"How interesting," Jillian stated, toying with the glass.

"Nope. Mac's made it real clear that he likes bein' a bachelor. 'Course, round here it's probably best for him to stay single. It's hard being a country doctor, and with all the distance and danger that sometimes comes on him, well, it would be plain hard on a woman to try to plan a life with a man like that."

Jillian nodded. She felt as if Mary were giving her a fair warning about Mac's heart, and it made her uncomfortable that Mary should even think there was a need to do so. Quickly, she shifted the focus of the conversation back to Mary's work. "I don't have much in the way of possessions," she told Mary, "but I would like to give you some money to help the Indians."

"Oh, child, that would be wonderful help. Maybe you would even like to come with me sometime to meet some of the folks."

Jillian nodded. "Perhaps." She wondered at the danger, imagining broad-chested, half-naked savage warriors standing guard at the entrance to some mythical village of tepees. Did Navajo people live in tepees? Jillian didn't have a clue.

Just then Mrs. Everhart passed by where they were seated with another woman at her side. They whispered and glared at Mary before moving on to join other women at another table.

"Why are they like that?" Jillian questioned aloud without thinking.

Mary shrugged. "A good number of folks can remember the old days when the Indian wars took the lives of those they loved. They never stop to think about the fact that the white soldiers took the lives of many of the Indians' loved ones as well. Others just don't like anything that's different from what they know. It scares them."

Jillian could indeed understand fear. She had her own fears when it came to dealing with things foreign and new.

"It's like they can't understand the Indians. Especially when they compare the various tribes to each other. The Navajo have their ways and manner of dress. The Hopi and Zuni have theirs. Some folks only remember the nomadic plains Indian tribes with their buffalo robes and tepees and find the adobe of the Pueblo and the cedar hogans of the Navajo to be strange."

Jillian smiled. "I have to admit I thought of tepees as well."

"Ignorance often breeds contempt and an air of superiority. We condemn what we don't understand and assume it just naturally has to be evil and bad."

Jillian nodded. "Fear makes us do the same."

Mary smiled. "Mac was right. You are a mighty intelligent and insightful young woman."

After circulating among the church congregation, Mary felt it was time to head home. It would take her the better part of an hour just to reach her small homestead, and while she knew she had the option of staying over at the Pintan Hotel and Laundry, her own home beckoned her.

Climbing onto her wagon, she smiled to herself as she thought of Miss Danvers and her obvious interest in Mac. Mac had become like a son to her in the last six years, and she didn't want to see him hurt.

He had suffered a great deal at the hands of a woman, and his heart, if not his entire being, had been seared by her deceit and cruelty.

Still, she recognized the light in Mac's eyes. It was a light she'd once known in her own husband's eyes. It was a light of interest—of possibilities—of hope. She chuckled and clucked to her mules.

Mac needed someone in his life. Someone who would love him and show him the loyalty he deserved. Maybe Miss Danvers could be that woman. She thought back on previous conversations with Mac and knew he highly esteemed the lady. He thought her witty and funny, as Mary recalled. She also seemed to have a sense for adventure, according to Mac. Of course, Mary had witnessed her setting off on her exploration of the countryside and knew Miss Danvers to show little or no fear in regard to experiencing life. Yes, maybe she was exactly what Mac needed.

———————

Jillian spent the rest of her day and evening off exploring the town. She smiled to herself at the sight of Gwen Carson and Zack Matthews in deep conversation. It seemed those two had taken a quick liking to each other. As they strolled together, careful not to touch one another, Jillian found herself almost aching to know the same companionship.

Funny, she hadn't really longed for marriage—or even courtship, for that matter. She had been so inundated with her mother's manipulations and good intentions that she'd always avoided having any entanglements of the heart.

Up ahead, Gwen and Zack paused in their walk, and Jillian realized she would have to either walk around them or head in a different direction. She chose to turn down the alley rather than intrude upon their private excursion. Jillian would have felt like an uninvited guest.

"I've been looking all over for you," Mac said as Jillian emerged from the alley onto Main Street.

"You have?" she asked curiously.

He pushed back his hat and smiled. "Yes, indeed. I had to find out how the rest of the social went. Did Mary talk your arm off?"

Jillian laughed. "She's a wonderful woman. So knowledgeable about the Indians. Does she actually speak their language?"

"Indeed she does. She speaks Navajo about as well as they do. She can also converse some in Hopi and Zuni, and I'm told she has a bit of Apache under her hat as well."

Jillian was notably impressed. "She's quite a woman."

Mac agreed. "That she is." They walked in silence for a few moments before Mac questioned, "Where are you headed?"

She shrugged. "I figured I'd go back to the Harvey House. I haven't had any supper yet and—"

"Have it with me," Mac declared.

"I beg your pardon?"

"Have supper with me," Mac suggested. "I know Mr. Harvey's food is probably the best you'll get in town, but there's another little café down on Second. The Andersons run it, and you can't beat what Mrs. Anderson does with a beefsteak."

Jillian felt a little nervous accepting his invitation. "I don't know if it would be right. It might raise some eyebrows."

"Not right? To have dinner with a friend? Why should that raise any eyebrows?"

She looked up into his eyes and felt an unexpected current course through her. "You're right, of course. Dinner with a friend shouldn't cause anyone to give it a second thought." She smiled, but inside her mind was reeling. Dinner with a friend was one thing, but dinner with this handsome man might be something entirely different. People would no doubt talk, and Jillian wasn't at all sure she was ready to deal with what they might have to say.

As if to prove her point, she had barely started toward Second Street with Mac at her side when Mrs. Everhart and her daughter appeared. Coming up the street from the opposite direction, Mrs. Everhart could only scowl at the sight of Jillian and Mac walking together.

"Well, I suppose the town must be in good health this evening if you have found time for an excursion with Miss Danvers," she remarked snidely.

"Indeed it is," Mac replied, completely undaunted. "Mrs. Bennett has delivered a healthy son, and the rest of Pintan seems to have made it through the day without mishap. We are just on our way to supper at the Andersons'."

Mrs. Everhart seemed unimpressed. She pulled Davinia close and tried once again to promote her daughter to the doctor. "Davinia made an apple crumb cake yesterday. I've never tasted anything quite so good in all my days. We'd be honored if you'd come spend the evening with us and share in her glorious cooking."

Mac glanced momentarily at Jillian and gave a quick roll of his eyes. "Would you like that, Miss Danvers?" He winked before turning back to face the older woman.

Mrs. Everhart stiffened noticeably, and Jillian wanted to laugh out loud. She knew full well she'd not been included in the invitation. Mac saved her before she had need to answer, however.

"I think we'll pass this time," Mac told Mrs. Everhart and Davinia. "I promised Miss Danvers one of the Andersons' special beefsteaks. I know Davinia's crumb cake is probably a masterpiece, but we're committed to our previous plan."

"Well!" Mrs. Everhart declared in a heavy expulsion of breath. Without another word to Mac and Jillian, she pulled Davinia down the street, muttering all the way.

"I suppose she won't have anything to do with me now," Jillian murmured.

Mac laughed. "You'd be one of the lucky ones if that were true. No, my dear Miss Danvers, you will most likely become one of her main items of interest."

Jillian looked at him in horror. "Please tell me you are joking."

Still chuckling, Mac shook his head and took hold of Jillian's arm. "Never fear, my dear friend. I will keep an eye out for you."

Jillian felt a sudden discomfort at his nearness. Mac was so unlike anyone she had ever known. Back home there had been such decorum, such rules. Mac would never have touched her so boldly in Kansas City. She stiffened, fearing that Mac would realize her feelings.

"Relax," he said, more seriously. "She can't really hurt you."

Jillian sighed. He'd taken her reaction for fear of Mrs. Everhart. Better that, she thought, than for him to think she was displeased with him.

C H A P T E R

5

NEARLY A WEEK LATER, Jillian found herself in the center of yet another controversial moment. Having been assigned to work a split shift in order to keep the dining room covered, Jillian took advantage of the quiet afternoon hours to get some shopping done. The heat of the day was pleasantly comfortable, and Jillian found the warmth of the sun upon her face to be most inviting.

The day seemed to promise solace and peace, without so much as a single cloud to mar the perfectly blue sky. Jillian found such simplicity suited her just fine. She tried not to worry about her parents and whether or not her father would come to fetch her home. Nearly a month had passed and no one had come for her yet, so she took courage in that and hoped for the best. And as she found strength in those thoughts, she also took pleasure in her new life. It was more than a little exciting and frightening, but Jillian had never felt more alive. *I like feeling this way,* she thought.

Pintan wasn't all that large. In fact, it was little more than a watering stop in the middle of a dry and desolate land. Natural underground springs fed into a decent-sized river, and these elements made it a necessary focus for the railroad. But like many other towns that had sprung up along the tracks, some found popularity and industry and others didn't. Pintan seemed to be among the latter.

Saloons seemed to be quite popular. Jillian knew of at least three in the town, and compared to the population and other businesses, it seemed a rather lopsided number. She'd overheard Gwen warning a new Harvey Girl of the dangers of walking in the vicinity of the saloons at night. Apparently cowboys frequented these businesses in the evening hours, and often after having too much to drink, they tended to be very brazen in their behavior. Decent women weren't out after dark, Gwen had told the girl, unless accompanied by a chaperone. Jillian took the advice to heart.

The dry goods store stood in the middle of a row of sadly weathered shops on Main Street. Jillian planned this as her destination. She didn't really need anything, but it gave her a good excuse to explore the town, as well as get to know the people better.

A wagon and two rather ancient-looking mules stood at the hitching post outside the store, but otherwise there didn't seem to be a soul stirring. It was almost as if the town had taken an afternoon nap. Jillian wondered at the stillness but decided not to dwell on it. The Harvey House always had plenty of action going on, and she figured maybe the rest of the town simply rode on its coattails. After all, it was hard to beat Fred Harvey's restaurants and hotels. The man had gone out of his way to make sparkling oases in the desert and prairie plains. Even Jillian had been impressed by his focus on the details. Fine china and crystal and only the highest-quality foods were allowed on Mr. Harvey's tables. Jillian was told that a person could expect the very best of service and food any place where Fred Harvey's placard marked the spot. It made her rather proud to be a part of the establishment, even if she was there under false pretenses.

Entering the store, Jillian was pleasantly surprised to find Mary Barnes. The woman was dealing with the store owner while a young Indian woman, heavy with child, waited near the door. When Mary saw Jillian, she paused in her bartering and smiled.

"Why, Miss Danvers, it's good to see you again. I was hoping to have a moment or two with you before I drove out to the village."

"That must be your wagon I passed on my way in here," Jillian replied, wondering how anything so rickety and worn could hold up to a jostling drive across the desert.

"Yes, indeed. That's Clarence and Dobbin standing ready and

waiting," Mary replied confidently. Mary turned back to the clerk. "So are you going to part with any remnant cloth today or not?"

The man looked a bit uncomfortable as Jillian, too, seemed to await his answer.

"Look, Mrs. Barnes, I already told you. There's some scrap pieces in the crate out back. You can have those. Otherwise, I've promised Mrs. Everhart I'd give her some remnants for her ladies' society."

"Ladies' society, my foot. She just wants to keep it out of the hands of the Navajo," Mary protested. "Well, how about I buy the cloth?"

The man perked up at this. "I can hardly say no to a paying customer."

Mary plunked down some change. "Give me whatever this will buy." The man scooped up the money and quickly went into the back room. Mary bit back further comment as Mrs. Everhart entered the store with a basket over one arm and her daughter, Davinia, on the other. Another woman, one Jillian recognized as Mrs. Mason, followed closely on Mrs. Everhart's heels.

All three women stopped in short order at the sight of Mary. Then their gazes traveled around the store and finally settled on the young Indian woman who stood not three feet away.

Mrs. Everhart pulled her daughter close and moved away from the Navajo. Then, with as much drama as she could muster, she reached into her basket and pulled out a handkerchief. "I cannot abide the stench in here," she announced, handing a cloth to Davinia before taking up another. Davinia raised the cloth to her nose and dabbed at it lightly, trying hard to look sophisticated.

Jillian thought the entire act appeared staged. It was almost as if Mrs. Everhart had known what she would find inside the store that day. Mrs. Mason, Mrs. Everhart's faithful follower, quickly imitated her mentor. Together they created a trio of handkerchief-waving forms. Jillian thought they all looked silly but considered it typical of the type of people she'd discovered the Everharts to be. Mr. Everhart was certainly no better. He ran the town's bank and assay office and doubled up by filing claims and land records for Pintan. He was quite outspoken at the church picnic, saying behind Reverend Lister's back that "the day he was equal to a low-down dirty Injun was the day pigs would fly and cows could knit." This had brought a hearty laugh from several of the listening townsfolk, revealing to Jillian just the kind of people Reverend Lister had to deal with.

"I simply cannot abide that you let the likes of this squaw stand inside the store," Mrs. Everhart said as the clerk came back with an armful of material. She frowned at the sight and added, "I thought we had an agreement regarding remnant cloth."

"Mrs. Barnes bought and paid for this," the man offered apologetically.

"Very well. If she chooses to spend her money on those savages, then let it be upon her head. They will no doubt abuse it anyway. Just as they abuse anything else offered them. Why, look at poor Mr. Cooper. He has tried over and over to help these people, and instead of being grateful and doing as they are told, they send that demon seductress to entice the poor man." She turned to stare at the pregnant Navajo. "The daughter of Satan is who you are. You, who would steal the very soul of that poor man. Plying your wares before him, then parading your consequences around town as though it's something to be proud of. You're nothing better than a—"

"Hazel Everhart, I'm half inclined to stuff this material down your throat," Mary said, interceding on the girl's behalf.

Jillian backed up a pace as Mrs. Everhart drew nearer. She had loosened her hold on Davinia, and both the girl and Mrs. Mason stood back as if to watch their heroine go to battle for them and all of proper society.

"Mrs. Barnes, you have forced this town to endure your meddling. However, you need not think you have the right to infringe upon our way of life by forcing us to approve the Indian ways as natural."

"I didn't ask you to approve the Indian ways. I merely ask you to accept that they are human beings with rights and privileges the same as you," Mary countered. "I hardly see how you can hold Little Sister responsible for what happened to her when you know yourself how Mr. Cooper can be. Didn't I hear you warn Davinia about the man?"

"That's beside the point. I don't want any daughter of mine married to an Indian agent. I would rather see her settled back East where civilization causes folks to remember their places."

"Their prejudices, don't you mean?" Mary asked.

Jillian saw how uncomfortable the young Navajo woman had become. She had no way of knowing whether the woman understood all that was being said about her, but Jillian felt confident that she understood the implication. The woman bowed her head and stared at the floor, as if deeply ashamed to even be seen.

"I do not consider it wrong to allow for each person to keep to their own kind," Mrs. Everhart replied. "Even the Navajo want nothing to do with the white way of life. They've made it clear."

"So you believe it is best to leave them to their own culture and ways, is that it?" Mary questioned.

Jillian could tell by the way Mary smiled that she was laying a trap for the snooty woman.

"I believe . . . well . . . I think that they should recognize that we have a better way. Our children can read and write. They know right from wrong, which is more than I can say for the likes of this pathetic creature," Mrs. Everhart said, marching toward the woman Mary had called Little Sister. She frowned at the girl as she raised her head to meet the older woman's glare. "She stinks to high heaven and she bears the consequences of her actions. She's a harlot, seducing a good man for whatever devious purposes she had in mind."

Anger coursed through Jillian, but she had no idea what to say. She had been raised to remain silent and allow her elders their say, but this seemed most unfair. By the time Mrs. Everhart had finished her harangue, Little Sister fled the store in tears.

Mary nodded to Jillian. "I'll talk to you later."

Jillian watched Mary walk proudly through the store. She paused in front of Hazel Everhart and, peering up over the stack of cloth, said, "Just remember, whatever you do unto the least of these . . ."

She let the words trail off and turned without hurry to march out the front door. The scene was so upsetting that Jillian couldn't even remember what she'd come for. Instead, she walked past the now silent women and stepped out onto the thin boardwalk.

"Come by any time, Mary," she called out to the woman who was now atop the wagon seat with Little Sister safely beside her.

"I'll do that, deary," Mary replied, then flicked the reins on the backs of the mules and moved off down the dusty street.

The dust rose up to swirl around Jillian and choke out the fresh air, but she hardly seemed to notice. Even this was pleasant compared to what she'd just endured inside the store.

Deciding to give up on her shopping, she walked over to Mac's, determined to talk to him about what had just happened. Not only that, but she was due to have her stitches out. Actually overdue, but she'd needed the extra time to work up her courage. No telling how painful this was going to be.

She knocked softly on the door and smiled shyly when Mac came to answer. He was dressed casually in jeans and a well-worn work shirt. He looked nothing like the properly attired doctor she'd first met.

"I've come to brave the removal of my stitches," Jillian said, holding up her hand. "If you have a bullet for me to bite, we can get started."

"Good to see you too," he said, then added in a whisper, "Jillian."

She stepped inside and followed him to the examination room where once again she took a seat and waited for Mac to wash his hands.

"Something very upsetting just happened," she began.

"Did it involve you breaking something?" he questioned with a grin.

She frowned. "No, this was very serious. It involved Mary and this young Navajo woman—although I hesitate to call her that. She seemed hardly more than a girl, yet she was with child."

"Ah, you must be talking about Little Sister."

"Yes, she's the one."

Mac nodded. "A most unpleasant situation, that one." He brought a tray with scissors and tweezers and sat down directly in front of Jillian. "Are you sure you want to hear the details? I mean, I know you aren't quite as worldly as your sister."

Jillian lifted her chin defiantly and replied, "I'm quite capable of dealing with the truth, Doctor."

Mac smiled. "I wasn't trying to be cruel, Jillian. It's just not a story I'd normally share with someone of your gender."

She nodded. "I suppose I can understand that. I know, however, that Mr. Cooper apparently got her that way."

"Jillian, the truth is . . . he raped her."

The word came as a slap to Jillian. "Raped?" she questioned hesitantly. "But Mrs. Everhart said—"

"I'm sure I know what Mrs. Everhart said. She suggests that Little Sister enticed the poor unassuming Mr. Cooper. That the girl has some sort of demon spirit and her powers left Mr. Cooper helpless to fight her off."

"Yes, that's pretty much the way it sounded," Jillian replied.

"The truth is that Mr. Cooper tends to have few limitations for himself and no moral values. Why he bothers to go to church is a mystery to me, but as Mary says, it ain't the well folks who need the doctor. Anyway, Cooper is the agent to the area tribes. His tasks vary, but he's lousy at all of them. Little Sister's brother, Bitter Water Bear, refused to deal with Cooper regarding the new school built last fall. Cooper suggested that Bear, as he's usually called, influence his people to accept the new mandates of public education and such, but Bear adamantly refused. Cooper tried to bribe him, sending a wagon full of gifts to Bear. Again Bear refused. Instead, Bear sent the gifts back by means of Little Sister."

"What a strange name for someone," Jillian said, thinking aloud.

"It's not her real name," Mac admitted. "Mary started calling her that because her Navajo name was hard to pronounce and it meant the same thing. I think the exact translation was something like *Girl Who Comes After*. Anyway, Little Sister took the goods back to Cooper, and he immediately took a liking to her. Well, maybe that's not the right word for it. He played on Little Sister's training and upbringing and ordered her to unload the wagon and bring the things into the house. She did so, and with the last load delivered, Cooper shut the door and barred her from leaving. He suggested she stay with him, but she refused, telling him that he was her brother's enemy. Cooper laughed at this. He tried to coax her, suggesting that he could help her people if she would just give him what he wanted. When she refused, he beat her and then forced himself on her."

Jillian shuddered uncontrollably. The thought of being anywhere near Cooper turned her stomach. "How can the people of Pintan tolerate him?"

"Most don't know, or if they do, they feel it acceptable to overlook. After all, it was just a Navajo girl. It wasn't like it was anyone important."

"That's unfair!" Jillian declared. "She's a human being. She's carrying his child."

"It's not the first," Mac replied sadly. "Two other women found themselves in the same situation. They're dead now."

"Dead?" Jillian questioned.

"They took their own lives. It was more honorable that way. Little Sister lives with Mary because her own people have disowned her. Cooper told Bear that she laid with him willingly and that when she tried to steal from him afterward, he punished her with a beating."

"Oh, Mac, don't say any more," Jillian said, lowering her head. "I didn't think such people existed."

Mac lifted her chin with his finger. "We have to acknowledge it in order to rid ourselves of it. I've written three letters to Washington suggesting Cooper be recalled on the grounds that he is mismanaging supplies and totally alienating the Navajo people. I haven't mentioned the situation with Little Sister because, frankly, I'm hoping the other things will be enough to see him removed."

"Let's hope so," Jillian replied sadly. She could still see the pain-filled expression of the young Navajo woman, and her heart ached for all that Little Sister had been forced to endure. "She's very brave," Jillian said, thinking of Little Sister's choice not to kill herself. "I wish I were brave. If I had been, I might have given Mrs. Everhart a piece of my mind."

"You're brave, Jillian. A coward would never have come west in her sister's place. A coward would never have desired to learn the truth rather than accept popular opinion. Now, stop being all gloomy. You can hardly be of any use to anyone if you give all your energy over to mourning what has already happened."

"I suppose you're right." She thought about it for a moment, then asked, "What do you suppose I could do to help the most?"

Mac shrugged. "I think Mary could probably tell you better than I can. I try to help Mary in whatever way I can. She's come to me for medicine and such on occasion, but for the most part the Indians won't use it. Can't say as I blame them. However, they have a wonderful system using herbs. Mary's been teaching me, and I've learned quite a bit. I've even used it on a few of the folks around here, but don't tell them." He grinned. "They wouldn't be able to abide knowing they were healed with Indian medicine."

"My lips are sealed," Jillian replied, smiling.

"So tell me," Mac asked, getting to his feet, "has anyone learned your secret yet?"

"No. I'm happy to report that as far as the good and sometimes not so good folks of Pintan are concerned, I'm Judith Danvers and my Harvey contract is up in June."

"Hmm, little over two months. Do you suppose you can pull it off that long?"

Jillian laughed. "Not if I have to deal with Mrs. Everhart too many more times."

"Oh, but that would be perfect," Mac said, leaning back against the counter. "Judith would have spoken her mind as well."

Jillian frowned. "Why didn't she say something about this, Mac? She never wrote about the problems. She only wrote about the good things."

"Maybe she didn't want to worry you."

"Or maybe she just didn't think I was up to the truth," Jillian replied.

"Either way, that's in the past."

Jillian looked at Mac's sympathetic gaze and nodded. "You're right." She contemplated the matter only a moment more before deciding she was ready for Mac to remove her stitches. "Well, let's get this torture over with."

"What torture?"

"The stitches," she chided him. "Remember, you were going to remove them?"

"I already have," he said with a devilish grin. "You just weren't paying attention."

She looked down at her hand and shook her head. "I shall have to pay particular attention when you are involved, Dr. MacCallister. You are too smooth for your own good, and I shall have to keep alert."

Mac laughed. "You're more like your sister than you know. I think if you give yourself a chance, you'll find out that you're just as bold and brazen as she ever was."

Jillian couldn't help but consider his words a compliment. "Thank you. Maybe I will."

———

That night, Mac settled into bed and picked up one of his many medical journals. He had allowed himself to get behind in his reading since Jillian's arrival in Pintan. Funny how she could be the identical twin of Judith, yet be so different. To Mac's way of thinking, they might share some of the same features, but there were things about Jillian that set her apart from her sister.

Smiling to himself, Mac couldn't help but remember the first moment he'd realized Jillian's identity. She had been so afraid of his telling on her, yet he found the whole thing a delightful break in the monotony of a normally quiet town. Oh, there had been some trouble with the local cowboys, but now that there was a new sheriff in town, even those disputes had calmed. Drunk and disorderly folks were still to be found on the street corners most nights, but with Zack Matthews in place, there were fewer gunshot and knife wounds. It made Mac's job a whole lot easier.

Opening the journal, Mac tried to focus on the article regarding diabetes, but his mind drifted to images of Jillian. He frowned as he realized the depth of his interest. There could be no one in his life— at least not a woman in the capacity of wife. Shaking his head, he couldn't help but think back in time. Back to his early days in Pintan. Back to *her*. It wasn't fair or right that she had been so heartless.

He had loved her more dearly than anything—maybe even more than God. Perhaps that was why things had gone so wrong. Mac felt a dull ache build in his heart until the pain felt fresh. Why had it gone so terribly wrong? Why couldn't she have loved him the way he loved her?

With a growl he forced the memories away. "I won't give in to that torture," he told himself. But even as he said the word *torture*, he couldn't help but think of Jillian. She had looked so frightened and helpless when she'd come to him earlier that day. She differed from Judith in that area. Judith had a way about her that suggested she feared nothing in life, while Jillian seemed afraid of a great deal.

"Well, this is one person she needn't fear," Mac said, turning back to the article. "She has absolutely nothing to fear from me. I'll be her friend, and when she's gone there will be nothing more." But the thought of Jillian leaving Pintan left Mac with a different kind of ache. He forced his gaze to the paper. "I won't make the same mistake twice," he promised himself. "I won't."

C H A P T E R

6

JILLIAN WAITED UNTIL HER next day off from the Harvey routine to see a bit of the countryside around Pintan. She contemplated asking to borrow Mac's horse, but that would mean riding astride, and she didn't have any riding skirts that would allow for such a thing. And, no doubt, Mac wouldn't have a sidesaddle. She continued to consider the situation when Kate came into the room and tossed her a letter.

"I had to come up to change me apron, and Sam had this letter for ya from the morning train." Sam Capper, the Harvey House manager, was always good about getting the mail delivered in short order. He knew how important a letter from home could be, and he cared about the girls as much as Gwen Carson did. If she were their housemother, he was, indeed, like a father.

"Thank you," Jillian said, picking up the missive with great reservation. It could have only come from one of two places: Judith or her parents.

Looking at the handwriting, Jillian immediately recognized her mother's penmanship. *Miss J. Danvers, Pintan, Arizona Terr.*, the address read. A wave of worry washed over Jillian. This letter would no doubt contain word from her father as to what he would and would not tolerate. It might even declare what train he would arrive on in order to bring Jillian home.

She waited until Kate had gone, then opened the letter and read. Her mother spoke of missing her dearly and of how the house was so very sad without her. She spoke of Judith's marriage as one of life's greatest disappointments, relating that her heart was completely broken by the missed opportunities for her daughter to be well established in society.

I have only wanted the very best for my girls, Jillian read, *and while your sister seems happy at this moment in time, I fear the day will come when she regrets her choice. Perhaps it is impossible for you girls to understand my concerns for your welfare, but marrying a man of little means will mean a hard life with great adversity.*

Judith seems content helping her husband put their business together. Why she should wish to soil her hands at such labor is beyond me, but I must find a way to resign myself to the matter.

The issue of Judith now put aside, Gretchen Danvers went back to her old nature and spoke of a handsome young earl who would be arriving from England. He had come to see the wild American West and to hunt, and Gretchen had it on the best authority that he was even interested in finding himself a rich American for a wife. Jillian rolled her eyes in exasperation, then continued reading. *He is said to be handsome and of good standing with the Queen of England. I think he sounds like a perfect match for you, darling Jillian.*

Jillian laughed. "Why, Mother? Because he's in good standing with the queen?" She failed to see her mother's logic. She finished the letter, then noted a smaller folded piece of paper. Her father's bold, almost arrogant script blazed off the page at her.

> *Jillian, I think you are six kinds of fool for having allowed Judith to coerce you into this ordeal. However, you make a good point regarding the business arrangement of this situation. Therefore, with reservation, I give my permission for you to stay on to finish out your sister's contract. After that, I want you on the first train home.*

Jillian felt a moderate amount of relief. She had her father's permission to stay, but her mother was still playing matchmaker. For the first time since Judith's marriage, Jillian actually envied her sister. Their mother could no longer play matchmaker for Judith. It was while contemplating this situation that Jillian hit upon an idea. Perhaps if she took Judith's example and began to stress the point of marrying for love, her mother would gradually change her mind. Maybe, if she saw that Jillian was truly happy, she would be content to let her daughter make her own choices.

Taking up pen and paper, Jillian began to write.

> *Mother,*
>
> *Life in Pintan is quite lovely. I've enjoyed my time at the Harvey House and find that working with my hands brings a great deal of satisfaction. I have made good friends, although they do not know my true identity. Please do not worry about me, and please do not try to arrange for me a husband. I am content to wait for love. In fact, I've met a wonderful man here in Pintan. He is handsome and quite civilized and charming. He is a doctor, and while I know you consider that to be beneath our social standing, he is quite wonderful. I have no interest in your earl, in light of my fascination with this man. I hope you will understand and let my heart judge who is best for me.*

She stared at the words for a moment, rather surprised at her boldness in expressing her feelings for Mac on paper. He *was* handsome and charming—not that she figured him to be anything more than a friend. In a few months she wouldn't even be here, and Mac would forget all about her and the deception she'd made him a part of.

Jillian reread the words and thought perhaps she should throw the letter away and start over. But a quick glance at the clock made her realize there simply wasn't time. If she was to get a letter back to her mother in time to dissuade her from further matchmaking, Jillian would have to hurry. She jotted a few more tidbits of information regarding her life in Pintan, then signed her name and blew on the ink to dry it more quickly. With any luck at all, this letter would put her mother in her place and force an end to the constant parade of suitors she had in mind for her daughter.

Jillian felt a bit guilty for involving Mac. After all, he'd been very kind to her, and she hated for it to appear that she was using him.

Maybe she should say something to him about it. She considered this, then cast aside the idea. It would be much too embarrassing to have Mac know of what she'd written. He might even get the wrong impression.

A light knock on her room door brought Jillian's thoughts back to reality. She carefully folded the letter and slipped it inside the envelope before opening the door.

"Good morning, Judith," Gwen said with a smile. "You have a visitor downstairs."

"Oh," Jillian replied, not quite knowing what to think. "Who is it?"

"Mrs. Barnes," Gwen replied.

Jillian smiled and nodded. "I'll be right there."

She took up her sunbonnet, something Judith had advised her to always wear when going outdoors, and the letter and made her way to the visitor's parlor. Mary sat waiting patiently, looking rather out of place in the artfully decorated room. Mr. Harvey not only had expensive taste but very particular taste, and the heavily polished English furnishings seemed rather misplaced in Pintan, Arizona.

"It's good to see you again," Jillian announced, coming into the room.

"Mac mentioned it was your day off," Mary replied, getting to her feet. "I thought maybe you'd be free to help me."

"With what?" Judith questioned, surprised that Mac knew her schedule so intimately.

"I'm taking a load of things to the Indian village. I'll also be bringing a load back. Little Sister is too far along to help me, and I'd like to get back to my place before dark so that she won't have to be alone all night. If we really push, we can make it."

Jillian felt a surge of fear at the idea of being out there among the Indian villages, but she shoved her emotions aside and nodded. What would Mary think if she refused to offer her a helping hand? "I'd be happy to help you. Just let me give Mr. Capper this letter to post." She paused as a thought ran through her mind. "Am I dressed appropriately?"

Mary's chuckle assured Jillian that such matters were probably not of great concern. "You look fine. Just make sure your boots are good for walkin' and your bonnet wide enough to keep the sun off your face."

Jillian nodded. "I had dressed in just such a manner. I suppose it was Divine Providence."

"God knew I'd need you," Mary said, then winked conspiratorially. "And God knew I'd be in a hurry as usual, so He readied you before I got here."

"I'm sure you're right," Jillian replied, though she wasn't all that certain. Mary talked about such things in the same way that Grandmother Danvers had always talked of her superstitions and omens. Was there really much difference just because Mary determined that hers came from God instead of stories handed down from family lore?

After leaving her letter to be posted and explaining to Mr. Capper where she was off to, Jillian climbed up into Mary's ancient wagon. Appearing more solid than she had expected, Jillian took a seat on the well-worn bench and waited for Mary to join her. Clarence and Dobbin hardly seemed concerned at Jillian's added weight as Mary flicked the reins. They moved out in a sluggish sort of disinterest that Jillian was sure must be their normal attitude toward the task.

"I was hoping to see more of the countryside," Jillian told Mary as she tied her bonnet securely.

"That mule expedition didn't show you enough, eh?" Mary questioned.

Jillian hated carrying on this deception. She had come to think of Mary as a friend, and maintaining her identity as Judith was causing her to lie to many people she had come to care about. Shifting uncomfortably, Jillian tried to think of something to say.

"I suppose seeing a bit of the landscape has only encouraged me to view more." *There*, Jillian thought, *that wasn't a lie*. She had been fascinated by her views from the train. Mile after mile of sage and tumbleweed, arid rocky mountains, and rugged piñon pine had drawn her attention all the way from Kansas City.

The Arizona landscape spread out before Jillian in a bevy of colors. Red and yellow sandstone rock, wild scrub, and tamarisk trees dotted the vast open expanses. At first it appeared quite desolate and lifeless, but as Jillian looked closer, she found much evidence to prove her initial conclusion wrong. Rabbits, mice, lizards, and snakes could be seen moving among the rocks and sage, and wild flowers were growing in abundance wherever the sandy dirt would allow growth.

"This is lovely," Jillian stated as Mary urged the mules forward.

"It is, isn't it? Takes a special eye to appreciate it, though," Mary replied. "Some folks just see the wasteland."

"Kind of like some folks just see the color of someone else's skin?" Jillian didn't know why she was compelled to bring up that subject, but it seemed appropriate, given their destination.

Mary nodded. "Just the same. Only the land doesn't get its feelings hurt if you say that it's ugly and useless."

"Tell me about the Navajo, Mary. How do they live, and what do they do with their lives?"

Mary laughed in a loud, guffawing way. Not at all the ladylike, almost lyrical laugh that Jillian had been taught as acceptable.

"Oh, girly, that's a loaded basket of apples. The Navajo are a fascinating people. They have many hidden talents and abilities, just like anyone else. You've seen their baskets and blankets, haven't you?"

"Yes, they're beautiful. How do they make those blankets? The patterns are so intricate."

"They weave them on looms. Have you never seen someone weave?"

"Never," Jillian had to admit.

"They claim to have been taught by Spider Woman."

Jillian frowned. "Spider Woman?"

Mary chuckled and gave a clucking sound to the mules. They picked up the pace as Mary continued. "Sounds a little strange, I know. Spider Woman's husband, Spider Man, constructed the first weaving loom from the cross poles of sky and earth cords—or so they say. Spider Woman taught the *Dine*, as the Navajo call themselves, the art of weaving on a loom. Spider Woman is quite important to them. She is very revered and honored. Some of the mothers even warn their children that if they won't be good, Spider Woman will come down on her webbed ladder and take them away to eat them."

"How awful," Jillian said, shuddering. "I can't imagine living with that kind of threat over me. Don't they worry about giving their children bad dreams?" She thought of her grandmother's threats and omens and knew the depth of fear a person could sustain when exposed to such stories.

"It's a hard life out here. You have to motivate the children in order to keep them safe. There are so many dangers."

"I can tell that much is true," Jillian replied. "Until coming here, I certainly never had to beat my clothing to make sure it was free from varmints. Still, I know what it is to live in fear that something bad might happen." Mary looked at her strangely, and Jillian couldn't help but elaborate—just a bit. "My grandmother held to superstitions all her life. She used to terrify me, particularly about death. I suppose she thought she was keeping me in line, but I found it cruel. I still do. I'm sorry if the Navajo think it necessary to train their children with such stories."

"The Navajo have a good system," Mary said, turning her gaze back to the mules. "Their children are their assurance of the circle of life continuin'. They wouldn't risk them by not teachin' 'em the hazards of life out here. It ain't like livin' in the city, where things are pretty much labeled for you. The Navajo have cultivated the earth, and in spite of the barren appearance of the land, they have found ways to grow crops and tend sheep. They get their wool for weaving from their own flocks. They are a very efficient people."

"But what kind of beliefs do they have? You said they revered this Spider Woman. Do they have other gods?" Jillian questioned, noting that there was now no sign of Pintan or civilization. How in the world did Mary stand traveling out here all alone?

"They have their Holy Ones, as they call them. But ultimately, they believe there is power and energy in everything. They believe the land itself is partly where they get their power for healing and life. They hold special regard for the four directions and believe they have bearing on their lives. The East is the place of dawn, which is their thinkin' direction. The South is a plannin' direction. The West is where they do their livin', so it's their life direction. And finally, the North is a place for evaluatin'. They find their satisfaction here and determine what changes they can make to improve their lives."

"It's all so fascinating," Jillian admitted.

They rode a ways in silence, and Jillian thought of the strange beliefs of the Indians who lived not so very far from her world. Yet because of the isolation she had known, Jillian felt as if she were the most ignorant person on the face of the earth. She was only now beginning to feel more competent at her job, but she still couldn't imagine trying to live life on her own out here in the desert. Mary seemed to take it all in stride. Her husband was dead and gone, and her home was probably all that remained of that portion of her life.

"Mary," Jillian said softly, "were you married for a very long time?"

Mary laughed. "I'll say. Sometimes it seemed forever and sometimes it didn't seem near long enough. I was married for thirty years before my husband passed on to his reward. He's been gone nearly ten years and that seems like forever." Sorrow edged her tone.

"I'm sorry. I didn't mean to make you sad."

"It's not really a sadness. It's a longing. I wish for nothin' more than to join him in heaven, but I know that my job on earth ain't done yet. When it is, God will come and take me home, but not a minute sooner." Again they rode in silence, until nearly twenty minutes had passed and Mary declared, "There's my place over there."

Jillian squinted to look out across the horizon. The small stone house seemed such a natural part of the landscape that at first Jillian thought it was nothing more than an outcropping of rock. As they neared, however, she could see that the little house was a combination of stone and cedar poles and even a little adobe. It wasn't anything to boast about, but it was shelter and apparently some comfort to the old woman, for she beamed proudly at the house as they came to a stop.

"My husband wasn't much of an architect, but it served us well. We always hoped to have a family here, but God never gave us any young'uns. So we devoted our time to the Navajo and Hopi. They became our children."

"How is it that they don't hate you like they do other whites?"

Mary stared at her hard for a moment. "I wouldn't say they so much as hate the white man. I think they are simply weary of their interference and constant attempt at indoctrination."

"But Mac said that you share the Christian faith with the Navajo. Aren't you striving to indoctrinate them yourself?" Jillian suddenly realized how her question sounded. "I didn't mean—"

Mary held up her hand. "I ain't offended by your honest questions, so don't go apologizin'. I share the light of Jesus with them through my work. I speak to them of the Word of God. The Navajo believe that words have great power. I tell them that I couldn't agree more. I speak of my Savior and His love for all people. But I don't beat them over the head with religion. I let God speak for himself, and I help them by buyin' their wares and tradin' goods with them because, frankly, their feet don't need washin'."

"What?" Jillian was confused.

"Don't you remember the part in the Bible where Jesus washed the disciples' feet?"

Jillian hated to admit that she wasn't very familiar with Scripture, but there was nothing else to do. "I'm afraid I don't."

Mary patted her arm gently. "That's all right. Jesus washed His disciples' feet as an act of love and servanthood. He showed them that we must come to people in love and service rather than from lofty ornate pulpits and gold-encrusted cathedrals. Jesus was tender with folks. He loved the truth into them. That's what I intend to let Him do through me."

"What a beautiful thought," Jillian replied. She felt a warmth spread through her at the idea of such tenderness.

"Well, come on inside. We'll need to get a move on if we're to get this wagon loaded and make it to the village before noon."

Jillian followed Mary into the open house and found Little Sister quietly weaving in the corner of the room.

"How wonderful!" Jillian exclaimed, moving closer to see the delicate patterns of blue and white.

"She's making a blanket for her baby," Mary explained. "Little Sister, this is Miss Danvers. She's going to help me today so that you can rest."

The shy girl looked up, her gaze barely reaching Jillian's face.

Jillian looked to Mary. "Does she speak English?"

"As good as you or me."

Jillian knelt down beside Little Sister and gently reached out to touch the girl.

"I'm sorry for what those women said to you in town. I felt helpless to know what to say, but I just want you to know that they were wrong to treat you so badly."

"Thank you," Little Sister said without raising her face. "Your words touch my heart."

"Miss Danvers is a good friend," Mary said. "Her name is Judith. I'm sure she won't mind you using it."

Jillian swallowed hard. Her lies felt even more painful to her now. "I wouldn't mind at all. I'd like to be a friend to you, Little Sister."

The girl looked up, and this time she held her dark-eyed gaze to Jillian's. "You aren't like the others."

"I hope not," Jillian replied. "I hope never to be like them again."

Little Sister nodded. "Thank you for giving me your name."

Jillian's conscience pricked her painfully. With a deep sense of regret and frustration, Jillian straightened and looked to Mary.

"So where are the things you need loaded?"

7

JILLIAN'S EXPOSURE TO THE NAVAJO way of life opened her eyes to yet another facet of existence. Poverty.

The houses, or *hogans*, as Mary had called them, were crafted out of cedar poles and were octagonal in construction. None of the walls appeared to necessarily match their counterparts in length or height, giving some of the hogans a rather odd look to them. Jillian wondered how safe they were and commented on this, but Mary assured her the houses were solid and quite nice inside. She reminded Jillian not to be overly influenced by outward appearances, leaving Jillian feeling guilty for her attitude once again.

Children played happily in spite of what seemed to Jillian to be a dismal existence. When they saw Mary, they came running and ran back and forth alongside the wagon until Mary pulled to a stop beside one of the many sheep corrals. Laughing and clapping, they extended grubby little hands to receive the peppermint and licorice sticks that Mary pulled from her skirt pockets. Apparently this was a normal routine, for Mary made no announcement in order to gather the children.

Mary glanced at Jillian and winked. "My ma always stood by the idea of catching more flies with sugar than vinegar."

Jillian grinned and watched the happy children dance around with their candy. Some were barely dressed, while others wore simple cotton tunics and pants or skirts. None of them wore shoes, however, as they seemed to enjoy the warmth of the sandy soil against their feet. Jillian wondered if they ever wore shoes. She wondered, too, if they ever took baths, for the children were coated in layers of dust and dirt.

Several of the Navajo women, dressed simply in long skirts and belted tunic blouses, sat on the ground at outdoor looms. Their rich black hair was pulled back into looped buns and secured with rawhide strips, while booted moccasins peeked out from beneath their skirts.

Jillian was immediately taken in by the lovely colors that marked the patterns in their weaving and also graced their clothing. "They wear such bright colors," she commented to Mary as she handed out the last of the candy and climbed down from the wagon.

"They use natural dyes from the land," Mary replied, motioning for Jillian to climb down. "They are very resourceful people."

Just as Jillian started to move, she caught sight of a stern-faced Navajo man. His appearance suggested an age somewhere near or slightly older than Jillian's twenty-three years. Straight hair touched his shoulders in blue-black ripples that waved in the warm desert breeze. He stood between two hogans that were set somewhat apart from the others, his gaze intense and clearly not one of greeting.

"Who is that?" Jillian whispered, nudging her friend.

Mary looked up. "Oh, that's Little Sister's brother, Bear."

"He doesn't look too happy to see us."

Just then another Navajo man went to Bear, and after speaking to him for a few moments, the two men went off together in the direction of one of the hogans.

"Bear doesn't like interference from us," Mary admitted. "He finds our ways to be harmful to his people."

"How so?" Jillian asked, helping Mary unload the crates she'd brought.

"Bear sees what has happened to the young girls, including his sister, and believes all white men to be corrupt and evil. He sees the cheating and manipulation of folks like Mr. Cooper and some of the army officials and believes that all whites must surely follow suit. He hates that I come here and trade with the women, yet he also knows me to be fair. And of course, he knows that Little Sister is living with me. It's kind of a love-hate relationship."

Jillian watched as some of the women came to greet Mary. They spoke in a mix of Navajo and English, and from time to time Mary would pull one thing and then another out from her wooden boxes.

There was nothing for Jillian to do but step back and watch the trading go on. She admired the way Mary conducted business, shaking her head no when the trade was not reasonable and beaming a smile of acceptance when a match could be made. Mary neither gave her things away, nor did she take more than was fair.

Jillian thought it a rather fascinating system. Mary would take the offered pottery, blankets, and baskets and sell them to her buyer. Then she would take the money and buy goods for the Navajo and trade again for more works of art. It seemed a very self-contained system.

By early afternoon, Jillian and Mary began to make their way back to Pintan. During the extent of their stay at the Navajo village, Bear had never seemed far from where they were trading, and now Jillian could feel his piercing gaze as they drove away. She thought him to be a fierce-looking man, epitomizing everything she had imagined when the word *Indian* was spoken. Funny how she had known people back East who lumped all of these native people into one simple word: Indian. Mary had told her that the Navajo were very proud and easily angered when it was suggested that they were merely Indians.

"They are Navajo," Mary had said quite seriously. "Just as the Hopi and Zuni are separate people, so the Navajo are separate as well."

The back of the wagon jostled with a number of ornate pots, causing Jillian to focus on the present rather than the past. Mary had packed them carefully, using straw to keep them as safe as possible, but the deeply rutted excuse for a road would not cooperate with the rickety wagon, and some amount of abuse was to be expected.

Still, the pots seemed quite solid. Jillian had thought it rather fascinating the way the women had painted intricate designs on the various vases, water jars, and bowls. But even this wasn't as wondrous as the delightful patterns woven into the wool blankets. The items were all quite lovely and Jillian couldn't help but admire them. She wondered what her father would say about such creations. Would he see their potential to become salable products? Perhaps he would. Maybe she could even write to him about it and suggest such a thing. Then Mary would have yet another buyer for the Indian work, and perhaps she could make the people even more money.

She frowned, however, knowing that money would never fix the existing problems between the whites and the Navajo. Money wouldn't change the color of Navajo skin or dispel the prejudice of the folks in Pintan. In fact, Jillian knew money couldn't even buy the Navajo approval in the eyes of the whites. She had seen poor immigrants back home who had made good and earned themselves hefty savings. Yet they were still shunned by upper society. Just because they had money didn't mean they had manners or the cultural background to give them acceptability in the circles of Jillian's parents and friends. So if money wasn't the answer, what was?

The trip home seemed endless. The rocky red cliffs cast ominous shadows across the ground, giving the landscape a strangely painted appearance. Mary had told her of an area even farther away, which many called the Painted Desert. The play of sun and shadows upon this area of land had given rise to the name. If it was similar to what Jillian saw in the land before them, then she could well understand why it would be called "Painted."

The patterns rather reminded her of the blankets, and Jillian wondered if that was where the Navajo women got their ideas for their designs. Glancing over her shoulder at the stack of blankets behind the wagon seat, Jillian knew she must have a memento of the day.

"Mary," she said as they slowly neared the town, "I wonder if I could purchase one of those blankets. The red-and-yellow one is my favorite, and I'd be happy to pay top dollar."

Mary smiled. "I saw you eyeing that one with particular interest. Of course you may have it." She pulled the wagon to a stop against the back side of the Harvey House and shook off some of the dust and sand that had accumulated on her dark gray skirt. "I surely do appreciate the help you gave me today."

"I appreciate that you asked me to go. I learned a great deal," Jillian said as she climbed down from the wagon. Though dirty and gritty from the long ride home, she felt a satisfaction in having expanded her mind. And maybe even her heart.

"Here, you don't want to forget this," Mary said, reaching behind her to pull the red-and-yellow blanket from a crate.

"Oh, do come inside and have dinner. I can run upstairs and get my money while you eat."

Mary looked at the angle of the sun. "I might have just enough time for a piece of Mr. Harvey's pie. After all, it's some of the best I've ever tasted."

"We have a great chef," Jillian said, patting her waist. "He may, in fact, be too good for my good. I've probably gained five pounds since coming here."

Mary laughed and maneuvered over the side of the wagon. "You look just fine. Even Mac said so."

"Mac?" Jillian felt her cheeks grow hot. Mac had spoken about her appearance?

"My goodness, you look as though the possibility were completely unthinkable. You're a handsome woman, and there aren't many women in these parts. Mac said the Harvey House had been losin' them left and right to area ranchers and miners. He also said that as pretty as you are, someone was bound to take an interest in you, and that it probably wouldn't be long before some prospector or railroad worker snatched you up for himself."

Jillian felt her moment of glory fade. Mac hadn't mentioned anything in regard to his thoughts being personal, just that someone else might find her worth the trouble of taking interest in.

"Well," she finally said, pushing aside a disappointment that she didn't understand, "Mac doesn't know everything. Once I take care of Ju . . . my contract . . ." she stammered, "I'll be on the next train to Kansas City."

They rounded the corner of the Harvey House just as Mr. Cooper entered through the front door. Jillian stiffened, and Mary announced, "Oh, good. I need to see that man in regard to the meat he's been sending to the reservation."

"You're on speaking terms with him?" Jillian questioned, finding it hard to imagine she could be so forgiving.

"Sometimes you have to face the devil head on," Mary replied.

Inside the Harvey House, Jillian watched as Cooper openly flirted with every Harvey Girl who passed his table. The ladies had been amply warned about people like Cooper, but some of them seemed to enjoy the attention. Jillian found her anger mounting as she considered all that she'd been told about Cooper. How could he have done such a violent thing to Little Sister and then show his face among decent people?

He looked up, seeming to sense her gaze, and smiled. Jillian shuddered and turned away, while Mary handed her the blanket and moved toward Cooper's table.

"Mr. Cooper, we need to talk," she announced.

"Why, Mrs. Barnes, it's always a pleasure," Cooper said congenially.

Jillian didn't wait to hear more. She hurried upstairs with her keepsake and went to find her money. She hadn't thought to ask Mary for the price of the blanket, so she tucked all of her money in her pocket, fixed her hair, then made her way back downstairs. She had just come down the hall and into the dining room when Mary, seated at Cooper's table, laughed heartily, then got to her feet.

"I'll be expectin' you to hold to that," she told the man, then spied Jillian. Coming to where Jillian stood in complete confusion, Mary said, "You're gonna collect flies that way."

"Huh?"

The older woman chuckled. "You keep your mouth open that way and you're gonna collect flies."

"I guess I was just surprised to see you laughing with that . . . that man."

Mary shrugged. "Business is business. Remember what I said earlier about catchin' more flies with sugar than vinegar?" She laughed and slapped her hand against her side. "Must have flies on my mind, they keep coming up in the conversation."

Jillian shook her head. What a strange little woman.

"I've changed my mind on the pie," Mary told her, moving toward the door. "I've got a feeling I ought to be gettin' home. It's a rough piece to drive in the dark. Maybe I'll be seein' you to church on Sunday."

"Actually, I have to work that day," Jillian admitted.

"Mr. Harvey should be ashamed of himself for having you girls workin' on the Lord's Day."

Jillian shrugged. "Guess as long as the trains run on that day, Mr. Harvey will see to the food. Oh, by the way, I brought you money for the blanket."

Mary shook her head. "You've already given me a good amount of cash as a donation for the Navajo. That's more than enough to buy a blanket. Thanks again for the help."

Jillian watched her go, then turned to go back upstairs. She caught sight of Cooper watching her and forced herself to give him a hard, distasteful stare. He grinned, causing her to realize this was not a game she could win. Realizing that, Jillian took herself upstairs for a long soak in a tub of hot water.

———

"I just wish he wouldn't even come here," Gwen told Zack Matthews. She glanced past the sheriff to where Cooper was just finishing up his meal.

"If he causes you any grief, just come get me," Zack told her.

Gwen smiled, feeling rather shy at his obvious protective nature toward her. "Sam won't tolerate much around here. He's a good manager and sees to it that the girls are safe and treated right. Cooper just makes me uneasy."

"Well, just forget about him," Zack said with a smile. "Why don't you sit down here with me and we can make some plans."

Gwen glanced around the room, and seeing that everything was in order, she nodded and took a chair. When Zack smiled at her, she felt giddy like a schoolgirl. Funny, she hadn't felt that way in years. When her first love had died years earlier, she had almost been convinced that her heart would never heal from the pain and loss she suffered. But now . . . well, time would tell, but she liked the way things were developing between herself and Zack. And she liked being able to feel happy again in the presence of a man.

———————

Later that night when Kate and Louisa had come to bed, Jillian found herself contemplating the day's events. She thought of the anger and hatred she had seen in Bear's expression. She remembered Mary's words and realized that Bear held his own prejudice against the white people. *He thinks we're all alike,* Jillian reasoned. *Just like many of the folks in Pintan believe all Indians to be the same.*

"May I ask you both something?" she questioned her roommates.

Kate looked up from the stocking she was darning and nodded. "Aye, ya can for sure be askin' me anythin' ya like."

"Me too," Louisa replied, her voice betraying her weariness. She plopped out across her bed, rolling to her side. "What do you want to know?"

Jillian sat down on her bed and tucked her legs up. "What do you think about the Indians around here?"

"What would ya be meanin' by that?" Kate asked, resuming her stitches.

"It's just that a lot of people really seem to hate the Indians. They feel that the Indians are sub-human or at least not equal to white folks. At the same time, I talked with Mary Barnes, and it seems some of the Indians feel the same about us. I just wondered what your opinion on the matter was."

"Me own people have suffered greatly for the snooty ways of folks. Ya know for yarself, as ya lived a life of privilege, most of the world sees us as a bunch of dumb ol' Micks. We get the washin'-up jobs and the muckin'-out jobs, but when it comes to doin' the nicer things or marryin' upwards in society, then folks remind us of where we belong."

Jillian frowned. She knew Kate spoke the truth. People were often cruel and heartless to anyone who spoke differently or dressed in ways that seemed foreign. Jillian had heard tales of the ugly riots and street fights when former slaves had tried to get work after the War Between the States. Worse still, she remembered an incident a few years back, when a terrible murder had taken place when a black man had tried to marry a white woman. The woman's father had shot the man through the heart, but the woman's reputation was ruined. Eventually, she succumbed to pneumonia and died, but the controversy lived on and was still talked about in hushed whispers.

Louisa spoke up rather hesitantly. "I . . . well . . . I know this might sound silly. . . ."

"No, it won't," Jillian said, focusing her thoughts back on the present.

"Well, the Indians scare me. I've put in for a transfer as soon as my contract is up."

"That doesn't sound silly," Jillian replied. "A good many people are afraid of the Indians. Do you know why they scare you?"

Louisa shook her head. "They just do. I suppose some of the stories I've been told about them going on the warpath and killing white settlers stick in my head. My father told me never to get far from town or one might steal me away and make me a slave. He told me horrible things about some Indian war in a place called Little Big Horn. He thought the government should have exterminated them all for what they did to General Custer and his men."

"Exterminate? Like the rodents that get into the pantry?" Jillian questioned softly. "But they're human beings. They're people just like us. How could anyone think of killing off a race of people for nothing more than being different than we are?"

"I'm supposin' it has more to do with the Indian Wars themselves," Kate suggested. "I mean, plenty of folks recall only too well bein' scared half out of their wits by threats of Indian raids. I don't imagine they give much thought to it bein' a matter of skin color so much as a matter of survival."

"But I hardly think we have much to worry about in this day and age. Why, it's almost 1900. Even the West is settling down. Soon you won't know the difference in living life out here or back East."

"Of course you'd say that, Judith. You're very brave, but I am not," Louisa said quite seriously. "I'd just as soon go back to Kansas, where I was trained. I don't like it here. It's out in the middle of nowhere, with nothing but snakes and lizards. I really hate those little creatures."

"It for sure ain't as hot in Kansas as it is here," Kate threw in. "I'm not lookin' forward to another summer here. Maybe I should go puttin' in for a transfer as well."

"Well, I for one plan to quit when my year is up," Jillian announced. Both Kate and Louisa looked at her like she'd said something of such surprise and importance that Jillian glanced quickly around the room. "What is it?"

"Yarself," Kate said. "Are ya really gonna quit?"

Jillian nodded. "That's my plan."

"Since when?" Louisa asked. "You've never once said anything about quitting."

"That's for sure," Kate said. "I thought ya liked yar independence."

"I do," Jillian admitted. She truly did love the freedom she'd found in her life. But if she were to abide by her father's wishes and honor him for the permission he'd granted her in fulfilling Judith's contract, she would have to return to Kansas City. At least for a time.

Yawning, Kate looked at her stocking, then put it aside. "I'm thinkin' for sure it's near time for lights out. Besides that, I'm havin' trouble keepin' me eyes open."

"Me too," Louisa said, looking over the side of the bed before getting up. They were always to check the floor before stepping out of bed, but it was a habit Louisa had down to a fine art form. "It's my turn to put out the lamp, so you both go ahead and get in bed."

"Don't be forgettin' to check your bedding," Kate admonished.

Louisa pulled down her covers and sheets and gave everything a generous shake. "Kansas City won't have scorpions and centipedes either."

Jillian laughed and rechecked her covers before settling into bed. "No, we don't have those."

Louisa turned down the lamp and climbed into bed. "Good night," she said, yawning most unladylike as she spoke.

Jillian smiled to herself. In spite of Louisa's poor manners and Kate's outspokenness, she liked them both very much. She thought about her sheltered life and how her mother would find such people to be quite intolerable. Why, neither one of them would have even been considered good enough to work in the Danvers household, much less to be friends of anyone in her family.

Jillian remember Reverend Lister's sermon and the words he'd read from the Bible. The attitude Jillian had been raised with all of her life was clearly not pleasing to God. It was, in fact, a sin.

This came as a hard revelation for Jillian. She had always considered herself to have lived a good and godly life. She didn't give religious matters much consideration, mainly because her father did the thinking in their family—as well as the spiritual reasoning. But here was a fact she could not ignore. It was given in the Bible, and she knew her father respected that book as the Word of God. Had he never read the passages that spoke to treating people differently because of their looks or education? Maybe he didn't realize that such a scripture was there. After all, it was a very big book.

Jillian found it impossible to sleep with all of this playing on her heart. Something was happening to her. Her safe, cozy world no longer seemed quite so nice. With each passing day, she saw new reasons to disdain much of what she had been raised to believe. How could she set everything straight and put it back in order? What could she do with these conflicting feelings?

A noise outside their window caught her attention.

"Did you hear that?" she questioned Louisa and Kate, but both of the girls had already fallen asleep.

Slipping from the bed, mindless of the thought that a marauding scorpion might lay in wait, Jillian moved to the window. Pulling back the heavy shade, she looked out onto the moonlit street below.

She had to suppress a scream as she noted a lone figure standing in the darkness. The apparition stood as still as stone—arms raised toward heaven—feet slightly apart. Jillian watched in fascination, wondering who it might be. He stood just far enough in the shadows that she couldn't make out the person's identification, but as if sensing that someone was watching, the figure turned and walked toward the building.

Jillian could now see, much to her surprise, that the man was Little Sister's brother, Bear.

He glanced up at the window, and she knew that he could see her watching him. She thought to drop the shade back into place, but something held her fast to the spot. He considered her for only a moment before heading out of town in a dead run.

Breathing heavily, Jillian crept back into bed, certain now that sleep would be impossible. As she lay awake, tossing and turning, it suddenly dawned on her the reason for Bear's stance in the middle of the street. He had stood directly in front of the Indian Agent office, where Mr. Cooper kept his quarters upstairs. With this revelation, Jillian shuddered. What did it mean? Had Bear planned the demise of this man who had so greatly harmed his sister? Should Jillian tell someone what she had seen?

C H A P T E R

8

JILLIAN FOUND IT IMPOSSIBLE to forget the image of Bear standing in the still of the night, the wind lightly blowing against his clothes and shoulder-length black hair, his hands raised heavenward. It gave her a chill whenever she thought of it, and she wondered if she should at least say something to someone. As the days passed, however, she gradually let the memory slip away, and by the time she received her third letter from home, announcing her mother's desire to send the earl to Pintan to meet Jillian, Bear was no more than a wisp of the past.

The earl has seen your picture and believes you to be exactly what he is looking for in a wife, Jillian read. *He is coming west to the Rocky Mountains to hunt for elk and believes it would be no trouble to make his way to Pintan.*

Jillian nearly dropped the letter right there and then. Her mother was determined to see her married to the earl of wherever it was he hailed from. She sighed. When would she ever be free of her mother's meddling? She looked at the letter again. Why, her mother hadn't even made mention of how happy Jillian was in Pintan. Couldn't she understand that this new life suited her?

Taking up a pen and paper, Jillian hurried to send her mother a reply. There would be an eastbound train at one o'clock, and Jillian intended that letter to be on board.

Glancing at the time, she realized she would be expected to be downstairs helping with the westbound lunch train in fifteen minutes. She hurried to the task at hand.

Dearest Mother,
    Please do not send the earl to see me. The man I told you about, Dr. MacCallister, has become most dear to me. He has become my best friend, and I find that I can talk to him about most anything. He is kind and considerate, and he makes me very happy. I know this will come as a shock, and I truly meant no disrespect to you or Father, but we have become engaged to be married.

Jillian looked at the words for a moment. A deep sense of dread and remorse washed over her. How could she tell such a terrible falsehood? She had already steeped herself in this deception of Judith's, and in a short time her contract would be up and she would be free to return home. Her parents would know the truth by then, for there would be no fiancé traveling with her, no husband to remain in Pintan to come back to. She sighed again. This web of deceit was only growing bigger. She thought of Mary's tale of Spider Woman and figured the Navajo deity could not have woven a bigger mess than Jillian had created for herself.

She hurried to complete the letter, stressing her deep love for Mac and adding that she had come to love the territory as well. As she reread the words, Jillian was struck with an overwhelming realization that the latter was true. She had come to love Arizona. The dry climate agreed with her, and the arid terrain appealed to her sense of beauty. She enjoyed the people, at least most of them, and for the first time in her life, she had true friends. Not just friends based on her social standing, but honest-to-goodness friends who liked her and sought out her company.

The revelation swept over her and from it sprang up a joy that was so real and tangible she could almost touch it. "I'm happy here," she stated aloud. "I'm happy with Arizona and the Harvey House. I'm happy with my friendships, and I love Mary and Mac."

Love Mac? Where had that come from? She shook her head and pushed the thought aside. But then as she reread what she'd just written to her mother, she could feel the compelling truth of her words. Mac had become most dear to her. Even now she could imagine his laughing face when she closed her eyes.

She remembered an encounter she'd had with him the evening before when he'd come into the Harvey House. He'd sought her out, making sure she would be the one to serve him.

"I'd much rather talk with you than the others," he confided. "In fact, why don't you plan to walk out with me after you're all finished in here? I haven't had a decent conversation all day." He then beamed her a smile and a hopeful look of expectation.

His words had made her feel warm inside—his expression even more so. He always made her feel as if she were the most important person in the world.

"But love?" she questioned, letting the memory go. She looked at the letter again and shook her head.

Surely it was just a friendship type of love. Mac had never shown her so much as the slightest indication that he could feel romantically inclined toward her. He showed her friendship—that was all.

It was rumored that Mac had some great tragedy in his past love life and therefore had determined to spend his life as a bachelor. If there was any credence to the rumors, then Jillian knew there was little hope that he would take a liking to her. But on the other hand, she smiled wistfully, he treated her kindly and discussed matters quite openly with her.

Another memory crept in and took her back to one Sunday when Mac had sat alongside her in the pew at church. He seemed as comfortable with her as she was with him. At least it appeared that way, and perhaps . . . perhaps that could be grounds for the beginning of something more.

Shaking her head at her own silliness, Jillian heard the distant train whistle and knew her time was up. In fact, she was late. She stuffed the letter haphazardly into the envelope, scrawled her mother's name and address, and took the stairs at a run. She nearly mowed over poor Sam in her haste, thrusting the letter in his hand and breathlessly requesting he post it for her on the first train to Kansas City.

Smoothing her apron, she hurried into the dining room, caught Gwen's disapproving frown, and bowed her head. There were strict rules of convention in Mr. Harvey's establishment, and because of those rules, normal operations ran smoothly and without disruption. An entire dining room full of guests could be fed a four-course meal in under thirty minutes, all because of Mr. Harvey's meticulous order. It only took one, such as Jillian, to put a kink in the works.

Gwen came to Jillian's station, her face revealing her intention to discuss the matter. Jillian bit her lower lip and tried to think of something to say.

"Miss Danvers, I cannot abide you taking time away from your duties. I know there was a letter from home, and while I hope there were no bad tidings, you must know that leaving your station to deal with such a matter is uncalled for."

"Yes, ma'am," Jillian replied, realizing she had no defense. Gwen already knew what she had been about.

"Very well, don't let it happen again."

With that, Gwen went off to the kitchen, and a clanging gong announced the arrival of the train passengers.

Jillian glanced around just as Kate came up to give her a brief pat on the shoulder. "Don't be frettin' none about Miss Carson. She needs ya too much to go a-firing ya. Besides, she likes ya better than just about anyone else here. Ya know it's always been that way."

Jillian tried to nod, but the truth ate at her. How would Gwen feel about her once she learned that she wasn't Judith? "I suppose I know that," she finally told Kate, "but there's no excuse for taking advantage of it. I shouldn't have left my station."

Kate eyed her seriously for a moment. "Ya've changed, Judith. Ya didn't used to care about such things."

"I am a different person," Jillian admitted.

Kate nodded. "Aye, I'm supposin' ya are."

Jillian didn't know if Kate really suspected her true identity, but it wouldn't have surprised her. Still, the Irishwoman seemed to be in no hurry to share her suspicions with anyone else.

The lunch crowd came and went, with Jillian making only minor mistakes. She served the wrong salad twice, spilled soup on the table, and broke one china plate when it slipped from her hands in the kitchen. When the eastbound train came through, slowing only long enough to snag the mailbag, Jillian was already stripping the tables in her station.

"Do you have a table for me?"

Jillian startled and dropped three crystal goblets, spilling the left-over contents out across the fine Irish linen tablecloth. The voice immediately took her back to the revelation of her letter.

"Oh, you gave me a start!" she exclaimed, trying to regain her composure.

"I didn't mean to," Mac said apologetically.

Jillian then looked into his face. Captured by his gaze, she realized the truth . . . she had lost her heart.

This can't be happening! she told herself.

She had fallen in love with Mac. And now that she knew it, Jillian suddenly felt quite shy around him. She quickly bowed her head and concentrated on cleaning up the mess she'd just made. "I know you meant no harm," she said rather formally.

"So what's for lunch?" he asked, sitting at the next table over.

"We have beef tips picante, fried flounder, or curried lamb," she replied, forcing her focus to remain on the table. *How could I have fallen for him so easily?* she wondered. "Of course, there are other things. I could just bring you the menu and let you decide who you love." She felt her cheeks grow hot. "I mean what you love . . . well . . . you know what I mean."

Mac laughed. "You're in a queer state today. How many dishes did you break at lunch?"

Jillian straightened and glared at him. "I only broke one plate."

He grinned. "I'm sure Mr. Harvey will be glad to hear that. You didn't douse anyone else in coffee, did you?"

Even as he spoke the words, Zack Matthews walked into the dining room. He immediately sought out Gwen, who blushed furiously when he presented her with a small collection of wild flowers.

"I'd say the good sheriff has taken an interest in your Miss Carson."

Jillian felt a pang of something akin to jealousy. Matthews was openly showing his affection, and Gwen was happily, although shyly, accepting. In fact, Jillian knew that Gwen had received permission from the house manager to spend time away from the Harvey House in the company of Mr. Matthews.

"Are you feeling ill?" Mac asked softly.

Jillian turned to look at him. "What?" She let her gaze linger on his face. That proved to be a big mistake. Why was it that yesterday, when she hadn't realized her feelings for Mac, she could laugh and joke with him and look at him without feeling her skin go all goosey on her?

"It's just that you look like you're feeling ill. Maybe it's just the heat. I keep telling them that you Harvey Girls shouldn't be wearing black in the Arizona sun. Why can't Harvey dress you all in white?"

Jillian shook her head. "I'm sure I don't know." She began to gather the dishes.

Turning to take her things into the kitchen, Mac called out after her, "Just bring me the beef tips and some vegetables. You know what I like."

She nearly dropped the dishes again. His words rang in her head. *"You know what I like."* She silently thought, *Oh, but you don't know what I like.*

Feeling rather breathless, she deposited her dirty dishes in the sink, then turned to give Mac's order to the cook. Within a matter of a minute, a steaming order of beef tips sent an appealing aroma from Mr. Harvey's finest china. The cook had accompanied this with buttered red beets and creamed peas with pearl onions. Another plate, which contained several slices of bread, all different in flavor and appearance, was handed to Jillian.

By the time she headed through the kitchen door, Jillian's nerves were getting the best of her. *I'm in love with him. How can I endure serving him without making a complete fool of myself?*

When she arrived in the dining room, Kate was pouring his coffee. *Good,* she thought, *I won't have to stay any longer than to deposit this food. Mac will have to understand that I have work to do.*

But instead of feeling relieved at the thought, Jillian felt almost disappointed. Why did she have to feel so torn? On one hand, she wanted only to run from the room, and on the other, she longed to go to Mac and share her heart. Was this what falling in love was all about?

Determined not to give it a second thought, Jillian picked up her pace and made her way to Mac. However, she didn't see the errant piece of lettuce, which had doubtlessly been dropped by one of the luncheon diners. Stepping down on the slippery piece, Jillian felt her foot begin to slide forward in an uncontrollable manner. Struggling to right herself, she whipped around and tried to regain her footing, but it was too late. Mac saw her dilemma and only made matters worse by reaching out to steady her. In a flash that could only be described as sheer disaster, Jillian felt Mac's firm grip on her as her feet went completely out from under her. Without any further ado, she landed squarely on his lap as the plate rained its contents down the front of both of them.

Mac began laughing uncontrollably, while Jillian sat in stunned silence. So much for being inconspicuous. She saw the red beets dripping down the front of her apron, then raised her gaze to Mac's laughing face, where creamed peas oozed down the side of his cheek. His laughter became contagious as Kate and some of the other girls began to laugh, and Jillian herself could no longer keep a straight face as pieces of beef picante began to slide down Mac's forehead.

Not thinking of the inappropriateness of remaining on Mac's lap, Jillian began to giggle and then to laugh until finally tears were in her eyes and she was edging close to hysteria. What a scene. She had truly outdone herself this time.

She didn't think about what she was doing as her hand went up to Mac's face. She began wiping creamed peas from his cheek, her fingers lingering on his clean-shaven skin. Tracing down along the lines of the sauce, she touched the edge of his laughing mouth and trembled. And for a reason that baffled her, Mac trembled too, and then stopped laughing. She grew sober, not at all sure what was happening.

Mac's blue eyes seemed to darken as they held her gaze. For a moment, Jillian could have sworn he was going to say something important. But before he could speak, Gwen interrupted.

"Miss Danvers, what in the world has happened here?"

It was only then that Jillian realized the intimacy of the moment. She quickly slid off of Mac's lap and stood up. Her uniform was covered in food.

"I slipped on something and, well, Dr. MacCallister tried to help me. . . ." She let the words trail off as the laughter from her fellow co-workers began to increase. Glancing around, she could see that Zack Matthews was laughing as well.

Gwen didn't need any more encouragement than this before she began to smile. "Oh, Judith. Go change."

Jillian nodded, then against her will she looked back at Mac. "I'm sorry," she whispered.

He shook his head and very seriously replied, "Don't be."

Kate and Louisa followed her upstairs, both still laughing at the incident. As Jillian undressed, Louisa poured water in a bowl while Kate beat any wildlife from Jillian's clean uniforms.

"Thank you for your help," Jillian said in complete defeat. She didn't understand Mac's serious tone, and she couldn't figure out what was happening to her heart.

Standing there in nothing more than her undergarments, Jillian felt tears come to her eyes, suddenly overwhelmed. *I don't know what to do to feel right again. Nothing seems to make sense.* She didn't understand why a simple mistake should make her feel so bad, but it did.

"They say confession is good for the soul," Kate told her as she brought a black shirtwaist. "Perhaps if ya offered some confession to us, we could help."

Louisa brought the basin to Jillian and nodded. "We don't want to see you hurt."

Jillian looked at her roommates for a moment, then suddenly realized they knew. They knew she wasn't Judith but had kept it to themselves anyway.

"I'm Judith's sister, Jillian," she said softly.

Kate nodded. "We know."

"I don't know exactly how you figured it out, but frankly, I'm glad. No, I'm relieved. The only other person who knows is Mac, and it's beginning to take its toll on me," Jillian said, plopping onto her bed.

"So where is Judith?" Louisa asked matter-of-factly.

"She eloped with her childhood sweetheart," Jillian admitted.

"Good for her," Kate said, taking up the washcloth from the basin. "Here, ya best clean up before ya dress." She handed Jillian the cloth, then asked, "So why did ya come here, Jillian?"

"Judith asked me to. She begged me to come in her place until her contract was up. She said she would lose half her back wages if she didn't complete the contract and stay until June. But she was so in love and she didn't want to give up Martin. So I agreed to come in her place."

"Does yar family know?"

Jillian wiped her face and nodded. "Yes. They were none too happy about it, but my father is a businessman of some means. He realized the logic in letting things ride. Otherwise, I feared he might well come storming into Pintan to drag me home."

"Well, it's glad I am that he didn't," Kate said with a smile. "Yar sister was a wild card, but we loved her dearly and now we love you just the same."

"Yes," Louisa said with a smile. "You and Judith are just alike."

"Not really," Jillian replied. "I've been trying hard to be like Judith, but honestly, I don't have her flair for adventure."

"Nonsense!" Kate declared. "Ya wouldn't be here if ya didn't."

"I'm here for Judith's sake," Jillian replied. "I didn't really want to come, but I've always wanted to please Judith."

"Well, whatever the reason, you're here now," Louisa replied. She held the basin out in order for Jillian to rinse the cloth.

"And ya still have a few short weeks left on your contract," Kate replied. "So we'll help ya keep yar secret and do what we can to make the time a bit easier on yarself."

"No, don't do me special favors," Jillian replied. "I need to pull my weight and do my job, the same as you."

"But we were trained for the job," Kate stated. "Yar doing a great job considering that ya've not had the training. Ya should have seen me in my first three months. I liked to have killed myself and nearly every diner who bore the misfortune of crossin' me path. There was no one more disorganized than meself." Kate's infectious grin caused Jillian to smile. "There, that's better," Kate said. "Now let's get ya dressed and back on the floor. I'm sure Dr. Mac would like to see if ya can find some other way to land in his lap again."

Jillian felt herself blush, and the look Kate and Louisa shared didn't help.

"He's as crazy for yarself as ya are for him," Kate said with a shrug. "No sense in denyin' it."

Jillian shook her head. "You shouldn't talk about such things."

"Why not? They're true enough."

Jillian put the cloth in the basin and took the blouse Kate offered. Her gaze locked on the Irishwoman's. "I don't think it is true. I think Mac just finds me amusing because of the situation. I've heard it said that he had his heart broken once before and has no interest in becoming involved with any woman, so I think it's best just to forget it. I think we'll all be happier that way. After all, I'll be leaving for Kansas City in a few weeks."

"Oh, will ya, now," Kate replied with a devilish grin.

Jillian nodded. "Yes. I will."

In the quiet stillness of her little house, Mary Barnes finished her accounting of the Navajo's money and goods and put down her pencil. She had managed to make a tidy sum for the Navajo, and while the money wouldn't begin to stretch far enough to make life really comfortable, it would ease things a bit.

A noise from the far side of the room caught her attention. Little Sister stood awkwardly and admired her finished blanket.

"And you worried that you wouldn't have it done in time. Looks like you did yourself proud," Mary said, going to where Little Sister stood.

"The baby will wait just a little longer," she told Mary, her hand going automatically to her swollen abdomen. "She's not ready to be born."

"So you're sure it's a girl, eh? Well, time will tell," Mary teased.

She could see the seriousness in Little Sister's expression, however, and sobered. "Try not to worry about the future. Remember what I told you. You can stay here for as long as all time, if necessary. You're safe here."

"But I'm not with my people," Little Sister said sadly.

Mary nodded. "I know you miss them. I've tried to talk to that brother of yours, but he won't listen to reason."

"He is very proud," Little Sister replied. "He thinks I have taken a white man to my bed. He thinks I'm like the others."

"Those women were just as misguided as some of the white women in town," Mary said, trying to reassure Little Sister. "Mr. Cooper is not an honorable man. I've written letters to our government, and hopefully they will take care of everything—put things back to right."

"They cannot take care of this," Little Sister said, patting her stomach. She looked up to meet Mary's watchful eyes. There were tears in her eyes as she added, "Your government cannot make my people know the truth."

"God knows the truth, Little Sister," Mary assured, switching easily to the Navajo language. "God knows. And believe me, He isn't happy about it either."

Mary watched the pregnant girl head outside and said a silent prayer for the child, then asked God to forgive the rage in her own heart. Cooper deserved to hang for what he'd done, especially given his unwillingness to admit to any wrongdoing. Still, Mary prayed to be able to forgive him and overlook his actions.

" 'For all have sinned,' " she reminded herself.

It was late, almost dark, when Little Sister came in for supper. She had fetched some water in a large jar and went about the task of re-filling the jars and jugs that held the legs to the two small beds where she and Mary slept.

"Don't worry over that now," Mary chided. "Come have some stew while it's hot."

"I'm not hungry," the Navajo girl said in a weak voice.

Mary instantly noted her tone and left the task of stirring the stew. "Little Sister, are you feelin' all right?"

The girl straightened and shook her head. "I think I am sick. My head hurts."

Mary reached out to touch her flushed face. "You have a fever. We'd best get you to bed. No tellin' what you might have caught."

Little Sister nodded. "I finish here first."

"No, come on." Mary took the water jar from her hands and set it to one side. "Let's get you into your nightgown and then to bed. I'll bring you some broth." She helped Little Sister take off her over-sized tunic and drawstring skirt, then brought a clean fresh gown.

Snapping it out several times, Mary helped Little Sister slip it over her head. Mary pulled it down over the young woman's protruding belly just as Little Sister began to sway.

Whipping back the covers with one hand and steadying Little Sister with the other, Mary quickly tucked the girl into bed, then stood back in concern. What manner of illness had overcome the girl? Just hours before, she had been perfectly well, and now she appeared as though she were seriously ill. Mary shook her head and went back to the kitchen, a silent prayer on her lips.

C H A P T E R

9

SEVERAL DAYS PASSED without Jillian catching so much as a single glimpse of Mac. She figured she had offended him somehow, but for the life of her, she couldn't understand why. It wasn't like Mac to be put off by a simple little accident. And he had laughed. At least at first.

Unable to make sense of it, Jillian swallowed her pride and decided to seek him out and make sure he knew how sorry she was for dumping food all over him.

Pintan was in its lazy, sleepy state of afternoon as she crossed over to Mac's side of the street. A warm breeze blew across the sandy dirt road, stirring up tiny bits that swirled into dust devils and danced down the street. Thick moody clouds draped the skies overhead, and Jillian couldn't help but wonder if they would be fortunate enough to get some rain. The thought only held her interest momentarily as Mac's placard came into view.

She felt a nervous tingle originate somewhere near the nape of her neck and spread down through her back and into her fingers and toes. The idea of seeing Mac gave her a sensation of excitement that she couldn't begin to deny. Her feelings and emotions were genuine and true, and they ran deep within her. Maybe this wasn't such a good idea.

But by the time she questioned the good sense of coming to Mac's, she was already knocking on his door.

Mac opened quickly and stared at her for a moment before questioning, "What have you done to yourself this time?"

The first words that sprang to mind were *I've fallen in love.* But of course she didn't say that. Instead, she shrugged. "I'm not here for medical attention. I just felt bad for what I did to you the other day. I haven't seen you since, and I figured I ran you off from the Harvey House with my clumsiness."

Jillian didn't understand the expression on Mac's face. It seemed to change from one of general amusement to something akin to pain. She hurried to speak, almost fearful of what he might say if she gave him a chance to talk.

"I know it was stupid of me. I didn't see the mess on the floor, and I know you were just trying to keep me from being hurt. I hope you aren't mad at me."

She knew she sounded almost desperate, but the thought of his anger or disappointment in her caused her to ramble.

"I wouldn't blame you if you didn't want me to ever wait on you again. I can arrange that, you know. Kate and Louisa are very understanding, and they'd be happy to help me out. I just don't want you to think you can't come to the Harvey House without fearing I'll bombard you with food."

Mac shook his head and reached his hand out to cover her mouth. "I'm not mad," he said simply. "I've just been busy."

He took his hand away from her mouth, but his touch caused Jillian to feel quivery inside. Her stomach did flips, and she thought she might actually need to sit down.

"I just felt bad about it," she finally managed to say.

He grinned, his expression suddenly turning very mischievous. "It was actually one of my more memorable and pleasant dining experiences."

She felt her cheeks grow hot and stammered for something to say. She didn't need to worry about it, however, as the rumbling and creaking of Mary Barnes' wagon interrupted their moment.

She waved to Mac and Jillian, then pulled Clarence and Dobbin up rather abruptly. Pushing her sunbonnet back, she called down,

"Mac, Little Sister is sick. She's running a fever and vomiting. I haven't been able to help her, and I'm afraid for her. I wondered if you'd take a look at her?"

Mac nodded. "Let me get some things together. Oh, and I'll have to change my clothes and saddle the horse, but I'll be quick."

Mary nodded. "Hello, Judith. How's life at the Harvey House?"

"Same as usual," Jillian said, moving to stand beside the wagon.

Mary wrapped the reins around the brake handle and climbed down. "I'm afraid Little Sister is quite ill," she said, her tone grave. "I'm not even sure she's going to make it."

Jillian felt overwhelmed by memories of her grandmother's death. She could still see the pasty complexion and hollow look in her eyes. Death had engulfed the house as her grandmother waited for it to finally settle upon her, and Jillian couldn't bear the memory.

"I'm sorry. I wish there was something I could do." Even as she said the words, Jillian knew that wasn't really the truth. She had no desire to help at Little Sister's bedside.

"You can pray," Mary told her quite seriously.

"I'm afraid I wouldn't know a great deal about that," Jillian admitted. "I've never done much of it. I've heard preachers do it, but I'm not at all comfortable trying it for myself in any length, much less for someone else. What if I said the wrong thing? What if I couldn't think of anything to say at all?" *And what if God won't listen to me because of my lies?* she thought to herself but remained silent.

Mary looked at her for a moment, then patted her arm. Her wrinkled expression was as gentle as her voice. "You just talk to God like you would your own pa."

Jillian laughed. "No one talks to Colin Danvers. They listen. My father is the one to do the talking and dictating."

"Well, God isn't like that. He listens. He cares about what we have to say. It's all there in the Bible. Many a time folks had to call out to Him. You should read up on it and see for yourself. The Psalms are full of prayers."

Jillian shook her head and looked away. "I'm afraid I don't have a Bible."

"No Bible? Well, then, I'll just have to be lending you mine," Mary replied.

"No, I couldn't do that," Jillian said quite seriously. "I'll talk to Reverend Lister about one or I'll write home to have my mother send me one, but I couldn't take yours."

Mary smiled. "I have another. Besides, you've been such a dear sweet girl and so helpful. I'd be proud to have you use it."

"Perhaps I could just borrow it for a short time," Jillian suggested. "Just until I get one of my own."

Mary nodded. "I'll send it back with Mac."

"What should I do with it? I mean, I know you say to read it and see the prayers and such, but Mary, I've never read the Bible before. I'm not sure I know how."

Mary gave her a hug. "Oh, Judith, you're such a dear. It's just like Reverend Lister says on Sunday. By gettin' better acquainted with God's Word, you get better acquainted with God himself. Why don't you start in the Gospel of John. Now, mind you, all the books are good, but John has a way of putting Jesus into flesh and blood, while keeping Him all holy. Read some of the Psalms as well."

Jillian nodded, but her conscience sorely bothered her. Mary was helping her to learn more about God—how could Jillian go on deceiving her? She glanced around her, and seeing that Mac was still nowhere in sight, Jillian determined to set things right.

"Mary, there's something I need to tell you."

The older woman stepped back and studied her. "It's something weighin' heavy on your heart, eh?"

Jillian nodded. "Very." She didn't bother to tell Mary that it was only one of many things, but instead she struggled for words to make her confession. "I've misled you, and I'm sorry."

"However have you done this?" the woman questioned.

"I'm not Judith. My sister—my twin sister—is Judith. I'm Jillian Danvers." Mary looked at her and her expression made it clear she didn't understand anything about this deception.

Jillian sighed. "My sister needed me to come here in her place so that she could marry the man she loved. She didn't want to cancel out her contract with Mr. Harvey, but neither did she want to wait until her contract was up in order to marry. I know it sounds rather silly, but at the time Judith made it seem like a necessary crusade."

Mary nodded. "Sisters have a way of talkin' you into matters. I have a sister myself. She was forever getting me in trouble." She smiled and reached out her hand. "I'm glad you told me the truth, Jillian. It means a lot to me that you'd trust me with your secret. However, I'd advise you to just come clean with Miss Carson and the rest of the town. Maybe if they know the situation, they won't mind keeping you on."

Jillian shook her head. "I don't know if that would be wise or not. After all, if Judith is made to pay the back wages, she'll be in grave trouble."

"Pray about it, Jillian. Lies only breed more lies, and all of it leads to destruction."

Just then Mac came around the house leading his sorrel gelding. "I'm ready, Mary," he said, tossing fat saddlebags over the back of the horse. He quickly tied them securely, then mounted.

Mary climbed back up in the wagon and took up the reins. "Remember what I said," she told Jillian, then flicked the reins and maneuvered the mules in a circle to head back to her desert house.

Mac smiled, tipped his felt hat to Jillian, and followed after the older woman. Jillian walked back to the Harvey House in silence. Mary had asked her to pray, but in truth, she didn't know what to say. She had said all sorts of little, rather insignificant prayers, but this was different. This was a prayer to save a life. To see a dying mother through the birth of her child. How should she pray?

Oh, God, you know I'm not a religious person. I don't know much about these matters, but Mary said you would understand. Please comfort Little Sister. And give Mac the ability to help her through this.

Mac urged his horse forward, leaving Mary to follow after him. He could beat her to the house in half the time, and given Little Sister's symptoms of fever and vomiting, he figured they had little time to waste.

But even with Little Sister uppermost in his thoughts, it was Jillian who crowded in to consume his heart. How could he have been so foolish? He knew better than to allow such emotions and distractions. Hadn't he stayed in this territory for that very reason?

A rattlesnake slithered off to find the shelter of a rock as Mac urged his horse into a dry wash. What was happening to him? Why couldn't he just keep Jillian in the role of a friend? He hadn't had any problem keeping Judith in that position, so why should Jillian be any different?

A distant memory crowded into Mac's mind. He could see her. Almost hear her. Shaking his head, he forced the image away. There was no room for her in his life now. He was different . . . and she was gone.

Still, he could see her smiling face and hear her laugh. She had worn her blond hair very similarly to Jillian Danvers. She had been pretty and sophisticated and everything that a lady of society should be.

He felt a familiar tightening in his chest. A guilt of sorts, a sorrow blended with regret and a touch of bitterness. He had loved her, and she had betrayed his heart. Why should Jillian be any different?

"God help me," he muttered, lightly kicking the horse's side. "Help me to put everything back in its proper place—including my heart."

MAC FOUND THE DAYS AHEAD weighted with concern for the young Navajo woman. He had made at least a dozen trips back and forth in as many days, always wondering what more he could possibly do to help Little Sister. Somehow she clung to life physically, but emotionally she was already gone. Mac had tried to talk to her about regaining her strength, but she held no interest. Her family had shunned her, her people had turned their backs on her, and because of this, she had lost the will to live.

Mary stewed and fretted, beside herself with grief for the young woman's condition. When Mac finally felt certain that Little Sister would die within the next few days, he broke the news to Mary. She had taken it well, but her initial thought was to find Bear.

"I can't stay here, Mary," he told her gravely. "I have to get back to town and check in on my other patients. And you can't leave Little Sister here alone."

"Maybe you could bring somebody out with you when you come back," Mary suggested. "Maybe Jillian would come."

He eyed her suspiciously. "Who?"

"Jillian. She told me all about her little deception. I suggested she come clean on the matter, but that's no nevermind. Why don't you seek her out and see if by chance she could come here in the next day or so? I should be able to make it to the village and back within a matter of hours, and if Bear isn't off tendin' to business elsewhere, it should be easy enough to find him."

"What if you can't convince him to come?"

Mary shrugged. "I don't know, Mac. I suppose I'll just cross that bridge when I get to it."

Mac packed his saddlebags and headed for the door. Once outside, he glanced upward at the blackening sky. "Maybe we'll get rain from this one."

Mary shook her head. "I wouldn't count on it. It'll probably blow on over to the east. We could sure use some, though. I'd hate to see us headin' into the summer only to sustain more drought. Bad enough to live where water is so limited, but to have a drought on top of it is sheer misery."

Mac nodded and mounted his horse. "I'll be back as soon as possible. If no one in town needs me, I might even come back yet tonight and check in on her."

"Don't forget to see about bringing Jillian."

"I won't," he promised.

By the time he'd ridden back to Pintan, a few sprinkles of rain were all that marked the passing of the dark clouds. The drops made strange little indentations in the dry sandy ground, giving it a speckled appearance.

In the west, the sun was already starting to lower. Mac would have to be quick about it if he was to return to Mary's yet that evening. Traveling the desert at night could be most dangerous, and he had no desire to cause his horse to misstep into a hole or meet up with something worse, like a bobcat or mountain lion.

Things looked to be quiet at the Harvey House. The trains had apparently come and gone, taking satisfied dinner crowds farther down the line to their destinations. Mac looked at his dusty clothes and thought it might serve him better to get a bath before checking on any patients or even Jillian's availability to ride with him back to Mary's. Spying Kate McGee on the opposite side of the street, Mac called out to her.

"Miss McGee, I wonder if I might impose upon you?"

Kate looked up and, seeing it was Mac, crossed the road. "And what would ya be needin' with the likes of me, Dr. Mac?"

"I'm wondering if Miss Danvers is available to speak with me. I have a problem, and Mrs. Barnes suggested I seek her out."

"I can be sendin' her over to yar place," Kate replied with a grin. "She's ironin' linens right now, but I'm sure she's nigh on to finished. If not, I'm sure she'll be a-hurryin' through when she finds out you've called for her."

Mac shifted uncomfortably. "Well, it's business."

"Oh, and for sure it is," Kate laughed. "I'll be sendin' her over in short order for . . . business."

Mac nodded in irritation. "That's fine. I'm going to clean up a bit and check on some patients, so there's no hurry."

Kate headed off to the Harvey House, but her laughter still rang in Mac's ears. Was it so evident to everyone in Pintan that he had feelings for Jillian?

The very idea of having feelings for anyone created a tug-of-war in Mac's heart. He enjoyed Jillian's friendship and found her intelligence and interest in things around her to be refreshing, but she was, after all, a woman. A very attractive woman. A woman with a background of luxury and wealth, and one who intended to go back into that setting once she'd fulfilled her sister's contract.

He thought of the fact that she'd opened her identity up to Mary's scrutiny. He knew the older woman would have advised Jillian to be completely honest with those around her, but he also understood Jillian's dilemma. It seemed rather harmless that she should lie about being Judith. Judith's tasks were still being taken care of, and it wasn't as if the deception was really hurting anyone. Or was it?

He sighed and clucked at the horse as he pulled him around back of the house. Why did she have to mean so much to him in such a short time? Was it the familiarity of Judith that had allowed him to settle easily into a friendship with Jillian? He smiled at the thought of her seeing herself nothing like her sister. *They are more alike than she can see,* he thought. Still, he'd never desired to hold Judith in his arms—to kiss her lips.

Laboring with these thoughts, Mac fed and watered the horse, then headed to the house to see to his own needs.

About half an hour later, Jillian knocked on his door. He ushered her in, feeling his heart pick up its pace when she smiled. Even in his exhausted state, he was happy to see her. He looked forward to the possibility of sharing a moonlit ride to Mary's with this lovely young woman.

"Kate said you needed to see me?"

"Yes. I'm afraid it's not good. Little Sister is gravely ill. She'll probably die within a short time. Mary asked if you would come and sit with Little Sister while she goes out to the Navajo village to find Bear."

Jillian shuddered noticeably, and Mac didn't know if it were for reasons of the stern-faced Bear or Little Sister's condition. She looked away, refusing to meet his gaze.

"I wouldn't know what to do. I'm not at all helpful in such matters. My mother never allowed me to tend the sick, and when our grandmother died, we were made to sit beside her, but she died anyway."

"It isn't a matter of needing you to do anything in particular," Mac replied, totally confused by Jillian's attitude. "Little Sister shouldn't be alone—even for the few hours it'll take Mary to get to the village and back. She might go into labor; then again, she may not. But if the baby should come, there would be no one there to help her."

"I . . . can't . . . can't do it, Mac," Jillian said, backing toward the door. "Why don't you . . . I mean . . . why can't you . . . get someone else?"

She was shaking and stammering, and for the life of him, Mac didn't know how to respond. "Mary asked me specifically to bring you."

Jillian shook her head. "You don't understand."

Mac was beginning to get a little irritated. "No, I don't."

Jillian reached for the door. "I can't explain it to you. I can't help you."

"Can't or won't?" Mac asked angrily. "Isn't a poor Navajo woman worth the effort?"

"That's not fair, Mac. You know me better."

"I thought I did," he replied. His confusion over her behavior was overriding his ability to reason the situation. "Just go on back to your safe little world, Jillian. You're probably right. You're probably not much good for anything more than looking pretty and entertaining." He said the words to Jillian, but it was another woman's face he saw.

The expression on Jillian's face betrayed her hurt. Mac's words had obviously hit their intended target, but he had no satisfaction in that. He didn't understand why she had suddenly become so irrational in her attitude. She seemed almost afraid, but why should she be? She'd been to Mary's before, and she knew Little Sister. Mary had even told him that she had befriended the Navajo woman and had easily shared her company. So what had happened since that time and this?

"I didn't mean to make you mad," she said, turning, as if she'd changed her mind.

"Well, you did a good job of it. I don't have time for games like this, Jillian. Mary can't very well go for Little Sister's family and sit at her bedside at the same time, and frankly, I don't know of anyone else, short of the Reverend Lister or his wife, who might be willing to help a dying Navajo."

"Reverend Lister would be a better choice, especially since . . . I mean, if she . . . dies."

Angry at himself for losing his temper, Mac nevertheless hit his fist against the wall. "Go home, Jillian. Go back to Kansas City, where life demands nothing more of you than you can handle."

"I'm sorry, Mac," Jillian whispered before fleeing from the room.

He pretended that he hadn't seen the tears in her eyes. Pretended, too, that he didn't care about whether she accompanied him to Mary's or not. But he did care and he didn't understand how she could be so callous about Little Sister. She had acted as though the very idea of accompanying him had terrified her. Was she afraid of him? Afraid that once they were alone in the desert, he might take liberties?

This thought calmed him a bit. Perhaps that was the answer. She had never had a romantic encounter. He knew this because she'd told him so one day when they were talking together. Maybe she was just afraid of what he might do to her. But Mac felt a sense of irritation in Jillian's lack of trust. If she did fear him and think him to just be using this as an excuse to get her alone, then he intended to give her a piece of his mind when he got back from Mary's.

Jillian had never longed more for Mary's company than she did in the hours that followed her entanglement with Mac. Mac had clearly been disgusted with her. He probably thought her as prejudiced as the rest of the town when it came to Little Sister and her condition. But it wasn't true. Jillian wanted to help Mary and Little Sister, but the thought of dealing with death overwhelmed her ability to reason.

Torn between hiring a horse and trying to find her way out to Mary's or waiting it out at the Harvey House until Mac returned, Jillian chose the easy way out. But hadn't she always? Rather than standing up to Judith, she always gave in and did whatever her sister asked of her. She said it was because she loved Judith, and she did. There wasn't anything she would have withheld from her twin because the bond between them was so deep—so strong. But she knew she also allowed Judith to push her around and get her into messes because it was the path of least resistance. Judith never demanded much of Jillian, and up until this stunt of posing as Judith, Jillian had never felt it was any real sacrifice to endure her sister's requests.

But the truth was, Jillian had let people push her around most of her life. She feared standing up to them, and she feared dealing with them head on. Her father dictated to her what she could and couldn't do, and she knew that had he forbidden her to stay in Pintan, she would have taken the first train back to Kansas City. She loved her father, though he could be demanding, and it just seemed more pleasant to let him have his way. Then there was her mother, who plotted and planned for Jillian's future. Jillian had never had the heart, until now, to put her foot down and demand her mother set such notions aside.

Letting people have their way seemed the most generous and loving thing Jillian could do. She might get walked on and pushed around a bit in the process, but if she did, it was her flaw that had caused it and not someone else's.

And until Mac had pressured her to face her fears of death, Jillian had felt it a fairly simple matter to endure this flaw in her personality. Now, however, Mac thought poorly of her—maybe even hated her for what he would misjudge as prejudice. She had to explain and make him see the truth. She couldn't just let this be swept aside, not when Mac thought her to be so heartless and cruel.

"I've made such a mess of this," she moaned, struggling to keep a positive outlook. It was bad enough that Mac knew her capable of living a lie; now he probably thought she'd lied about caring about the plight of the Navajo as well. Mary might agree with his conclusion. Jillian bowed her head in sorrow. "I've probably lost my two dearest friends."

It was nearly nine-thirty when Mac rode back into Pintan. Jillian had watched for him faithfully from her upstairs window, hoping and praying that she might be able to sneak out before curfew and explain her actions to him. How could she have refused him help? Then again, how could she have gone, knowing what she would find at Mary's? She hated her fear of death. Now Mac probably hated her, and she had no way to explain it . . . except to tell him the truth. But would he believe her, knowing her for the liar she was? Why should he trust her for the truth? Especially when the truth sounded so un-founded—so silly.

How could she explain to a man of medicine that her grand-mother's nonsensical superstitions about death and dying had man-ifested unnatural terrors in Jillian's heart and soul? From the time Grandmother Danvers had moved in to share their home, she had tormented Jillian with death lore. Jillian had suffered horrible night-mares, certain that the Grim Reaper would soon pay her a visit. Grandmother had warned her never to be in the room when a person died, or she might be the next one to go.

Jillian shook her head and wiped an errant tear. How could she expect Mac to understand?

She slipped from the room quietly, not explaining to either Kate, who sat penning a letter home, or Louisa, who worked intently stitch-ing together a new sunbonnet, that she was going out. With any luck, they'd just think she was going out to see to her personal needs before bedtime.

Creeping down the back stairs, Jillian knew she might not be back in time for curfew, but it was a risk she was willing to take—no matter the consequences. Somehow, the idea of climbing the latticework alongside the building didn't seem nearly as bad as leaving this misunderstanding to stand between her and Mac.

Silently she opened the back door and stepped out into the darkness. She felt a rush of wind against her face, and remembering Bear's nighttime ritual of a few weeks past, she trembled. *I'm such a coward. Judith would have gone with Mac and no doubt would have never given Bear a second thought.*

She walked slowly, hoping to give Mac plenty of time to put his horse away and take his things into the house. She was halfway across the street when she saw a glow of light in Mac's house as he moved from one room to the next, obviously carrying a lamp with him. The shadows danced eerily on the walls inside the house, and through the open window, Jillian could see Mac's almost ghostly form move in the muted light.

Steadying her nerves, Jillian reached for the door, knocking almost hesitantly. She then thought better of her irrational decision to sneak over to see Mac, but she squared her shoulders, determined to tell the truth. Jillian hated that he thought less of her and couldn't bear her conscience any longer.

When he opened the door, Jillian began to tremble anew. "Mac, I have to talk to you," she said in a pleading voice.

"Not now, Jillian."

"Please, Mac." She knew she was begging, but she was desperate.

He stared at her for a moment, his eyes hard and unyielding. "No." He shut the door hard, leaving her to stand alone in the darkness.

A sob escaped her as she turned to run from the house and back to the safety of her bedroom.

Going through the back door, Jillian nearly ran over Gwen and Zack as they shared an intimate moment.

"Judith? What's wrong?" Gwen questioned.

"Nothing. Everything," she replied, so tired of the lies.

Jillian looked up to see the sympathetic expressions of both Gwen and Zack. She desperately wanted solace, but they weren't the ones to offer it.

"Has somebody hurt you?" Zack questioned, glancing past Jillian to the open back door.

Jillian sniffed back her tears. "Not in the sense you're talking about, Sheriff."

"Is it Dr. MacCallister?" Gwen asked softly.

"No, not really," Jillian replied. "It's me. I did something unforgivable as far as he's concerned, and maybe even as far as I'm concerned. He asked for my help and I refused it."

"That hardly seems unforgivable," Zack said, relaxing now that he better understood Jillian's emotional state.

"Please don't worry about it," Jillian replied. "I shouldn't have said anything. It's all my own fault. I just went over to apologize, and he won't hear me out."

"You want me to go talk to him?" Zack questioned.

"No!" Jillian's voice raised as she shook her head. "Please don't. I have to take care of this matter."

"If you need more time to try again," Gwen began, "I can leave the door unlocked for a short time."

Jillian wanted nothing more than to settle the matter with Mac. She looked out through the open door to where she could still see the light gleaming from his window.

"Go ahead. He may be stubborn, but I've a feeling you're just as determined as he is," Gwen encouraged.

"Thank you," Jillian answered. "I'll give it a try."

She turned and walked out of the Harvey House with new determination, glancing over her shoulder in hopes of receiving one last smile of encouragement from Gwen and Zack. Instead, she found them to have totally forgotten about her. Standing very close, they seemed to be murmuring endearments in their farewells for the evening. Jillian's heart ached at the thought that theirs was a true and honest romance. A mutual attraction that would allow for a strong and binding love.

Leaving them to their secrets, Jillian turned away and faced Mac's door. She bolstered up her courage once again and wiped her eyes. Knocking lightly, she waited, barely breathing.

He opened the door and scowled. "I told you I'm not in the mood to hear any excuses. Why won't you just leave me be?"

"Because I won't be able to sleep if you don't let me explain about this afternoon," she said, feeling her words catch in her throat. "I know I hurt you, and I'm sorry. I was being unreasonable, but I was afraid."

Mac leaned back against the door, his expression clearly one of disbelief. "Afraid? Of what?"

"I don't handle these things well, Mac. I've never been strong when it comes to . . ."

"Something outside of your perfectly ordered world?" he questioned angrily.

"That's not fair," Jillian retorted. "It's not my fault that my father sheltered me. He believed women were to be cared for and watched over." Jillian knew she sounded defensive, and had it not been such a serious matter, she might have laughed at the thought of defending her father. "I'm the first one to admit that I've not had to handle much discomfort in life, and I was wrong to refuse to help you."

"Yes, you were," Mac replied, not giving her an inch of consideration.

Jillian looked down at the floor. "I came to apologize. I'll help you in any way I can. I have tomorrow off, and if you want me to go out with you to help Mary with Little Sister, then I will." She looked back up to meet his expression, hoping to find forgiveness . . . and maybe something more.

Mac's expression did change, but not in the way Jillian had hoped. It grew even harder, and the words that came from his mouth were given in a cynical tone. "There's no need."

"Don't be like this, Mac. I said I was sorry, and I am. This isn't easy for me and I don't expect you to understand it, but I'm trying to do the right thing."

"Well, you're too late. Little Sister has already given birth to a daughter." He paused before adding, "She passed away shortly afterward without ever having a chance to hold her."

Jillian felt the room begin to spin. "She's dead?" She barely managed to croak out the words.

"Yes, Jillian. She's dead."

"Oh, Mac." She stumbled and reached for the doorpost.

"Are you all right?" For the first time that evening his words softened in concern. "Jillian?"

She held fast to the post, but her grip was weakening as the fainting spell overtook her body. "I'm sorry," she whispered as Mac caught her in his arms. "I'm so sorry."

Mac looked at the unconscious woman and waited only momentarily before lifting her into his arms. He carried her to the sofa, uncertain of how to treat the situation. He didn't feel the need to act as doctor to her when it was obviously the shock of the moment that had brought about her condition. Still, he was a doctor first and foremost, even if his heart was aching over their wounded friendship and Little Sister's death. He checked Jillian's pulse, then gently slipped his arm under her neck to lift her head.

"Jillian?" he said in a professional manner, patting her cheeks to bring her around. "Jillian, wake up."

She moaned softly and began to regain consciousness. "I . . . what . . ." she murmured, struggling to open her eyes.

"You fainted," he said, brushing back an errant strand of blond hair. Holding her close, Mac felt torn between his anger with her earlier attitudes and his emotions at seeing her so helpless. He realized how deeply he'd come to love this woman, and that fact was almost more troubling than the disappointment he'd felt in her refusal to help Little Sister. It wasn't mere infatuation as he had hoped, or even a love born out of isolation and loneliness. She had become an integral part of his life, and Mac was hard-pressed to let her go now that he knew how important she'd become.

"God help me," he prayed. *Help us both*, he added silently while glancing down at the woman in his arms. There was no way this was going to be easy. For despite his love for Jillian and a deep desire to keep her in his life, Mac knew the hopelessness of the situation. He could never keep her. He could never marry her—not with so much in his past to condemn him.

C H A P T E R

11

WATCHING JILLIAN REGAIN HER COMPOSURE, Mac was amazed at the flood of memories that came to him. He hated that the past just wouldn't die. People died. Why couldn't their memories be as obliging?

"Oh, Mac," Jillian whispered, not even trying to get away from his hold. "I'm sorry."

He felt his anger subsiding. "Don't worry about it. Obviously you have something troubling you quite deeply. Are you sure you're not sick?"

Jillian shook her head. "Not in the sense you're suggesting. It's a long, long story, Mac, but honestly, it has nothing to do with feeling anything against Little Sister. I truly admired her. She could have taken her life as the others did, she could have sought revenge with her brother, but instead she did nothing for herself. I would have come to help, but . . ."

"But?" he asked, his hand gently stroking her hair.

"But I was too afraid," she whispered.

"Afraid of what?"

All at once Jillian seemed to realize the intimacy of the moment and attempted to sit up. Mac very discreetly withdrew his hold on her.

"Slow down, you don't want to pass out again."

"I'm sorry," she muttered, inching away to put distance between them.

"You've already said that a few times too many," he replied, getting to his feet. "Now, why don't you tell me about this—starting with why you fainted."

Jillian licked her lips and lowered her gaze to the floor. "I can't abide death, Mac. My grandmother told me such horrible stories that I can't bear to even think about it. She told me if I were in the same room with someone when they died, I would be the next to go. Tales about how if you were the first one to touch someone after they died, they could take over your body. She also told me that dead spirits stayed in the room until a living person came in and allowed them a flesh-and-blood body to take over.

"Grandmother lived with us for about five years, and even before that, she was always telling her stories and warning us of different things. Once when a bird flew into her house, she went positively hysterical, saying that it was a sure sign someone was going to die. Sure enough, two days later my uncle died in a carriage accident. Another time, I accidentally rocked her rocking chair and it turned out to be another sure sign that there would be a death in the immediate family. A week later, we got word that my grandfather on my mother's side had passed away. Grandmother Danvers never let me forget that I had caused it by rocking that chair."

"That's all nonsense, Jillian," Mac replied, trying to sound patient. In truth, he wanted to laugh out loud. It seemed so funny that a grown woman could have such fears.

"I know it's nonsense, but it scares me still." Her voice sounded strange, and Mac worried that she might start to cry. He wasn't at all sure what her tears might do to his resolve to keep his distance.

"I didn't mean to suggest that you weren't within your rights to be scared," Mac finally said. "Your grandmother's actions and words were cruel. And I was wrong to get so mad at you. It's just . . . well, I was tired and I knew the end was coming. I didn't think the baby would even make it. I figured I'd be burying them both by morning."

"I know I've been a ninny, and if I hadn't, then maybe Little Sister could have had her brother's comfort in her final hours," Jillian said, looking up mournfully at Mac.

He shook his head. "Bear would never have come. He'd rather die than step foot in a white man's house. He'll come now to take her home and give her a proper funeral, but he wouldn't have come before then. Mary knew it, same as I did."

"Oh, Mary must hate me," Jillian said, burying her face in her hands.

"Mary doesn't know about your refusal," Mac said softly. "I just told her you were busy. It wasn't exactly a lie."

"If I'd been there . . ."

"Little Sister would still be dead and you would be hysterical." Mac tried to keep his tone from sounding too condemning. "Jillian, I understand, and I'm not mad anymore. In fact, I'm pretty embarrassed about the way I acted. I didn't give you a chance to explain, and I'm sorry. I'm just so used to people being unwilling to help when it comes to the Indians, I jumped to the wrong conclusion. There are so many different tribes in the area, and even so, most folks—most of *our* people—won't lift a hand to befriend them or treat them decently. Instead, they just demand that the Indians be contained on reservations. It's easier to pretend they don't exist if you can keep them out of sight." He paused, realizing he was rambling.

Jillian watched him with wide blue eyes and an expression that melted his heart. "Forgive me?" he questioned with great hope.

"There's nothing to forgive you for," Jillian replied. "I'm the one who was in error. Do you forgive me?"

He reached out to help her to her feet. "You acted on what you knew. I'm sorry you were so afraid. I'm sorry that you've suffered because of one old woman's superstitious notions. As a doctor, I can tell you that none of that stuff has any bearing on real life. Birds can fly all over the house, stars can fall from the sky, but it doesn't cause death. You know, if Mary were here, she'd tell us about eternal life in Jesus and how we don't need to fear death because He's already overcome it."

"Do you believe that, Mac?" Jillian asked.

Mac thought about it for a moment. "I was raised to go to church every Sunday, mainly because my father was the one doing the preaching. I used to think I understood this religion thing pretty well. You did as you pleased through the week, and on Sunday you came to church all bathed and gussied up and you told God how sorry you were for all the bad things you'd done. You talked to folks about heavenly matters, leaving each other with a hearty 'God bless you' and 'See you on Sunday.' Then you left just in time to go socialize and get an early start on the sins for next Sunday."

Jillian grinned, and Mac was relieved to see the color returning to her cheeks.

"But I now know there's a whole lot more to being a Christian than going to church on Sunday."

"What changed?"

"My parents, for one. They began to see that God has something more in mind for them. They decided they were called to the mission field, and before I knew it I was staying with my grandparents and my folks were thousands of miles away." He remembered that separation as being one of the most painful in his life, and he knew the tone he took betrayed it. "It was hard to lose them."

"I'm sorry, Mac. I didn't have any idea."

"Of course not," he said, smiling. "I can't say that their change of heart changed me. I'm still not sure where I stand or how I look at spiritual things. Mary's helped me to see that it's all a very personal matter."

"How?" Jillian questioned.

Mac laughed. "She once asked me outright if I was a Christian. I told her, of course I was. She asked me how I knew it, and I told her my folks were Christians and I'd been going to church all my life." Mac could remember the older woman's reaction like it was yesterday. "She laughed at me and asked me again how I knew I was a Christian. I told her I sat in church every Sunday and that folks who weren't Christians wouldn't do such a thing."

Jillian smiled. "What did she say?"

"She told me she could drag Dobbin into church every Sunday but it still wouldn't make that mule a Christian—or human, for that matter."

Jillian giggled. "She does have a way with words."

Mac nodded. "I finally understood, nevertheless. She asked me if I knew where I was going when I died. I hadn't really given it much thought. I'd always presumed it would be heaven, so I never worried much about it." He shrugged. "I suppose it sounds a bit foolish."

"Not at all," Jillian said, suddenly sobering. "It sounds all too familiar."

"Well, maybe that's something you should discuss with Mary. She says it's all about a personal relationship with Jesus Christ. She says we can sit in a pew until our backsides are grafted to it and it still won't change our hearts. I wasn't always sure I understood, but tonight I think she finally got through to me."

"How?" Jillian questioned, watching him carefully, as if he were about to impart some great universal mystery to her for safekeeping.

Mac pushed back the hair that had fallen across his forehead and said, "She told Little Sister she'd see her soon. I came to realize that I didn't have the same confidence in my eternal destination as Mary did for herself. I intend to spend a little time praying on the matter, and tomorrow I'm going to go talk with Reverend Lister."

Jillian stood completely still for what seemed an eternity. Finally she nodded. "It gives me much to think about. I'll be interested to know what he tells you."

Mac reached out and took hold of her shoulders. "I'm truly sorry for the way I acted. You've been a good friend, and I wouldn't want to do anything to cause that to end."

Jillian nodded. "You've been a good friend too. I could hardly bear the idea of spending three months in a place like this, but you've made the time go fast."

Mac felt a pang of regret stab at his heart. In a very short time, Jillian would return to Kansas City and he'd never see her again. Of course, he could give up his life in the desert and follow her back East. He had lived in cities before; surely he could do it again.

She suddenly appeared to grow uncomfortable. Maybe she could read his mind.

"I need to get back. They'll lock me out otherwise, and I'm not sure I'm up to climbing that trellis, even if Judith could."

Mac smiled. "Let me walk you back."

"No, that's not necessary," Jillian said, pulling away rather quickly. "I wouldn't want anyone to get the wrong impression. All it would take is one of those nosy women from town seeing us together. Tongues would no doubt wag unmercifully."

"You think they don't already wag?" Mac questioned.

Jillian paled. "What do you mean?"

He felt sorry for her and decided not to press the issue. "I'm just suggesting that the women who gossip will do so with or without anything concrete on which to base their conversations. It wouldn't really matter if I walked you back or not. If they decide there is something to this, they will merely fill in the details from their imagination."

Jillian moved toward the door. "That's why we'd be wise not to give them any fuel for the fire." She turned the handle and glanced back over her shoulder. "Thanks, Mac. Thanks for understanding and for caring about my feelings."

He nodded, not trusting himself to speak. He cared about her feelings, all right. And if Jillian Danvers cared about him the way he cared about her, the town would have more than a little bit to preoccupy itself with.

He watched her walk back to the Harvey House and test the back door. It opened and she slipped inside without anyone seeming the wiser. Mac felt an emptiness invade the house. She was gone.

"You're being foolish, Mac old boy," he said aloud, closing the door. "She couldn't be happy living on here as a doctor's wife. The desert would eat her alive." Mac slowly shook his head. "No, it's better you let it go. Let her go. Don't even try to love her."

But in his heart he knew it was too late. He did love her. And just as he had loved once before, only to be on the losing side of romance, Mac was certain that this time would be no different. It wasn't just that Jillian reminded him of *her*. It was that history seemed to be repeating itself, and Mac knew he wasn't strong enough to endure that kind of heartache again.

CHAPTER

12

JILLIAN LOST HERSELF IN HER WORK at the Harvey
House in an attempt to push aside thoughts of Mac and the gentle
way he'd held her. But she found it was almost impossible to forget.
So instead, she listened to the customers speak of their travels and
woes. She focused on Fred Harvey's routine, setting the tables with
meticulous care. Only the finest china and crystal, each piece closely
inspected for flaw or chip. Only the whitest linens, pressed and arranged to perfection.

From the moment the gong announced the passengers' arrival
until it sounded again to warn them that they were soon to board,
Jillian gave her entire heart and soul to the job at hand. She hadn't
broken a single dish in the last four days, and her tips had improved
dramatically. Men flirted with her as they did with the others, two
had proposed, and one had firmly announced that she was destined
to be his wife. She'd had to laugh when she came back to the table
to find that he hadn't tipped her so much as a penny.

But when the passengers had gone and the tables had been cleared
and reset, Jillian found herself with way too much time to think.
Nighttime was the worst yet. She lay in her bed for long hours before
sleep would finally give her any peace, and all she could think about
during those hours were Mac and Mary and Little Sister. Sometimes
she would think of her family as well, remembering, sadly enough,

that it wasn't much longer before her contract was up and she'd be expected to return home. But could she go back to what she'd known before, knowing what she did now?

Could she live among her mother's camelback sofas and Persian rugs, listen to her father compete for men's properties and goods as if the world depended on his skill? Could she dine every evening at exactly seven-thirty, wearing Worth gowns and boasting the latest in hairstyles, all while knowing that in Arizona children went to bed on mats, often hungry because of a lack of food? Could she sit in her pious cathedral, listening to the unmoving sermons and droning voices and not remember the way Reverend Lister's simple words had stirred her heart?

Jillian never found any answers for her questions—perhaps because she pushed the thoughts away as quickly as they came. She simply didn't want to deal with them. They were painful reminders that she would soon part company and leave Mac and Mary and all the others who had been so kind. And for what? Obedience to her demanding father? Lack of courage to do anything else?

Finally her mind came to rest on the lies she'd created. Few people knew who she really was, and while it didn't really hurt anyone that she was posing as Judith, Jillian was growing increasingly uncomfortable with hiding the truth. She knew Mary, although forgiving and understanding, had been surprised by her declaration. For a moment, Jillian had felt as though Mary had been hurt by her deception. This in turn grieved Jillian. She hadn't thought it would matter to anyone. She hadn't figured her identity to be of any importance.

What would the others say when she let the truth be known? Would they be angered she had led them on falsely? Tossing and turning in her bed, Jillian realized that she had come to detest her actions. What could she possibly do to right her wrongs, short of revealing herself and getting Judith into trouble?

———

Thursday dawned bright and warm, and before Jillian was even fully awake, she remembered it was her day off. In all the time since she'd come to Pintan, her days off had varied. Kate said that Judith had allowed Gwen to alternate her schedule rather than giving her a fixed day, so that if one of the other girls needed to be away, she could simply change times with Judith. It seemed like the kind of thing Judith would enjoy, but Jillian longed for a bit more order in her life.

Getting up, Jillian went quickly to her morning chores, dressing carefully in a lightweight muslin blouse and a dove gray skirt. The temperatures in Pintan were gradually climbing, and by listening to those around her, Jillian knew the heat would only continue to rise. She didn't really mind the added warmth—at least it was dry. Back in Kansas City, summer days often felt sticky and uncomfortable when the air became humid. That wouldn't be a problem here in the Arizona Territory.

She decided early on to seek out Mac and see if he might escort her out to Mary's place. She'd already spoken to her house manager, receiving permission to be in Mac's company for the day. Sam had smiled knowingly and said it was perfectly acceptable for her to court the good doctor. Jillian hadn't any chance to set him straight on his thinking because at that moment, Louisa burst into the office and declared that the kitchen was on fire.

Jillian and Sam both ran to see about the situation, finding that the cooks had easily controlled the flames.

"Sorry to give you a fright," the head chef told Sam. "Some rags were left too close to the stove. They've been moved away and shouldn't cause any more concern."

"See that they don't," Sam said. "A fire out here would spell disaster for sure."

Jillian decided this was the best moment for slipping away and quickly exited out the back door before anyone could question her further.

Mac's door was wide open, as was nearly every window in the tiny house. Jillian couldn't blame him for allowing the breeze inside. The air smelled sweet, scented with the blooming vegetation from the surrounding desert landscape. Though unlike anything she had ever known in Kansas City, she loved it nevertheless.

"Mac?" she called at the door. "Are you in there?"

"I'm here," he replied, wiping his hands on a towel as he

approached the door. "Is there a problem?"

"No." Jillian shook her head, suddenly feeling a bit self-conscious. "I was just hoping to ask you a favor."

He smiled. "When Judith came to me asking for favors they usually involved a great deal of energy and time."

Jillian couldn't help but smile. "Well, then, I'm more like my sister than I imagined. I was hoping you could take me out to Mary's place."

Mac seemed to consider it for a moment before nodding. "I think that can be arranged. I'll see about borrowing the buckboard from Reverend Lister. It's certainly sturdy enough to endure the drive."

"Thank you, Mac. It means a lot. I've been meaning to talk to Mary about a great many things, and since I have the whole day off, I was hoping you could help me out."

Half an hour later they sat side by side on the wagon seat, Jillian very aware of Mac's nearness. He smelled of freshly washed clothes and cologne. The cologne was a spicy scent, and Jillian wondered if Mac had put it on just for her. He hadn't been wearing it when she'd arrived at his door, neither had he worn it before.

"So did you have your talk with Reverend Lister?" she asked, trying to think of something to say.

"We met this morning and talked some," Mac admitted. "I still have a lot of questions, but he's a good one for supplying answers."

"Mary's good for that too. I don't suppose she'll be too happy with me for not telling everybody about who I really am, but I just don't want to mess things up for Judith. I don't want her in trouble, even if she did break her word."

"Sometimes people need to face the consequences for their actions," Mac answered.

Jillian nodded. "I know that's true, but she's my sister and I love her very much. I know she's happier now that she's away from my father and mother and married to the man she loves."

Mac fastened his eyes on her. "Tell me about your homelife, Jillian."

The request didn't seem all that unreasonable, but it made Jillian uncomfortable nevertheless. How could she possibly explain her family to Mac? They were such a strange lot.

"Well, my mother descended from European royalty, as she proudly tells everyone and anyone who will listen. She met my father in New York City while on a holiday. They fell madly in love, and my father so impressed her father with his ability to make money that when my father pledged to finance a business adventure for my grandfather, he eagerly agreed to their whirlwind courtship and marriage.

"My father's background accounts for his business acumen. His father and his father's father were both businessmen. They would participate in bits of this and that. Father calls it 'diversifying one's interests,' but I think Father is a great deal like Judith. He becomes bored easily and has to have something new to focus on. He dabbles in banking and stocks and real estate, as well as a dozen or more businesses. He's done quite well for himself, but he is very demanding and often hurts people to get what he wants."

"I'll keep that in mind," Mac said, glancing at her with a smile.

"Well, hopefully you'll never have reason to do business with him," Jillian replied. "He is ruthless and I wouldn't wish him on my worst enemy."

Mac nodded. "So is it just you and Judith as far as children?"

"There were two others, but they died very young. We are the youngest of the Danvers children, born and raised in Kansas City. Father moved his family first to Chicago, then St. Louis, and finally Kansas City. He picked up wealth as he went, much as a farmer might take up vegetables as he walks through his garden. Father just has a knack. Anyway, he settled in Kansas City and two years later Judith and I were born. Grandmother Danvers said twins were a bad omen and that nothing good could befall the family after that."

"I don't think I would have liked your Grandmother Danvers," Mac said matter-of-factly.

Jillian giggled. "I didn't like her much myself. And you know how Judith felt."

"Yes, I suppose I do. What did she die of?"

"The doctor said it was a kind of cancer," Jillian said quite seriously. "But if you want my opinion, I think she died from a hard heart. She was very much like my father. Ruthless and unyielding, not caring a bit who she hurt so long as she got her own way."

"How did your mother figure into all of this?"

"She spent her time having parties and social teas, and being seen in the right place at the right time. When Judith and I were old enough to come out of the nursery, she sent us off to boarding school and then a prestigious ladies' finishing school. Once we returned home, we were finally interesting to her. She took up the task of finding rich, handsome husbands for us and . . . well, she continues to this day."

Jillian tried not to think about the fact that she hadn't heard from her mother since writing to tell her that she and Mac were engaged. She wondered if the lie had done the trick. She felt only a small amount of relief, however, even if she had managed to stave off her mother's irritating meddling. After all, once her contract was up, what could she do but head home to the same nonsense as before? It wasn't like she could stay on in Pintan. Or could she?

"Mac, I've been thinking about something," she said, deciding to get his opinion on her idea. "I know I have to tell Gwen about who I really am. But do you suppose that given the time I've been here and the improvements I've made, plus the fact that she's shorthanded . . . well, do you suppose she might let me stay on? I mean, even after she knows I'm not Judith?"

Mac reined back on the horse and turned to look at Jillian as if she'd said something quite profound. "You'd actually want to give up your life in Kansas City and live in Pintan?"

Jillian felt uneasy with the tone of his voice. He made her feel like she was incapable of enduring such a thing. "Yes, that's what I'm proposing to do. I suppose you think that I wouldn't make a good Harvey Girl on a full-time basis."

Mac shook his head very slowly and pushed back his hat a bit. His face, although still shadowed by the hat, seemed to express hurt. "I didn't mean that at all. You shouldn't assume the worst of me. I simply find it amazing that you would like the territory enough to stay."

Jillian sighed. "I guess I jumped to the wrong conclusion. I seem to be quite good at that."

"I think we've both been guilty of that," Mac replied. "Still, are you sure you wouldn't miss the city?"

Jillian looked out across the land. "I love it here. I didn't realize it until the other day, but I really do. I don't miss the abundance of trees or water, I don't pine away for the city and all its amenities. But I do think I would miss this. There's such a serenity and peace about this place. I realized it when Mary brought me out here the first time. It seems like a nice place to call home."

Mac stared at her for a moment before slapping the reins against the horse's back. "Few people feel that way," he finally murmured.

"Well, I guess I'm just one of the few," Jillian replied softly. "I suppose I would have much to learn. I'm not very well suited to do much of anything."

"Mr. Harvey would probably argue that point," Mac said with a grin.

"Mr. Harvey is probably still tallying up his monetary losses from my escapades with his china. Gwen says in the history of her time on the job, she has never known anyone who has broken more dishes than I have."

"See there," Mac said encouragingly. "Everybody is good at something. Now, if we can just find a use for your talent, you should be quite content."

The laughter that erupted from Jillian seemed to revitalize her soul. "I shall keep my eyes open for something I might accomplish using broken china."

As they approached Mary's little house, the screams of an unhappy baby reached their ears from nearly half a mile away.

"Is Mary caring for Little Sister's baby?" Jillian questioned as Mac pulled the buckboard alongside the house.

He secured the brake and reins before jumping down. "Yup, she knew the little girl would die otherwise. The Navajo won't take her, and there aren't any whites in the area who would want a half-breed for a daughter."

"How awful," Jillian declared as she allowed Mac to help her down. As Mac's hands encircled her waist, a current of energy coursed through her body from his touch.

"You eating these days?" he questioned lightly.

She forced her thoughts to cooperate with her mouth, but it wasn't easy. She felt weak-kneed and breathless as she replied, "Of course I'm eating. Why do you ask?"

"It's just that your waist is so small. You aren't lacing your corset too tight, are you?"

"What a question!" Jillian said, her illusions of romance shattered. "You really should mind your manners, Dr. MacCallister."

The baby's insistent cries kept Mac from replying. Instead, he turned to make his way to Mary's door. The woman was coming out to greet them even before Mac could knock.

"Oh, you two are a godsend. Here," she said to Jillian, pushing the crying infant into her arms. "I have to go milk the goat."

"What? But wait!" Jillian exclaimed. "I've never held a baby."

Mary laughed and went for a bucket. "Ain't nothin' to it, child. You just hold on and don't drop her."

Jillian looked down at the squirming bundle. The baby cried with a fury that Jillian wouldn't have thought possible. Her face was all red and scrunched up, but her eyes were surprisingly void of tears.

"What's wrong with her?" Jillian questioned as Mac came to peer over her shoulder.

"I'd say she's probably hungry."

"She's always hungry," Mary chimed in. "Mainly 'cause nothin' agrees with her. She can't stand cow's milk or canned. I'm gonna try goat's milk and see if that makes any difference. Poor mite. The only thing she's got in that tummy of hers is sugar water."

"You go ahead and get the milk," Mac told Mary. "I'll give the baby a quick look-over, then settle her and Jillian in the rocker and come out to help you."

"I won't need help, Mac, but given the greenish appearance of Jillian's face, I'd say she might."

Mary laughed as she passed by them and headed to the tiny corral where she kept her goats.

"Come on," Mac instructed. "Bring the baby inside."

Jillian held the infant tightly, desperately afraid she might stumble and drop her. This firm grip only made the tiny girl scream louder.

"I'm hurting her, aren't I?" Jillian questioned nervously. "Here, take her."

Mac laughed. "Stop being so afraid. She isn't going to bite. Just relax and take a few deep breaths. You aren't going to drop her."

Jillian forced herself to do as he said. She eased her hold on the child and took a deep breath. As if sensing her efforts, the baby stopped crying and fixed her dark eyes on Jillian's face.

"See, you're a natural," Mac said as he spread a blanket atop Mary's small kitchen table. "Now put her down here, and I'll make sure she's doing okay."

Jillian reluctantly placed the baby on the blanket and watched as Mac unwrapped her and gently began examining her.

"With babies you have to be particularly careful of this spot on their heads," Mac said, showing her. "It stays soft for a long time. Those bones haven't come together yet, and there isn't any protection for the brain at this point. It'll firm right up in a few months, but in the meantime, it's a pretty vulnerable spot. My grandmother used to say it's where God ran out of materials."

Jillian thought of her own grandmother. "Mine would no doubt have said it had something to do with mankind being evil and needing someplace to let the bad humors go in and out."

Jillian then watched in amazement as the baby grasped Mac's index finger with her own tiny fingers. How wondrous to see the intricacy of this new human being. Tiny toes and fingers, a flat little button nose, and eyes the color of charcoal.

"She's beautiful," Jillian finally managed to say.

"She is lovely, isn't she?" Mac said, rewrapping the baby. "There you go, you can pick her back up now."

Jillian felt a moment of nervous anxiety, but she was drawn to this child in a way that she didn't understand. Reaching out tentatively, she looked to Mac for encouragement.

"Go ahead. You can do it."

She smiled weakly and lifted the baby slowly.

"Support her neck and head with your left hand while you put your right hand around and under her bottom," Mac instructed.

"I see what you mean," Jillian replied, cradling the baby close to her breast. The baby instantly began to nuzzle against her, instinctively seeking food. Jillian felt her cheeks grow hot as Mac began to laugh.

"I think I'd better hurry Mary along. Why don't you sit over here in Mary's rocker, and I'll be right back."

Jillian nodded and let Mac help her to the chair. She watched the baby in silence, feeling a strange rush of emotions. How could anyone despise this child? How could anyone say she didn't deserve life?

"Poor, sweet girl," Jillian whispered, gently stroking the thick black hair. "It's so sad that your mama had to die." She shuddered involuntarily at the thought that Little Sister had died in this very house. She wondered whether Mary had arranged for Little Sister's burial or if Bear had come and taken care of the matter. Maybe Mac had taken care of the burial.

"Here we go," Mary said, coming in with Mac. "I'll pour some of this in a bottle and we'll see how it goes."

Jillian watched Mary work with the feeding contraption, carefully pouring the goat's milk inside.

"This has to work," Mary said softly as she brought the bottle to Jillian. "There isn't a whole lot more I can do."

"What about a wet nurse from the tribe?" Mac suggested.

"I doubt anyone would care to help. Bear actually came to take Little Sister's body, but he wanted nothing to do with the baby," Mary replied. "No doubt he's set everyone against this little one, just as he set them against Little Sister."

As if realizing the gravity of the moment, the baby easily latched on to the rubber nipple and began to drink the milk. She didn't scream or turn away, but instead watched Jillian with great interest while being fed.

"I think she likes it," Jillian said, her voice full of hope.

"I think she just might. She's usually throwin' it all up by this time." Mary patted Jillian's shoulder and moved to the bucket that held the remaining goat's milk. "I'd best put the rest of this in a jar and save it for later."

Mary had just finished this task when someone could be heard calling her name in the distance. Mac went to the door and looked out.

"There's a young Navajo coming this way. A girl," he said, turning back to Mary. "She sounds pretty upset."

Mary put the jar aside and wiped her hands on her apron. Jillian remained seated, watching in fascination as the baby sucked greedily at the bottle.

"Dancing Star," Mary called out to the girl from the door. Waving her forward, she urged, "Come inside, child, and tell me what's wrong."

Jillian wondered at the scene. She supposed it wasn't common for the Navajo to come to Mary, but she couldn't be sure.

"Bear and the others . . ." the child gasped and fell silent.

"Bear and the others did what?" Mary questioned, handing the child a cup of water.

"They . . . they burned . . . the school," the child managed to say after downing the water.

"Oh no!" Mary exclaimed. "Oh, dear Lord, help us."

"What does this mean?" Jillian questioned.

"It means trouble," Mac replied. "The army will never stand for this."

Mary went to Jillian and helped her to position the baby on her shoulder. "You need to burp her like this after she eats, otherwise her tummy will hurt her. I'll pack up some more milk for you and Mac, and you can take the goat back to town with you."

Mac nodded, but Jillian was still not sure what Mary was saying. "Why should we take the goat?"

"Child, I'm going to have to go with Dancing Star and see if I can't intercede with the army. Bear's just lashing out because of Cooper. I'm actually amazed that the man hasn't already killed Cooper, but he believed for so long that Little Sister brought this whole thing on herself. I set him straight when he came for her body. I probably shouldn't have, but I told him the truth. I told him about the rape. He pretended not to hear me, but I know he did. And now this."

Mary's face was stricken and filled with worry. *She looks to have aged ten years,* Jillian thought.

"Here, now," Mary said, putting Jillian's hand on the baby's back. "Give her a few good pats and when you hear her burp, you can feed her a bit more or let her go to sleep."

Jillian tapped very lightly against the baby's back. It felt awkward to hold the child in this position, but she supposed Mary knew what was to be done.

"No, no," Mary said as she went about the room, picking up an assortment of things for the baby. "You aren't going to hurt her. Pat her a little more firmly."

Jillian complied, feeling like she was surely harming the baby. Instead, with a great whoosh of air, the baby burped. It so surprised Jillian that she started and Mac laughed.

"I guess you've never had to burp a baby."

"Have you?" Jillian asked indignantly.

Mac laughed. "Only once, but I wasn't anywhere near as successful as you."

"Here," Mary said, handing a rolled bundle to Mac. "There are diapers and clothes, blankets, and even another one of those bottles. I hate to impose this on you, but there's no other way. I can't take her with me."

"We understand," Mac spoke, taking the bundle.

"No, we don't," Jillian replied, looking at them both as if they'd lost their minds. "What's going on?"

"I need for you to take the baby," Mary replied. "She can't stay here alone, and I don't know what I'll find when I get to the village. The army may have . . ." She halted in mid-sentence, realizing Dancing Star was listening. "I just need for you to take her back to town and keep her there until I can come for her."

"But I have to work at the Harvey House. What should I do with her?"

"Surely the girls will help," Mac suggested.

Jillian felt completely overwhelmed by the prospect of this new task. "But I don't know anything about babies."

Mary smiled. "You'll learn. Ask your Miss Carson. Seems I remember she has younger brothers and sisters."

Jillian remembered Louisa having mentioned caring for younger siblings. Surely she could help too.

"You go ahead, Mary. We'll see to her," Mac said, helping Jillian to her feet.

"Does she have a name?" Jillian questioned, looking down at the now sleeping infant. Funny what a difference a little food and care had made.

"No, I haven't named her. I figured I'd let someone else do that," Mary replied. "I had hoped on findin' her a ma and pa to raise her. But you go ahead and name her, Jillian. I'm sure you'll come up with something just fine."

Jillian nodded. It seemed no less reasonable than giving the baby over to her care. After all, giving her a name couldn't harm her.

Mac led the way to the wagon and took the baby long enough for Jillian to climb up. He touched her very gently at the elbow with his right hand as his left cradled the sleeping baby. Once again, Jillian felt a current move through her. She trembled from the touch and tried to compose herself as Mac handed her the baby.

Mac looked around and nodded. "The wind has shifted and that cool air suggests a storm. Let's get you both back to town before it turns bad."

Jillian looked to the skies and saw a band of gray clouds on the horizon. The air had cooled, but it certainly wasn't the reason for her trembling. And it wasn't even her fear of caring for this newborn. No, her trembling was born out of something much more powerful. Her trembling was born of desire and unbidden love.

Mac jumped into the wagon and reached across Jillian to release the brake and take up the reins. He looked into her face for just a moment, and Jillian knew he saw something there that she'd not been able to hide in time. Before she knew it, he had reached up to touch her cheek ever so gently.

"You'll do just fine," he told her. "The baby will be all right."

She nodded and looked away quickly. Let him think that this was the only reason for her mood. Let him believe it had only to do with the baby and the storm and even the Indian troubles. Just don't let him know it has to do with loving him.

By the time Mary arrived at the little collection of hogans, the women and children were in utter chaos. Dancing Star jumped from the wagon and went in search of her mother, and before Mary could even bring the wagon to a halt, several women had come to approach her.

"Our men are gone," one woman said. "They will hide from the army."

"Will the army kill them?" another asked.

"Will soldiers kill us—kill our children?"

"Whoa, now!" Mary said, raising her hand for silence. She looked into the worried faces of the women. "I can't say I know for sure what will happen. Can you tell me how this started? Is it true that Bear burned down the school?"

The women nodded, their dark eyes pleading with Mary to make things right.

"Bear say it will bring Mr. Cooper," Dancing Star's mother related.

Mary nodded. "I figured as much. He's planning on killing Cooper, ain't he?"

The woman nodded and tears came to her eyes. "He say Cooper killed his sister and left an evil spirit behind in her baby."

"Nonsense. You need to put that from your mind. The baby is beautiful. She looks just like Little Sister. There's nothing evil about that child."

The women comforted their own children and said nothing. It was as if they expected Mary to work some sort of miracle, and when Dancing Star's mother spoke again, Mary was certain that was exactly what they expected.

"You talk to your God and have Him work His Spirit magic."

Mary shook her head. "I'll talk to God, but He isn't a magic worker. He has a plan and an order for all of this." She reached out and patted the head of a small boy and couldn't help but wonder what his future would be. In the distance thunder rumbled, and Mary re-alized that it might rain. They desperately needed it, but not only that—the rain would slow down the army and maybe give the Navajo men a chance to get further into hiding.

BACK AT THE HARVEY HOUSE, everyone crowded around Jillian and the baby.

"Oh, she's so tiny," one girl said, reaching out to touch the baby's fingers.

Louisa popped a look over Jillian's shoulders. "She won't be any trouble. They mostly sleep at this age."

"I know it's a problem," Jillian said, looking at Gwen's worried expression. "But I promise I'll see to all her needs. You won't have to worry about a thing."

Gwen shook her head. "No, Jillian. If you are to have her here, we'll all help. Poor little mite. She can't help her circumstances."

Jillian smiled but it quickly faded as one of the newest replacements, a young woman of eighteen or nineteen, chimed in, "But she's an Injun."

"She's a baby, Miss Stamos," Gwen countered before Jillian could say a word.

Jillian threw Gwen a grateful look. "Thank you for understanding."

Just then Zack Matthews came bounding into the dining room. "I just heard from Mac about the school," he said, coming to Jillian and Gwen. "Miss Danvers, do you know what route Mary took?"

"No, not really. I rode with her once when she was trading goods, but I don't know which trail we were on or how she got there. Mary said the Navajo have many areas where they've congregated to live together. She said there were several roads and many settlements throughout the reservation. Why, Mr. Matthews? Is Mary in danger?"

"I'm afraid she might be. Bear might have counted on someone going to her for help. He may have laid in an ambush for her and any other white man to head his way."

"No," Jillian gasped, pulling the baby closer. "Mary is only trying to help Bear. The Navajo are good, peaceful people."

"Except when you push them around," Zack suggested. "They haven't been happy with the new schools, and now that they've actually taken matters into their own hands, the army will step in and see to it that the perpetrators are punished. Unfortunately, a great many innocent people may be punished as well."

He looked briefly at Gwen, and it was while watching this tender exchange that Jillian was more certain than ever that they had fallen in love.

"Miss Carson, I'd like a moment to speak with you before I head out."

Gwen paled but nodded. "Girls, get back to work," she ordered before following Zack from the room. "Oh, and, Judith, just take the baby upstairs and I'll be up directly to help you."

Jillian moved down the hall to the back stairs, then carefully cradling the baby with her left arm, she pulled up her skirt with her right hand and made her way up. She entered her room and after searching the bedding, she placed Little Sister's baby in the center of her own bed.

"What am I going to do?" she questioned, staring at the infant. "I don't know anything about taking care of children." She tried to remember all that Mac and Mary had told her. Mac had taken the goat home with him, promising to bring extra milk within the hour. But that wouldn't solve all of her problems. Feeling inadequate, Jillian realized that she didn't even know how to change the baby's diaper.

"They're really not that much of a mystery," Gwen said from the open doorway.

"Oh, I would beg to differ with you," Jillian replied in complete exasperation. "I don't know why I agreed to this. I've never had the opportunity to so much as hold a baby before today."

Gwen stood beside her. "It'll be all right. We'll all help."

Jillian turned to look at her housemother. The worried expression on her face told Jillian that Gwen's concern was for more than the child before them.

"Has Mr. Matthews gone after Mary?"

Gwen nodded and looked away.

"I know you're worried about him, but he seems very wise in dealing with these matters. Not at all the kind to go off without thinking it through."

Again Gwen nodded. She reached into her pocket and pulled out a folded piece of paper. "He gave me this to keep for him."

Jillian took the paper and unfolded it. The sketch was of a house with a woman who looked remarkably like Gwen, standing to one side, looking off at some distant rider.

"I didn't know he could draw. He's quite good."

"Yes, he is."

"But it's more than that, isn't it?" Jillian stated more than questioned. "You're in love with each other."

Gwen looked at her rather apprehensively and nodded. "But don't go telling anyone. It's almost more than I can believe."

Jillian smiled and refolded the paper. "I think a good many folks already suspect."

"Well, it just wouldn't do to go stirring up gossip and such," Gwen said. She paused a moment, then added, "It's just that, well, I was engaged once before to a wonderful man. We were so happy, Judith."

"What happened?" Jillian questioned, feeling awkward that Gwen was pouring her heart out to the wrong sister.

"He was killed in an accident at the factory in which he worked." Her voice clearly revealed the sorrow that she had known. "It took a long time to get over that. It's been over five years now."

"I'm sorry," Jillian replied. "That must have been terribly hard to endure."

Gwen nodded and tears came to her eyes. "If anything happens to Zack, I don't think I could bear it. I wasn't going to let myself fall in love with him, but now I've gone and done it and I just can't stand the thought of him going out there to possibly be killed."

Jillian reached out and patted Gwen's arm. "Mary says we should pray when things like this come upon us. I'm not one to understand such matters too well, but Mary seems to know what works."

"I know that prayer works," Gwen admitted, "and I feel bad that I can't just say that because I've prayed for him, I'm not worried about him. I suppose it's a big sin to pray to God about something, then worry the whole time afterward."

"If it is," Jillian replied, "I'm sure He understands our fears. He made us, so He must realize how we feel."

"Please don't say anything about this to the other girls, Judith," Gwen said, gripping Jillian's hand. "I just don't want a scene about this. Zack has asked me to marry him when he comes back. That's what this picture is all about. He drew the house he wants to build me. He said he always wants me waiting there for him to come riding home to."

"I promise I won't say anything, but I have my own confession to make," Jillian stated. She gathered her courage. "You probably won't like it, but I'm begging you to hear me out and try to understand why I did what I did."

Gwen eyed her suspiciously. "What in the world are you talking about?"

Jillian moved away and went to look out the window. The time to tell the truth had come. "I'm not Judith." She turned and saw that Gwen didn't understand. "I'm her twin sister, Jillian. Judith came home for our grandmother's funeral and couldn't bear the thought of leaving the man she's loved all these years. She gave him all the money she had saved from her Harvey House job, and he invested it in a business and home for them.

"You have to understand, Judith and I have always been very close. But even more so, Judith has a way of getting what she wants, and I can't usually fight her when she comes to me with such sincerity and hope."

"So she asked you to come here in her place?" Gwen questioned.

"But why? Girls were resigning their positions left and right to marry. Why did she not do the same?"

"Because her contract wasn't up and she would lose half her back wages," Jillian replied. "And she needed that money for her new life."

Gwen shook her head. "Mr. Harvey very seldom demands that money. Although I have seen a time when he did, it was just to teach someone a lesson. Leave it to Judith to worry about such a matter."

"It wasn't just that," Jillian continued. "She cared a great deal about all of you here in Pintan. She didn't want to leave you without help. She asked me to come here and fulfill her contract, and now that I have nearly done so, I'm asking you to let me stay on and finish it out. But more than this," Jillian said, stepping toward Gwen, "I'm asking you to let me stay on afterward."

"Why?" Gwen questioned. "Now that you know Judith would suffer little or no consequences for what she's done, why would you ask to finish out her term and stay on?"

"Because I've come to love it here, Gwen. I know I'm still kind of clumsy, but I've never had to do things for myself until now. I know, too, that you're shorthanded and that no one wants to come to a small dining house in the middle of the Arizona heat. But I've come to love Arizona as well."

Jillian went to where Gwen stood and pleaded, "Please, Gwen. Please try to understand that I wasn't seeking to hurt anyone with this deception. I only wanted to help Judith."

"Lies are never the way to fix a problem. You've allowed people to believe in you, to give you their confidences."

"I know," Jillian said, wringing her hands together. "I've been feeling horrible ever since . . . well, since I've come to care so much about everyone. Kate and Louisa guessed it. I suppose given the fact that I didn't have the same wound on my arm from when Judith burned herself and all the little subtle differences you see when you room with someone, they were able to see through my facade. They were very kind. But I know I don't deserve kindness or to be excused. I'm just begging for you to forgive me and allow me to go on with my life here."

"Well, it certainly explains a great deal," Gwen said thoughtfully.

"I thought Judith must have been beside herself with grief given her inability to perform her tasks properly."

"It was simply a lack of experience, I assure you. Haven't I improved?"

Gwen nodded. "Yes. Yes, you have. I'm amazed, however. How you managed to keep everyone besides Kate and Louisa from knowing your true identity is beyond me."

Jillian looked to the floor in embarrassment. "Well, I didn't exactly keep it from everyone. Mac found out right away. When I had to have my hand stitched up, he wanted to look at Judith's burned arm."

"Oh my," Gwen said, grinning, "I would imagine that was quite a shock."

Jillian laughed and nodded. "It was, but he agreed to keep my secret, and for that I'm eternally grateful. He has always been very good to me and I . . . I have always appreciated his help."

"I would imagine there is something more than appreciation between you two. Sam told me you were courting." Jillian flushed and opened her mouth to contradict this, but Gwen continued. "I am short on available help, and because of that—and the fact that I like you—I'll let you stay for as long as you want the job. In fact, consider Judith's contract fulfilled. I'll write up a new one just for you."

"Truly?"

"Truly. But Jillian, no more lies," Gwen stated softly. "I won't pretend to understand the full reason you would allow such a drama to play out in your life, but our lives here at the Harvey House are founded on openness and honesty. If you can't give that to me, then don't stay."

Jillian swallowed hard. "I understand. I don't want there to be any more lies, either."

Gwen smiled. "Good. Now we need to be thinking about this baby. I'll see if there isn't a crate or an extra trunk for keeping her in. We have to keep her safe from the varmints around here," Gwen said, moving toward the door. "And, Jillian, thank you for keeping my thoughts on Zack to yourself."

"I think most everyone knows your heart for Mr. Matthews," Jillian said with a smile. "But I'll keep quiet."

"I think we should let everyone know the truth about you," Gwen said as she paused at the door. "I think most everyone will understand, but you should probably be prepared for some to be unforgiving. Not everyone will care about your reasoning."

"The people I care about have already forgiven me," Jillian replied. "Still, I know it was wrong to impose upon the trust of so many. I don't want people getting the wrong impression about me."

"I don't imagine they will. Especially after they think about it and remember Judith's way with folks."

Jillian grinned. "She does have a way, doesn't she?"

Gwen laughed. "So do you."

Jillian thought of Gwen's words long after her housemother had taken herself off in search of a proper bed for the baby. *Maybe I have more courage and daring than I thought,* she reasoned. *After all, I'm here, like Mac pointed out. And I've taken on the task of a baby and a job and now I'll have to take on the task of standing up to my mother and father, as well.* The latter thought filled her with apprehension.

The girls were all true to their word. They came in various shifts to offer help with the baby, and when they all gathered together that evening after the dining room had been closed for the night, the most important task of all was considered: What should they name the baby?

"I don't know any Navajo names," one girl threw in.

"I don't think it should have to be a Navajo name," Louise replied. "After all, the Navajo don't want her."

Jillian rocked the baby gently in a borrowed cradle that Mrs. Lister had managed to come up with. The entirety of the cradle rockers had been placed in a large pan of water, a necessity since a scorpion sting or spider bite would most likely be the death of the infant.

"What about something like Mary?" someone suggested. "After all, Mrs. Barnes is the one who will go on caring for her after she comes back."

"If she comes back," another girl added.

The idea of Mary never returning hadn't occurred to Jillian. What would she do if Mary ended up dead in some ambush? The baby would truly be homeless then. Could Jillian go on working at the Harvey House and keep the infant with her? She would just have to have hope that the future would work itself out.

"I'm thinkin' somethin' biblical would be good," Kate suddenly declared. "Maybe somethin' like Sarah or Ruth."

"Mary's biblical," the girl who'd suggested the name countered.

"What about something like Faith or Patience?" Kate questioned.

"Why not Hope?" Jillian suddenly said.

"Yes, Hope is perfect," Louisa agreed.

"Aye," Kate said. "She looks like a Hope."

They all agreed that the name was perfect, and long after they had all gone to bed and Jillian sat feeding the infant girl her midnight bottle, Jillian still thought the name fit to a T. They would all need hope if they were to get through this conflict between the Navajo and the government.

"I'll bet even Mary will like the name," she whispered to the baby. Her heart ached at the thought that Mary might not return. After all, there had been no news or sign of Zack or Mary. What if Bear had ambushed them and killed them? What if he was putting together an entire army of warriors to come and kill everyone who had caused the Navajo harm? Jillian felt her body tremble. How she longed to hear Mac's reassurance that everything would be all right. How she longed to feel his arms around her, comforting her, loving her.

"Oh, Hope, this is a hard world you've come to live in. But Mary says that God can make even the hardest places soft and smooth." The baby's dark eyes watched Jillian as she spoke. She seemed so observant, and it was almost as if she knew exactly what Jillian was saying.

A strange noise came from outside in the street, and Jillian immediately thought of Bear and the night he'd stood in front of Mr. Cooper's office.

Carefully, she placed the baby in the cradle and went to the window. Pulling back the shade, Jillian stared out into the darkness. The street was empty. She shuddered and quickly dropped the shade back into place. Just then she heard the wind pick up and the rain start to fall. How refreshing the thought of rain could be, but in this moment, she worried that it would thwart Zack's efforts to find Mary.

God, please help Mary and Zack, she prayed. *Please help us all.*

CHAPTER

14

TENSION MOUNTED in the following days when there was still no word from either Zack or Mary. Gwen and Jillian shared brief concerned glances, nodding as if to reassure the other that they were still thinking on the matter—still praying for intercession.

Jillian had never known such exhaustion as the ordeal of trying to keep up with a baby and work for Fred Harvey. When Sam brought her a telegram one morning, shortly after the westbound train pulled out of the station, Jillian merely tucked it into her pocket and continued with her duties. She yawned in complete exhaustion, trying hard to mask her weariness. She desperately wanted to show everyone that she was capable of handling both tasks.

Everyone had pitched in to help with Hope, and everyone had been extremely nice about the whole Jillian/Judith ordeal. They had, for the most part, thought it amusing and quite entertaining. Jillian felt relieved to be able to be herself again, but upon finding that luxury, she wasn't entirely sure who she was anymore. She didn't seem like the old Jillian. Her eyes had been opened to too much, and her mind and heart were occupied in ways they had never been before.

A deep growing love for Hope was present in her heart, as was a romantic love for Mac. The only problem, Jillian realized, was that neither one of them belonged to her in any form of permanency.

"You look dead on your feet," Mac announced, coming alongside her.

Jillian had been so preoccupied that she'd not even seen him approach. "I am tired, but I'm okay. Are you here to eat?"

He nodded, his dark hair falling lazily over his left eye. Jillian reached up without thinking and pushed it back. Mac's gaze burned into her as she pulled back in embarrassment.

"I'm sorry. I don't know why I did that."

"No harm done," Mac replied. He looked as if he might say something more, but then Gwen entered the conversation.

"Dr. Mac, have you heard any news?"

He shook his head. "Not a word. I tried telegraphing the fort to see if they had any word for us, but so far no one's responding."

She nodded. "I see."

"Look, if you don't mind, I'd like to give Hope a brief examination. I just want to make sure she's thriving," Mac told them.

"She's asleep upstairs," Jillian said, yawning. She was getting as remiss in her manners as Louisa. "I can go get her."

"I'll get her, Jillian," Gwen announced. "You look like you're ready to fall over."

"Thanks," she murmured and tried to turn her attention back to the table. She was tired—completely exhausted—but Mac's presence was also taking its toll. It seemed like her love for him was growing stronger every day, and she worried that sooner or later she'd go and do something stupid like make a public declaration. It was bad enough that she'd just brushed his hair out of his eyes. That was the touch a mother might give her child—or the way a wife might adjust her husband's appearance.

"You should get some sleep," Mac said softly.

She smiled. "Tell that to Hope."

"I will," he replied.

Gwen arrived with the sleeping infant and held her out to Mac. "She's a good baby for the most part. I know Jillian's had to do battle with her at night. I figured tonight Hope could sleep with me and give Jillian a break."

"No!" Jillian replied, coming fully awake. "I mean, I don't want to do that. I'm all right. Hope's no trouble."

Mac and Gwen both eyed her curiously for a moment. Before turning his attention back to the baby, Mac suggested, "Perhaps, Miss Carson, you could allow Jillian to work in split shifts so that she could get some sleep during the day."

Gwen agreed that this was acceptable. "In fact," she told Jillian, "why don't you go ahead and go upstairs to bed. I'll take care of Hope while you get some rest."

The thought of resting for even a short time appealed greatly to Jillian. She didn't know why it mattered so much that she should be the one to care for Hope in the night, but for some reason, yielding the child's care in the daylight hours didn't seem to bother her nearly as much.

"I'll get myself something to drink and go upstairs," Jillian murmured.

Turning from Gwen and Mac, Jillian made her way to the kitchen. It was then that she remembered the telegram. Reaching into her pocket, she withdrew the missive and opened it to read.

With a gasp and a cry that edged on terror, Jillian backed into the cook's assistant, sending him crashing against a stack of pots. This in turn caused the pans to fall clattering to the floor, knocking the poor man against another of the chefs, who in turned juggled a bowl of soup, only to lose the battle. Jillian reached out to help but slipped on the wet floor, and before she knew it, she had landed in a heap alongside the pots and pans.

Mac and Gwen, along with several of the Harvey Girls, came running to see what the commotion had been about. Mac laughed when he saw that Jillian was at the center of the matter. He stopped laughing, however, when Jillian began to struggle to her feet, only to cry out and fall back down.

"What is it?" he asked her, squatting down beside her.

"My ankle. I think I've twisted it."

Mac reached out and pushed back her black skirt. He gently moved the foot back and forth, but when Jillian cried out, he stopped. "I'd say you've twisted it pretty badly. It's already starting to swell."

He lifted her into his arms without giving her a chance to protest.

Jillian wrapped her arms around Mac's neck, fearful that he might drop her. He seemed completely unconcerned with her weight.

"Miss Carson, I'll need some ice. Will someone show me the way to Miss Danvers' room?"

"I can be showin' ya," Kate said, moving toward the back stairs. "Just come this way." Kate hurried ahead of them, calling out, "Man on the second floor! Man on the second!" This was the rare time when anyone of male persuasion was allowed to venture into the sanctity of the Harvey Girls' quarters.

Jillian had never known such humiliation. She struggled between the desire to cry and the overwhelming urge to laugh. Laughter seemed to be a good way to cover up her embarrassment, but spying the telegram she still clutched in her hand, laughter was the furthest thing from her mind.

Kate opened the door to their room and quickly checked the covers and bedding before Mac deposited Jillian on the bed.

"I'll be fine, really I will," she said in protest as Mac directed Kate to remove Jillian's shoe and stocking on her right leg.

Kate wouldn't hear any protest from her friend. She quickly and discreetly released Jillian's garter and slipped the stocking down, then pulled her shoe off, taking the stocking with it.

"Here's the ice," Gwen announced, bringing in a large bowl. "I've also brought some cloth to pack it in."

"Good thinking," Mac replied. He went to Jillian and grinned. "You do have a way of getting yourself into trouble, don't you."

"If you only knew the half of it," Jillian muttered and fell back against her pillow. How in the world could she ever explain this one to him? From downstairs, Hope began to cry and Jillian attempted to get up.

"Stay where you are," Mac half growled at her. "You aren't going anywhere."

"But the baby—"

"Miss Carson or one of the other girls can see to the baby."

"If you don't need us," Gwen said, "Kate and I will do just that."

Jillian thought to protest but figured she'd have to face Mac sooner or later with the truth. Maybe now would be the perfect time.

Perhaps he'd have more sympathy for her since she was hurt.

"Mac, there's something I need to tell you. Ow!" she exclaimed as he manipulated her foot.

"It isn't broken, but it's going to hurt pretty fierce for a day or two. You're going to have to take it easy and stay off of it for a while."

"But I can't. I have a job to do, and then there's Hope. . . ."

"You've gotten yourself pretty attached to that little girl, haven't you?" he questioned, looking her straight in the eye.

"Well, she's . . . she needs me and I . . . think she's special."

Mac nodded. "She is and so are you. Mary was right to give her over to your care."

"I sure hope Mary is all right," Jillian murmured, momentarily forgetting about her confession.

"I'm sure she is." Mac propped the leg up with a pillow, then proceeded to pack ice in cloth and place it around Jillian's swollen ankle. "We have to trust God to watch out for Mary. Now, you want to tell me what this is all about? What happened down there?"

"Well, it's just that . . . you see . . ." Jillian fell silent. This wasn't going to be easy to explain. She'd brought all of her troubles on herself; having to admit her actions to Mac was more than a little overwhelming. "I did something really foolish."

He looked at her oddly, then pulled up the rocking chair she had been using while caring for Hope. "I can see I'm probably in for a pretty big ordeal. Maybe I should sit down."

She nodded. "I don't know where to begin, but first, you have to know how sorry I am."

"I hate it when folks start out like that," Mac said apprehensively. His eyes narrowed as his right brow raised and his voice lowered. "Jillian?"

Jillian bit at her lower lip and nodded. "It's really not all that bad—maybe you'll even find it amusing." She laughed nervously.

"So you'd best get to explaining."

Jillian fell back against her pillow and sighed. "My mother has been pestering me ever since I came to Pintan. She has this earl in mind for me to marry, and she kept writing about having him come here."

"And now he's coming here, is that it?"

"No," she said, shaking her head from side to side. "I told my mother there was someone else. Someone here in Pintan. I told her not to bother with the earl because I was already in love."

"I see," Mac replied, easing back in the chair. He crossed his arms and looked at her curiously. "Did she buy it?"

"Not at first." Jillian tried to think of how best to break the news. "She kept talking about coming here with the earl. I just couldn't stand any more of it. You have to understand, she's done this to me ever since I came of age. It's her desire to see her daughters married off to wealthy men with titled backgrounds."

"So what did you do to convince her that she shouldn't send him here?"

Jillian licked her lips, but her mouth was so dry that it did little good. "I told her I was engaged to be married."

Mac laughed. "I'll bet that put her plans to send the earl here to a grinding halt."

"It did, only now my mother and father are coming to Pintan to meet my fiancé. They don't like that I've gone behind their backs and gotten myself engaged, but because I've described such a wonderful man, they've agreed to come and consider him as a potential son-in-law."

"I see."

"No, you don't," Jillian replied, feeling absolutely horrible. She wanted to crawl into the cracks between the hardwood floor panels. "It isn't that simple."

"Why not?"

"Because they're going to be here in three days."

"So?" He looked at her as if she were speaking a foreign language.

"So we have a real problem here."

"We?" he questioned, shaking his head. "Why *we*?"

She had no other recourse but to just lay out the truth. "Mac, I told them I was engaged to you."

He looked at her in stunned silence for a moment, then began to chuckle. Only he didn't just chuckle. Soon he was nearly howling with laughter. "Oh, that's a good one, Jilly."

He'd never called her that before, and somehow the nickname only made her feel worse. It suggested an intimacy that she would have cherished under different circumstances.

"I'm sorry, Mac. I didn't think it would ever come to this. But now they're on their way—or soon will be. I didn't even read the entire telegram. I feel just awful. I know I shouldn't have lied, but I was already steeped in deceit. Telling them about you seemed to be easy enough and, I thought, harmless."

"Well, there's just one thing to do about it," Mac told her, sobering rather quickly.

"What?" The word was barely a whisper, she was so nervous.

"I'll just have to ask you to marry me and you'll just have to say yes, and when your folks step off the train, we'll greet them like any other loving couple."

"You'd do that for me?" Jillian questioned, incredulous. "Oh, but Mac, I couldn't ask you to do that. That goes beyond friendship."

"And right into matrimony," he said with a grin. "So what about it? Will you marry me, Miss Danvers?"

"But we can't just keep on lying. I promised Gwen I would not deceive her anymore. I just can't continue to lead everyone on like this."

Mac took hold of her hand. "So don't make it a lie. We can always call it off later." His expression caused her heart to beat faster as he added, "Or not."

"Not a lie?" she questioned weakly. How she wished he were serious.

Mac grinned. "Not at all. Folks get engaged and unengaged a lot out here. We can cross that bridge later. It might be fun to be engaged to you. Who knows where it might lead us? After all, we like each other, right?"

He sounded so enthusiastic that Jillian began to see the possibilities. "I don't know, Mac. It wouldn't really be right, would it?" Though her mind was hesitant, her heart pleaded with her to be convinced.

"We're the two who are getting engaged," he said softly. "We know the truth of the matter, and we'll work on it as we go."

Jillian saw no other way out. Her father would descend upon them both, no matter what she did. And if he came all the way to Arizona on a farce, he would be livid.

"But what will we do once we convince them we're engaged? I told them we were going to marry right away."

Mac shrugged. "Don't borrow trouble. Maybe we'll have a hideous fight and break if off after they get here. Or maybe—"

"But you don't know my father," she interrupted. "He's used to having his way about things. He might force me to return to Kansas City."

"Jillian, you're a grown woman, fully of age. You have a way to make a living for yourself and a good head on your shoulders. Why not just stand up to your father respectfully and let him know how you feel? He sounds like the kind of man who appreciates honesty and strength."

"Both qualities that I seem to sorely lack," Jillian moaned.

Mac laughed. "Just answer my question and we can get on with this. Will you marry me?"

Jillian's heart ached. How she would love to hear Mac ask that question for real. "Yes," she murmured. "But I still don't see how we're going to pull this off. After all, the entire town knows us and knows that we aren't engaged."

"We'll get that resolved real quick. After all, what are small towns good for if not spreading gossip? Besides, we really are engaged now. I just asked and you just accepted." He smiled, seeming quite pleased with the outcome of this situation.

Just then Gwen returned to check on Jillian's condition. "Will she be all right? Is it broken?"

Mac grinned at Jillian, then met Gwen's concerned look. "No, it's not broken. It's just a sprain. She'll have to stay off of it for a few days." He stood up and struck a roguish pose. "Oh, by the way, we want you to be the first to know that we're engaged to be married."

CHAPTER

15

MAC FOUND HIMSELF WHISTLING a lot over the next couple of days. The idea of being engaged to Jillian Danvers was just fine by him. Now his only problem was how to change their make-believe situation into reality.

He had thought himself resigned to a life of solitary existence, until meeting Jillian. The idea of marriage had never appealed to him, given his past and the tragedy that haunted him. But Jillian had a way of making him forget the past, even as she awakened in him memories of love and joy.

However, he never would have allowed himself to consider marriage to Jillian had she not spoken of her love of the territory and of the desire to remain here rather than return to Kansas City. No one would be forcing her into a life in the middle of nowhere, for she had already chosen it for herself. She had come to love this arid, sage-covered land. Now if only she could come to love him as well.

Sitting on a chair outside his front door, Mac worked at sharpening a knife on a whetting stone as this thought played in his head: *The entire town thinks she's mine. Even Jillian doesn't seem to mind the idea, but then again, she's trying to hide from the lie she's told her parents.* A lie that seemed to draw everyone into plans for their wedding. Images of Jillian smiling up at him from behind a wedding veil made his heart race a little faster. He whistled and contemplated what his next move should be.

"Congratulations, Doc," one of the town's old-timers called. "Heard you was getting' hitched up with one of them Harvey gals. Sure are the purtiest thangs I ever saw."

"Thanks, Zeke. I have to agree with you," Mac replied, then put his attention back to the knife. He glanced up to ask Zeke how his rheumatism was acting when a cloud of dust on the horizon caught his attention.

"Riders are a'comin'," Zeke said as Mac realized it for himself.

Mac went inside and deposited the knife and stone. Hopefully the riders would include Zack Matthews and Mary Barnes. The entire town had been on edge since word had come about the school being burned down. It hadn't been that long since the government had arrested neighboring Hopi men for interfering with their children being educated in the white man's schools. Those men had been taken to Alcatraz Prison in the San Francisco Bay. The government officials believed this would be a very visual lesson to others who might protest, but it hadn't worked. Mac could have told them that it wouldn't. The Navajo and Hopi would rather die than rob their children of their heritage and culture.

Mac returned to the street to watch the riders draw near. It became clear that a company of soldiers were approaching, along with six or seven mounted Navajo men. The Navajo had been bound and tied to their mounts with leg-irons that looped under the bellies of their horses from one ankle to the other. Bear sat proudly at the head of the group. He looked neither left nor right as the soldiers brought him into town.

Not far behind this group of riders came Mary Barnes and Zack Matthews. They looked very unhappy, but none the worse for their two-and-a-half-day adventure.

Mac hailed Zack and Mary. "Anybody hurt?"

"Nothing too bad," Zack declared. "Frankly I'm surprised, given the stubbornness of both sides."

Mary nodded. "They act worse than a bunch of children."

"You doing all right, Mary?" Mac questioned, seeing the weary expression on her face. Dirt caked the wrinkles in her skin, and her hair poked out in odd directions from the haphazard bun on her head.

"I've had better days," the old woman admitted. "How about you?"

Mac smiled. "I'm not too bad off, considering."

Zack watched the soldiers as they headed for his jail. "I've got to get down there. They're going to put this bunch in my jail while they go out and find the others. They believe there to be about twenty altogether who either plotted or actually carried out the destruction of the school."

"What'll happen to them?" Mac questioned.

Zack shrugged. "Who knows? Given the army's delight in making an impression, I'll be real surprised if they don't line them up and shoot them."

"What's going to happen with the children?"

Mary answered before Zack could speak. "That Colonel Windbag or Winthrop or whatever his name is has already ordered them to be packed up and moved not far from Fort Defiance."

Mac shook his head. He could only imagine that this was only the beginning of the problems to come. The Navajo were a proud people, and they held their culture and heritage in high regard. Now their children would be forced to live away from their people and wear white man's clothes. The boys would have their hair cut very short, and no one would be allowed to speak their native Navajo language—all in order to Americanize them. Never mind that the Indians didn't even have the right to vote. Never mind that no one wanted to allow them to be educated in universities and rewarded with prestigious positions or live in their neighborhoods. Let the Indians become civilized, but don't welcome them in as friends or leaders.

"I'll catch up with you later, Mac," Zack told him, nudging his horse's flanks.

"How are Jillian and the baby holding out?" Mary questioned as Zack sped off to catch up with the soldiers.

"She's doing real well. She named the baby Hope."

Mary grinned a wide, toothy smile. "That fits. I knew she'd come up with the right choice. She's got a good head on her shoulders, even if she does let herself get a little mixed up now and then."

Mac nodded. "I couldn't agree more. In fact, there's something you should know."

A gunshot rang out, giving both Mary and Mac a start. "Now what?" Mac growled. "I suppose I'd better get my bag and make sure no one has been injured."

"I'd go with you, but that colonel has already forbid me to accompany them further. I'm going over to the Harvey House." She grunted a bit and tightened her grip on the reins. "I'd like to give him a piece of my mind, but I just get mouthy when I'm around that bunch. Then Colonel Winthrop just takes his anger at me out on the Navajo."

Mac nodded. "I'd feel better if you stayed away from that bunch as well. They don't cotton to women interfering in army matters, and I fear someone would just end up hurt. I'll come over and let you know what's happened." He went inside for his bag, and as he came back out, Mary was already positioning her wagon at the back door of the Harvey House.

"Oh, ask Jillian to tell you about her big plans!" Mac called out as he hurried off down the street. He grinned to himself. Maybe if enough people told her what a good idea it was to marry Mac, Jillian herself would begin to believe it. Then maybe he could turn this temporary engagement into something more permanent.

"I swear she looks like she's grown six inches," Mary declared, holding Hope up for inspection. "Life with you must agree with her."

"Oh, Mary," Jillian said, watching her fuss over the baby, "she's such a sweetie. Everyone here simply adores her. But what about you, Mary? Are you all right? What happened out there?"

Mary continued to play with the baby as she spoke. "I made it to Bear's settlement, but all the men who were involved with destroying the school were gone. I stayed with the women and tried to give them encouragement by praying and talking of God's love. Several decided to trust in Jesus and became believers, saying that they knew my faith had to come from something very real, and they wanted that for themselves.

"Anyway, the army came and ransacked everything in sight. They stopped short of beating the information out of the women, but I'm not sure they would have if I hadn't been there."

"Oh, how terrible!"

"It was. Most of the soldiers were angry and wouldn't listen to much in the way of reasoning. They were following orders and seemed happy to comply. I finally threatened their windbag of a leader, saying that if they touched so much as a single hair on the heads of those women and children, I would have a telegram off to the president of the United States, giving such detail that he'd be sure to come under his scrutiny. Then I promised I would take the story to every newspaper I could find willing to run the story. He didn't seem to like the idea of such negative publicity and settled for merely stalking around the women in an intimidating manner."

"I was so worried for you. Hope kept waking me in the night, and when I'd get up to feed her, I'd think of you. I prayed too, although I don't suppose they were very good prayers."

Mary smiled and cradled Hope in her arms. "Prayers are prayers and God hears 'em all. He knows the heart and that's what counts. Well, I knew you'd be anxious to get back to your own life, so I figured to come and take the baby home with me."

"You're taking her?" Jillian questioned, trying to remain calm.

Mary didn't seem to notice the hesitant tone in Jillian's voice. "I figure we'll do all right for ourselves until the good Lord sends a family for her. Say, Mac tells me you have some sort of plans going on that I should ask you about."

"Oh, he did, did he," Jillian more stated than questioned. "Well, much has happened since you've been gone. I twisted my ankle, but it's much better now. Hardly hurts me at all to walk on it. And my parents are due in on the train tomorrow." She hesitated to say more.

"Wonderful. What a treat to get to meet them."

Jillian shook her head. "No, it won't be a treat, I'm afraid."

"Why not?" Mary questioned, pausing only long enough to coo

at the drowsy baby. "You haven't seen them in some time. Won't you be happy to have them here?"

"They're coming because I told them I was engaged to be married." But before Jillian could relay the whole story, Mary jumped in and wouldn't allow Jillian a single word more.

"Well, that sly dog. No wonder Mac told me to talk to you. I knew he'd figure out sooner or later that you were the gal for him. I was beginning to think I was gonna have to hit him over the head or draw him a picture!" She chuckled, then continued. "The two of you will make the perfect couple. Did you tell your folks that you wanted to stay out here after you were married? Well, of course you must have 'cause they're comin' here to see you. So I take it the wedding will be right away. That's perfect. What a great time we'll have of it."

"But, Mary, I need to tell you—"

Mary held up her hand. "You needn't fret about a thing. I'll take Hope back to the house with me and we'll be just fine. A gal's gotta have time to prepare herself for these things. A wedding! We'll just have us one great celebration."

Mary got up and began gathering the things that obviously belonged to the baby. Just then Kate came in, grumbling something about her apron.

"Well, Kate, it's quite the news, ain't it. Our Jillian and Dr. Mac finally seeing sense."

"Aye, I've figured 'em to be half-sick with love for each other since she had to have him stitch up her hand," Kate agreed. "But I can't say that the bride is all radiant-like. She seems more worried than happy."

"You don't understand," Jillian tried to explain.

"Of course I understand," Mary replied. "I've gone through it myself. There wasn't a more jittery bride than me. Say, do you have something special to wear? Is your ma bringin' something from Kansas City?"

"No," Jillian answered. "I mean, I don't think so."

"Well, don't be frettin' about that," Mary said, grinning. "We'll see to that if they don't."

Jillian gave up trying to explain and sat back down in complete frustration. She was going to take Mac to the woodshed for this one. She might be able to pretend to the entire town—even her parents—but Mary was different. She simply couldn't lie to Mary. Not after all she had done. No matter that Mac said they were really and truly engaged, their actions were veiled in deception. They didn't plan to stay engaged or go through with the wedding that everyone had embraced as the perfect excuse for a celebration.

Kate quickly changed her apron and hurried from the room, mumbling as she had when she'd entered. When Mary appeared to have run out of comments about Jillian and Mac's upcoming wedding, Jillian decided to try again to explain the situation. But it was no use.

"I think this is God's timing, deary," Mary said before Jillian could speak. "I mean, Mac has been so lovesick for you, and you obviously have strong feelin's for him. Now there's Hope to consider as well."

"What do you mean?" Jillian asked hesitantly. The now sleeping baby hardly seemed to mind that Mary was bouncing around the room, collecting her things.

"I mean that this baby will need a ma and pa. You and Mac would be perfect for the job. You both accept who she is and, given the love you have for each other, well, that love will just naturally pour itself out on her too. I'd say God was workin' extra time to make this all work together for good."

"You want us to raise Hope?" Jillian questioned, her stomach aflutter. The idea was so instantly appealing that Jillian momentarily forgot that the wedding plans were staged.

"Well, I think you'd make the best choice," Mary said, pausing to look quite sternly at Jillian. "That is, unless you think you and Mac would prefer to have more time to yourselves. I know young couples need a good amount of time to get used to each other, but you and Mac just seem to come together natural-like. I wouldn't want to be pushy in the matter, but Hope needs to be with a family. On the other hand, unless I've misjudged this and you don't want to take her—"

"No!" Jillian declared, coming back out of her chair. "That's not the case. I love her. I can hardly stand that you're taking her away."

Mary smiled and nodded. "I thought as much. Look, it'll just be for a few days. Your folks will come and you'll get them all acquainted with Mac. I'll bring Hope in to town to see you or you and Mac can just ride out to my place. After the wedding and some time alone, you just come on out and get her."

A train whistle blew in the distance and Jillian startled at the sound. "Oh my! I'm going to be late. I was supposed to get Hope to Gwen, but now I suppose I don't have to worry over that. Oh, Mary, this is all too much to explain right now, but we have to talk. Things aren't exactly as they appear."

Mary took Hope and walked from the room, calling over her shoulder, "They never are. We'll have a nice long talk whenever you like. Come on out to the house and we'll make plans."

Jillian pulled on her apron. "Probably not the ones you intend, but we'll definitely have to make plans." Mary had already gone and didn't hear her reply, but it made her feel better to say it, just the same.

Coming downstairs, Jillian froze in place. There at the bottom of the stairs, kissing quite passionately, were Gwen and Zack. Sensing her presence, they paused and looked up without breaking their embrace.

"We figured if you and Mac could get hitched, we might as well take a chance too," Gwen explained, blushing profusely.

Zack grinned. "I always did say that Mac showed a lot of good sense. Congratulations."

Jillian sighed. "Thanks. Congratulations to you two as well."

"Maybe we should make it a double wedding," Gwen said softly as she turned to gaze into the face of the man she so obviously loved.

"I'm sure Mac would love that," Jillian replied rather absent-mindedly.

"I'll talk to him about it," Zack offered, then, after quickly kissing Gwen one final time, he pulled away. "I've got to go. I'll see you later tonight."

Gwen stood staring after him until long after he'd gone. "Oh, Jillian, I'm so happy."

Jillian gave Gwen a hug. "And I'm happy for you, Gwen. You deserve this."

Gwen smiled, tears glimmering in the corners of her eyes. "So do you, Jillian. I know you and Mac will be perfect for each other, and together we shall all be great friends."

Before Jillian could reply, the gong sounded in the dining room. "Oh, the passengers are coming!" Gwen exclaimed. "Come on, Jillian. We can dream about the men we love while we serve Mr. Harvey's finest meals."

Jillian watched her housemother scurry down the hall. "I'll dream about him, all right, but that's all I'll have. Dreams." She shook her head, envious of Gwen's happiness.

C H A P T E R

16

THE TRAIN WAS DUE TO ARRIVE within the hour, and Jillian could hardly stand the wait. She reasoned with herself that this wasn't the end of the world. Gwen had given her three days off in order to be with her parents and make plans for their upcoming double wedding. The wedding was already set for Sunday afternoon, although Jillian had no idea how she was going to set things right by that time. She had hoped that Mac would come to her rescue when Zack and Gwen requested the double wedding, but instead he had thought it a capital idea. Then Jillian had hoped that when they mentioned their desire to marry right away, Mac would either back out or ask them to put it off. But he hadn't—in fact, he'd seemed quite pleased that the wedding should occur in such a short time.

How Jillian wished that his emotions were genuine. She could hardly bear seeing Mac, watching him smile at her in his lazy, endearing manner, without longing for their plans to become reality. Unable to endure her tangled emotions any longer, she'd determined to speak to him about the whole matter, but every time she tried to see him, something or someone interfered.

And now she was supposed to meet her parents, and they in turn would expect to meet her fiancé. A fiancé who didn't exist.

Jillian knew that once her parents were in town, there would be no resting—no quiet moments for settling matters. She had hoped to enlist Gwen's help, but her housemother was much too giddy with her own wedding plans.

Gwen had admonished her to relax and enjoy the preparations and forget about her worries, but Jillian had no way to explain the situation. Lies were entangling her from every angle. There were already wedding gifts to deal with, little trinkets of good luck given to her by some of her Harvey sisters.

"Oh, God," she prayed, "I know this can't be right. This can't be what you had in mind for me. I just don't know what's right anymore. I love Mac, but that isn't going to fix this."

Realizing she was praying, Jillian pondered the spiritual side of things for a moment. She had longed to sit down and talk to Mary about God, for Mary had a light inside her that Jillian longed for. She knew she had to find a way to talk to Mary and tell her the truth.

"But the truth is very uncomfortable right now," Jillian murmured, heading outside the Harvey House for a bit of a walk. She was too nervous to simply sit around and wait for the train. Forgetting her bonnet, Jillian rather enjoyed the wind in her hair. She had styled her hair very casually that morning, leaving it down but clasped into a bulk at the nape of her neck. She did this in spite of the fact her parents would disapprove. Or maybe because she knew they would disapprove. Maybe it was her own little act of rebellion. But wasn't that rather childish for a grown woman?

The day felt warm and breezy without a single cloud to mar the crystal blue sky. It would have been the perfect day to welcome visitors to her new home, but Jillian had no heart for it. She missed Hope, and she hated the situation she'd created for herself. *Why did I have to lie? Why didn't I just make myself clearly understood and not fret over Mother's desires to matchmake?*

"You look like you've lost your last friend."

Jillian started at Mac's voice. She turned and found him watching her curiously. He leaned against the side of the Indian agent's office, seeming unconcerned with the afternoon's planned events.

She had never seen him look more handsome. He'd dressed smartly in a lightweight navy blue worsted wool suit with a fresh white shirt and black tie. Atop his black hair sat an equally black derby hat, giving him an air of sophistication and elegance.

"Mother will think you quite dashing," Jillian murmured without thinking.

"What your mother thinks isn't half as important to me as what you think," Mac replied.

Jillian smiled weakly. "I always think you look dashing."

"Really?" He grinned and came toward her in deliberately slow steps. "Then why have I never heard about this until now?"

Jillian felt herself blush. She lowered her head. "I guess because I didn't think it proper to say so."

"But it's proper now because we're engaged, right?"

She looked up, regret and sorrow written across her face. "Oh, Mac, I'm sorry to have involved you in this. I promise to get things straightened out." She paused and looked away before adding, "Although I'm not at all sure how I'm going to do that. You could have saved us both a great deal of trouble if you would have just put an end to the idea of a double wedding with Zack and Gwen. What were you thinking?"

"I thought it sounded like fun."

"But, Mac . . ." Her words trailed off as she shook her head. There were no words to explain how painful this was becoming. Why couldn't he just love her as she loved him?

"Jilly, you worry too much," he said, seeming to understand her turmoil.

She couldn't help but smile at the nickname. "That's the second time you've called me that."

"Do you mind?"

She shook her head. "No, but it just seems . . . well . . . I don't know."

"Personal? Intimate?" he questioned, looping his arm through hers. "It's intended to be that way. Engaged folks often have terms of endearment for one another."

"But I don't have such a term for you," Jillian said quite seriously. She could feel her pulse quicken at his touch and found herself longing to speak of her true feelings. Why did this have to be so hard?

"Sweetheart or dear—even honey would be fine by me," Mac replied with a laugh.

"Stop teasing. I'm serious."

"So am I," Mac replied, sobering. "Look, if you want your folks to believe us to be engaged, there are a few things we should get straight. First is this." He stopped and pulled a small box from his pocket. "This should prove to that father of yours just how serious my intent is." He let go his hold on Jillian and opened the box. Inside was a ring with the largest cluster of sapphires Jillian had ever seen.

"Oh, Mac, it's wonderful. But why in the world did you buy a wedding ring for a wedding that will never take place?"

He frowned. "I didn't buy it. This belonged to my mother. She bequeathed it to me. It's been in the family for generations and didn't seem fit for life in the jungles of South America. She left it with my grandfather with instructions to give it to me when I came of age."

"Well, I'm sure my father and mother will be impressed. Material wealth usually appeals to them."

"But not to you?" he questioned softly.

She looked at the ring and smiled. "I love beautiful things, Mac. But I love it here and I love my simple life. I don't have to worry about the latest fashions because Mr. Harvey dresses me like a nun in a convent anyway. When I do have days off, it seems completely acceptable to dress as I am now, in a very simple manner."

"You do look quite beautiful. I was going to tell you earlier, but you got me sidetracked."

She glanced over her shoulder at the train depot and tracks. Soon her parents would arrive and her world would be turned upside down.

"Don't worry," he said softly. "It's all going to work out."

She shook her head. "You don't know my father. He's so demanding. He won't give you a moment's peace. He'll harangue you and cut you to shreds."

"You don't have much faith in me, do you?" Mac said, his tone sounding hurt.

"Oh, don't get me wrong, Mac. I admire you greatly. You have strength and courage and a genuinely good heart. You're kind and considerate and . . ." She stopped in mid-sentence, realizing he was grinning. He seemed to enjoy hearing her sing his praises. "Well," she continued, not wishing to take any of it back, "you're my dearest friend, along with Mary, and I'd hate to see you hurt."

Mac reached out to take hold of her shoulders. "Like I said earlier, you worry too much. I'm fully capable of taking care of myself. I don't recall if I told you, but my grandfather MacCallister was a bear of a man who demanded I walk a straight and narrow line. He refused to deal with excuses and he always commanded every situation. I know how to deal with men like your father."

Jillian looked into his eyes. He seemed completely confident of himself. Surely he knew his own limitations. And she hadn't demanded he participate in this—he'd volunteered. Apparently he wasn't overly concerned, so why should she worry? But Jillian knew it was much more—she wanted Mac for herself. She wanted their engagement to be more than a farce. She wanted to explain her heart on the matter and hear him say that he felt the same way.

"I'm twenty-three years old, Mac," she muttered, still thinking.

"And I'm thirty. What of it?"

He was eyeing her quite seriously, and Jillian couldn't help but quake at the realization that she was very nearly in his arms. She licked her lower lip nervously and felt her breath quicken. If she didn't know better, she'd think he was about to kiss her.

The train whistle sounded in the distance. A mile away to be precise. The spell was broken between them, but rather than turn away from Mac, Jillian threw herself into his arms and clung to him. It didn't matter that they were in broad daylight in the middle of town—she needed his strength.

"I'm going to be sick," she whispered.

Mac held her close as her quaking increased. "You aren't going to be sick."

"How do you know?"

He laughed and hugged her close. "I'm a doctor, remember?"

She said nothing but held tightly to him. It was the most wonderful feeling in the world. To be held by Terrance MacCallister and to feel his arms around her, his fingers lightly toying with the hair at the nape of her neck. Why couldn't this be true love for him as well as her?

"Mac," she said without pulling back to see his reaction, "you've come to mean a great deal to me." She gathered her courage. She would just tell him how she felt. Explain why she had used his name when telling her mother about the man she'd come to love. Because she did love him and it seemed only fair that he know it as well. She thought she heard him moan, low and soft down deep in his throat. Perhaps—just perhaps—he loved her too? A hope sprang fully born from her rapidly beating heart. Could he love her?

The whistle blew again.

"Mac?" She said the name questioningly. She had to know the truth.

He broke his hold on her and stepped back. His eyes darkened in intensity, and for just a moment, Jillian was certain that what she saw there was a mirrored reflection of her own passion and need. He looked away and tucked the ring box into his pocket.

"I'd better get back to my office. You said earlier that you wanted to meet them alone."

She nodded, not at all sure what she had done wrong. Perhaps he'd been offended by her brazen embrace. Maybe she didn't know him as well as she liked to think. Her hope of true love began to fade.

"All right," she said, barely able to force the words from her mouth.

He gave her one quick glance, then took off for his place. "This is all going to work out, Jilly," he called over his shoulder.

She nodded. If only that could be true.

Slowly, she walked back to the front of the Harvey House and over to the depot platform. She prayed for strength, not completely convinced that God would hear her prayer. There was a great deal that lay unresolved between her and God. What if that kept Him from listening to her heart?

The train pulled in, churning black smoke from its stack and spewing white steam puffs from pressure spigots. The groaning and grinding of metal on metal was enough to set her teeth on edge, but Jillian stood fast and waited for the porters to lower the steps.

Then before she had time to think about anything else, Jillian saw her father step from the train. He had dressed in a light brown suit and sported a stylish straw skimmer. No doubt he thought this fashion would be cooler protection against the Arizona heat.

He reached back to assist her mother from the train. True to her need to outdo those around her, Gretchen Danvers wore an elaborate traveling ensemble. Tailored to her petite frame, the alpaca traveling suit of burgundy and black drew everyone's attention. First, because it was quite smart and the woman wearing it looked very lovely. Second, however, seemed because those around were wondering how long it would be before the poor woman succumbed to the heat and passed out from her layers of clothing.

Leaning on her husband's arm, Gretchen Danvers lifted a parasol over her elaborately ribboned hat and glanced around her.

Jillian stepped forward with a smile. "Father, Mother," she said in greeting. "It's so nice to have you here."

Colin Danvers gave a grunt. "I don't suppose we had a choice. Where's this man you plan to marry?"

Never one to waste time, Jillian's father had simply skipped past the proprieties and moved right into the pertinent information he desired.

"He's in his office. I asked him to allow me to greet you privately," Jillian replied. "I thought perhaps you would both feel better if you had a chance to go to your hotel room and freshen up a bit."

"Well, I suppose it couldn't hurt," her father replied, surprising Jillian.

"I thought we might all meet at supper this evening, and you could rest and prepare yourselves in the meantime. You both might prefer to wear something lighter. It stays quite warm until the sun goes down, and Mother looks quite spent."

"I'm perfectly fine, Jillian." Gretchen Danvers spoke for the first time since alighting from the train. "This is quite fashionable back home." She was always rather reserved in the presence of her husband.

"Yes, I'm sure it is, but here you will quickly see the folly of wearing too many layers of clothing."

"I will remind you, young lady, to address your mother in a more respectful manner."

Jillian felt herself cower under his words. "I assure you, Father, it wasn't meant in disrespect. I simply would hate for Mother to faint on the depot platform." She tried to keep her voice steady and sure. She had to show her father that she was capable of making choices and decisions for herself, or he might never allow her to remain in Arizona.

"If you're ready, I'll show you where to check in to your rooms. They'll bring your luggage over so you needn't worry about waiting for it."

"I suppose we might check in," her father muttered. "Come along, Mrs. Danvers. We *should* get you out of this heat. I must say, it's hard to think much of a man who would come here to make a way for himself. Are you certain that doctor of yours has all his senses?"

Jillian sighed. It was going to be a long, long evening.

Once inside the hotel and out of the ghastly heat of the afternoon, Gretchen Danvers seemed to come alive. When they had settled her in her own room upstairs, with her husband in the adjoining room, she became quite animated.

As soon as her husband dismissed himself to go inspect the town, Gretchen took Jillian aside and motioned to the three trunks that were stacked at one end of the room. "Your father has hired a hotel maid to come and unpack for me, but I must tell you about the contents. I've bought you the most beautiful wedding dress. You're going to love it. I had it handmade in that little shop on Fifteenth. You remember the one, don't you? The woman who owns it is French."

Jillian nodded. "Yes, Mother."

"The dress is the epitome of fashion. The style is straight out of Paris. I don't imagine there will be another gown like it west of the Mississippi. Maybe not even in the entire United States."

Jillian knew such matters were important to her mother. Being the best, the first, the finest—all of these were important social status marks to be claimed for one's own prestige.

"I've also brought along all the proper necessities for a decent wedding, although you must realize it isn't at all what I had hoped for you."

"I know, Mother."

Gretchen studied her daughter for a moment. "It isn't too late, you know. The earl is in Denver, and I have his address."

"No, Mother, that won't be necessary. As I told you, I'm in love with Mac." At least this wasn't a lie.

Her mother let out the tiniest hint of a sigh. "Very well, but you certainly could have done better for yourself. Love isn't everything, and if a man cannot support his wife, misery will follow. I suppose I shall simply allow your father to make the final decision in the matter."

"What do you mean?" Jillian questioned.

"Well, he hasn't exactly given his approval of this union. He'll have to meet this doctor and decide whether it's acceptable for you to marry him. He isn't one of us, you know. He's a mere doctor."

Jillian frowned. "Mother, don't you ever tire of such thoughts?" She knew the words were harsh, but her irritation had been stirred. "I mean, the way you speak, I believe you think that others are less deserving of goodness and happiness merely because they have a different social setting or culture."

Gretchen nodded. "But of course, this is true. You can't expect me to feel otherwise. I was raised with nobility."

"Perhaps that's the problem. After all, they lock themselves away and rule from distant thrones. They have no first-hand knowledge of their people, but rather trust the intermediaries who act in their stead. Frankly, I've met a great many people here in Arizona—some very, very poor in possessions but rich in spirit and love. I've even had encounters with Indians, Navajo to be precise, and they are wonderful people."

"Oh my," Gretchen said, sinking to the straight-backed chair beside her dressing table. "You can't be serious."

Jillian went to kneel in front of her mother. "But I am serious, Mother. People are people. They have feelings. They get hurt. They bleed just as we do. You can't go around the rest of your life believing that just because they are poorly educated or have a different color skin, that they aren't just as precious in God's eyes as we are."

Just then a loud bang from the adjoining room let them both know that Jillian's father had returned.

"Please don't talk like this in front of your father, Jillian. He wouldn't take well to it," Gretchen pleaded. "And you want to have him approve of your wedding."

Jillian got to her feet and nodded. There was no sense in beating them over the head with their prejudiced ways. "Very well. Unless the matter comes up by another means, I won't say a word."

Colin Danvers entered the room and looked at both women in silence. Then, with a narrowing of his eyes, he focused on Jillian.

"Now, I want you to tell me why you've dragged me to this hideous place. What do you mean, getting yourself engaged to someone without seeking me out on the matter?"

"Well," Jillian offered nervously, "it just sort of happened. Look, I know you think me incapable of making my own choices, but, Father, I've grown up a good deal and I'm not the same person I was in Kansas City."

He nodded. "I can see that for myself."

She couldn't tell if he approved or disapproved as he crossed his arms against his chest. "I want you to understand that I love both of you very much, but I want to make a life for myself. I am twenty-three, after all, and I feel like you both still see me as a child." She took a deep breath and tried to focus on her father's firmly fixed chin. If she didn't have to look him in the eye, maybe she could manage to somehow work through this and send them back to Kansas without having to involve Mac.

"I don't feel like I need anyone's approval or disapproval in choosing a husband. As a grown woman, fully in my majority, I feel that I can reasonably ascertain what is best for my life."

Her father half grunted, half laughed at this. "Next thing you know, you'll be expecting to get the vote."

"And why not?" questioned Jillian. "I read the newspapers and keep on top of the affairs of my community. Why may I not also vote on the people who make choices and changes for the land I live in?"

Colin Danvers shook his head. "This is ridiculous. You leave home for three months, and already you sound like your sister."

"Good!" Jillian replied. "I love Judith, and since we're twins, we should share similar views."

"Well, I don't think much of it!" declared her father. "I raised you to be respectful and honorable. You should care what I think of your young man, because maybe, just maybe, I'm a better judge of character than you are. Did that ever cross your mind?"

Jillian shook her head. "I don't suppose I worried much about what judgments you wished to pass on him, Father. I love him. That should be enough." She immediately regretted her confession.

"That's exactly what I'm talking about," her father countered. "You women and your idealistic romantic notions. Love won't see you through when the bank forecloses on your property. Love won't mean much at all when you have no food in the cupboards or on the table." His voice took the bitter tone of one who knew these things first hand. "Love doesn't keep people alive. No, your feelings of love mean very little in this, Jillian. I will be the judge of whether or not your doctor is worthy of marriage to my daughter. Until then, you do not have my permission to marry."

Jillian balled her hands into fists and held them tightly to her sides. "I didn't ask you here, nor did I ask for your permission." She stalked from the room, feeling an overwhelming urge to hit something. At the top of the stairs, she punched her fist at the banister, instantly feeling the pain of her folly. Rubbing her sore knuckles, Jillian shook her head and made her way down the stairs. The only thing left to do was hope and pray that her father would tire of this game and go home.

"Or I could just pray that Mac might want to elope for real," she murmured. Either one would be perfectly acceptable to her way of thinking.

CHAPTER

17

MAC FORCED HIMSELF TO FOCUS on the work at hand, but the medical journal he normally devoured each month held no interest for him now. Putting it aside for the tenth time, he got to his feet and began to pace the room, feeling like a man possessed. Her image was all he saw. When he closed his eyes, he could see her face— read the fear and anticipation of what was to come.

Since becoming engaged to Jillian Danvers, Mac had barely known a restful moment. It seemed someone constantly needed his medical skills or he was being called upon to participate in something regarding the town. The Indian situation was still unresolved and would no doubt remain that way for some time to come. But regardless of where Mac took himself or what his activity, it was Jillian who haunted his every thought.

Why would she have thrown herself into my arms if she found the idea of being with me repulsive? She must enjoy my company. She said I meant a great deal to her. He reasoned all his feelings and thoughts. What could he say to her to make her understand how much he loved her? How could he get her to agree that this engagement should become a marriage?

But even as he questioned this, he wondered at his own madness. He knew the pain of a love gone bad. The past rose up as an ugly reminder of all that could go wrong. Did he really want to risk his heart—again?

Continuing to pace, he glanced at his watch and nearly fell over his chair. It was time to go to the Harvey House for dinner. He and Jillian had agreed that this would be the best place for their first meeting with her parents. He longed to know how she would respond to him in front of them. He had advised her to appear loving and devoted, but would it put too much pressure on her? Could she pretend to feel something more for him than she felt?

But she trembled in my arms, he reasoned, then just as quickly pushed the thoughts aside. "She was afraid because her parents were coming," he announced aloud. "That's all it was."

He grabbed up his hat and walked to the door. Whispering a prayer for strength, he walked out the door just as Zack Matthews stalked by.

"Evenin', Mac."

"How are your prisoners doing?" Mac questioned as Zack paused, pushing up the brim of his hat.

"They're keeping well enough. That Bear doesn't say a word. He just stares at me like he wishes he could drop me dead in my tracks. If looks could do the job, you'd be burying me now."

Mac nodded. "Mary says his rage runs deep. But who can blame him? He's buried a sister and other members of his family—most of whom have perished at the hands of the white man, in one way or another. He's not old enough to remember the Long Walk, but he knows those who are and he remembers the stories. They moved the entire Navajo nation from their homeland. Many of them died . . . even more wished they could."

"Glad I wasn't around for that. My own pa's told me stories of Indian wars and the bad times that followed. I can't imagine them moving an entire group of people off their land and marching them off to resettle elsewhere. I just don't see how we have the right to be interferin', so long as the Indians don't expect to be runnin' our lives."

"I'm not sure what the answer is, to tell you the truth. Mary talks about their need to fit in with the scheme of the future, yet she respects the need to hold on to tradition and culture. A person's family and ancestors should have a place of importance, but sometimes I don't see it making it through to the twentieth century."

Zack nodded. "There's a lot of hate out there, Mac. A lot of hate."

"On both sides."

Again, Zack nodded. "That's for sure. Well, guess I'd better go round up their meals. The Harvey House has been furnishing the grub, and for that, I'm grateful."

"Are the Navajo eating it?" Mac questioned.

"For the most part. It's that or go hungry. Frankly, I think they may be plannin' an escape or hoping for some sort of intercession on the part of the government. Mary promised to telegraph the authorities and see what could be done."

"No doubt she's kept to her word, but I wouldn't bet on the authorities caring much one way or the other."

Zack shrugged and made his way to the back door of the Harvey House, while Mac followed behind and passed him by to head around front.

"Wish me luck," he said to Zack.

"You meetin' Jillian's parents?"

Mac nodded. "I feel like a lamb led to the slaughter."

Zack laughed. "I'll have to sketch that out. A lamb with your face, and the executioner can be Mr. Danvers."

"Don't laugh. It's not that far from the truth."

Zack was still chuckling as Mac rounded the corner of the building and headed to the front door. He scrutinized the dust on his black shoes and wondered if he should pause long enough to wipe them off with his handkerchief. Surely the Danverses wouldn't be that particular.

Inside, the pacing was much slower than when the train passengers were being served. Ten to twelve people, including some railroad workers, sat at the formal-looking tables.

"Jillian's in the front parlor with her folks," Gwen said, coming alongside of Mac. "She thought perhaps you'd rather meet up with them there."

Mac nodded and asked, "What did you think of them?"

Gwen met Mac's gaze. "Her father is overbearing, bossy, and

opinionated. Her mother is docile in comparison but gets her thoughts in nevertheless."

Mac had hoped she'd say something to relieve his nervousness, but her words didn't help. "I suppose there's no putting this off."

"I don't suppose so," Gwen said sympathetically. "After all, you wouldn't want to be late."

Mac shook his head. "No, that would no doubt be a poor omen of things to come."

He quickly made his way out of the dining room and back down the hall to the front parlor. Immediately he spied Jillian. Radiant and lovely in a gown of lavender muslin, she met his entrance with warmth and enthusiasm.

"Here he is now!" she announced, getting to her feet. She rushed to Mac's side and held her hand out to him. "This is Dr. Terrance MacCallister." She paused and met Mac's eyes. "My fiancé."

Mac held her gaze for a moment. He knew he didn't have to pretend to give her a loving look, for the great love he felt for her was no doubt evident in his expression. He looped her arm around his own before proceeding to meet her parents.

"This is my father, Mr. Colin Danvers of Kansas City," Jillian announced very formally.

"Mr. Danvers," Mac said in greeting.

"Dr. MacCallister," Danvers replied. "I had begun to think you were a figment of my daughter's imagination."

"No, indeed," Mac said with a smile. "And you must be Mrs. Danvers." He turned to Jillian's mother, who extended her hand. Mac took hold of her gloved fingers and expertly lifted them to his lips. Not quite touching his mouth to her hand, he bowed. "It's a pleasure to meet you."

The expression on Gretchen Danvers' face registered pure surprise and delight. He had presented himself as a gentleman of refinement, something she had evidently not expected. *Good*, Mac thought. *Let me keep them guessing.*

"Our daughter has written much about you," Gretchen said as Mac released her hand. "I am happy to see that she did not exaggerate. You appear to be everything she said you were."

"Oh?" Mac turned to Jillian and grinned as she blushed a brilliant red. "We shall have to find a moment to discuss what she put to paper."

"I don't think that would be necessary, dear," Jillian said, emphasizing her endearment. "You wouldn't want my parents to think you a prideful man."

Colin Danvers continued to watch him wearily, so Mac did nothing more than nod. "But of course, you're right."

"What kind of name is Terrance?" Jillian's father asked suddenly. All heads turned to the older man as if he'd lost his senses.

"Father, does it need an explanation? Apparently it's the name his parents gave him," Jillian replied.

Mac patted her arm soothingly. "It's actually a name I cannot abide, so most folks call me Mac. We're rather informal around these parts, and titles and other formalities soon go by the wayside."

"I would have figured as much," Danvers replied.

Jillian tensed on his arm. "Shall we go ahead to dinner? The food is quite good and the dining room is not so crowded that it shall exclude serious conversation." Her voice came in a tight, controlled manner.

When no one replied, Jillian simply turned for the door. "Come, then. Mac and I shall lead the way."

They moved quietly into the dining room, allowing Gwen to show them to the special table she'd prepared for them. Kate and Louisa both were on hand to wait on them, and after ordering more food than any four people could consume, Mac decided to jump right in and lead the conversation.

"Did you have a pleasant trip?"

Danvers grunted. "As pleasant as you can have riding into the middle of nowhere. What brought you to these parts anyway?"

Mac showed no surprise at the man's boldness in skipping the formalities. "I heard there was a great shortage of doctors in the West. I grew up and took my training in Philadelphia. My married sisters live there still."

"Oh, so you know about society," Gretchen interjected. "Good breeding is so important. Do your parents live there also?"

"My parents have passed on to their reward," Mac replied.

"I see," Gretchen said, looking quite disappointed.

"What did your father do for a living?" Colin Danvers asked as Kate served them their first course.

Bluepoints on the half shell, stuffed mangoes, and currant soup decorated the table in an inviting manner, and Mac allowed Kate time to serve each of the Danverses before he replied.

"My father started out as a minister, and then my parents took up a job of missions work. They spent a good deal of my childhood in South America. This made it necessary for my grandfather, a man of some varied industrial interests, to raise me."

Danvers eyed him quite seriously for a moment, his thick face seeming to turn to iron. "Your people were religious?"

Mac thought he denoted disapproval in Danvers' voice. "They were," he replied, deciding that a simple answer was better than a lengthy explanation.

Jillian remain focused on her dinner, while Mac felt his level of nervousness mount. It hadn't dawned on him until just that moment that Danvers might ask some very personal questions about the past. About . . . *her*. Mac looked to Jillian, wondering what she would think about the truth—about his life and his past.

As if realizing he contemplated her reaction, Jillian glanced up and smiled reassuringly. Mac felt torn between grabbing her up, running from the room, and blurting out his feelings of love. Colin Danvers, however, took the matter from his hands.

"So you grew up in Philadelphia and attended school there. You became a doctor and moved to Arizona. Is that the sum total of your life?"

"For the most part," Mac replied, hoping the man would be content to move on to the present.

"And now you wish to marry my daughter."

The statement was delivered in such a way that there seemed to be no need for reply. Mac looked Danvers in the eye. The sternness of his adversary's expression might have withered a less worthy opponent, but not Mac. To Mac, it was almost as if his grandfather had come back to life.

"Can you support a wife?" Danvers questioned.

"I can," Mac answered in calm assurance.

"You say that very confidently," Jillian's father replied. "Have you reason to believe this to be the case? Have you been married before?"

The question had come so unexpectedly that Mac nearly dropped his fork. He had no time to prepare a lie, so he simply told the truth. "Yes."

Jillian did drop her fork. It clattered loudly onto the highly polished wooden floor. "Oh my," she said apologetically. "Please forgive me."

Kate quickly came and replaced the utensil, taking the dirty fork away before anyone could so much as comment on Mac's declaration.

Mac could see the stunned look on Jillian's face, even though she tried so hard to hide it. If he recognized it, no doubt her parents would as well.

"Perhaps you should explain," Danvers stated as Kate and Louisa took away their plates in order to serve the next course.

Mac nodded. "I married quite young. A local girl from a well-regarded family was chosen by my grandfather for me to marry, and I found that it was not an unappealing idea to propose matrimony. We were married for less than a year."

"What happened?" Gretchen Danvers asked. She all at once realized that she'd spoken aloud and bowed her head as if she'd committed some unforgivable breach of etiquette.

No doubt, Mac thought, Danvers liked his women silent. He smiled reassuringly at Gretchen as she glanced up. "She was a frail person. She caught pneumonia and died."

"You were a doctor and you couldn't save her?" Danvers questioned.

"I wasn't with her at the time. We had moved to the Arizona Territory. She had gone home to spend time with her parents. The life here made her homesick, and we both agreed it would do her well to make the trip."

"Apparently you were in error."

"Father!" Jillian declared. "That's hardly fair to say."

Mac appreciated her defense, especially after springing such a surprise on her. "I was in error, sir," he admitted. "I was in error about a great many things. Including the idea of taking one so young so far from home. And also in allowing my marriage to be arranged for me based on business rather than love."

"Marriage is as much a business arrangement as anything you will ever know in life," Danvers replied sternly. "Emotions and female notions will not hold a family together in hard times."

"Neither will money," Mac replied confidently.

The rest of the dinner passed in an awkward series of questions and answers. Mac felt drained of all energy by the time Danvers announced that he would like to retire for the evening.

Jillian and Mac escorted them to the hotel, and while Mac waited patiently, Jillian kissed her mother's cheek and bid her father goodnight. When they had gone and Jillian and Mac were left to themselves, Mac felt the need to apologize.

"Would you walk a bit with me?" he asked.

Jillian nodded. "If you'd like." She sounded shy and hesitant.

"I feel I need to explain about Abigail."

"Mac, you don't owe me any explanation," Jillian countered. "After all, you're only going along with this to keep me out of hot water with my father."

Mac took hold of her arm. "Please just hear me out. It's important that you know. I care about you, and I want to be completely honest." Jillian looked up at him oddly but said nothing more. Mac drew a deep breath and began. "I didn't exactly tell the whole truth."

"Oh?"

"Abigail and I did marry too young, and I did move us here, leaving her feeling completely distraught. The reason, however, had little to do with her parents and everything to do with another man in Philadelphia."

"Oh, Mac, I'm sorry."

Her heartfelt words warmed him and gave him the courage he needed to continue. "I was too. I thought I really loved her. I thought she really loved me. My grandfather saw it as a good match. He and Abigail's father were business partners, and they saw this as a joining of the power they had created. Abigail and I had been intended for each other for some time, and I had thought we both were keen for the idea."

"Only she wasn't?" Jillian questioned softly. She looked up at him with such an expression of concern that Mac wanted to hold her close.

"She pretended to love me. It made a good cover for her escapades with the man she really loved. After we married and moved, however, I learned the truth of the matter."

"How?"

"She had remained distant, weepy, and cold to me from the night of our wedding. She didn't want my love or affection. My attempts to romance her were rejected. She'd have nothing to do with me—nothing."

Jillian nodded knowingly, and Mac appreciated that she had taken his meaning without offense at the delicacy of the subject matter. "Two months after living this farce of a marriage, she could no longer hide the fact that she was pregnant. Unfortunately, the baby was not mine. She had been expecting even when we had married."

"Oh, Mac, how betrayed you must have felt."

He looked at her for a moment, pausing in their walk. "I vowed to never love again. Only now . . . now I see that was wrong."

Jillian said nothing, but looked away quickly. "What did you do when you found out about her . . . her indiscretion?"

Mac began walking again, pulling her close alongside him. A full moon illuminated their path, and Jillian seemed in no hurry to be rid of his company. Mac relished the feel of her being so near. He longed to share his heart with her and explain everything in detail, but a part of him held back, fearful of the rejection that might come. Remembering the pain of the rejection that had come.

"I was willing to forgive her and accept the child as my own. It hurt me to realize that she had only married me out of obligation to her family, but I told her we could make a new start. She laughed at me and said she didn't want to start anything with me. She wanted to go home to the father of her child and make her life there. I told her I wouldn't give her a divorce, that I didn't believe in such things.

She told me she'd find a way to make it happen. But she never had the chance."

"What happened?" Jillian asked.

By now they had walked past the Harvey House and the train depot. The night air had grown cool, and seeing Jillian shiver, Mac decided it was time to take her home. He slipped his coat off and put it around her shoulders. Smiling her gratitude, Jillian pulled the coat close.

Turning back for the Harvey House, he continued. "She went home about three weeks before Christmas. Somewhere along the way she came down sick, and when she arrived in Philadelphia she was already quite ill. Her parents telegraphed to say that she was failing fast and that I should come right away. She never told them about the other man, and I never learned who he was. She died before I ever got to Philadelphia. There was an elaborate funeral, and hundreds of sympathetic people told me how sorry they were for my loss. They didn't know the half of it.

"Three weeks later, my grandfather had a heart attack and died. He left everything to me, surprisingly enough. I sold off most of the businesses and invested the money elsewhere. Then I kept what I wanted from the house and sold it as well. My elder sister wanted the place, so her husband bought it at a very reduced price. Then I split the money with my sisters and returned West."

Mac began to walk toward the front of the Harvey House, but Jillian nodded in the direction of the back. "I'll go in back here," she whispered. "That way I won't have to face everyone and answer all their questions."

Mac nodded. "I hope I did the right thing in telling your father the truth."

They came to stand outside the back door to the restaurant. Jillian turned and smiled up at Mac. "You did wonderfully. I couldn't have asked for more. I hope you know how sorry I am for the pain you suffered." Her words were sincere and pierced to the heart. "No one should have to feel such rejection and hurt. I can't imagine that this wife of yours had any good sense at all—not if she put another in your place when she could have had you all along."

Without realizing what he was doing, Mac reached out and pulled Jillian into his arms. He ached to hold her close. In fact, ever since she had thrown herself into his arms in fear that afternoon, Mac had longed to draw her back. She didn't protest his embrace, and when she turned her face up to look into his eyes, Mac felt certain that he saw a longing there to match his own. Perhaps it was just the moonlight, but he was willing to take the chance.

Lowering his mouth to hers, he kissed her tenderly. He felt her respond to his touch, felt her hands circle up to touch his neck. She wanted this kiss as much as he did, of this he was certain. Perhaps if he just told her the truth of his heart, she would open up to him and admit the same.

He pulled back just far enough to speak, but instead of seeing the expression of pleasure he had hoped for, Jillian looked almost pained. She shook her head and moved away from him as if he had somehow hurt her.

"I suppose you think me rather silly for doing that," he said, trying to make light of the matter.

"I don't understand," she said, barely whispering.

Mac shrugged, feeling like quite the cad. "It just dawned on me that your father, being the nosy sort of man he is, might ask you more intimate questions of our relationship. He would surely have expected me to kiss you by now. If he asks about it, now you can tell him the truth—that we have kissed."

She nodded, but the pained expression remained. "I'm sure you're right. He's just that sort of man."

Mac wanted to reach out again and hold her. She looked so lost and hurt. "You'd better go inside," he muttered instead.

She nodded again and opened the back door. "Mac," she said, pausing on the threshold.

"What?"

"I don't know how to manage all of this. I'm really confused. My father—the wedding—what are we going to do?"

He thought for a moment her words might hold more than the obvious meaning, then dismissed the idea as romantic nonsense. "It'll work itself out, Jilly. Don't worry about it."

"I hope you're right, Mac."

She went inside, leaving him to stand alone in the dark. "I hope I'm right too," he murmured. "I pray I'm right."

C H A P T E R

18

TO JILLIAN'S ABSOLUTE HORROR, she learned that there was to be a party and street dance held in honor of the couples about to wed. Even Mary thought it a wonderful idea and showed up early Friday afternoon with Hope happily wrapped in a cradleboard. The baby seemed content enough, but Jillian's heart ached to hold her. Playing and fussing over the baby, Jillian realized how intensely she missed this little girl.

As the afternoon passed into evening and Jillian saw that there was no way to get out of the party, she resigned herself to play yet another scene in this senseless production she'd authored. She dressed carefully in a rose-colored gown her mother had brought from Kansas City. The silk taffeta gown had been designed with much more prestigious parties in mind, but Jillian knew it would make her mother feel good and perhaps it would even catch Mac's attention. She waited impatiently as Kate laced her corset tight enough to allow her to fit into the narrow-waisted creation. She had put on weight out here in Mr. Harvey's desert, but everyone told her she looked healthy and lovely.

Kate helped her with the dress, bringing it over Jillian's carefully styled blond hair. The gown fit perfectly, blooming out gracefully in yards and yards of shimmering skirt around Jillian's ankles.

"Oh, yar so beautiful," Kate announced as she finished doing up the buttons.

"You don't think this neckline is too low?" Jillian questioned uncomfortably. After months of mostly wearing her modest uniform, the rounded, lace-edged neckline seemed a bit risqué.

"Yar not showing that much skin," Kate said, adjusting Jillian's lacy capped sleeves. "This lace is like some me mum used to make."

"It's certainly beautiful," Jillian agreed. "No doubt my mother had it made by that sweet little Frenchwoman on Fifteenth Street."

"What now?"

Jillian shook her head at Kate's puzzled expression. "Never mind. I wish this would all just go away."

Kate laughed. "It's just pre-wedding jitters. All brides get 'em. Ya'll settle down well enough after Sunday."

But Jillian knew that wasn't true. Sunday would no doubt be the worst day of all. She felt horribly guilty as she thought of Gwen and Zack's romantic notions and excitement. They were planning a real wedding. Their future together was more than the pleasant daydreams of an overactive imagination.

Kate gave Jillian one final look-over before turning to the mirror to adjust her own ebony curls. "Who knows, maybe I'll be findin' me a nice young man to settle down with. There's some cowboys in from the local ranches. I might even find me an Irishman."

Jillian smiled. "You'd give up all of this?"

Kate laughed. "If I could marry someone as wonderful as yar Dr. Mac, I'd leave it all in a minute. Yar blessed to have him, Jillian. He's an honest and trustworthy man."

Jillian frowned and looked away quickly so that Kate couldn't see her reaction. Mac *was* a good man, and she felt as though she'd somehow corrupted him by forcing him into this lie.

"Well, come along, Mrs. MacCallister," Kate said, laughing.

Jillian shook her head. "You can't be calling me that yet."

"I'm just tryin' it on for size. It suits ya, don't ya think?"

Jillian nodded. It suited her just fine. Too bad it wasn't for real.

Music could already be heard coming from the impromptu band at the end of Main Street. Everyone who had a fiddle or guitar had congregated at the end of town where the street had been quartered off for dancing and other festivities. Long tables generously laden with a variety of food stood alongside the street. Jillian noted that several of the church ladies, including Mrs. Everhart and Mrs. Mason, were busy putting order to the tables and instructing hungry cowboys where to begin.

Jillian and Mac had agreed to meet at the hotel, where Jillian would first find her parents and then await his arrival. However, when she managed to make her way through the crowd to the small establishment, Mac and Mary both were already in deep conversation with Colin and Gretchen Danvers.

Jillian paused and watched them for a moment. Four of the five most important people in her life stood congregated in one room. They were probably talking about her, and for the first time in many weeks, Jillian desperately wished her sister, Judith, might be here to advise her.

The sea of people seemed to swirl around her and part just in time for Mac to glance up and see her standing in the doorway. The look on his face was one of pure admiration. Jillian warmed under his scrutiny. *Why can't you be in love with me as I am with you?* she felt her heart question.

Mac came to her and took her gloved hand in his. "You look incredibly beautiful. Fine gowns do suit you, Miss Danvers."

"So does black-and-white homespun, Dr. MacCallister."

He grinned and inclined his head to where Mary was still in a heated discussion with Jillian's father. "They're talking politics."

"Oh dear," Jillian replied, looking at the stern expression on her father's face. "I hope he won't hurt Mary's feelings."

Mac chuckled softly and leaned to whisper in her ear. "I hope your father will survive Mary's berating. He made an offhanded comment about our Indian troubles, and of course Mary couldn't let that just pass without educating the man on the true nature of things around here."

Jillian smiled. "Bless her. I should have known that if anyone could stand up to my father besides Judith, it would be Mary."

As if hearing her name mentioned, Mary caught sight of them and motioned them to the group. "You can whisper sweet nothin's to her later," she called out, causing Jillian to feel her cheeks grow hot.

"You look so sweet when you blush," Mac murmured.

Jillian tried to hold her smile firmly in place while replying, "It seems I do a lot of blushing when I'm around you."

They joined the threesome, and Jillian kissed her mother lightly on the cheek. "You look wonderful, Mother," she commented. And it was true. Her mother was always dressed in the height of fashion. Tonight, dressed in a royal blue satin with a jet-beaded black mantle and dripping in sapphires and pearls, Gretchen Danvers could clearly hold her own with any of the younger women. She was only in her forties, after all, and time had been very kind. Her blond hair was nearly as bright and silky as Jillian's or Judith's, and her figure was just as trim.

Jillian turned and saw the complete contrast of fashion in Mary's simple well-worn skirt of navy serge and her full-sleeved blouse that Jillian recognized as her "Sunday best."

"That dress does you up real fine," Mary told Jillian. "I'm surprised Mac hasn't run away with you before now."

"I would have," Mac declared, "had I thought I could have gotten away with it."

He sounded so sincere that Jillian found herself unable to comment. There was really no need to worry about a lapse of conversation, however, as Mary quickly continued where she'd left off with Colin Danvers.

"Your daughter could tell you quite a bit about life out here. She's even accompanied me to help with some of the Indians. We have a group living not far from here, and I often go and trade the things they need for pieces of Indian art."

"I've heard tell there's some good money to be had in Indian art," Danvers replied. "Perhaps that's the incentive you folks need to put forward in order to calm the situation around here."

"What do you mean?" Mary questioned.

"It's just that this whole Indian uprising and war against conformity could probably be settled by putting forth a plan of benefits. There isn't a man alive who can't be bought for a price."

"Do you include yourself in that, sir?" Mac interjected.

Colin Danvers actually laughed, completely surprising Jillian. "Of course I do. I can be swayed for a price in most cases. But that price is quite high. You'll find, Dr. MacCallister, that most men have never bothered to consider it, but there is that place where we all must look to know ourselves a bit better. What man wouldn't lay down his life for his family? He would pay whatever price to keep them from harm—from making irrevocable mistakes."

Jillian got the distinct impression her father had moved the conversation over to the idea of her marriage to Mac.

"People usually learn from their mistakes," Mac answered. "Sometimes a fellow has to fall into the mud to appreciate being clean."

"Nonsense," Danvers replied, staring hard at Mac. "I can see that mud and muck are not a pleasurable source of entertainment. I can appreciate the finer things in life without having to suffer and live in the poverty-ridden shacks of the poor. I can relish a glass of fine brandy without having to drink rotgut. Your analogy holds no weight in my mind."

"I agree that some things can be seen that way," Mac replied and Jillian felt him tense. "As a doctor, I don't have to be suffering myself to know that pain hurts. But having suffered pain, I better understand how it feels to be in such a situation, and I believe it gives me a greater compassion for those I care for. It's no different with the poor and needy. Having known hunger, I'm more inclined to seek ways to help others avoid it. Knowledge and understanding are strength."

"The Indians are the same way," Mary declared. "The Navajo, for instance, believe they find their source of strength and power by living between the four sacred mountains. That is one of the reasons they refuse to be moved. They will fight to the death, if necessary, to keep their people on this land. Ask your daughter. She's worked with me. She knows how they feel."

Colin looked to Jillian and laughed harshly. "Look at her and tell me that she belongs in the filth and squalor of an Indian camp. She was created for a world of beauty. She learned from an early age to grace the home of the men who care for her. She can't possibly fit into their world because her own world knows nothing of those things."

"That isn't true, Father," Jillian said, feeling bold with Mary and Mac at her side. "I believe I can be capable in both areas. I know very well how to host a dinner party and entertain guests in a drawing room, but I also know how to make a fire for myself now, and I'm starting to learn how to cook. I love caring for Hope, the Indian baby Mary helped to save."

"That's right," Mary said, nodding. "I'm hoping Jillian and Mac will be parents to the baby after they marry."

Mac slipped his arm through Jillian's and pulled her a little closer. "Jillian is quite capable with Hope. I think she'll make a wonderful mother."

"But you can't think to raise an Indian child," her mother said in horror. "What will our friends say?"

"Your friends don't have to know, if it bothers you that much," Jillian replied, getting caught up in the conversation. She no longer even considered the fact that they were talking about a fictional wedding and future.

"But you'll be right there among them," Gretchen replied.

"What are you talking about, Mother?"

"Your mother is talking about your life in Kansas City. Either as wife to this man or as daughter to us," Danvers stated with authority.

"But we have no plans to live in Kansas City," Jillian replied, looking up to catch Mac's clenched-jaw expression.

"That's right," Mac managed to add in a steady voice. "We have no plans to leave Arizona."

"Nonsense," Danvers said as though the matter were settled. "You can't make a decent living here in the West. I can set you up in business in Kansas City, and you'll make a hundred times over what you could in this hole."

"But we happen to like this 'hole,' as you put it," Mac said, clearly irritated. "And we have no plans to move to Kansas City."

Danvers smiled cynically. "As I said earlier, there isn't a man alive who can't be bought. You desire to marry my daughter. There's a price for everything. If you want to do business with me, you'll have to pay that price."

"Father!" Jillian declared, completely embarrassed by his ruthless attitude in regard to her marriage.

"Jillian is of age, Mr. Danvers. She seeks your blessing, not because she can't marry without it, but because she prefers to marry with it. It won't stop us from marrying, however, so don't think you can practice your same roughshod business dealings with me," Mac said quite seriously. "You may have controlled the women in your family by keeping them cowered in fear and acquiescence, but I desire a wife who uses her mind and can think for herself. I prefer a wife who can stand up to me and point out when I'm making a fool of myself so as not to completely humiliate myself in public."

The meaning of Mac's words were clearly understood, and Jillian had never seen her father so taken aback. No one spoke to Colin Danvers in such a manner and got away with it. There was always a price to pay, and just as he had suggested earlier, Jillian knew most men were eager to pay it in order to align themselves with her father.

"I think I've heard entirely enough," Danvers stated, taking hold of his wife. "We will retire for the evening."

"What about the party?" Jillian questioned, hoping to knit some semblance of peace between the foursome.

"I'm not in a mood for a celebration," he replied and, pulling along a teary-eyed Gretchen, exited the hotel lobby and made his way up the stairs to their rooms.

Jillian, Mac, and Mary all stood staring up at the now empty stairs long after the Danvers had departed.

"There you two are!" a voice called out.

Jillian turned and found Zack Matthews and Gwen. Zack gave a whistle of admiration, and Gwen's face shone in pure delight.

"You two look like something out of a magazine," Zack declared.

"Jillian, your gown is incredible," Gwen said, breaking away from Zack's hold to come for a closer inspection.

"My mother seemed to feel that my simpler fashions were leading me to a life of misery and despair. She brought two trunks full of clothes just for me. She didn't want me showing up in Kansas City looking like some misfit."

"Kansas City? Are you and Mac going there for a wedding trip?" Zack questioned.

"We certainly are not!" Mac said, anger edging his tone. He turned to Jillian. A harshness she had never known seemed to override his gentle features.

"Mac?" she questioned softly. "Please don't let my father ruin your evening. I told you he was quite the taskmaster. He's treating you no differently than he treats anyone else."

"It's disgusting, if you ask me," Mary threw in, coming to give Mac a comforting pat on the back. "That man is rude and inconsiderate. Excuse me for saying so, Jillian."

Jillian shook her head. "There's nothing to excuse. The truth is the truth. He is rude and inconsiderate. He's also demanding, unreasonable, unwilling to back down, and unfortunately," she sighed and felt her spirit sink, "used to having his own way. He always manages to get what he wants."

"Well, he's not getting it this time," Mac replied. "We aren't moving to Kansas City after the wedding and that's that. You'll be my wife first and his daughter second."

Jillian looked up at this with surprise. The others chuckled. No doubt they thought Mac quite gallant in staking his claim, but Jillian realized he had managed to get caught up in the farce they'd created for her parents.

"Mac?" she said, drawing his attention. "Perhaps we should take a walk and calm down before joining the party."

He looked at her for a moment, the fierceness still evident in his expression. Then, as if realizing the things he'd said, he nodded. His face softened and he put his arm around her shoulder. "I believe you're right. It's time to let cooler heads prevail."

Mary laughed. "You two go have a few minutes to yourself. Just don't forget that you'll be expected to make a showin' at the party. Don't want you two elopin' or runnin' off just to get away from that dictator you call a father."

Jillian smiled at this. "If only we could find him a country to control."

Outside, as they strolled to the opposite end of town, Jillian and Mac remained silent. Moonlight shone down, and stars overhead twinkled against the milky glow as if God himself had turned on every light in heaven in honor of the couple.

"I'm sorry about all of that, Mac," Jillian finally began. "I tried to warn you."

"He's insufferable," Mac replied.

She nodded. "Yes, he is. But I've tried to respect him, and I've always been a dutiful daughter—at least until three months ago."

"He's being unreasonable to expect us to allow him to order us about."

Jillian paused and looked up into Mac's face. "It's all a game, Mac. None of this is real. I don't know how we're going to make this right, but listen to yourself. There isn't going to be a wedding. There aren't going to be any of the things my father is presuming upon." She turned away and buried her face in her hands. Moaning, she continued. "I am so sorry I put you through this. Mary was right. Deception only leads to more deception and people get hurt."

Mac pulled her hands away and tilted her chin upward. "Jillian, I'm sorry if I made you feel bad."

She shook her head. "You don't understand. I . . . care about you, Mac." She exhaled rather loudly, as if those words had cost her everything.

"I care about you too," he said softly. "I care a great deal."

"I don't want you hurt," she continued. "I only want your happiness."

"And I only want yours," he countered.

Jillian shook her head and moved away. They were still playing games. They weren't saying the words they really needed to say. She needed to tell him that she loved him—that she wanted this wedding to go through as planned. That she wanted to be his wife and share his life forever.

"Mac," she said, turning back to see him watching her very

intently. "I need to tell you something. It's important that you understand."

"All right. Go ahead."

She nodded and moved to stand closer, her taffeta dress rustling softly as she walked. "I think you know that I've come to love a great many things about this territory. I don't want to leave it, neither do I want to leave . . . to leave . . ." She struggled with the words. "You." His expression altered in such a way that Jillian immediately worried that she'd put him off. "I've never had a friend quite like you," she hurried to continue.

"A friend?" he questioned softly. "Is that what I am?"

Jillian knew she had to tell him the truth. "I . . . you're . . . more . . ."

"Hey, Doc! They're waiting for you and Miss Jillian! They're gettin' ready to make the toasts and wish you well," Sam Capper called from down the street.

Jillian quickly looked away. "We'd better get back," she whispered, feeling that she might break into tears.

"But we need to talk," Mac said, taking hold of her again.

"Maybe later," she said, trying to appear in control of her emotions. She offered him a brief smile, then quickly looked away. Later.

CHAPTER
19

THE FOLLOWING MORNING Jillian met her parents, as planned, in the Harvey dining room. As they sat down to breakfast together, Jillian tried hard not to say or do anything that would bring about her father's disapproval. She knew her mother had spent a good deal of the night crying, as her eyes were red and swollen, and the last thing Jillian wanted to do was cause her to cry now.

They ate silently, or very nearly so. Jillian asked them if their rooms at the hotel were acceptable, and Colin Danvers commented that they were tolerable. Jillian thanked her mother again for the party gown, pretending to be more excited about it than she really was. The falsity of her words and actions was weighing on her like a smothering shroud. It threatened the very breath from her body, and guilt ate at her constantly. What was it Mary had said about God freeing you from such guilt? The truth would set you free, she had told Jillian. It stuck in Jillian's mind like a counterbalance against all that she had allowed to put her into bondage.

They were just finishing with their meal when Mac appeared. He walked to the table with deliberate strides and stopped long enough to bow and smile to both Jillian and her mother before facing Colin.

"I received your note," he said matter-of-factly.

Danvers pushed back from the table and got to his feet. "Let's be about it, then."

Jillian shook her head. What was going on? The two men quickly exited the room, leaving her no recourse but to question her mother. "Why did Father send Mac a note?"

"He wished to talk to him. They have a great deal to settle, you know," Gretchen replied. "My dear, we have an appointment at the hotel. I have hired a local seamstress to come in and see to your final fitting of the wedding gown. There's no sense in appearing shoddy on your special day."

"I wish you wouldn't have gone to so much trouble," Jillian replied, then instantly regretted her words as her mother's countenance fell. She reached out to pat her mother's hand. "It's just that I know it's so hard on you. I don't wish you to be overworked on my account."

Gretchen nodded. "It has been difficult, but I shan't rest until the wedding is a success. Judith disappointed me by running off and leaving me without a wedding to plan. I simply can't have you dismiss me from your wedding as well."

Jillian felt consuming guilt. Here her mother was trying hard to make the best of a bad situation and Jillian was ruining it. What would her mother say when the truth came out and she learned there was to be no wedding at all? Then a thought came to her. Perhaps Mac would argue with her father and formally break their engagement that way. It seemed like a wise thing to do. It hurt to imagine that after being seen everywhere as an engaged couple, honored with toasts and congratulations at the party the night before, that Jillian would soon go back to being nothing more than another Harvey Girl.

"I suppose we could go for the fitting now," Jillian said, trying to put the image of Mac and her father aside. She got to her feet and helped her mother from the table.

Gretchen seemed happy again, and Jillian realized that she would have to figure out a way to ease her mother's distress once her wedding to Mac was officially cancelled. Maybe she could return home for a short while. After all, it wouldn't cost her that much in time or effort to see her mother through what would be an obvious disappointment. The idea of returning to Kansas City held no interest for Jillian, but she loved her mother and didn't want to see her suffer.

Outside, Jillian tucked her mother's arm close to her side and headed toward the hotel. To her immediate frustration, Jillian found herself forced to encounter Mrs. Everhart and her daughter, Davinia.

"Miss Danvers," Mrs. Everhart said quite haughtily, "I have not yet made the acquaintance of your mother."

Jillian nodded. "Mrs. Everhart, Miss Everhart, please allow me to introduce my mother, Mrs. Gretchen Danvers of Kansas City."

The two women nodded, each seeming to try to outdo the other in formality. Davinia, her mousy brown hair blowing lifelessly in the breeze, peered around her mother's shoulder as if to acknowledge herself to Jillian's mother.

"I hear tell that once your daughter and our good doctor are wed, they will return to Kansas City."

"We have no plans to return to Kansas City," Jillian interjected before her mother could speak.

Mrs. Everhart looked down her nose at Jillian. "I was speaking to your mother. Have the good manners to respect the conversation of your elders."

"Please do not reprimand my daughter," Gretchen spoke, surprising Jillian. "She is a grown woman of good breeding. She has attended the finest schools and has been finished by Madame Duvereau herself."

Jillian realized that Mrs. Everhart would have no idea who Madame Duvereau was. The stately old woman ran the most elite finishing school for women in the Kansas City area, and Jillian had placed at the top of her class in all subjects. Her mother was fiercely proud of this, for it showed all of polite society Jillian's potential as a wife and hostess.

"I don't imagine her good breeding would allow for the lies she's told while living here or for her taking on the ghastly task of serving in these Harvey Houses. Why, I'm appalled that such women are even allowed in the church on Sunday."

"Just what are you implying?" Jillian questioned before her mother could speak.

"I have it on the best authority that Mr. Harvey's 'Girls,' as you call yourselves, are no better than a higher class of street harlot."

"You take that back!" Jillian said, stepping forward. "I have never disgraced my parents in such a way, nor would I. I can't believe the things that some people will say in order to cast hurt and insult on others."

"I have no desire to take back the truth," Mrs. Everhart said, sneering at Jillian. "Although I realize the truth is something you may not be well acquainted with. After all, you did come to this town on false pretenses. How would we know if you were telling the truth or not?"

"Let God be my judge, then, Mrs. Everhart. I'm sure He needs no help from you."

Gretchen gasped, and Davinia stepped back as her mother squared her shoulders for battle. "The good Lord puts certain people on this earth for the purpose of maintaining proprieties. You may sway the minds of weak-willed men who find your beauty a thing to possess, but you are not fooling me. My eyes are open to you, Miss Danvers. You, who chased the poor doctor, throwing yourself at him and stealing him away from my Davinia. You, who keeps company with Mrs. Barnes, a woman of questionable repute, to be certain."

"I will not stand for you to impugn the reputation of such a saintly woman as Mary Barnes," Jillian said, stepping forward. "You take back your accusation."

"I will not!" Mrs. Everhart declared, pressing herself forward. "The woman goes into the desert alone and lives for weeks with only God knows whom, doing God knows what."

C-R-A-C-K! The slap Jillian delivered to Mrs. Everhart's face was unexpected by both parties. For a moment neither one did anything, then as her face turned red and mottled in fierce indignity, Mrs. Everhart continued her harangue.

"You are just like her. Of course you find her acceptable company. Her ways are your ways. Just as it was with that conniving little squaw."

By this time a crowd had gathered and Jillian knew she was making a spectacle of herself. But her anger was intense. That Mrs. Everhart would insult the reputation of Mary and Little Sister, knowing full well that Mary strove only to share her faith and that Little Sister had been forcibly raped, was more than Jillian could stand.

"You listen to me," Jillian said, seeing the stunned look on her adversary's face. "Little Sister had no say in what happened to her, and you know it." Just then Jillian looked past Mrs. Everhart and caught sight of Mr. Cooper. "That man took her innocence and left her with his child, then refused to do any decent thing to make amends."

Several people in the crowd let out sounds of surprise, and Jillian knew she'd crossed the point of no return. She would have her say now, and it would no doubt forever change how she was received in this town. Perhaps it would be her death knell, and she would be forced to return to Kansas City.

Jillian remembered something Louisa had told her in confidence and threw it into the conversation. "Tell me it isn't true, Mrs. Everhart. Tell me that you didn't warn your own daughter about Mr. Cooper."

More gasps accompanied by a couple of chuckles followed from the crowd this time. Mrs. Everhart was fairly steaming by this time.

"You little brat! What I do with my daughter is none of your affair. What Mr. Cooper does with those animal Indians of his is also none of your affair."

"He violated a young woman," Jillian countered, moving toward the older woman. "She was not an animal, but a living, breathing girl—not even as old as your daughter."

Jillian spied Mr. Cooper, who stood to one side, appearing to rather enjoy the entire showdown. "You should be ashamed of yourself. You shouldn't even be allowed to share the company of decent people."

He smiled and spoke smoothly, "Now, Miss Danvers, aren't you just a bit worked up?"

Jillian forced her hands on her hips to keep from putting them around Cooper's neck. Struggling to maintain control, the past and the pressures of the future were taking their toll. She felt consumed by her anger.

"I intend to write letters to the proper authorities," Jillian said in a low, menacing tone. "My father knows important people, and you, sir, should number your days, because I intend to see you dismissed from this position and, if possible, thrown into prison for your deeds."

"No one is going throw me into jail for sharing the bed of a squaw," Cooper said laughing. "They might question my acceptability in polite society, but they couldn't care less about those heathens, and you know that very well. The government didn't know what else to do with them, so they forced them into the poorest quarters of dirt and left them there hoping they'd rot to death. You aren't going to see anyone mourn the loss of that ignorant woman you call Little Sister."

"What about her daughter?" Jillian shouted. "What about *your* daughter?"

"That Indian brat is no child of mine. Who knows who else she laid with? You can't make me responsible for this—she was just a dirty squaw."

Cooper couldn't see the way the crowd was reacting to him, but Jillian could. People were moving away from him a little at a time, whispering among themselves, eyeing him with contempt. Perhaps his punishment would come from his peers after all.

Jillian was livid. "Is that the way you see it?" She looked out at the crowd and then turned to look at the gathering of Harvey Girls behind her. Gwen stood on the edge, as if to come to Jillian's rescue, but she said nothing.

Jillian saw the looks on the faces of the people; some appeared deeply ashamed, and others acted as though they didn't know quite how to take her. "Is that the kind of thing this town approves of? Because if it is, then I want no part of you!"

At that point someone touched Jillian's shoulder. She whirled around to see Mac's compassionate expression. He took hold of her hand very gently and pulled her toward him.

"Come with me," he said softly.

She saw that her father had taken his place beside her mother. She saw, too, that Gwen had begun to cry, as had many of the other women in the street gathering. Jillian didn't care, however. They could have stopped this a long time ago, and now it had escalated to a full-scale war with the army still out hunting down Navajo men. Why should the Navajo want to send their children to the white man's school when the white man stood by and allowed such heinous acts to continue?

Mac rounded the Harvey House and headed for his office with Jillian, but she stopped him in midstep. "Let me go, Mac," she said firmly, pulling away.

"I think we should talk and get you calmed down."

"I don't want to calm down!" she said, her voice nearly as loud as it had been a moment ago. "They could have stopped it. You could have stopped it. Why didn't you, Mac? Why did you allow for someone like Cooper to keep walking the streets? Why do you tolerate people like Mrs. Everhart with her gossiping lies and prejudiced ways?"

"Jillian, you're upset and rightly so, but you don't need to take it out on me," Mac said, reaching out for her again.

She jerked away and stomped her foot. "Don't touch me! You're just as bad as they are! You could have stopped Cooper a long time ago, but you didn't."

Mac crossed his arms. "What would you have had me do? Shoot him? Mary and I have tried to get the law in the area to take notice, to care about the situation. We've written letters to the proper authorities and tried to go about this the right way. Short of killing the man, however, I don't know what else you would have me do."

Jillian felt her energy draining rather quickly. Mac made too much sense, but she didn't want to admit it. She was hurt by Mrs. Everhart's insults. Hurt by her father's demanding ways. But most of all, she was hurt because she loved Mac and she was living a lie.

"Leave me alone!" she cried and ran for the back door of the Harvey House.

"Jillian!"

He called to her several times, but she ignored him and closed the door tightly. Running up the back stairs as quickly as she could manage, Jillian locked herself in her room, mindless that Kate or Louisa might need to get in. Then, without checking her bed, she threw herself across the mattress and sobbed. With any luck at all, maybe something poisonous would bite her and she'd die.

Oh, God, I've done nothing right since coming here. What am I supposed to do? How can I make everything right?

WITH FEELINGS OF SHEER EMBARRASSMENT for the way she'd acted, Jillian spent the rest of the day and evening refusing to speak to anyone. When Kate came to knock on the door in order to change her apron, Jillian reluctantly allowed her entry. But even when Kate applauded the way she'd dealt with Mrs. Everhart and Mr. Cooper, Jillian refused to comment on it. She couldn't believe that she'd so thoroughly disregarded her upbringing to make such a public spectacle of herself.

Kate mentioned before leaving that Jillian's parents were looking for her.

"Please don't tell them I'm here," she pleaded with Kate.

"If they ask, I'll tell them I haven't seen ya," Kate agreed.

"No!" Jillian declared, shaking her head. "No more lies. If they ask, just tell them I refuse to see anyone. That's the truth of the matter."

Kate nodded and took her leave while Jillian took down her hair and began combing it out. The blond tresses were silky, having been freshly washed that morning, and Jillian couldn't help but wonder why blond hair was so acceptable and black hair so abominable. At least it was when it was accompanied by brown skin.

Having stayed in her room alone, Jillian was ready for company again when Kate and Louisa came to retire for the night. She was almost herself again until Kate reminded her that the following day was to be Jillian's wedding day.

Just as Jillian thought to reply, a knock sounded at their door and Gwen peeked in. "Jillian? Are you all right?"

Jillian nodded. "I'm fine but sorry for having made such a ninny of myself earlier. I just couldn't seem to stop."

Gwen smiled. "I thought you were wonderful. Zack did too. He came and dispersed everyone and told me later that the general feeling among the townsfolk was that you did a good thing."

Jillian sat down on the edge of her bed and shook her head. "Then why don't I feel better?"

"I don't know, but give yourself time. Oh, and here's a note from your folks," Gwen said, reaching into her pocket. "I almost forgot that was the reason I came here."

Jillian reluctantly took the piece of paper and for the first time in days felt as if she'd been given a reprieve. "They want me to wait on the wedding. Judith has telegrammed that she wants to be at the wedding and will arrive on Tuesday." She looked up at Gwen, trying to seem disappointed, but inside she couldn't help breathing a sigh of relief.

"Tuesday? You can't get married with us tomorrow?"

"We are very close, Judith and I," Jillian began. "I'd really like to wait for her."

Gwen nodded. "Then Zack and I will wait too."

"Nonsense," Jillian replied, getting up. "You go ahead and get married tomorrow, and Mac and I can get married on Tuesday."

"You sure you wouldn't mind? I mean, the double wedding sounded like great fun."

"I don't mind," Jillian said honestly. "But I'd better go fill Mac in on the details." She looked at the clock and realized it was nearly curfew time. "I promise to hurry."

"You go ahead," Gwen said conspiratorially. "I'll leave the back door unlocked for you. We women in love must stick together."

Jillian smiled. "Thanks. I shouldn't be too long." She looked at herself in the mirror and shook her head. "I suppose I should pin my hair back up." She reached to fasten the top buttons of her blouse with one hand while taking up her brush with the other.

"Nonsense," Gwen said, interceding. "Just go." She took the brush from Jillian and pushed her hand away as she worked with the tiny buttons. "You're covered better than you were in that gorgeous gown you wore last night. Just go!"

Jillian laughed at her encouragement. "I'm going! I'm going!"

She hurried down the back stairs, and suddenly pangs of guilt washed over her. What was she going to say to Mac? She'd treated him horribly. What could she say? She knew he hadn't deserved her tirade, but her nerves were raw and it seemed that her grief over Little Sister and her misery over her situation were all too much to take.

Creeping out the back door and across the street to where Mac's house stood gleaming in the moonlight, Jillian resolved herself to plead insanity and beg for mercy.

Knocking lightly so as not to alert the rest of the town to her actions, Jillian waited until she saw the unmistakable glow of lamp-light appear, and finally, there stood Mac, rumpled and bleary-eyed.

"Jillian?" he questioned, setting the lamp on the stand beside the door. "Are you hurt?"

"Yes," she said honestly.

"What is it?" he questioned, becoming fully awake. "Show me."

"I can't," she said softly. "It's my heart that's hurt."

He instantly seemed to understand and nodded.

"Oh, Mac, I'm so sorry. I never meant to hurt you. I never meant to say those horrible things. I wouldn't blame you if you never spoke to me again, but please understand that I didn't mean a word I said."

He reached out and pulled her into his arms. "Oh, Jilly, I know you didn't." Holding her close, he stroked her waist-length hair and sighed against her ear.

She snuggled against him, grateful for his forgiving heart. "I feel like I'm walking against the wind," she whispered. "There's so much in conflict right now. So much I can't resolve."

He tilted her chin upward and gazed longingly into her eyes. "It's going to work out. You'll see. You just have to have faith."

"In God?" she questioned.

"Yes, in God. In yourself. In me."

Before she realized what was happening, Jillian found herself touching Mac's face. Oh, but he was handsome! He was loving and good-hearted and everything she had hoped for in a husband.

"Mac." His name was the only word she managed to speak before he closed her lips with his own.

"I suppose you have a good explanation for taking these kind of liberties with my daughter," Colin Danvers said angrily.

Jillian and Mac came apart like two kids caught with their hands in the candy dish.

"Father!"

"Don't even speak to me," he said, holding up his hand. "I suppose you've spent the entire day and night with this man. Now I have no choice but to see you married to him. Is that how you planned it? Is that why you were angry with that woman in the street today? Did her words hit too close to home?"

"Mr. Danvers, I'm a patient man, but I would advise you against insulting Jillian any further. She's innocent of what you suggest. She merely came here tonight to apologize."

"And to show him your note," Jillian said, grateful for her presence of mind. She held up the note as proof. "I needed to tell him that we weren't getting married tomorrow."

"What?" Mac questioned.

"That's right," Danvers said. "You aren't getting married tomorrow, you're getting married tonight!"

"But, Father—"

"This is how it's going to be, Jillian. Your mother would be appalled if she knew you were here with him like this. Why, the man isn't even properly dressed—and look at yourself. Your hair is down and you're not even properly buttoned! How do you expect me to believe this is something completely innocent?"

"I don't much care what you believe," Mac said, taking hold of Jillian's hand. "We haven't done anything wrong."

"Good. Let's keep it that way," Danvers said, not sounding a bit as if he believed them.

"That's fine by me," Mac answered.

"Now is as good a time as any," Danvers replied.

"Again, that's fine by me," Mac stated evenly.

"Get your coat, MacCallister."

"Why?" Jillian asked, totally confused by the conversation that seemed to be taking place without her.

"Because you're coming with me to the preacher. You're getting married to this man tonight."

Mac felt a sense of relief as Jillian's father pointed them toward the church. All day long he'd wrestled with the question of how to convince Jillian to marry him for real. Now her father was taking care of the matter rather neatly.

He wanted this wedding. He wanted Jillian for a wife. The only problem was, he couldn't be entirely sure that this was what she wanted. He wished they could have a moment alone so that he could talk to her and convince her of his heart in the matter. Maybe if she understood how he felt, how he'd only gone along with this in the hope that the truth might be born out of the deception they'd created . . . maybe then she'd share her heart with him.

Mac could feel her tremble. She clung to him so tightly that her hold was almost painful to him, but Mac would never have told her. He could see the kind of opposition she'd been up against her entire life. Danvers was not the kind of man to listen to his children or wife. He was the take-charge kind of man who would plow through a planted field if it suited his purpose. No wonder Jillian had felt the need to lie. Well, there would be no more need for that now. He would marry her, and one way or another, he would see to it that she was happy about the situation.

Jillian found she had no choice in the matter. The two angry men had taken the matter out of her hands. She marched obediently, clinging to Mac as they made their way to the tiny house where Reverend Lister lived with his wife. Unable to fathom that Mac was really going to go through with this, Jillian tried to force herself to calm. Mac would think of something once they were with Reverend Lister. He'd find some way to deal with Father, and everything would go back to normal.

Oh, why did I have to lie about all of this? she asked herself. But in her heart, Jillian knew her feelings for Mac were in harmony with the evening's plan. She desperately wanted to marry this man. She loved him, but could a marriage work if only one person desired the union? Mac would be legally bound to her, and it would take another legal act to separate them. Surely they needed to put a stop to this. But how?

"What about the license?" she asked, suddenly seeing it as her way out.

"Preacher already has it in preparation for the ceremony you planned for tomorrow," her father sternly replied.

Desperate, she dropped her hold on Mac and took hold of her father's arm. "What will Mother say?" she questioned. "You know she has her heart set on giving me a wedding."

"She can still do that on Tuesday. But no daughter of mine is going to spend the night with a man and not be wed to him."

"But I didn't—"

"Jillian, you know nothing of men. This man might tell you all manner of things, make you all manner of promises, but often what a man promises and what he actually carries through with are two different things."

"But I didn't do anything wrong!" Jillian declared a bit louder than she'd intended. Lowering her voice, she added, "Go ask Miss Carson. I've spent the entire day and evening at the Harvey House. I only went to see Mac to tell him about the note."

Her father shook his head, and for a moment, Jillian thought she saw a veil of sorrow pass over his expression. It almost seemed as if the moment brought him some unexpected pain. In the next minute, he stunned her with a totally uncharacteristic statement.

"I've seen women—their reputations—destroyed by men who made promises they never intended to keep. I can see for myself that you fancy yourself in love with this man. I have no way of knowing what liberties he's already taken, but I've heard the talk in this town. Jillian, you must marry him." The statement was offered without anger or malice. "Whether you stay in Pintan or move elsewhere, I want this scoundrel to realize he has an obligation. He's the one who wooed you and allowed you to lose your heart."

"But, Father, it wasn't that way," Jillian said, pleading with the older man to hear her out. "Mac has done nothing wrong."

"It never seems that way," Danvers said with a frown. "I'm going to tell you both something. Something I would never have shared while my mother still lived, but perhaps it needs to be told." He actually appeared less than confident for a moment. "At fifteen, my sister, Katherine, gave her heart, among other things, to a young man whom she fancied herself in love with. She was completely taken in by this scallywag, and when the moment arrived for him to deal honorably with her, he was nowhere to be found. Finding herself deserted, my sister pined and mourned for her young man, certain that he had met with a fate equal to or worse than death. Weeks passed, however, and the young man was soon seen frequenting some of the rougher taverns in town. I went after him as a good brother should, but the man refused to honor his word. He wanted nothing more to do with my sister."

Her father's haunted expression troubled Jillian. She'd never heard anything about this in all her years. Why, she scarcely even knew she had an Aunt Katherine. The only mention was of a sister who had died tragically at a young age. Jillian stiffened, suddenly knowing how her father's story was about to end.

"My sister was unable to deal with her grief. She took her own life." He let the statement settle for a moment before turning to Jillian. "I won't see that happen again. I should have forced that scoundrel to marry my sister. I didn't, but I should have. I won't make the same mistake twice." His anger seemed to return, and he twisted his arm away from her touch and pounded firmly on the front door of the parsonage. "I'll expect both of you to act respectably."

A sleepy Reverend Lister opened the door, candle in one hand, the other hand working to pull together the ties of his robe.

"I need you to marry my daughter to this man," Danvers told the reverend impatiently. "I don't care what it costs, I want it done now!"

Lister looked confused. "I thought they were marrying tomorrow afternoon."

Mac said nothing, but Jillian sent him a pleading look. She

couldn't help but hope that he had figured some way to fix this situation. Instead, he seemed quietly at ease with the entire matter.

"I want them married now. Her sister arrives on Tuesday, and we'll have a proper wedding then, but for now I insist on this." Danvers pulled out a wad of bills and handed them to the uneasy pastor. "This should cover your troubles."

By this time Mrs. Lister had come to see what the trouble was. "Oh, Jillian! Mac! How romantic. You two are eloping, I see." She seemed not to notice the tension among the three visitors.

"Well, come on in and let's get this over with," Reverend Lister finally said, stepping away from the door. "Hannah, light a lamp, please."

The older woman quickly complied. "We haven't had a midnight wedding in some time," she chuckled. "Guess you two are anxious to start your new life together."

Jillian felt faint. This was madness. Was Mac going to tolerate her father's interference in their lives?

Reverend Lister took up his Bible and nodded. "Mac, you take hold of Jillian's hand."

Mac did just that, but Jillian tried to pull away. "Mac?" she questioned, looking up at him.

He held her hand fast and refused to look down at her. "We're ready," he told the preacher.

Jillian's mind whirled in a million different directions. Her dream of marrying Mac was actually coming true, but it wasn't at all in the way she had expected it. Forcing a man into marriage couldn't be good, she reasoned.

She looked at the determined expression on her father's face and found herself stepping a little closer to Mac. He believed her to have been compromised. He believed the worst of her, and yet never once had she ever given him a reason to carry such notions. It angered her suddenly to realize the thoughts that were in her father's head.

Resolving to speak out when her chance came, Jillian wondered what she should say. Should she just blurt out that while she loved Mac dearly, she couldn't marry him because it had all been a lie? Could she bear additional humiliation? Mac's hand held her fast, and she couldn't help but allow her feelings for him to surface. How could she fight this kind of love? The power of it overwhelmed her.

When Reverend Lister finally asked her if she would take Mac for her husband, Jillian could no longer deny her feelings or heart in the matter. Knowing it was probably the wrong thing to do, Jillian nodded and said, "Yes."

The entire ceremony took less than ten minutes, and at the end of it, Mac turned to her and instead of kissing her, glared over her shoulder at her father and spoke in a low, hard voice. "Let's get out of here and let these good folks get back to sleep."

Outside, Colin Danvers, true to form, turned to his daughter. "You'd do best to get yourself back to that Harvey House and stay there until the wedding on Tuesday. I won't tolerate you shaming your mother."

"Excuse me," Mac said, holding Jillian possessively. "She's my wife now and she's coming with me."

Jillian began to tremble as her father's eyes narrowed and the truth of the matter began to dawn on her. She had just become Mac's wife.

"You'll further compromise her reputation," Danvers replied, then shrugged. "But given the fact that you won't be here much longer, I suppose it doesn't have to be that detrimental."

Mac's grip on Jillian's arm became painfully tight. "As I've told you before, Jillian and I are going to remain here in Arizona."

"But I thought we'd come to an understanding about that earlier today," Danvers said.

"*You* came to an understanding. You offered money and the promise of an incredible future if I would move to Kansas City with Jillian. But you also offered me money if I'd leave her altogether and head west. Exactly which understanding were you expecting me to follow through with at this point?"

Jillian felt sick. It was as if they were bartering for her future. Her father treated her as if she were one of his businesses and he was negotiating the trade or sale of a valuable commodity.

"You know full well that I'm speaking of you moving with Jillian to Kansas City," Danvers replied. "My wife desires to have her daughters close, and if that means tolerating the likes of you, then so be it."

"Well, it doesn't," Mac stated. "I've married your daughter for one reason and one reason alone. I love her. I don't want your money or your demands. And please believe me when I say if I had not wanted to marry Jillian, your little escapade here tonight wouldn't have made a bit of difference to me. No one pushes me around and tells me how to run my life. My soul belongs to God, and He directs my steps . . . not you.

"Now we're going home, and I suggest you go back to the hotel and tell your wife what you've done. If Jillian wants a big town wedding on Tuesday, then we'll have one. If not, then we'll forget about it. Understand?"

For once, Colin Danvers had truly met his match. Jillian felt a mixture of pride and wonder as Mac fought for her. He had said he loved her. Dare she believe that this was the truth? Dare she hope that Mac had married her because he wanted to, not merely because her father had chosen to make a scene?

Danvers' expression changed to one of resignation, something Jillian had not ever witnessed. "Very well." He turned to go, then turned back to stare hard at his daughter. "I hope you'll remember your mother's delicate feelings on this matter."

Jillian nodded. "I will," she promised. "The wedding can take place Tuesday just like you requested." Danvers said nothing but turned and walked back toward the hotel.

"Come on," Mac said, loosening his grip to put his arm around Jillian's shoulders.

Trembling from head to toe, Jillian now realized she had an entirely different matter to deal with. She had to face Mac and learn the truth. But maybe more importantly, she needed to tell him the truth herself.

CHAPTER

21

WATCHING JILLIAN CLOSELY, Mac opened the door to his home. Their home. Without a word, he lifted her into his arms, smiling as she gasped in surprise.

"It's tradition to carry the bride across the threshold," he said softly against her ear. He could hardly believe she was really his wife, the very desire of his heart.

Jillian said nothing, and even after he set her back down and turned to close the door, she remained silent. Turning, he found her scrutinizing him. She backed up a step as if afraid, then licked her lips.

"Mac, I'm so sorry about my father. I had no idea this was going to happen. You have to believe me. I would never have allowed this. In fact, I was sure you were going to stop it."

She rambled on and on in her nervousness, and Mac might have laughed had the fear not been so evident in her eyes.

"I don't know what to do now. I feel awful. This only started because I wanted my mother to leave off with her matchmaking. I took advantage of you and that was so wrong. I appreciate what you did for me, but, Mac, you can't just marry someone to take them away from bad circumstances. My father is overbearing and ruthless, but you shouldn't have let him force you into a marriage you were only pretending to want."

He stepped forward at this and put his finger to her lips. "No one could ever make me marry anyone. Your father knows that. He offered me a great deal of money to leave you, but he also offered me money to marry you and return to Kansas City. I turned him down, just as I mentioned earlier, on both counts. I married you because I wanted to."

As if to show her proof, he took her into his arms and kissed her long and passionately. She yielded easily, but Mac couldn't help feeling a little guilty. After all, just because he wanted to marry Jillian didn't necessarily mean she wanted to marry him. Suddenly her outbursts took on a new meaning to him. Perhaps she was saying all of this because she was unhappy with him for forcing himself on her.

Mac broke the kiss and looked at her for a moment. Her eyes were still closed as if she were lost in the kiss. Slowly, she opened her eyes and met his gaze. She seemed content enough.

"Jillian, I know this is probably confusing for you, but we can make this work."

"I thought you never wanted to marry again. I thought the pain of what you suffered with Abigail had put you off of the idea of ever sharing your life with another person."

He nodded. "I thought so too." He grinned and reached up to touch her cheek. "Then you came to town."

"So you don't mind?" she asked weakly, almost fearfully.

Mac laughed. "Mind? Being married to the most beautiful woman in the world? Should I mind being married to such a loving and generous soul who fights with such fervor to right the wrongs of injustice?"

Tears formed in her eyes, and Mac released her to offer his handkerchief. "I didn't mean to make you cry."

She sniffed and dabbed at the tears. "It's not your fault."

He could see she was still shaking and so he led her to the sofa. "Here, sit down and talk to me about this." He squatted down beside her and took hold of her hand. "Is it really all that bad? Is the idea of being married to me so terrible?"

She looked up at him with such an expression of disbelief that Mac wasn't at all sure what she would say. But Jillian never had the chance to speak because the sound of a bell clanging from the far end of town brought both Jillian and Mac to their feet.

"Fire!" someone shouted in the stillness of the night.

"Fire?" Jillian barely breathed the word.

"Stay here and I'll find out what's going on," Mac instructed. He disappeared into his office, then grabbing up his black bag, he went to the door. "I'll be back as soon as I can."

He left her standing there and rushed out into the night. In the distance he could see the red and amber glow against the star-dotted night skies. Running at full speed, Mac rounded the corner coming onto Main Street just in time to hear Mr. Everhart shout that they were under Indian attack.

This halted Mac in his tracks. Indians? The Navajo? He looked around him at the gathering crowd of hysterical people. Men toted rifles and shotguns, fully prepared to do whatever battle became necessary to defend their loved ones. Mac felt almost silly carrying his doctor's bag as he noted the glances of the other men as they acknowledged his presence.

"What's going on?" he finally asked the nearest man.

"Injuns set fire to the jail, is my guess. The wind has spread the flames. It's gonna be hard to keep it from burnin' us to the ground."

"Get your buckets!" someone yelled. "We ain't gonna stand by and let them savages burn us out."

Cheers went up from the crowds as women and men scrambled for every available bucket and watering can. Mac moved off down the street toward the jail. Zack Matthews instantly came to mind, and he wondered if Bear had somehow overpowered the young sheriff— or worse yet, killed him.

Glancing out of the corner of his eye, Mac tried to be wary of any movement on the side streets or between buildings. He could distinguish moving shadows but had no idea to whom those shadows belonged. They could be Navajo, they could be townsfolk. Either way, knowing the jittery nerves of his neighbors, someone was bound to get hurt before it was all said and done.

As he approached the jail, Mac could see the flames. He prayed that no one was still inside, knowing that it would be impossible to survive. Coming around the side of the small building, Mac made out the shadowy form of someone lying in the alleyway. He rushed to the body and rolled the man over. In the dancing glow of flames, Mac easily identified the man as Zack.

"Matthews!" he called out, feeling the heat from the fire. "Wake up, Matthews. Talk to me."

Zack groaned and seemed to try to open his eyes, but he quickly fell silent. Mac had no idea what was wrong with him but knew he had to get Matthews away from the intense heat. As he slipped his arm around Zack's body, Mac instantly became aware of a wetness. He held his hand up to the light of the flames and saw that he was covered in Zack's blood.

By now other people were starting to gather around. He stood up and motioned to Zack. "I need some help getting the sheriff to my office. He's bleeding pretty badly."

A couple of men came forward, and one man took hold of Zack's arms while the other grabbed his legs. Mac nodded. "If anyone else is hurt, come to my place." He left the rest of them fighting the fire and hurried after the men. Mac feared the shock of seeing Zack might be too much for Jillian, so he quickly bypassed the men and raced to his door.

"Jillian!" he called out. "We've got an injured man."

Jillian stood in the middle of the room, apparently pacing. She stopped, however, and looked past Mac as if expecting the man to be right behind her husband.

"It's Zack Matthews," Mac said.

Jillian's expression changed to one of extreme concern. "Is he badly hurt?"

"He's bleeding," Mac replied, as if that said it all. He turned and motioned. "In here, men," he instructed as the two men maneuvered through the door with Zack's body. Mac stood between them and Jillian, hoping to protect her from witnessing something that would further upset her. He knew how she was about the superstitions regarding death. How in the world would she face the possibility of watching this man die?

"I'll get Gwen," Jillian told Mac.

He nodded. "That's probably a good idea." He forgot about his arm and hand being stained with Matthews' blood as he reached out to her. She paled instantly.

"Is that from him or are you injured?" She trembled noticeably but held her ground.

"I'm fine. It's Zack's blood."

"I'd better hurry," she managed to reply. Mac would have loved to have comforted her for a moment, but there was no time. Sooner or later she'd have to learn that as the wife of a doctor, there would be many unpleasant moments where life and death hovered in the balance of his actions.

He went to work lighting several lamps and placed them around his examining room just as the men managed to deposit the good-sized sheriff onto the table.

"Thanks," Mac told the men. They left as quickly as they had appeared, and Mac set to work on his patient.

Examining Zack's head, Mac found a gash about three inches long on the back. Someone had hit him hard, knocking him unconscious and leaving him for dead.

He set to cleaning the wound, causing a fresh oozing of blood, just as Jillian and Gwen returned to the house.

"Mac!" Jillian called out as she entered.

"In here," Mac replied. "Come and help me."

Jillian came into the room with Gwen close on her heels.

"Is he all right?" Gwen questioned, sobbing at the sight of her fiancé.

"I hope he will be," Mac told her, "but I can't be sure. Someone has hit him pretty hard. I'll know better when he regains consciousness. Jillian, I need a basin of hot water and some towels. You should find everything you need over in that cabinet, but you'll have to set a fire in the stove and get some water on to boil. Can you handle that?"

Jillian nodded. "I can do it, and Gwen can help me. Come on," she said, pulling at her housemother's arm. "Mac can handle this part without us." Gwen refused to move, however, and Jillian went to the cabinet to retrieve the needed items without her.

Mac glanced up to give Gwen a reassuring nod. "He doesn't look too bad, but I need to get his head stitched up. Go ahead and help Jillian."

Gwen nodded and reluctantly joined Jillian. No sooner had she gone than Zack moaned, twisting away from Mac's hold.

"Whoa now, Zack. You're safe," Mac told him.

Zack's eyes opened and closed very quickly in succession before he finally managed to hold them open. "What happened?"

"I was hoping you could tell me."

Zack closed his eyes and shook his head. "I don't remember."

"I figured as much. It's not a problem. You have a bad gash on the back of your head. I'm going to have to stitch it up. Gwen and Jillian are getting me some hot water."

"Gwen's here?" he asked weakly. "Thought I wouldn't get to see her again."

"Nah, you're too hardheaded to pass on from a mere blow."

"How'd you find me?"

"Someone set fire to the jail. I'm presuming it has something to do with your Navajo guests. I'm hoping they escaped before the fire was set."

Zack opened his eyes and looked up at Mac. "I figured they were up to something. They were just too quiet. Cooper came and tried to talk sense with them, but apparently it didn't help matters."

Mac nodded. "Just try to rest. You aren't bleeding too badly right now, but you've lost a good bit of blood."

Zack let out a long breath and closed his eyes. "You're the doc."

"You need any help in there?" Mary Barnes called out before entering the examination room. Her hair was knotted in a hasty bun and her clothes showed marks of soot.

"Have they managed to contain the fire?" Mac questioned.

"For the most part. Ain't a whole lot close enough to catch fire since they moved the livery away from the jail."

"Do you know if anyone else is injured?"

"Didn't hear anyone say they were," Mary admitted. "They know you're here working on the sheriff, so I figure they'll come here if needed."

"Mac, this water is hot. Where would you like it?" Jillian announced as she came into the room with Gwen right behind her. "Mary! Are you all right? Is Hope all right?"

"We're both fine. I left Hope with Kate and came on over here to see if Mac needed help. I figured you'd be with your folks."

Jillian shook her head. "It's a long story, Mary, but one I promise to explain."

"Right now we need to get this wound sewn up. Jillian, you may put the water on the counter here and then you and Gwen rest in the other room while Mary helps me."

Jillian looked as if he'd somehow hurt her feelings, so Mac quickly added, "Mary's done this before, but soon I'll train you to help me." She nodded, seeming to understand, then reached to take hold of Gwen's arm.

Gwen moved forward, then turned away and went quickly to Zack's side. Leaning down she pleaded, "Oh, Zack, please don't die." Tears slid down her cheeks and onto Zack's face.

Opening his eyes, he gave her the tiniest smile. "Can't die. I'm gettin' hitched tomorrow."

Mac laughed. "See, there's too much orneriness in him to die. Everything is going to be just fine."

"Couldn't hurt to pray, though," Mary told the women.

Jillian smiled. "Mary's right. We should have done that first thing. Come on, we'll get started."

After she and Gwen left the room, Mac turned to Mary. "You best say one for me, as well."

Mary laughed. "You're a fine doctor, Mac. What has you so stirred up?"

He gathered his instruments and sat down at the head of the table to work on Zack's head. "I'll explain it all later. Suffice it to say, God has His work cut out for Him."

C H A P T E R

22

BY THE TIME MAC FINISHED UP with Zack and felt confident about putting him to bed in a room just off the examination room, it was nearly two in the morning.

Yawning, Mac suggested they all get some sleep. "Morning's going to come before we know it."

"I don't want to leave him," Gwen announced. "Please let me stay here with Zack."

Mac nodded. "There's another cot in that room. If you don't think it will tarnish your reputation too much, you're welcome to stay."

Mary yawned. "Well, I'm heading back to the hotel. You want to walk with me, Jillian?"

Jillian looked at Mac, uncertain what she should say. She opened her mouth to speak, but Mac took charge.

"Jillian will be staying here as well. We . . . ah . . . well, that is to say," he stammered, actually looking ill at ease. Blushing like a schoolboy, he blurted out, "We got married tonight!"

"What!?" Both Gwen and Mary declared.

"It just sort of happened." He grinned sheepishly and shrugged as though that explained everything.

"Well, not exactly," Jillian replied, feeling the need to explain more. "I don't know exactly how to say this, but my father forced our plans. He found me talking to Mac and unfortunately assumed the worst."

Mary chuckled and Gwen hid a smile. "Well, this is some wedding night," Mary said. "You sure you wouldn't like me to stay here with Zack?" She looked directly at Mac as if Jillian had no say in any of it. "You two could go take my room at the hotel."

Jillian swallowed hard and turned away. She'd tried unsuccessfully not to think about those moments when she'd have to be alone with Mac. They hadn't finished their conversation, and she still longed to tell him all that was in her heart. She hoped he would believe her when she told him how much she loved him. But what if he didn't?

"We'll stay here, Mary," Mac announced. "I want to be close in case Zack needs something more."

Mary nodded. "Well, I guess I'll see you in the morning, then."

After Mary left, Mac arranged Gwen in the sickroom, leaving her with extra blankets should Zack grow chilled in the night. He quietly came back through the examination room and took Jillian by the hand.

"I know this is a difficult situation and it's very late," he said, pausing by the bedroom door, "but I feel there are some things that must be said."

Jillian knew he felt her trembling. Why did she have to be so obvious in her fear? Although it wasn't really fear—it was more an anxiety of sorts. She hadn't expected this turn of events, and now she wasn't at all sure what was expected of her.

"I don't have any of my things," she offered weakly. It was all she could clearly think of to concentrate on.

"That's all right. You can use one of my nightshirts." He said it as though there was nothing at all unusual about having a woman share his things.

He opened the door to the bedroom and gave Jillian a light nudge in the small of her back. "Sorry for the mess."

Jillian smiled at the sight. Medical journals stacked haphazardly around the room vied for space with thick dusty books. Clothes had been strewn carelessly over the back of a chair, the end of the bed, and on the bedpost itself.

"I'm not much for housekeeping, I guess," Mac said, turning her to face him. He studied her for a moment, making Jillian quite uneasy. "I don't want you to regret this. I know you didn't plan on becoming my wife. I know this was all a game to you, but now it's not. Now we're married, and I don't believe in divorce. I guess I should probably have told you that from the beginning. I know some folks get them, but I won't be one of them."

Jillian lowered her head to keep from smiling. She wasn't about to get a divorce from the only man she'd ever fallen in love with. "I understand, Mac," she said softly.

He gently touched her chin with his finger. "Look at me, Jillian." She did and found his expression almost pained. "I want you to be sure about this. I know you started this out to put an end to your mother's meddling, but now it's gone beyond that."

"I know that, Mac. I'm not a child," she said, feeling slightly irritated at his speech.

"No, you most certainly are not a child," he said, his voice low. "I want you to be sure about our marriage. I want you to share my bed, but only when you can say that you love me."

"But—"

Mac put a finger to her lips and wouldn't let her continue. "Marriage has to be more than feelings and more than plotting against someone else's plans. My parents loved each other a great deal. They filled a need in each other. I thought I might have that kind of love with Abigail, but it never happened. I want that kind of love with you."

She thought he might kiss her, but instead, he moved away and began gathering up his clothes. His separation, even of a few feet, caused Jillian an immediate sense of loss. "I'll put these aside," he continued. "You sleep in here tonight, and I'll take the sofa. That way if Zack needs me, Gwen won't have far to come."

Jillian had planned to tell Mac of her love for him, had fully anticipated explaining how she had kept her true feelings a secret, but now the words stuck in her throat. Maybe she did need time to think this through. After all, until her mother had insisted on coming to meet Mac, Jillian had never discovered the depth of her feelings for Mac.

Then another thought pricked her conscience. Mary had said that a person should be right with God before binding themselves to someone on earth. Jillian had longed to better understand how to make herself right, but she'd never taken the time to talk to Mary— or Reverend Lister for that matter.

Unable to suppress a yawn, Jillian suddenly felt very weary. The events of the week had caught up with her and all she longed for was a warm bed and time to rest.

"This ought to serve you well enough for sleeping," Mac said, pulling a nightshirt from the closet. He shook it out and snapped it hard several times to assure them both that it was free of desert crea-tures. "Let me check the bed for you." He handed her the nightshirt, then after seeing to the bed, he moved across the room to the door. "If you need me . . ." He left the rest unsaid.

"Good night, Mac," Jillian whispered, clutching the nightshirt close.

He looked at her, the desire evident in his eyes. "Good night, Mrs. MacCallister."

After he had gone, Jillian sat down on the edge of the bed to con-template what had just happened. If she understood everything, Mac loved her and was happy to be married to her. This idea should have left her with a heart overflowing with happiness, but instead, Jillian felt a strange emptiness. Well, it wasn't exactly emptiness.

My life here has been based on lies from the start, she reasoned. *I came here as one woman when I was truly another. And now I feel I've become someone else again. I don't think or feel like I used to.* That Jillian Danvers existed in a refined and elegant world. A prison, really. She wasn't worth much. She was afraid of everything and everyone.

Staring at the closed door, Jillian pondered her transformation. "I'm not that woman anymore," she murmured. She thought of Little Sister and baby Hope. She thought of the Navajo and of Mary's desire to share the light of Jesus with them.

I want that light too, she realized. And then she knew it wasn't an emptiness in her heart, so much as a longing. A longing for a relationship with God like Mary had and so clearly demonstrated.

I don't know how to get that, and if I find it, will that make things right again? Will my life finally make sense?

She ran her hand lightly over the soft woolen cover on Mac's bed. She thought of the contrast between this and her richly decorated room in Kansas City. Mac's bed could boast nothing more than an iron head railing and a lumpy mattress. Her bed at home had been fashioned out of the finest oak. The mattresses were the softest goose down, and the bedding had cost a small fortune, having been imported from one of her mother's trips to London.

Arizona had shown her another side of life, and strangely enough, Jillian found this world more inviting. Oh, there were those folks who had given her misery and unhappiness, but that was to be expected no matter where you traveled or lived. Jillian yawned and stood to stretch. She began unfastening her blouse, realizing that only hours before she had stood before Reverend Lister. *What a strange wedding night,* she mused.

———————

After what had seemed like only minutes of sleep, Jillian found herself being shaken.

"Jillian, wake up," Gwen called.

Slowly, as if coming through a veil of mist, Jillian opened her eyes. "Am I late for work?"

Gwen laughed. "Yes, you are."

Jillian sat straight up and yawned. "I'm coming." Then she noticed her surroundings. "Oh." She felt incapable of saying anything more.

"Kate just sent me a message," Gwen explained. "It seems that our romantic celebration from the night before last and the fire from last night have left us shorthanded at the Harvey House."

"How so?" Jillian questioned, swinging her legs over the edge of the bed.

"Well, apparently we lost another couple of girls," Gwen replied. "Two for sure and possibly three."

"I still don't understand why that's our fault." Jillian forced herself from the bed and laughed at the way Mac's nightshirt puddled on the floor. "Next time I'll bring my own clothes."

"That would probably be wise," Gwen agreed with a grin. "Look, from what Kate said, two of the newest girls, Ellen and Matilda, have run off with local cowboys."

"But they came shortly after I did," Jillian said in surprise. "And now they've up and quit and run off to get married?"

"Apparently so. Another of the girls, the one who came just last week, hasn't been seen since last night during the fire, when she hysterically declared that life out here was too wild for her and she was going home to her mother in Boston."

"She's got to be around here somewhere. There won't be an eastbound train through for at least an hour or two," Jillian said, shedding Mac's nightshirt to reveal her chemise. She laughed at Gwen's curious look. "Mac's nightshirt is kind of scratchy," she offered as an explanation. She picked up her corset. "Will you help me with this?"

Gwen nodded and came to lace Jillian into the contraption while Jillian continued. "How's Zack this morning?"

"He's fine. He's complaining of a powerful headache and an empty stomach, so I figure he'll make it."

"I suppose you'll have to put the wedding off until he's back on his feet."

Gwen laughed and pulled the laces tight. "He's already on his feet. He won't be kept down. He knows that Mr. Everhart or Mr. Cooper has no doubt already wired the fort to tell them that the Indians have escaped."

"There's only going to be more trouble now," Jillian said sadly. "Poor Mary. She's worked so hard to show the Navajo that not everyone is like Mr. Cooper or the soldiers."

"Some soldiers are good," Gwen offered, finishing with the corset.

Jillian slipped her skirt on first and then her blouse. Doing up the buttons she said, "I suppose it's just that there are bad folk among every type of people. Just as there are good folk among the same. Not all white people are honorable and not all Indians will be either."

"That's true enough," Gwen replied, waiting while Jillian finished dressing.

Jillian looked around the room for a brush. "I suppose my hair will have to wait. I guess I'm ready."

Mac came into the front room just as Jillian was following Gwen out the door. "Escaping me, eh?"

Jillian paused and smiled shyly. "I'll be back. I live here now, remember?"

Mac's eyes warmed. "How could I forget."

Jillian felt a strange current run through her. "I need to go help Gwen. Apparently we've lost more help at the Harvey House."

He nodded. "We can talk later."

"I'd like that," Jillian said softly. "I have a great deal to say to you."

She hurried after Gwen, hoping that she would have a chance to talk to Mary before she came back to explain things to Mac. She longed to have answers for her questions, and she knew Mary would understand.

The first train arrived, and with it a load of hungry and cranky passengers. Spending the night on the train made even the stout of heart downright uncomfortable. Sleepy-eyed children accompanied by equally weary women and men shuffled into the dining room. Jillian circulated among the tables, asking what everyone wanted to drink and arranging cups and saucers in accordance with Mr. Harvey's system of order. Kate and two other girls followed, quickly filling those cups with coffee, hot tea, and milk. Once this was done, huge platters of food arrived. Breakfast in Fred Harvey's restaurant was no less a grand celebration than lunch or dinner. The portions remained huge and the quality impeccable.

When a commotion was stirred up on the far side of the room, Jillian just happened to look up in time to see a rail-thin woman berating her petite teenage daughter to take her place in a high chair. The high chairs were reserved for smaller children, but because youngsters ate for half the price of adults, people were often found to try this method of saving pennies. Gwen usually allowed them to get away with it, but it always made Jillian feel rather sorry for the child involved. And today was no different. The girl was in tears as the woman demanded she do as she was told. Finally, a stranger came from across the room.

"Madam," he said politely. "It would be my honor to purchase your daughter's breakfast. Perhaps she would feel more comfortable seated here at the table, however." He graciously held out a chair for the girl.

The teenager dried her tears while the pinch-faced woman stared at the man in a manner that suggested she wasn't at all sure how to take this man's offer.

"And who might you be?" she finally asked the man.

He smiled and gave his bearded chin a little stroke. "Why, I'm Fred Harvey," he told her. "And this is my restaurant."

As the name was spoken throughout the dining room, Jillian watched Gwen pale noticeably from across the room. The great man himself had come to dine in their little house. Jillian thought it rather strange and amusing that he would take his breakfast here in tiny Pintan, instead of one of the nicer, larger facilities elsewhere. Why, Winslow wasn't that far away, and they were renowned for their atmosphere and service. Nevertheless, he was here, and she knew Gwen would be counting on all of them to make certain there were no mishaps.

"Please, God, don't let me break anything," Jillian muttered.

The rest of the meal passed without incident, and when the final boarding call was given, Mr. Harvey shook hands with Gwen and Sam Capper and thanked them for a pleasant meal. Jillian and the other girls had lined up as if they were soldiers for inspection.

"You've done a fine job here," Mr. Harvey told them. "Keep up the good work."

When the train pulled out, Gwen sighed openly. "I'm so glad we came to work this morning. Imagine if I hadn't been here what might have been said."

"You are a good housemother," Jillian told her with a smile. "I do believe that whether you were here to present yourself to Mr. Harvey or not, everything would have run smoothly. You've trained us well, and if I can turn into a capable Harvey Girl under your tutelage, anyone can." Everyone laughed at this, easily remembering Jillian's clumsiness.

There came a bit of a crowd after church later in the afternoon.

Folks tended to like to continue their fellowship after the services and often they would grace the Harvey House for lunch.

"Miss Danvers," one nicely dressed woman said from her place at the table. "I'd like to say something to you."

Jillian smiled down at the women seated around the huge oak table. "Why, of course, but you'll have to forgive me for correcting you. I'm Mrs. MacCallister now. I eloped last night." Jillian stated this in hopes that anyone who might have witnessed her coming from Mac's house early that morning would have their accusations stifled before they were issued.

The woman gasped in surprise, then offered her words of congratulation as Jillian showed off the ring Mac had put on her finger.

"How wonderful!" the woman who had first called her attention replied. "My dear, we are delighted to have you as a part of our town. What you said yesterday . . . well, it needed to be said for some time. My husband intends to see Mr. Cooper run out of town. He's gone with some of the others to help locate the soldiers, but not because he hates the Navajo. Rather, he'd like to see some order and peace brought out of last night's tragedy—and that would include Mr. Cooper's resignation."

Jillian felt blessed as the women continued to praise her efforts and assure her of their support.

"We've long been ramrodded by Hazel Everhart, and I think it did us all a bit of good to see you slap her and call her on her rudeness and obvious lies."

Jillian's cheeks grew hot. "I should never have lost my temper, but I appreciate that you would be so kind to me after the way I spoke."

"She's quite the gal, ain't she?" Mary said from behind Jillian. She came to put her arm around Jillian's shoulders. "I knew she was somethin' special the first time I laid eyes on her in church."

The ladies agreed. "We'd like to invite you to take part in a quilting party we have scheduled for a week from Saturday," one of the older women announced. "My daughter is getting married, and we're putting together a special quilt."

"Thank you," Jillian said, feeling an immense sense of gratitude. "I would love to."

Jillian turned to her mentor. "Mary," she said with great enthusiasm, "I'm so glad you're here. I simply must talk to you. Can you spare me some time after lunch?"

Mary nodded. "I've got a few things to discuss with you as well. Why don't you come over to the hotel? You can play with Hope and tell me all about what's on your heart."

SETTLING DOWN TO FEED HOPE, Jillian knew a sense of satisfaction that normally eluded her. The precious baby seemed more alert and interested in her surroundings than she had only a few days earlier, and it fascinated Jillian.

"She's changing so much. So quickly."

Mary nodded. "Babies have a way of doing that." The older woman sat down on a nearby straight chair and eyed Jillian seriously. "So what was it you wanted to talk about?"

Jillian touched the downy softness of Hope's ebony hair. "I wanted first to apologize."

"Apologize?" questioned Mary. "Whatever for?"

"Mary, you've been the one friend I could truly count on since coming here, and I've deceived you over and over. I didn't set out to be that way. I can't honestly say that I was ever given to lying before now, but it seems the last few months of my life have been nothing but one tangled-up mess."

"Lies have a way of doing that to a person. It's kind of like getting your ball of yarn all tangled and then finding that you only make matters worse as you try to straighten it out."

"Yes, it's exactly like that," Jillian said, nodding. "I came here under false pretenses, and that just started the ball rolling. Before I knew it, I was lying to everyone, including my parents and you. I even lied to Little Sister and that breaks my heart now. She was so touched that I would give her my name, but I didn't give her my name." Sorrow overwhelmed Jillian in the memory.

"But you've already told me about pretending to be Judith," Mary offered.

"I know, but I didn't tell you about lying to my parents about being engaged to Mac," Jillian said, looking back to Hope. She was so ashamed of having lied to Mary. "I wouldn't blame you if you never wanted anything more to do with me, but I hope you will hear me out."

Mary laughed. "I've had folks do a whole lot worse and I still talk to them."

Jillian smiled and met Mary's compassionate gaze. "Mary, I wasn't really engaged to Mac. I mean, we're married now, but even that came about through a collective misunderstanding."

"What happened?"

"I wrote to my mother telling her that I had met a wonderful man."

"Mac."

"Yes, Mac," replied Jillian. "Mary, that part wasn't a lie. I've always thought Mac was a truly great man. He was kind and sweet and generous."

"Good-lookin' fellow too," Mary teased.

"That didn't hurt matters," Jillian said, grinning. "But you see, my mother was so insistent on seeing me married off. She had been plotting and planning for years on how to see me married to nobility or at least to someone very wealthy. So when her letters started arriving and she was still suggesting the idea of bringing suitors out here to Arizona, I decided enough was enough."

"You told her you were marrying Mac and she believed you." Mary's statement explained away most of the remaining issues.

"Yes. We told everyone in town that we were engaged, mainly because my mother and father were on their way to meet Mac. Mac thought it very funny and decided it would be a good time, but last night my father was livid when he found me talking to a half-dressed Mac. My hair was down and my buttons weren't completely done up, and he presumed I was coming from an evening with Mac."

"Oh my. I guess that set him on his ear."

"To say the least. He marched us to the preacher and saw us properly married, only now—"

"Only now there's no way to explain to everyone that it was just a make-believe engagement."

Jillian nodded. "Trouble is, I never wanted it to be make-believe."

"What are you saying, deary?"

Jillian put the bottle aside and shifted the baby in order to burp her. "I'm saying I love Mac. I've loved him for a long time. The things I wrote to my mother were true, with the exception of actually being engaged. I wrote of falling in love with a wonderful heroic man. And I had."

"So what's the problem?" Mary asked softly.

"The problem is, Mac thinks that this was all just a game. He said he cares and said he wouldn't have married me if he didn't really want to, but I'm still worried that he only did it out of pity for me."

Mary guffawed loudly. "Oh, girlie, that boy wouldn't have married anyone out of pity. He's been so heartsick with love for you that it ain't even funny. I've watched him pinin' for you when you were too busy to notice he was even in the same room."

Jillian's eyes brightened. "So you think Mac is telling the truth? You think he married me because he truly loves me?" she questioned hopefully.

"I know it as sure as I know my name. Is that all you're worried about?"

Jillian shook her head. "No, there's more. Mary, you've been so good to share your love of God with me. I want to know more. I feel a horrible emptiness within me when I look at you and your life. You have purpose and you have direction. Your life seems to mean something."

"Only because God gives it meaning," Mary offered. "Jillian, have you ever accepted Jesus as your Savior?"

"Sure, I've gone to church all my life. I know Jesus is Savior."

"No," Mary said, leaning forward, "I didn't ask if you knew it, I asked if you'd accepted it—accepted Him."

Jillian felt puzzled. "I don't suppose I really know what you mean."

Mary leaned back, nodding. "It's not enough to warm a pew on Sunday, Jillian. It's not even enough to believe there is a God and that He has a Son named Jesus. If you don't accept Jesus as your personal Savior and friend, you will go on feeling empty inside."

"What do I have to do?" Jillian questioned, patting the baby gently.

"Just pray and ask Him to forgive you of your sins. Repent and turn away from the old way of doing things—"

"The lies?"

"Yes, the lies. Satan is the Father of Lies. You sure don't want to be doing anything to benefit his cause. The lies have to stop, Jillian. They are hurtful and often destroy the people we love. Jesus wouldn't want you lying to save yourself from an uncomfortable situation."

Hope was already beginning to fall asleep, and after she finished feeding her, Jillian wrapped her tightly in a blanket and cradled her close. "Mary, is this the truth that you said would set me free?"

The old woman smiled knowingly. "It's that and so much more. You know the Navajo people work a great deal with sheep. Up until coming out here with my husband, I knew very little about sheep, but now I know a whole heap more. The sheep are funny. They know their shepherd. Without him, they are silly ninnies always running themselves into trouble. Jesus said, 'I am the good shepherd, and know my sheep, and am known of mine.' There are plenty of examples in the Bible of us bein' like the sheep. We tend to run willy-nilly without a shepherd to guide us. We head in the wrong direction and do the wrong thing. But you know, Jesus is a compassionate and caring shepherd, Jillian. He'll come after you, even if you're the only lost sheep left on the open range. You mattered enough to Him, long before you were placed on this earth. You mattered so much, in fact, that He decided to help you find your way back to the heavenly Father. He's the way, Jillian."

Jillian felt tears streaming down her cheeks. "Sometimes I've felt very lost," she admitted. "I didn't know why. I thought maybe I was just homesick."

Mary smiled. "You were, child. Just homesick for a different home. A heavenly one."

"And all I have to do is repent of my sins and ask for Jesus to be my shepherd?" Jillian questioned hopefully.

"That's right," Mary said softly. "You want to do that with me now? I can help you pray the prayer if you don't have the words."

Jillian sniffed back tears. "I'd like that very much, Mary."

The old woman knelt down beside the bed and waited for Jillian to place Hope in the middle of the bed and join her on the floor. Kneeling there together, Jillian prayed with Mary.

"Father, I'm askin' you to bless Jillian as she comes to you," Mary said softly. "She's willing to repent of her sins, and she's askin' for your forgiveness."

"Yes, Lord," Jillian prayed, "please forgive me my sins and lead my life. Let me seek you always. Save me from evil and give me eternal life in Jesus."

"Amen!" Mary said, squeezing Jillian's hand.

"Amen."

Mary laughed. "Feel better?"

"Only partially," Jillian said, suddenly remembering something Mary had mentioned. "Mary, I don't know for sure if Mac will understand all of this. I don't know if he's a Christian. I mean, he told me he was working on making peace with God. He said he'd gone and talked to Reverend Lister, but I don't know where he stands. Will he think me silly for all of this?"

"Does it matter what Mac thinks in regard to your decision for Christ?" Mary asked as Jillian helped her back to her feet.

"I remember you saying that a person ought to attach himself to God before attaching himself to someone else. I've done that now, but what about Mac? Will it be a problem for us if Mac doesn't believe this way?"

"I think it would probably be a real stronghold for the devil to get in and stir all kinds of grief," Mary replied. "Why don't you just ask Mac how he feels and find out for certain?"

Jillian twisted her hands and looked away. "I don't feel like I have the right. I feel like there's so much I need to talk to Mac about and this is just one more thing—one very big thing."

"Would you like me to find out about his spiritual stand?" Mary questioned.

"Would you?" Jillian asked, looking up rather quickly. "Could you just talk to him, at least? Tell him about my choice—ask him if that will be a problem."

Mary laughed. "I'll go right now. I wanted to see how Mr. Matthews was doin' anyway."

"Oh, he isn't there. He was getting ready to go out to search for Bear and his bunch early this morning. Gwen was beside herself for fear he'd get hurt."

"Men are like that sometimes," Mary said knowingly. "Well, if you want to stay here with Hope, I can go talk to Mac." She walked to the window and glanced out. "I'm glad it's staying light for longer periods of time. Too bad it'll allow the army longer hours to search for Bear."

Jillian felt sorry for Mary. "You love those people so much. I can't even begin to comprehend all you feel for them. I love Hope and felt a kinship with Little Sister, but you know them all so well."

Mary smiled. "Well, not all of them. You know there are quite a few Navajo living out there on the reservation. We only saw a handful who happened to live nearby. There are so many folks out there, though. Folks who are suffering and doin' without. Folks who haven't got anything but dislike for the white men who put them there and took away their freedom."

"Someday it'll be different, Mary. Someday they'll know about Jesus, and it'll be because of you and your love for them."

Mary shook her head. "No, child. My love is quite limited. It'll be because of God and His love. He sent His Son to die for them, same as you and me. When Jesus went to that cross, it wasn't just for white-skinned folks. In fact, if you'll look at folks from that part of the world, you'll see their skin is more the color of the Navajo. Someday maybe skin color won't matter. Maybe later, maybe sooner, but someday maybe the love will be enough."

Jillian embraced Mary in a fierce hug. "Oh, Mary, love just has to be enough. It just has to be."

C H A P T E R

24

"JILLIAN DID WHAT?" Mac questioned the feisty woman who'd just marched through his door.

"I said she sent me to talk to you," Mary replied.

"Why didn't she come herself?"

Mary chuckled and looked her friend over. Mac had become like the son she'd never had. He had helped her many a time, and now she intended to return the favor.

"Mac, Jillian is worried about this marriage."

Mac sat down hard. "I knew it. I just knew it. Here I thought I was doing the right thing." He looked up with a lopsided smile. "Well, maybe not the right thing, but a good thing. I thought surely she wouldn't mind being married to me. But she hates me, doesn't she?"

Mary took pity on him as he ran a hand through his hair in exasperation. "You're worse than any lovesick cowpoke I've ever known. You'd think you were a boy still wet behind the ears to listen to you talk." She put her hands on her hips. "Terrance MacCallister, you ain't usin' the sense the good Lord put in that head of yours."

Mac looked at her, his blue eyes searching her face for answers. "What are you saying, Mary?"

"I'm saying that Jillian didn't send me over here for any such notion as to tell you that she hates bein' married to you."

He started to look hopeful. "Then what did she send you for?"

Mary smiled. "I just came from listenin' to your wife take Jesus as her Savior."

"Jillian?" Mac said with a grin. "That's what this is about?"

With a nod, Mary pulled up a chair and continued. "Mac, she wants to know where you plan to spend eternity. She cares a mite deeply about you and wouldn't want to be fussin' and lovin' over a man bent for hell."

"Loving? Did she say that word?"

Mary laughed. "I ain't here to talk about your matrimonial bliss. That's up to Jillian. I'm simply here on a spiritual mission. Have you set things right with the Lord, Mac?"

He nodded as if he were a ten-year-old boy being asked if he'd studied his ciphers. "I knew the way, but my pride kept interfering. God helped me to see that I wasn't fooling Him or anyone else with my self-reliance and strong-willed ways. I had a long talk with the Reverend. I asked God to forgive me—to take me back."

"Good. Then Jillian has nothin' to fear," Mary said, slapping her hands on her knees.

"Jillian was afraid? Of me?" Mac questioned.

"Don't look so heartbroke. She's listened to those sermons preached about folks being unequally yoked, not to mention the things I've told her privately. She's grown up a piece since comin' to Arizona. Don't you think?"

Mac nodded. "I think she's wonderful, and knowing that she is at peace with God and the other situations in her life—well, who could want more for the woman he loves?"

Mary felt a strong sense of satisfaction in listening to Mac's declaration. "Mac, there's another matter I'd like to ask you about. I mean, I know I've spoke out of turn about it, but I'd like to know if you and Jillian would consider taking Hope to raise her for your own."

"It's a tremendous responsibility," Mac replied. "However, I think we'd be hard-pressed to get that baby away from Jillian."

"She's caring for her right now. I don't know when I've seen a more natural mother. She's going to make a fine wife, in spite of its start as a ploy to fool her folks."

"She told you?" Mac questioned in startled bewilderment. "I didn't figure she'd tell anyone. I mean, it's kind of embarrassing."

"Her conscience was hurtin' her somethin' fierce. I'd imagine your own conscience wasn't feelin' too healthy these last few days."

"Ah, but I wanted to marry Jillian."

"Then why didn't you just ask her?" Mary questioned. "Why all these games and lies?"

Mac shrugged. "I was afraid she wouldn't feel the same way about me. I guess I was just so overwhelmed by feeling something so strong for a woman after all these years, and it scared me to think that she wouldn't feel the same way. When she told me that she'd been writing letters back home to her parents, telling them that she'd fallen for me and that we were going to get married, well, frankly, I was as pleased as punch. I just didn't see it going this far. I didn't plan on her father thinking untrue notions about her, and I didn't figure on forcing her into a wedding she didn't want."

"Well, at least you haven't got that to worry over," Mary said with a mischievous wink. "I ain't never seen a woman more happily married."

"Are you sure, Mary? Don't tease me about this."

"I'll let Jillian come and tell you herself. She's practically bustin' at the seams to do the deed," Mary said, getting to her feet. "Zack Matthews doing okay?"

"He's too stubborn to stay around long enough for me to make certain, but I think he's doing fine. He rode out of here earlier, much to Miss Carson's consternation."

"Well, that's what love'll do for you," Mary said with a laugh.

Mac got up and walked out with her. "Why don't I accompany you to the hotel? That way, I can walk my wife back home."

Mary nodded. "Sounds like a reasonable plan to me."

The sunlight was fading against the horizon, where purple streaks shot out against the burnt orange, gold, and crimson skies. Thick, billowy white clouds lazed across the skies heading east into the navy blue of twilight. It seemed to Mary that the artistry of this land was often overlooked because of its seemingly barren state, but how could anyone not find God's glory in a sky such as this?

Mac kept a tight grip on her arm as a number of cowboys rode hard and fast down Main Street. They were heading for O'Sullivan's Saloon or the Mad Dog Saloon or any number of other drinking establishments. If they had one thing in abundance, it was places to get a drink and play a hand of cards. Mary was grateful for Mac's escort, but she couldn't help but feel her age as the cowboys went by, yelling and acting up for the sake of impressing the few ladies who were actually out on the streets.

I was young once too, she thought and smiled. *And I wouldn't go back to being young again for all the gold in Arizona.*

Mac helped her inside the hotel just in time to come face-to-face with Gretchen and Colin Danvers.

"Why, Mr. and Mrs. Danvers," Mary said, greeting them with genuine warmth.

"Mrs. Barnes," Colin Danvers replied coolly. "Dr. MacCallister."

"You gonna call him that now that he's your son-in-law?" Mary questioned. She knew Danvers' type. She knew that asking a bold question such as this, one that would put him on the spot, was the only way to deal with him.

"I hardly think calling him 'son' would be appropriate," Danvers replied, scarcely missing a beat.

"How about Mac?" Mary suggested. "Everyone else calls him that. You might as well."

Danvers ignored her. "Where's my daughter?"

Mary smiled. "She's upstairs in my room taking care of Hope."

"That Indian baby?" Gretchen questioned in horror.

"That would be the one," Mary replied. She felt sorry for Jillian's mother. The woman looked as though she might faint, and from the sight of her narrow hourglass figure she could probably manage that easily enough without a shock to the system. Why these women of high-bred society insisted on lacing their corsets so tight as to be unable to draw breath was beyond Mary. She herself might sport a thick waist, but at least she could breathe. Besides, at her age, nobody was going to be caring about her waistline.

"See here, Mrs. Barnes," Colin Danvers began, "I don't appreciate your putting ridiculous notions in my daughter's head. It is completely unacceptable for her to even consider raising that baby as her own."

"*Our* own," Mac corrected.

Danvers eyed him harshly. "You have no idea what you'd be up against. Society will never accept her. She'll never be white enough to pass as white, and her darkness will separate her from everyone in our social circles."

"But as we've discussed before, we won't be living in your social circles," Mac replied, his grip tightening on Mary's arm.

"Look here, gentlemen," Mary said, hoping to smooth things over, "the life of one infant shouldn't cause so much upheaval. Not to say that children don't manage to cause a ruckus when they come into a household, but this baby needs parents. Her ma is dead and her pa might as well be, for all he cares."

"And her people have rejected her," Danvers added.

Mary nodded quite soberly. "That's true enough. No one outside of me and your daughter and son-in-law cares enough to keep this child alive."

"Well, maybe that should have been considered before now."

"Danvers, I'm going to try to forget you said that about your new granddaughter."

"She's no granddaughter of mine. She's a half-breed!" Danvers replied angrily. "Better she would have died at birth. Better she'd be taken into the desert and left to die," he growled. "She'll never know anything but suffering. She'll be mocked and taunted no matter where she goes."

"So was our Lord, Mr. Danvers," Mary replied, "but He proved himself to be of great value."

Colin Danvers narrowed his eyes but said nothing more. She felt sorry for the man—even more so for the poor woman who stood teary-eyed at his side.

But then Mary began to truly wonder if giving Hope over to Jillian and Mac was such a good idea. The Danverses would obviously shun the child, and when Mac and Jillian started having a family of their own, it would be evident to Hope that she wasn't being treated the same.

"Mac, I guess we've worn out our welcome. If you'll see me to my room, you can collect your wife."

Mac nodded. "Come on, Mary."

They moved to the stairs, ignoring the fact that Danvers' face was turning beet red in anger. He obviously wasn't used to being dismissed, Mary decided.

"I wouldn't pay him much mind," Mary told Mac. "Fellows like that usually come around. You've just taken his daughter away from him and he's lickin' his wounds."

"He's just as rude and demanding as Jillian ever painted him. How could he be so cruel to Hope?"

"Many folks have made their own thoughts clear in that area, and, Mac," she said as they reached the top of the stairs, "your father-in-law is right about one thing."

"What?"

"Hope is going to have a tough life ahead of her. She'll never be easily accepted. No matter where she goes, someone is going to make trouble for her."

Mac nodded. "I know. It's just so unfair. She didn't ask for this, Mary. And Little Sister wasn't responsible for the rape. She had no power over Cooper."

"Speaking of Mr. Cooper," Mary questioned, "where did he get himself off to? I don't even remember seeing him at the fire."

Mac shrugged. "I can't say. He hasn't been showing his face much since Jillian's little outburst."

Mary laughed. "Good thing that wife of yours doesn't carry a gun." She reached out to unlock her room door but felt it swing open. "That's strange, I thought for sure I locked this. Jillian," she called, "I'm back, and look who I've brought."

Both Mac and Mary stood completely dumbfounded, however, when they caught sight of Jillian tied to a chair and gagged. Tears were streaming down her face as she struggled against the ropes that bound her.

"Jillian!" Mac declared before Mary could speak. He rushed to his wife's side and quickly untied her gag. "Who did this to you?"

"Oh, Mac," she cried in earnest now. "He's taken her."

"Taken who?" Mac questioned.

"Hope," Mary said, looking around the room to see where the baby might have been. "Someone has taken Hope."

Jillian nodded. "Mr. Cooper. He came here shortly after Mary left." Mac finished untying her as she told them the story. "He was so angry. He said he wasn't going to have anyone holding his mistakes over his head for the rest of his life. I told him to leave, but he . . . he . . . slapped me—"

"I'll kill him," Mac declared.

"You'll do no such thing," Mary replied calmly. "Jillian, how long ago did he leave with Hope?"

Jillian shook her head. "It seems like forever. I know it was still light outside."

Mary nodded. "Maybe half an hour to an hour ago?"

"Yes, that would be about right," Jillian replied.

"Did he say where he was taking her?" asked Mary gently.

Jillian's tears came anew as Mac took her into his arms. "He said he was going to eliminate his problem. That's all he said. Oh, Mac, what if he kills her?"

Mac held his wife tightly and looked at Mary over her shoulder. Mary wished she could comfort them, wished she could convince Jillian that there wasn't anything to worry about, but she was scared half out of her wits herself.

"We need to pray about this," she suggested. "We need to pray good and hard."

C H A P T E R

25

MAC TOOK JILLIAN BACK TO THE HOUSE and wondered how they would ever manage through the night. He worried that if left alone, Jillian might cry herself into hysterics—or worse, try to sneak off to find the baby.

"I want to go look for Hope," she said as Mac went around the room lighting lamps.

"Jillian, we can't. It's the dead of night and there are wild animals, angry Navajo, and soldiers out there, none of whom will care that you are on a mission of mercy. We'll do something about it in the morning."

"But morning might be too late. Oh, Mac," she started to tear up again. "What if he just leaves her out there in the desert to die?"

"I wouldn't put it past him," Mac said, barely containing his anger. He reached out and pulled her into his arms. "But right now we're going to pray and give it over to the good Lord."

"But—"

He put a finger to her lips. "Listen to me, please." She nodded. "I left a note for Zack with Gwen. She'll see to it that he comes here and checks in with us when he gets back. I've scouted around town, and Cooper is nowhere to be found. Mary wouldn't hear reason, and she's headed back out across the desert, in spite of the hour. So we've done all we can do—tonight."

"I know," Jillian finally managed to say.

Leading her to the sofa, Mac pulled her down with him. He put an arm around her shoulder and eased Jillian closer until her head rested against him. "Jillian," he breathed her name and sighed. "I want you to listen to me now. I have to say some things. Some things that should have been said a long while back."

"I'm listening," she said, her voice sounding very much like a child's.

"I love you. I think I've loved you since you first walked through my door. I didn't think I could ever love another woman after what had happened to me, but I love you so much it scares me."

She rose up and touched his cheek. "Oh, Mac, I love you too. Everything I told my mother in those letters was true. I fell in love with you, but I didn't know how to go about making it a mutual feeling."

He smiled and took hold of her hand as it caressed his cheek. "Oh, sweetheart, the feeling was already mutual. I got the cold sweats every time I saw you. If I hadn't known the truth, I would have thought I had malaria."

"So falling in love with me made you sick?" she asked, giving him a weak smile.

"Fearing that I'd lose you, that you'd go back to Kansas City— that made me sick. Then when all this happened, I worried that you'd just married me out of being forced into it."

"I wanted to marry you, Mac. I've never wanted to marry anyone but you."

"And you didn't just do this to avoid your mother's other suitors?" he questioned lightly, but inside he desperately needed to know that she felt as committed as he did.

"I kept wondering how I was going to pull it off," she began softly. "Here my parents were expecting a wedding, but you knew it was just a game to put them off. The days were narrowing on me and I wanted to tell you the truth, but I was so afraid of being . . ." She paused, seeming to search for the right word.

"Rejected?" he questioned, understanding that kind of heart-break.

She nodded. "Yes. I was worried that you would laugh and think it great sport that I had lost my heart to you. I worried that you'd make light of it and then I would have to make light of it, too, in order to save face with everyone. But mostly I worried that when it was all said and done, I'd have to get on the train and head somewhere else in order to try to forget you."

He lightly kissed her mouth and shook his head. "I would never make light of your feelings, and had you left town, I would have had to follow because I cannot imagine life without you."

"Oh, Mac," she whispered, laying her head on his chest.

In one fluid motion, Mac pulled her across his lap, cradling her in his arms. "No regrets, Mrs. MacCallister?"

She looked into his eyes and shook her head. "Not where you are concerned."

He knew her mind had drifted back to the baby. How could he expect it to be any other way when his own heart was still contemplating whether there was something else to be done?

"God sees everything, Jillian. He sees the sparrow fall, my mother used to tell me. It's in the Bible. He sees even the tiniest bird and knows its needs. We have to trust that He'll know Hope's needs as well. We may not be the best ones to care for her, and if she never comes back to us, we have to trust that the Lord has seen a better way."

She lay quietly against him. "I guess this is what faith is all about. Mary said it was a fiercesome thing at times."

"Faith?"

She sat back up. "Yes. Mary said faith on a sunny day when everything is going right is nice, but in order to be strong, faith has to be used. And during those times when nothing goes right and everything looks—"

"Hope-less?" Mac interjected with a grin.

Jillian smiled and nodded. "Good point. Anyway, she said faith could be quite fiercesome then. If it's strong enough, it can stand up to even the most powerful storms."

"I suppose it's like anything else," Mac said. "It takes time and constant use to make faith grow. I know it's the kind of faith my mother and father had. It's the kind of faith I want," he admitted. "I couldn't really say that a few months back, but God has managed to get my attention. I see that His Word is real and that we can count on Him to be faithful, even when the world or other people hurt us. I got on my knees, Jillian, and gave my heart and soul and life to God. I asked Him to cleanse me and heal my hurt, and I asked Him to give me a Christian wife. I asked Him to give me you, and God answered my prayers."

Jillian eased back against him. "He answered my prayers in that area as well," she murmured.

"Then trust Him to answer our prayers now," he whispered. She sighed, and Mac knew that she was finally allowing her faith to take strong root.

Mac held her close, his desire for her strong. God had given him a woman to love, and one to love him in return. The images from the past were finally laid to rest. Abigail could no longer hurt him.

———

Jillian woke up first with the pale light of dawn falling muted through the dusty windowpane. She yawned and stretched and then remembered the man at her side. Smiling, she leaned up on her elbow and studied him for a moment. His dark hair fell across his forehead in that rumpled look she had come to love. Reaching up, she gently pushed back the strands and leaned closer to kiss her husband's cheek.

His eyes opened slowly. "I thought I was dreaming," his husky voice murmured.

"Nope, this is your life, Dr. MacCallister."

He came more fully awake and brought her lips back to his own. "I think I can tolerate it."

He had barely started to kiss her when a knock sounded furiously on the front door.

"Hope!" Jillian declared, pulling away from her husband. "Oh, Mac, do you think maybe they've found her?"

Mac shook his head. "I don't know. You get dressed while I go see who it is."

Jillian jumped from the end of the bed and pulled on her robe. "I'm coming with you. After all, I'm going to need some help getting dressed, and you're the only one here to see to it."

The knock sounded again, and Mac nodded, even as he pulled on his shirt. "Come on, then."

They opened the door to Zack Matthews, who looked at them both with a worried expression. "I came as soon as I heard. I didn't even get back to town until a few minutes ago."

"I don't suppose you saw anything of Cooper while you were scouting for Bear and his bunch."

"No," Zack replied. "Are you all right?" he questioned, looking to Jillian.

"I'm fine," she replied. "But Cooper has bad plans for Hope. He told me he planned to eliminate his problems."

Zack shook his head. "I should have known he'd take the news in a bad way."

"What news?" Jillian and Mac asked in unison.

"He's being replaced. A telegram came recalling him to Washington. Apparently Mary caught someone's attention."

"And he knew this last night?" Mac questioned.

"Yup. Matter of fact, word came to him Saturday night."

"Then there's no telling what he's up to," Mac said, tucking his shirt in his pants.

"He didn't say anything about where he planned to go?" Zack asked, looking to Jillian for answers.

"No. He came to Mary's room last night and knocked on the door. I thought it was Mary and went to open it. He pushed me back and stalked into the room like he owned the place. He locked the door and grabbed me." She shuddered at the memory. "I tried to scream, but he told me if I didn't stay quiet, he'd hurt Hope." She felt tears come to her eyes. "I told him I'd be quiet and begged him not to hurt her. He laughed and said he wasn't going to have anyone holding his mistakes over his head the rest of his life. He said some other ugly things, and I told him he had no right to barge into Mary's room and threaten the life of a baby. He slapped me, then dragged me to the chair and tied me up and gagged me."

"Then he took the baby and left?" Zack questioned.

The tears flowed freely by now. "Yes," her voice broke into a sob, and Mac put his arm around her supportively. "He put her in a carpetbag. She . . . she . . . slept through it. She's a good baby." Collapsing against her husband, Jillian cried quietly while the men discussed what was to be done.

"Where's Mary?" Zack asked.

"She wouldn't listen to reason and stay here. She harnessed up those mules of hers and drove out of town to go search for Cooper. I couldn't very well go after her with Jillian needing me here, and I wasn't about to let Jillian go scouting around in the dead of night."

Jillian tried to compose herself a bit and stood up straight. "I want to go look for her now." She tried her best to sound determined.

"I think you'd do more good if you stayed here," Zack told her. He looked at her compassionately. "I'm afraid of what might happen if we get too many folks out there. Those Navajo are still missing, and the army won't take too kindly to us stirring up the countryside and interfering with their tracking."

"We can't just sit here and do nothing," Jillian protested.

"I know," Zack told her. "And I don't intend to do nothing, trust me."

"Do you want me to go with you?" Mac asked.

"No, I'd rather you stuck around. Someone might end up hurt, and we'll need to know where the doctor is. I'd feel a whole sight better knowing where to send folks."

Mac nodded. "We'll stay put, then."

Jillian pulled away. "But there has to be something we can do to help."

Zack nodded. "Pray."

"Folks have been telling me that all night," Jillian said in exasperation, "but it just doesn't seem like enough."

Zack smiled. "I bet it will accomplish more than my efforts will. You just pray and let the good Lord work."

———

Mary Barnes had never taken the easy road for a single day in her life and she wasn't compelled to start now. Even so, she knew a bit of fear as she moved deeper into the canyon. The Navajo women had finally told her where she could find Bear, and now, with all that had happened, she had to find him.

Dawn had been upon them for twenty or thirty minutes, but even with this meager lighting, the canyon remained dark and foreboding. Shadows danced off the walls, creating spectral images, and strange sounds echoed around Mary as she pushed Dobbin and Clarence forward.

At least now she had hopes of finding Bear, and because of his hatred for the white man, she had a strange feeling she might also find Cooper. Or at worst, learn where he was.

It hadn't been easy to get information out of the closed-mouth Navajo women. Most were completely distraught about the soldiers rounding up their children for schools in faraway places. But Mary had appealed to their motherhood and told them the story of Cooper and baby Hope. Finally the women had opened up to her. Years of building trust had convinced them that Mary only meant to see good come to them.

The canyon walls rose up on either side of her in an impressive barrier of crimson sandstone. Mary squinted her eyes to see any detail that might betray the presence of another human being, but there was nothing. Deeper and deeper she pushed into the silent sanctuary. She could easily see why Bear would choose this place to hide. Not only had it been difficult to find, but with its twists and turns and jagged walls, it made the perfect place for an ambush or defense.

And then suddenly Mary knew she'd come far enough, sensing the presence of another person before seeing proof of it. Right in front of her, Bear came to stand on the edge of a rocky outcropping. He had blended perfectly with the scenery until he allowed her to see him.

"Why are you here?" he asked.

"I need your help," she said, never taking her eyes off Bear's stern face. He jumped from the rock with the grace of a puma and came to stand beside Dobbin. Well-muscled and fierce looking, he did nothing but watch her for several moments. Mary knew he was trying to intimidate her, but she wasn't afraid. "Will you hear me out?"

"I don't need to," he replied. "You have come for the child of my sister."

"You have Hope here?" Mary questioned. "But how? When?"

Bear shrugged, then added as if it explained everything, "We have Cooper."

Mary felt a chill go down her spine. "Bear, you haven't killed him, have you? It's bad enough they want you for burning down the school, but if you've killed a man, the army will shoot you as soon as look at you."

Bear's eyes narrowed. "The white soldiers will have to find me first."

"But I found you, and Mr. Cooper apparently found you."

"We made deal with Cooper. He knows this place only because we let him know. He can't tell anyone now."

"So you have killed him," Mary said, feeling rather overwhelmed.

"He not dead yet. Soon," Bear explained.

"Let me see him," Mary demanded. "Let me see if there's anything I can do to help him. You don't need to die for this man, Bear. He's evil and what he did was unacceptable, but you can't go rightin' wrongs this way."

Bear said nothing more, but he took hold of Dobbin's harnesses and pulled himself on the back of the animal. Mary fully expected Dobbin to protest, but the animal remained still until Bear urged him forward. Holding the reins very loosely in her hands, Mary couldn't help but wonder about Bear's plan.

She didn't have long to wonder, however. He negotiated a narrow passage that Mary would never have believed would allow for her wagon, then moved them out into a small opening. In the middle of the opening lay Cooper. He was staked out spread eagle on the floor of the canyon. He had been severely beaten and his face was swollen almost beyond recognition. There was blood all over his body, indicating knife wounds—torture mostly likely, Mary decided. But worse still, Mary could now see as they drew nearer that Bear had tied a rattlesnake to each of Mr. Cooper's limbs. Whenever the man cried out in pain or tried to struggle, he irritated the snakes into biting him.

"Oh, Bear," Mary whispered as they came to a stop. "This wasn't the answer."

She climbed down from the wagon and went to the Navajo. There was nothing she could do for Cooper. "Where's the baby?" she asked softly.

Bear pointed and Mary followed his gaze to where several other Navajo men sat. In the middle of these men lay Hope on top of the carpetbag.

Mary went to the baby and lifted her into her arms. Hope seemed no worse for the wear, but Mary knew she wouldn't feel better until she had the baby safely back with Mac and Jillian.

Bear came to stand across from her. Mary looked up at him. "What did you mean about making a deal with Cooper?" she asked.

"Cooper come to me and say he get us out of the jail and out of the hands of white man."

Mary raised her brow. "And what did you have to do for him in return?" she questioned, knowing without a doubt that Cooper hadn't performed the act out of the kindness of his heart.

"He asked us to get rid of the baby—and you."

"And you agreed to this trade?" Mary asked, feeling her nerves go taut. "You would take the life of your sister's child—your own niece? You would kill me as well?"

Bear smiled, but there was no humor in his expression. "He is a stupid man and soon he will be dead. He say your letter make many people mad. He think they would come here to see him and he not want baby to be here. He not want you here to tell them what he did."

Mary shook his head. "Folks still knew his deeds, Bear, and whether you believe it or not, most folks are appalled. They don't believe it was right for him to do the things he did. He cheated your people and the same as killed Little Sister. Whether folks like the idea of acceptin' the Navajo as equals or not, they are still saddened when people do bad things."

Hope began to fuss, and Mary lifted her onto her shoulder and began patting her back. "So what happens now, Bear? You're going to let Cooper die slow and painful-like, and I don't suppose I can do anything to change your mind on that. But what about Hope and me?"

His expression changed to one that Mary had not expected. He looked almost mournful—regretful.

"She did not ask to be half white," he said simply.

Mary laughed, for she'd never heard anyone regret being white, only the other way around. "You're right, Bear. She didn't ask for any of this. But she's Little Sister's daughter. Little Sister's life is here in this baby."

He nodded. "She is Navajo."

"True, but only half."

"She should be with her people."

"She has people in both worlds," Mary replied.

"Your people will never accept her," Bear stated.

Mary knew he spoke the truth. It would be hard for Little Sister's daughter to be accepted by the whites. She thought of Colin Danvers' bitter hatred toward the idea of his daughter raising an Indian baby. Suddenly, in spite of knowing Jillian's attachment to the child, Mary wondered if the best thing for Hope wouldn't be to remain with the Navajo. Would they accept her? Would they see her as Little Sister's daughter instead of Cooper's?

"She is Navajo," Mary said, cradling Hope in the crook of her arm. The dark-eyed baby watched her for a moment, then blinked against the growing light and closed her eyes.

Bear looked at Mary with a pained expression. "You were good to my sister even when I was not."

"I loved her dearly. Just as I love her child," Mary replied. "Can you say the same? Can you love Hope and see to her well-being?"

Bear looked past Mary to where Cooper was tied to the ground. "I will be hunted down. I cannot give her a home, but my people will. Will you take her to them? Take her to the daughter of my mother's sister."

Mary nodded. "I will take her if that's your wish. You're her uncle, the only family she'll have left. You have that right."

He turned away and spoke in rapid-fire Navajo to the men around him. Quickly they gathered their things and got to their feet.

"We go now."

"What about Mr. Cooper?" Mary questioned.

"He is dead."

Mary wondered about taking Cooper back to town, but given his condition, she knew it would only stimulate the people to war against the Navajo.

"Would you help me bury him?" she asked Bear. "Even a bad man deserves a decent burial."

Bear eyed her for a moment, then nodded. "We will do this, but only because of your goodness. Not because he deserves it."

Mary hugged Hope close and watched as the men went about the business of freeing Cooper. She wondered how in the world she would ever explain to Jillian the choice she'd made today. In some ways Hope would have an easier life should she return to be brought up by Jillian and Mac. No doubt she would never go hungry and she would sleep in a nice bed and wear good clothes. But her looks would betray her, and the only person of her parentage to love her was her Navajo mother. Was that not reason enough to raise her in the Navajo way?

C H A P T E R

26

WORKING AT THE HARVEY HOUSE did nothing to take Jillian's mind off the obvious problems. The town was still in an up-roar over the recent happenings, and it was the topic of every con-versation after the train passengers went on their way and the local folks took to the dining room.

Jillian spent most of her time between serving meals polishing silver tea and coffee urns to the Harvey standards. She caught bits and pieces of conversations among her own co-workers and recog-nized a thread of fear evident in everything that was said.

"The Indians burned down the jail," someone whispered. "They'll probably burn down the depot and the Harvey House next."

"Is the telegraph still working? Can we get help?"

"They'll probably burn the whole town down!"

Jillian shuddered at their statements. For all she knew, they could be right. Mary said the various tribes no longer believed a thing the government officials told them. If they all banded together to fight the army, it could get very ugly.

She began to wonder at the sensibility of living in such a remote area. Maybe she had been foolish to fall for the hidden beauty it pos-sessed. After all, Mary herself had said it was a harsh and unforgiving land.

"What's a fellow got to do to get some service around here?" Mac questioned, coming up from behind her.

Jillian, whose nerves were already taut, let out a yelp and jumped. Realizing, with great embarrassment, that it was nothing more serious or threatening than her husband, she forced herself to calm down.

"I'm sorry, sweetheart," he said, cautiously touching her shoulders.

"No, I'm the one who's sorry. Have you any news?" she asked hopefully.

He shook his head. "No. Nothing. I've made my rounds and checked in on a few of my patients, but no one knows anything. Has Zack come back?"

"No, and Gwen is beside herself. I don't know how she'll ever manage being married to a lawman."

Just then Gwen entered the room, and spying Mac talking to Jillian, she made her way over to the couple. "Have you heard from Zack?" she asked eagerly.

"No, I was just asking Jillian if you'd heard from him. I'm sure he'll contact us as soon as he can."

Gwen nodded somberly, her face clearly betraying her emotions. "I was just hoping he'd be back by now."

"I know," Mac said sympathetically.

Seeing that there was nothing else to be said, Gwen headed off to tend to her duties. Jillian looked to her husband for reassurance, but Mac's expression didn't offer her any comfort.

"It's in God's hands, Jilly."

"But with all He has to take care of these days," she said with a weak smile, "He might overlook something."

Mac laughed and kissed her forehead. "Not likely. You know better." He stepped back and admired her work. "I see Mr. Harvey's silver is benefiting from your concern."

Jillian looked back at the sideboard and noted the gleaming pots. "I suppose so. It's better than sitting with nothing to do."

"How long are you going to keep working here, Mrs. MacCallister?"

Jillian frowned. "I don't know. We've never really discussed my working, have we?"

Mac shook his head. "I presumed if we were to take over the task of caring for Hope, you would resign your position here. Also, there's always plenty I could keep you busy with. I could teach you to be a first-rate nurse."

"I doubt that. I get queasy every time I so much as see blood."

He grinned. "That could be a problem."

Jillian sighed and reached out to touch her husband. "They will find her, won't they, Mac?"

He pulled her close and stroked her cheek. "I'm sure they will, Jilly. I'm sure they will."

After finishing with the silver, Jillian went to work polishing the oak tables in the dining room. She remained at work because the idea of doing anything else was unthinkable. Mac was off setting the leg of a busted-up cowboy, and to sit idle at home would have caused her to go mad.

In the afternoon her mother and father came into the dining room. They weren't looking to be fed, but rather desired a private audience with her in the parlor. At least, she figured, it was a diversion. Gwen quickly gave her permission, and Jillian led them down the hall to the more private of the two rooms.

Feeling rather uneasy, Jillian closed the door and turned to greet them. Before she could say a word, however, her father addressed the current affairs of the town.

"Jillian, this life is not for you. Your mother has been beside herself—barely sleeping or eating. You must listen to reason and heed my advice. You're my daughter, and I won't see you thrown into harm's way."

"I'm not merely your daughter anymore," Jillian said, taking her seat on a brocade-covered chair. "I must yield to my husband's decisions, and Mac desires a life here." She paused, realizing that she made it sound as if this were all Mac's idea. "And," she quickly added, "I love it here and want to stay as well." Despite her earlier worries,

Jillian knew her heart in the matter. Life anywhere had its dangers.

Gretchen began to sob quietly into a lace-edged handkerchief. For all her mother's emotional trauma, Jillian had never seen her without an adequate supply of handkerchiefs.

Jillian attempted to ease her worries. "It's not a bad place to live. You just happen to be here when some upsetting things have occurred. It's actually quite peaceful most of the time. Why, in all the time Judith lived here, she said that nothing overly exciting ever happened." Mentioning her sister gave Jillian an idea for changing the subject. "By the way, when does Judith arrive?"

"Tomorrow," her father replied sternly. "She's coming to see you and the doctor married."

This seemed to perk her mother up. "Will there still be a wedding?"

Jillian instantly felt sorry for her mother. Fretting over Hope wouldn't make things any better, and perhaps Jillian would even feel better if she focused on her mother's plans. At least it would fill the time. "Of course there can be a wedding. If it means so much to you, Mother, we can have a lovely wedding at the church and then bring everyone over here for the reception. I know Gwen will approve."

Gretchen dried her eyes. "And you'll wear the dress I had made for you?"

Jillian nodded. "Of course."

"This is madness. You two sound as though you're planning tea parties in the middle of a war. This land lacks civilization, and I won't stand by and watch you waste your life here. I want you to use your influence to persuade your husband to move to Kansas City. I won't deny you anything you need. I'll set him up in business, even see to him being added onto the staff of the most prestigious of hospitals. I'll gift you with a new house, any house you like—just convince that man to move east."

"I won't do that, Father. Mac is a good man and he knows what is best for him, and I like to believe he knows what's best for me as well."

"He doesn't show that he knows what is best," Colin Danvers countered.

"Why? Because he wouldn't take your money? Frankly, Father, I would think you'd rather honor and respect the man for the fact that he can stand up to you. As far as I can tell, Mac is the only person in the world who hasn't fallen at your feet in the hopes that you'll throw him a bone. Mac is content to make his own way and to care for me. I would think that would make you happy."

Her father sat looking at her for a moment, saying nothing, seeming to consider her words. Finally he stood. "I only came here because your mother has her heart set on this wedding. Judith will be just as bad, I'm afraid."

Jillian stood and walked over to her father. She had always feared him, but seldom had she allowed herself to feel love for him. Colin Danvers wasn't one for allowing much affection and had certainly never tolerated public displays of emotion.

Without warning, Jillian stood on tiptoe and placed a kiss on her father's cheek. "I do love you both," she said and turned to kiss her mother. "I know it's hard for you to understand, but money and social standings mean little to me. I've had both all of my life and neither one has ever made me happy. I have fallen in love with a wonderful man, and that has brought me the happiness I had only dreamed of. I can only hope that we will share half as much love as you two have known."

This seemed to soften her father, who looked awkwardly away. Her mother, however, began to regain her composure. She looked to her husband with open admiration, causing Jillian a warm wash of happiness. Everything would surely be all right.

Obviously embarrassed by Jillian having turned the tables from something he understood and openly felt comfortable with, Colin extended his arm to his wife. "We should be getting back to the hotel. I have a meeting."

"Here?" Jillian questioned.

He nodded. "Just a little business. We'll be tied up through dinner, so don't expect us here this evening."

Jillian watched them go, feeling content and confident. She had taken a stand and her father respected her now—maybe for the first time—and he would be more willing to see value in her decisions.

Toward evening, Jillian made her way back to the same parlor where several of the Harvey Girls relaxed and discussed the affairs of the town. Word had come that Mac was having trouble with the wounded cowboy and would probably be late getting back into town. Jillian couldn't help but wonder if this was how it would always be.

Kate came to Jillian and offered her a comforting smile. "Yar lookin' a bit worn, Mrs. Mac."

Jillian nodded. "I feel weary to the bone." She dropped onto the sofa and sighed.

Kate sat down beside her and reached out to squeeze her hand. "I know this is hard for ya. I know yar worried about Mary and the baby, but surely God is watchin' over them both."

Jillian knew Kate was right. It didn't do any good to fret about the situation. "I should be getting home," she said with a sigh. "Mac's off on some ranch patching up a wounded cowboy, and I don't know when he'll return. He didn't come here for supper, so he'll probably be starving."

"Ya could probably get Cook to give ya a wee plate to take home. Ya don't want to be worryin' over cookin' at a time like this."

Jillian smiled. "That's a good idea. I'll go get him some of that wonderful baked chicken." She got to her feet with new determination. At least this gave her something to focus on.

The Harvey chef was very accommodating, and with food in hand, Jillian stepped out the back door and made her way across the street to Mac's little house, now her home as well. To her surprise, light shone brightly from the front room. Apparently Mac had made it home and hadn't yet come to tell her.

Opening the door, she was startled to find not only Mac but Mary as well. "Mary! You're safe! Oh, thank God!" Jillian exclaimed. She thrust the plate of food at Mac and embraced the little woman in a powerful hug.

"Where's Hope?" she questioned, pulling away and glancing around the room. "Is she safe? Oh, please tell me she isn't hurt."

"She's just fine, Jillian. I left her with the Navajo," Mary said, reaching out to take her hand.

"Why? I thought you said they hated her." A growing sense of dread caused a lump to grow in Jillian's throat.

"They never had much of a chance to know her," Mary replied, then added, "until now."

Jillian looked at Mac and noted the worried expression on his face. His blue eyes were fixed upon her, as if awaiting her reaction. Jillian tried to make sense of what Mary was saying. "You gave her to the Navajo? Forever?"

Mary nodded. "It's a long story, Jillian, and I'd like to be able to explain it all to you."

Jillian forced back her tears. "All right." She let Mary lead her to the sofa, where both women sat.

"I found Hope with Bear. It seems Mr. Cooper had some sort of arrangement with Bear. Cooper helped him escape, and the agreement was that Bear would take Hope and do with her what he would. Cooper had heard that my telegraph to the Bureau of Indian Affairs had raised quite a ruckus. This, along with the other complaints and the obvious problems in this area, caused them to recall Cooper. They announced that a replacement would be sent and Cooper was to board the first train east.

"Instead, Cooper decided to exact his revenge. He knew the Navajo would be happy for help in escapin' the jail and soldiers. Apparently it was Cooper and not one of the Navajo who hit Zack over the head and set fire to the jail."

"Oh my!" Jillian said, shaking her head.

"I think he figured on grabbin' Hope that night in all the confusion. But I took her to the Harvey House, thinkin' I'd find you there, and left her with Kate instead. There was no way for Cooper to gain access to the Harvey House, much less to the second floor where the women were, so I guess he decided to bide his time until he could get another chance."

"That's when he came to your room and tied me up," Jillian offered.

"Yes. He took Hope and went to an agreed-upon location, where he figured he'd give the baby over to Bear and work out an agreement for payment. The best I can figure, he freed Bear and his men for the satisfaction of being a thorn in the side of the U.S. government, but

I think he also figured on Bear being angry enough about the baby that Bear would see to ending her life. After all, Bear had threatened to put an end to Little Sister in order to purge her shame."

"Oh, he didn't hurt Hope, did he?" Jillian asked quite anxiously.

"No. He finally put his anger aside enough to recognize the life of his sister in the baby. We discussed the situation, and we both agreed that Hope would be better off among her own people."

"You didn't think I could do a good job for her, is that it?" Jillian questioned, sniffing back tears.

Mary patted her hand. "Now, deary, you know that ain't true. But Hope's life in the white world would have been difficult at best. Your father and mother's feelings would only be the start of it. You know how folks would treat her, and no matter how hard she tried to fit in and how nice you dressed her, she'd still be bullied and picked on. At least among the Navajo her appearance won't be so unusual. She's going to be dark like her mother, and even though she's half white, she'll probably never look it."

Jillian began to see the logic in what Mary was saying. "So because people are unwilling to set aside their prejudices and see a child for who she is, instead of her ancestry, Hope is lost to me?"

Mary's expression held a great deal of sorrow. "I know this is hard for you. But I wouldn't have done it if it hadn't seemed right. I prayed about my decision, and I think she'll be better off growin' up Navajo. She's going to be raised by some of Little Sister's extended family."

"Will they be less judgmental when considering her white blood?" Jillian questioned. She felt angry and knew her tone betrayed this, but she didn't care.

"I hope so," Mary replied. "Little Sister was greatly loved before Bear told the people that she had betrayed them. Bear set the record straight, and now the Navajo mourn the loss of Little Sister. But with the baby, they can celebrate her life as well. They seemed quite pleased to take her, and before I left, I saw that she was already a part of the family."

Jillian got to her feet. Mary's words made perfect sense, but her heart ached to realize she would not be the one to raise Hope as her own or even to be a part of her everyday life.

"I know you did what you thought was right, Mary." She wiped at her tears and looked at Mac. "I suppose I can see the sense in it, but it doesn't hurt any less, just because I understand it to be the better choice."

"Of course it doesn't," Mac said, opening his arms to her. Jillian hesitated a moment, then walked into his embrace. "It's one of those times, Jilly," he whispered in her ear, "one of those times of having enough faith to trust that God knows what He's doing."

Jillian nodded and looked into Mac's loving gaze. "I know you're right, but it hurts so much. I'm going to miss her, Mac."

"Me too. But there will be others, I promise you," he said with a cocky grin. "I intend to have a big family, and I already know you'll make the perfect mother."

Jillian blushed. "And you'll make the perfect father." She glanced at Mary, who watched them in silence. "And they'll need a grand-mother nearby," Jillian finally said, pulling back enough from Mac to extend her arm to Mary. "One who isn't full of superstitious nonsense and scary stories."

Mary came to them and smiled. "I've got a few scary stories," she admitted, "but they're all true and usually good for teaching a lesson here and there and keeping curious children out of danger."

"Just don't tell them that Spider Woman is going to eat them," Jillian stated quite seriously. "That one still gives me a queer feeling."

Mac and Mary chuckled, causing Jillian to smile. She would sur-vive this sadness. She would find strength in her faith that God knew what was best. Because the alternative was quite unthinkable. For if God didn't know best, who did?

CHAPTER
27

JILLIAN TRIED NOT TO BE DEPRESSED. After all, it was her wedding day—again. She and Gwen agreed to resume plans for the double wedding that had been earlier suggested, and although the issue of Bear and his men had not yet been resolved, Zack agreed.

Plans for a party of grand proportions took shape at the Harvey House, and a telegram arrived from Mr. Harvey himself issuing the house manager to draw on Harvey House funds to pay for the party. Mr. Harvey might run his restaurants on a tightly organized list of rules, but he loved his girls and had a generous heart. It wasn't the first time someone had known him to throw a party for an engaged Harvey Girl, and it probably wouldn't be the last.

Gwen, although nervous about the evening's events, had confided in Jillian that she feared that Zack would forever be off searching for someone and that they might never actually get married. This opened the conversation for Jillian.

"I don't mean to meddle, but are you sure you're up to being married to a lawman? I mean, you've fretted and fussed so much over the last few days, and naturally so. But still, it won't be easy."

Gwen's expression changed to one of concern. "I know you're right, and it is a worry. But I love him so much. I talked to him about these fears and we prayed about them." She smiled ever so slightly. "But, Jillian, to not deal with my fears over this would mean to lose him. I can't do that. I'd rather have him for a short time than no time at all."

Jillian hugged Gwen and sniffed back tears. "I know how you feel. I hate it when Mac has to go riding off out there into the wilds of the country. I worry that he'll encounter a wild animal or poisonous snake. I fret that bandits might come upon him or that his horse will lose its footing. But Mary told me that worrying about it was a sin. She said I might as well say that God can't do His job and that He isn't faithful to His Word."

"I never thought of it that way," Gwen admitted, wiping at her own tears.

Jillian smiled. "Now, come on. This is our wedding day and we aren't supposed to cry, at least not yet."

Later in the afternoon, Jillian sat working with her hair while Gretchen fussed around the hotel room. "Your sister should be here any minute. I hope she remembered to bring her mauve silk. I want a photograph of this day, and the silk always reads best in photos."

"Where did you find a photographer?" Jillian questioned, securing a curl with a long hairpin.

"Your father brought him in from Winslow," Gretchen replied. "Your father really is a good man, Jillian."

Jillian stopped in her task and looked at her mother. "I know he is. I regret that he wasn't very affectionate. I regret, too, that often his business always seemed more important to him than his family."

"But that isn't true," Gretchen said to her daughter. "He wasn't raised with much affection. You know, he wasn't a man of means when he was young. He made himself what he is today. He's widely respected and held in esteem, something his father never had. You can't understand how it was for him, but his family suffered greatly when he was a child."

"Then why does he have such little compassion for the poor—the Indians? Why does he worry over my social standing in Arizona and desire to see Mac and I live in Kansas City?"

"He doesn't want to see you suffer, Jillian. He doesn't want you to know what it is to do without. He watched his mother shed tears of anguish as she sent her children to bed hungry. He had nightmares for years after we were married, recalling the horror of watching siblings die because there was no money for a doctor. Then, too, he watched his father die at the hands of a physician who bled him to death."

"So that's why he's never had much use for doctors?"

Gretchen nodded. "It's also why he's never had much use for religion and God. By understanding these things, perhaps you won't judge him so harshly. Maybe they even explain your grandmother's strange concerns and superstitions. She had lived a life of misery and suffering until your father managed to make a fortune for himself. I suppose her superstitions were all she had to make sense of the world."

"They terrified me," Jillian said, turning back to the mirror. "I used to lie awake at night and worry that some clumsy mistake of mine had caused the death of someone in the family. I worried that she would come back to haunt me and blame me for her own death."

Gretchen came up behind Jillian and hugged her. "I had no idea. I thought you knew it was nonsense."

"I do now, Mother. I've found something real, however." She turned and gently touched her mother's shoulder. "I found that God loves me and has given His Son to save me from eternal death. It isn't at all like those piously spoken words we heard in the church back in Kansas City. God really does love us, Mother. He doesn't want any of us to go to bed afraid of dying, and He doesn't want us to hurt one another by showing prejudice and snobbery. Do you know that the Bible says it's actually a sin to treat someone badly because he's poor or sick or not dressed as nicely as you are?"

Gretchen shook her head. "I suppose I didn't."

Jillian nodded. "I didn't either. But, Mother, it has changed my life—forever."

Gretchen looked at her daughter quite seriously. "Yes, I can see that."

"Jillian! Mother!" It was Judith calling out at the top of her lungs as she burst into the hotel room.

Jillian turned to find her twin rushing to her for an embrace. Her blue feathered hat was askew on her rather disheveled hair, and her blue serge traveling suit was smudged here and there from soot, but otherwise, she was just as she had always been.

"I see you're still in one piece," Judith declared as she hugged Jillian. "You didn't fall off the ends of the earth, which, by the way," she said, grinning conspiratorially, "is just west of Flagstaff."

Jillian laughed. "Neither did I get swallowed up by scorpions or snakes. Although I have seen several of each."

Gretchen shook her head. "You girls will be the death of me with your spirit for adventure."

Judith put her arm around her mother and kissed her on the cheek. "Well, speaking of adventure, guess who is going to have a baby!"

Jillian watched her sister's face light up in evident pleasure. "A baby! Oh, Judith, congratulations!"

"A baby?" their mother questioned. "I'm going to be a grandmother?"

Judith nodded. "Yes, and hopefully Jillian won't be too far behind me. I want our children to be close in age, and I want there to be at least a half dozen of them for each of us."

"I'll tell Mac," Jillian laughed.

Just then their father came into the room, directing the hotel bellboy as to where he could deposit Judith's bags.

"You'll tell Mac what?" her father asked rather gruffly.

Jillian grinned. "You called him Mac."

Her father flushed a bit at the collar and looked away. "I was merely repeating you."

"Well, Judith just announced that she's to have a baby, and she figured we should both have at least a half dozen children."

"You'll need them for company, if for no other reason," her father replied. "This territory seems rather empty."

Jillian went to her father and touched his arm, looking at him as if for permission to speak. His expression softened just a bit, and Jillian beamed him a smile. He was changing. He'd considered her words, of this she was sure, and he was changing his mind about her husband and their new life.

"Some wealthy entrepreneur could always figure out a few new businesses to help boost growth for an empty territory," she said softly.

Her father actually smiled at this. "What makes you think I'm not already working on that? After all, I've got to have some reason to make frequent trips out here."

"You'll always have a reason to come if I'm here," she said, putting her arms around his neck. "You will always be welcome in our house."

He hugged her close and kissed her lightly on the forehead. Then, as if the intimacy of the moment were too much for his stern nature, he set her aside.

"Mrs. Danvers, we have a wedding to attend in a few short hours. I would suggest you get our girls prepared."

Gretchen smiled. "With pleasure, my dear. With pleasure."

———————

Mac pulled at his starched collar and wondered why he felt so nervous. It wasn't like he and Jillian weren't already married, so what was the fuss?

He checked his black suitcoat a second time and picked furiously at several pieces of lint.

"You're gonna wear a hole in that suit or this floor if you don't settle down," Mary chided.

"I don't know why I feel so nervous. I mean, she's already my wife. She can't back out now," he said with a stilted laugh.

Mary chuckled and came to help him on with the coat. "You need to be gettin' on over to the church. We'll have just about enough time to walk leisurely."

Mac nodded. "I'm glad you're here, Mary. I don't know what I would have done with myself if you hadn't been."

"Could I have a word with you?" Colin Danvers called through Mac's open door.

Mac straightened and tried his best to look self-assured and confident. "Of course, come in."

Mary squeezed his arm. "I'll be waitin' for you at the church." She slipped out the door just as Danvers opened it. "Good to see you, Mr. Danvers," she said.

He tipped his bowler hat to the old woman, then turned to Mac. "I've come to say something—something important."

"If you're hoping to talk us out of getting married, it's too late. Remember?" Mac said, trying to sound amused. In fact, he was quite guarded and fearful of what Danvers would try. He didn't want to see Jillian's special day ruined, but he knew this was just the man who could do the job.

Danvers fidgeted with his hat and cast his gaze downward. "I've actually come to apologize."

Mac stood completely silent, uncertain what he should say. "Apologize?"

Danvers squared his shoulders and looked Mac straight in the eye. "I was wrong, and when I'm wrong I say so. I shouldn't have tried to interfere with your life or with Jillian's. If you and my daughter are happy here, then I should find that satisfactory."

"And do you?"

Danvers smiled. "I'm learning to. It won't be easy. Jillian and Judith have been the light of my world, along with their mother."

"I'm not sure Jillian's ever known that," Mac replied.

"I'm not sure she has either. I'm not sure any of them know it, but I intend for them to learn. If you can forgive an old fool, I'd like to offer this as a wedding gift." He handed Mac a bank draft.

Looking at the generous sum, Mac said, "I don't know what to say. This seems like an awfully large wedding gift."

Danvers laughed. "It's only money, my boy. I think I can see that now."

"And you aren't trying to buy us in some way? After all, you were the one who said everyone had their price," Mac said suspiciously.

Sobering, Colin Danvers nodded. "I said a great many things that I regret. You proved to me that not all men can be bought off. I respect that in you, and I know my daughter is getting a decent man for a husband. I won't worry that someone else will come along to entice you to leave her. I won't worry that you'll put your profession ahead of her well-being."

Mac nodded. "I might have been that man at one time, but I'm someone different now. I promise that I love your daughter with all my heart. I'll never willingly hurt her."

"If you do, you'll answer to me," Danvers replied gruffly, then with a smile he nodded toward the door. "I think we're going to be late if we don't hurry."

———————

Mac watched Jillian come down the aisle of the small church on the arm of her father. A vision in white satin and lace, he smiled proudly at the knowledge that this woman belonged to him. Through the filmy veil that covered her face, he could see her smile at him. It was almost as if she was now reassuring him instead of him reassuring her.

Next, Gwen came in on the arm of Sam Capper. Gowned in a simple creation of bleached muslin and lace, she looked no less regal as she took hold of Zack's arm.

The ceremony itself was brief but lovely. Mac felt a surge of sheer delight when Reverend Lister pronounced them husbands and wives and allowed for a marital kiss to seal the ceremony.

"Mrs. MacCallister, I believe," Mac said, lifting Jillian's veil.

"Dr. MacCallister," she whispered as his lips closed over hers.

The congregation burst into applause and cheers, and before he knew what was happening, Mac and Jillian were headed out of the church and on their way to the Harvey House for what promised to be an exceptional celebration.

Catching sight of the prune-faced Mrs. Everhart and her daughter, Davinia, standing in front of the Indian Affairs office, Mac nudged Jillian. "Did someone not get their invitation to the wedding?"

Jillian giggled. "They were invited but chose not to attend."

Mac nodded. "Good. Isn't there some superstition about having a sour-faced, bitter old woman at the wedding being bad luck?"

"Oh, Mac," she laughed. "Behave yourself. You know we don't believe in those things."

Inside the Harvey House, the wedding party went on until nearly midnight. Jillian and Mac danced and ate and laughed until they were both certain they would drop from sheer exhaustion. Mac felt a deep sense of gratitude when Mary pulled them both aside and shoved them toward the back door.

"Get out of here, you two. You've been here long enough."

Jillian leaned over and kissed Mary on the cheek. "Thank you for everything."

"Get on with you," Mary said, waving her off. "You'd do the same for me."

Jillian stopped in her tracks and looked at Mac. "Now there's an idea. We need to find a husband for Mary."

The old woman's laughter threatened to bring down the house. "That'll be the day!" she declared, slapping her knee in a very unlady-like manner.

"You never know," Mac said teasingly. "I once said I'd never marry again." He looked back to Jillian and reached out to touch her cheek. "But I was walking against the wind, and somehow it seemed the better course to change directions and walk with it."

Jillian reached up to place her gloved fingers over Mac's hand. "God has a way of pointing us in the right direction, even when we aren't expecting it," she said softly.

Mac realized his heart was near to bursting with love for this woman. She had touched him in a way that he was only now beginning to realize. She made him laugh and she brought him to his knees in prayer over her sorrows. Everything he had ever longed for in a wife was found in the lovely form before him.

Tucking her arm close to his side, Mac grinned at Mary. "Don't look for us for about a week."

"What will Mr. Harvey do without Jillian to keep his customers happy?" Mary teased.

"Mr. Harvey will just have to make do," Mac replied. "She's taking care of this customer, and I can be a very needy soul."

Jillian rolled her gaze heavenward, then cast a glance over her shoulder to Mary. "Just tell Mr. Harvey that I fulfilled his contract and have set out on another. A contract of the heart rather than of the stomach."

Mary's laughter rang out as Mac pulled Jillian out the back door and across the street. "Does that mean you don't intend to feed me?"

he questioned as he lifted her into his arms to carry her once again across the threshold.

"Did I forget to mention that I can't cook?" Jillian asked almost sheepishly.

Mac kicked the door shut with his foot and smiled. "I have it on the best authority that you are quite trainable."

She grinned. "I *can* boil eggs."

"See there, we shan't starve. We'll feast on love and boiled eggs."

She frowned in mock distaste. "Maybe we can just eat at the Harvey House."

Mac nuzzled his lips against her throat. "Maybe they'll deliver."

Jillian sighed in unmistakable satisfaction. "I love the way you think, Dr. Mac."

"I just love you," he said, the contentment in his voice matching hers.

And without a doubt, Mac knew that their future was set on a course that would engulf them in love and hope. They would strive together to right the injustices of the world—or at least of their little town. God had been good to drive away his demons of the past and give him a second chance at love. It was a gift, pure and simple. A gift he didn't intend to waste.

A Word From the Author

PINTAN, ARIZONA, is a fictional town; however, there were many Harvey House locations along the Santa Fe line throughout Arizona. Today, La Posada, a Harvey hotel resort in Winslow, Arizona, remains a tourist attraction, giving visitors a flavor of Mr. Harvey's standards of gracious living.

Many people see Fred Harvey as having been the father of "fast-food service." His desire to provide affordable quality meals along the Santa Fe line did much to settle the southwest. His growing interest in native-made crafts and goods also brought widespread awareness of the cultures and traditions of the various Native American tribes on the Santa Fe rail line.

The "Harvey way" became a well-known phrase and stood for the integrity and quality of service that Fred Harvey had known would keep customers coming back for more. It is quoted that upon his deathbed, Fred Harvey's dying words to his sons were "Don't cut the ham too thin, boys."

I want to thank a couple of people for their helpfulness during this series. First of all, thanks to Brenda Thowe, who heads up the modern-day Harvey Girl organization for the Burlington Northern Santa Fe Railroad. Thanks also to Janice Griffith with the Winslow Historical Society, for providing much detail and information on Arizona, as well as historical research related to the Winslow Harvey House.

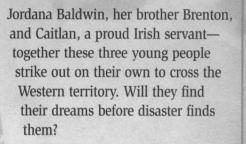